9TAIL FOX

9TAIL FOX

JON COURTENAY GRIMWOOD

GOLLANCZ

LONDON

The right of Jon Courtenay Grimwood to be identified as the
author of this work has been asserted by him in accordance
with the Copyright, Designs and Patents Act 1988.

First published in Great Britain in 2005 by
Gollancz
An imprint of the Orion Publishing Group
Orion House, 5 Upper St Martin's Lane,
London WC2H 9EA

A CIP catalogue record for this book is
available from the British Library

ISBN 0 575 07615 1 (cased)
ISBN 0 575 07713 1 (export trade paperback)

1 3 5 7 9 10 8 6 4 2

Typeset at The Spartan Press Ltd,
Lymington, Hants

Printed in Great Britain by
Clays Ltd, St Ives plc

www.orionbooks.co.uk

Bulgakov – to whom I owe my black cat, my passion for weird plots and (bizarrely enough) my marriage . . .

'The real voyage of discovery consists not in seeing new landscapes, but in having new eyes . . .'

Marcel Proust

PART I

CHAPTER I

Friday 6 February

'Okay,' said Bobby, 'show me how you shot him.'

He handed his .44 Magnum to the child and watched thin arms tremble as Natalie Persikov tried to keep the gun steady.

'Like this,' Natalie said.

Taking the Colt from the girl, Sergeant Bobby Zha placed it on a table, next to one of the many photographs in her grandfather's dining room. 'Now show me.'

The eleven-year-old struggled to lift the gun. When she finally did, it was using both hands and its muzzle wavered between the door and a high sash window, which overlooked Tamsin Steps, one of the more exclusive areas of San Francisco's Russian Hill.

At eleven, Bobby Zha's own daughter had been wearing mascara and her mother's Gucci sling-backs. Natalie Persikov had sandals, wore her blonde hair tied back in a loose ponytail and looked like the child Bobby remembered eleven-year-olds being. She was also thin as a stick. The recoil from a Colt .44 Magnum would have snapped her wrists. At the very least, it would have sprained them.

'And he came in that window?'

Natalie nodded.

'How did you know he was a burglar?'

The child looked at Bobby Zha as if he was stupid. 'He was wearing a mask.' This part was true. The dead man had been wearing a Russian ski mask made from black silk, with the label cut out. Forensics were still liaising with Moscow to identify the maker.

Then there was all that stuff with the icon. This sat on a wall by the window, a sour-faced virgin with Christ squashed onto her lap. *Opportunistic insurance fraud*, Bobby would have said. If not for the fact the family were stupidly rich and Dr Misha Persikov notoriously honest. Apparently, reporting the icon missing had been a mistake.

Outside the window Ozzie, the family's odd-job woman, continued raking the tiny lawn for cigarette butts and plastic coffee cups left behind by a camera crew, while inside, industrial cleaners had already returned the dining-room carpet to a surgical purity it probably never possessed.

'Did the gun make a loud noise?'

Natalie glanced at where her grandfather had stood until Bobby sent him from the room.

'Very loud,' Natalie said, her chin going up.

This was also true.

'How about recoil?'

The girl looked blank.

'Guns often kick back,' said Bobby, 'when you fire them. It's called *recoil* . . .'

Natalie Persikov nodded doubtfully. She knew he was trying to trick her, Bobby could read that in her narrow face. She just wasn't sure what form his trickery would take.

'Did the gun move?'

Was that the trick? The police officer was waiting so she nodded, making her choice. 'Of course it moved,' Natalie said crossly, putting Bobby's revolver down on the table.

'And did it move up or down?' He was being unfair, Bobby knew that. The tears backing up behind the small girl's eyes said she knew that too. Pushing children so far was not something Bobby did willingly, but this was different.

If the girl was telling the truth, then Natalie Persikov had picked up her grandfather's unlicensed revolver and shot a burglar through the head. She did this from across a dining room bigger than some people's apartments, at dusk, when the light was almost gone and the victim little more than silhouette against an already darkened sky.

It was either the world's luckiest shot or someone was lying. And it didn't help Sergeant Bobby Zha's nerves that Moscow's embassy in Washington seemed unwilling to confirm that the amalgam in the dead man's fillings was typically Russian.

So what Bobby had was one eighty-year-old doctor, a pillar of respectability and friend to at least two of the city's last three mayors, one eleven-year-old girl and a dead burglar with every single label cut out of his clothes. The child was adamant she shot the man. Sergeant Zha's instinct said Mihail Persikov was responsible, but since the doctor was blind that seemed unlikely.

'Come on,' said Bobby, returning the revolver to the girl. 'Tell me, did the gun move up or down?'

Taking the weapon, Natalie held it out in front of her, hands trembling, as if holding it so might give her the answer. A boy of that age would have threaded one finger around its trigger from instinct. Natalie held the gun as she might a snake, barely able to touch it.

'Down,' she said.

Bobby smiled. 'Okay,' he said. 'We're done.' He resisted the urge to ruffle Natalie's hair, in the way he would once have ruffled the hair of his own daughter, before things changed and Kris grew too old for that. He also resisted telling Natalie everything would be all right, because it wouldn't. Either the child had killed or she was being used as camouflage for someone who had.

'I have to go now,' said Bobby. 'And fill out lots of forms, like home-work.' That usually earned him sympathy, from boys at least.

'I like homework,' announced Natalie.

'So does Kris, but only sometimes.'

The girl frowned, waiting for Bobby's explanation.

'Kris is my daughter.'

She looked at him then, as if to say, *you have a daughter*? It made Bobby wonder what she saw. A small man, in faded jeans and black T-shirt, an SFPD badge on a tape around his neck and tinted glasses hiding tired eyes . . . ? Natalie hadn't wanted to talk to him today, her silence holding until – in the end – Bobby sent her grandfather from the room.

'It's an odd name,' Natalie said finally.

'What is?' asked Bobby. 'Kris?'

'Zha . . .'

A mixture of Cantonese, Catalan and Scottish, Sergeant Zha looked foreign, no matter where he was or who he was with, whereas the child looked Russian, from her cheekbones and blonde hair to the speedwell blue of her troubled eyes. He was *za zhong*, which translated politely as *mixed race*, less politely as *bastard*. She was born and brought up in San Francisco and held an American passport. All the same, she looked as if she'd stepped out of an old Soviet poster, one advertising deter-mination and youth.

5

'My grandfather,' said Bobby. 'He came from China.'

'Ahh . . .' The child nodded, looked serious. 'About the gun,' she asked. 'You believe me now?'

Bobby debated lying and decided not. 'No,' he said, 'I don't think I do . . .' Picking up the revolver, he slid it into a holster. The original was in an evidence locker at 850 Bryant Street but this was as near as damn in size and weight, even if it was a replica. Bobby Zha wasn't the kind of man to put a real gun into the hands of a child.

'I did it,' insisted Natalie.

'Gun's jump up,' said Bobby, 'it's got to do with how your elbow pivots. And if you'd held the gun like that it would have broken your fingers. Someone else shot that man . . . Was it your grandfather?'

'No.'

'Are you telling the truth?'

'Of course I am.' There was real anger in the child's voice. An anger that Bobby suspected she either did not usually release: or, perhaps, wasn't often allowed to do so. 'He's blind,' she said. 'And he'd never shoot anyone anyway.'

'Whereas you would . . . ?' Bobby stopped, seeing panic blossom behind Natalie's eyes.

'I did it,' she said, shaking her head.

Conflicted, it was such a great word. 'You know,' said Bobby, as he put the holster containing the replica into a carrier bag and put the carrier bag inside a cheap briefcase. 'There's one thing that puzzles me.'

'What?' said Natalie.

'If your grandfather really is innocent . . . why would you take the blame for someone else?'

The odd-job woman was pruning police tape from a gate with a pair of scissors, Doctor Persikov sat by the porch, and two old men were watching from across the narrow street when Bobby walked Natalie back to the car in which she'd arrived.

He ignored them all.

Instead Bobby nodded to the uniform driving. She was someone he vaguely recognised. Hispanic, probably in her early twenties, full breasts under a blue shirt and a waist already beginning to spread over her regulation belt. She looked impressed to meet the famous Sergeant Zha, despite having seen him once already that afternoon, which was

6

how Bobby knew she must be fresh out of the Academy. Anyone else would have been around long enough for such innocence to rub off.

'Sir.' The officer sat up straight in her car.

Eighteen years before, within ten days of being sworn in, Bobby Zha took a bullet in the back to save the life of his partner, a man twenty years older who was meant to be keeping Bobby safe. Medal or not, it didn't make Bobby a hero, it just made him unlucky, a kid straight from training in the wrong place at the wrong time.

He'd spent a lot of his career trying to live that down.

'Take her back to eight-fifty Bryant,' said Bobby.

'You want a lift?'

'No, I'm going to look around.'

'CSI have already . . .' The young officer stopped, suddenly unsure. The crime scene crew had crawled all over every inch of the house and the garden, taking photographs and plaster casts of footprints, lifting fingerprints and bagging up cigarette ends for DNA testing. Obviously enough, the scene had since been released, otherwise the camera crew would still be waiting, instead of having been and gone.

'I know,' Bobby said. 'I'm just winding CSI up.'

She grinned, taking it as a joke.

Bobby wondered if the teks had been surprised by how many times Natalie had touched the glass of the broken window, the door handle to the dining room and the gun. If fingerprints were to be believed she'd even thumbed back the hammer when she fired, not to mention extracting the spent .44 case they found in the back of a drawer in her bedroom.

'If you're sure you don't need a lift?'

He was. 'In you go,' said Bobby, opening the door for Natalie. Putting his hand up to bend the girl's head, Bobby prepared to feed her into the back seat of the Cadillac, only to realise this was unnecessary, because the child was not resisting and, anyway, Natalie was so small she could climb into the vehicle quite happily, without needing to bow her head.

Bobby had offered Natalie Persikov the chance to ride in something anonymous but the child had wanted the full works, lights on top and sirens. There was an element of defiance in her choice.

'We'll talk again,' Bobby promised.

Natalie grunted.

7

From Bobby's daughter that would have been the height of communication, since Kris had spent the last six months ignoring him altogether. For Natalie it was positively rude. All the same, she'd talked to Bobby and that was more than she'd done to anyone else in the last forty-eight hours.

CHAPTER 2

Friday 6 February

'So,' said a voice. 'Worked your magic?'

The drawl was unmistakable. Pio Xavier Sanchez had left the Mission District a good Hispanic boy and returned a cowboy, in most senses of that word. Pete liked to keep cases simple and was rumoured to play fast and a little loose with his fiancée, Beatrice de la Paix; but he worked hard, said the right things at seminars, always arrived ten minutes early for each shift and did everything with a smile.

After a degree in criminology at Houston, closely followed by a masters and a doctorate, he'd come into the SFPD on the ACE program, one of the department's newest accelerated career entrants. The brass loved Pete Sanchez, almost as much as they loved their jazzy little acronyms. Despite himself, Bobby Zha was developing a soft spot for the man too.

'What are you doing here?' Bobby demanded.

'Yeah.' Officer Sanchez laughed. 'Good to see you too . . .' He glanced after the car. 'How'd it go?'

'As you'd expect. The kid swears she did it. All the evidence says she didn't.'

'Sergeant . . .'

'Bobby,' corrected Bobby. Officer Sanchez was given to calling those senior to him by their rank, and when that rank got to lieutenant or above he began calling them *Sir*. It was proving a hard habit for Bobby to break.

'You could have gone anywhere,' he said suddenly, looking at the younger officer. 'Special Investigation Section. Auto detail. Hell, you could have put in a couple of weeks with Fugitive Recovery. Why choose me?'

'You're a legend.'

'In my own lunchtime,' agreed Bobby. 'What's the real reason?'

'I needed a rest,' said Officer Sanchez, then held up his hands in mock surrender. 'Sorry . . . That wasn't meant the way it sounded. I'm interested in what you do. This empathy thing you have with kids and street people.'

'Rest from what?' Bobby demanded.

Sanchez looked behind him, but all Bobby could see was the gardener rolling police tape into a plastic ball and Mihail Persikov stood in his own front door, listening for echoes of a car now long gone.

'I'm not really meant to say,' said Sanchez, 'but I was on the Osip case before everything got fucked. You know, scut work. Helping chase down the money trail so the treasury could freeze any local accounts. We were getting nowhere fast when the bomb went off . . .'

Bobby remembered. A dead financier, billions missing and an explosion aboard a yacht, all under the cold eye of the international press; even this had to be a rest after that.

'It wasn't going well?'

Sanchez pulled a face. 'We had one photograph and that was out of focus. Second richest person in Russia, maybe third . . . And no one could tell us a thing. I'm not even convinced Osip came ashore.'

The Russian had bought a house on the cliffs south of Fort Point Rocks. A photograph in the *San Francisco Chronicle* had shown officers from the SFPD searching the place after Osip died. Bobby tried to remember if Sanchez had been among them.

'You know,' said Sanchez. 'Getting back to Natalie . . . Kids kill.'

'Not that one,' Bobby said, 'and not without reason.'

'The dead guy was climbing in a window. Wearing a mask. How much reason do you want? Natalie's fingerprints are all over the gun. She dialled nine-one-one herself and told us she'd killed someone . . .'

'On her own phone.'

Officer Sanchez sighed. 'What is this?' he said. 'The famous Bobby Zha intuition?'

'Yeah,' said Bobby. 'Something like that. I find it hard to believe she walked out of the dining room, ignored the house phone in the hall and carried straight on past her grandfather's study door, where Dr Persikov had managed to sleep through the entire shooting. She then went upstairs, unpacked her school bag and called us, using her phone.'

'Her prints are all over the gun.'

Bobby nodded. '*All over it*,' he said.

'And that's suspicious . . . ?'

Pete Sanchez held the view that if someone's fingerprints were on a weapon then that helped prove guilt. It was a perfectly reasonable position. One held by most of CSI and Captain Nash at Central. So now the city prosecutor was done talking to Natalie's lawyer and half a dozen people from 850 Bryant and City Hall were busy tying up some deal behind the scenes. The Persikovs were that kind of family; trip a single sticky strand and some pretty important spiders came crawling out in sympathy.

Natalie was three years under the age of criminal responsibility and no one was keen to find clear proof she might have known what she did was wrong. So the deal was simple. Court guidance, therapy, and as little publicity as the local press would allow. The plea bargaining had taken about ten minutes and eight of those were pleasantries.

It was Bobby's boss, Lieutenant Que, who messed everything up by suggesting Sergeant Zha talk to the girl. Maybe check she really had pulled the trigger. No one was better than Bobby at talking to traumatised kids, it was ordinary, everyday adults who gave him a problem. This wasn't quite true, because Bobby Zha also did a mean line in talking to those touched by poverty, despair, drugs and God.

There wasn't a panhandler or whore in Chinatown whose name he didn't know, from Colonel Billy himself down to the newest kid to crawl off a bus and start selling herself for crack.

'What are you going to tell the lieutenant?'

'That Natalie didn't do it.'

'And he's going to say what . . . ?'

'Your guess is as good as mine,' said Bobby with a shrug. Then began to re-walk the crime scene with Officer Sanchez trailing behind. It didn't matter that the teks had finally released the scene two days earlier or that most of the footprints were new – photographers from the *Chronicle*, a camera crew from KPIX, the usual collection of neighbours who suddenly wanted to renew their acquaintance – because he'd seen it all before, earlier that morning.

Everything that could be found had been bagged. Bobby was just being bloody-minded. Although he was probably being unfair to the neighbours. One old woman had stopped Bobby as he arrived at the house. She wanted to say how upset she was and from the hollow look in her eyes she meant it. Tamsin Steps occupied an area where the edges of Russian Hill merged with Pacific Heights. It was a nice neighbourhood.

Nice gardens, nice people, nice cars. The place backing onto the Persikovs, which wasn't even officially on Tamsin Steps, was on the rental market for more a month than most people in the city paid a year. Mind you, Begley House came with seven bedrooms, an octagonal tower and sea views.

Murders didn't happen in Tamsin Steps. Actually, if Bobby was being honest, such things tended not to happen at all in San Francisco, unless you were poor or black, and then there were a dozen such killings a year, mostly gang related.

'Why would she dial nine-one-one from her room, then go downstairs and pick up the weapon again?'

'She's a kid,' said Officer Sanchez. 'Why do kids do anything?'

'They have their reasons.'

Sanchez grunted.

A glazier had recently repaired the glass in the dining room, adding his footprints to those trampling down the flowers in a small bed outside the window. The small chair just inside the window had been taken for cleaning, then replaced with something new and less expensive. The original would go to auction, probably in Europe.

On being told its brocade seat was splattered with brains, the doctor's first instinct had been to burn the thing. Only the chair was original, early eighteenth century, and its nearest match was in the Victoria and Albert Museum in London. In the circumstances . . .

'You want a lift back?'

'No,' said Bobby, 'I'm not done. I want to walk the scene one more time.' This earned him another grunt, and it was only after Officer Sanchez had climbed into a squad car that Bobby realised he still didn't know what his partner had been doing there in the first place.

CHAPTER 3
Friday 6 February

In April 1991, the small sliver of central San Francisco bounded by Geary, Market and Larkin Streets got its own SFPD task force. The Tenderloin TF. Based out of a basement in the old Hibernia Bank building, the TTF policed an area thick with prostitutes, pimps, pushers and the highest ratio of parolees anywhere in the world. Ten years later, a purpose-built SFPD building opened at 301 Eddy Street, the new Tenderloin Station.

About five years after that, a similar decision to cut Chinatown out of Central and turn the area into its own SFPD district created such outrage from those within the local community that the whole plan was put on hold, indefinitely. Civic pride, however, needed saving and City Hall's compromise saw Chinatown merged with the Financial District and given quasi-autonomy as a SFPD sub-district within Central, which was, itself, one of five stations within Metro.

As merely a sub-station within Metro, Chinatown didn't rate its own captain, so it got a lieutenant instead. Rumour said that when Lieutenant Que retired the new Chief and the mayor had plans to slot the Financial District and Chinatown Station straight back into Central.

'Zha . . .'

Bobby shut the door behind him.

The old man in the blue uniform didn't ask Sergeant Zha to sit. They were well beyond that and the days when Lieutenant Que would have offered Bobby a coffee or asked how Ellen was doing and whether Kris liked her new school were distant memories. The lieutenant knew how Ellen was doing, which was not well. As for Kris, the whole station knew how Kris was doing. She'd been pulled in for underage drinking at a club in the Tenderloin.

Like it or not, fake IDs and underage drinking were a fact of life, but the club had been Zil's Kabaret and Kris was younger than most of the whores. Asked by Alphonse daVilla, the owner, what she was doing there, Kris replied, 'Looking for my dad.'

Bobby Zha had been somewhere else that night. He'd have liked to tell Lieutenant Que where that was, only Bobby had been too far gone to remember. It wasn't that he fell off the wagon, because Bobby was teetotal from choice. It was just that sometimes the pressure of work got so much he climbed aboard and crashed the thing on purpose. This happened maybe once a year.

Mostly Bobby made do with cleaning out his desk or stripping down an old Norton 500, oiling every part and putting the bike back together again. And again. A clean mindless obsession that bought him a day or two when the only thing to matter was which bit of metal went where. From habit, he stripped and rebuilt the bike on the floor of the kitchen. Something his wife had long since ceased to find endearing. It was years since he'd actually ridden the thing.

'You sure?'

Bobby wanted to ask how anyone could be sure of anything. Instead he nodded.

'Okay,' said Lieutenant Que. 'I'll pass that up the line. We'll see what the captain has to say . . .' They were talking about the Persikov case. 'What else are you working on?' The lieutenant wore his authority with ease, and one had to know the man well to hear the quaver in his voice put there by approaching retirement and a cancer that ate at his prostate.

Bobby thought about it, decided not to lie. 'Not much,' he admitted.

'I asked Officer Sanchez,' said Lieutenant Que. 'He told me you were working several cases.'

Great, thought Bobby. So now I owe Pete.

'Can we get coffee?'

Lieutenant Que stared at him.

'Alternatively,' said Bobby, 'we could skip the shit and you could just let me resign.'

The coffees were black and hot, although the uniform who brought them remembered to say *without milk*, which marked her out as one of the new intake. Once coffee would have come with donuts, only the lieutenant was dieting. At least that was what he told everyone. It was better than admitting to an ever-growing list of things his doctor had told him he could never eat again.

The lieutenant had two doctors. A general practitioner in Sun View and a small woman named Madame Han who kept a store on one of the side streets running up from Grant Avenue. She was even older than Lieutenant Que and was the only person he knew who could supply fresh civet cat. The lieutenant was pretty sure the civet was on some endangered list somewhere, but was careful not to check.

'What do you think of Sanchez?'

'A good officer.'

The lieutenant snorted.

'He puts in the hours,' said Bobby. 'He fills out the forms. The man's intelligent and makes friends easily. He'll go far.'

'You don't like him . . .'

'I do,' said Bobby. 'Just not sure the feeling's reciprocated.'

'Tell me what you're really working on,' insisted the lieutenant, as he watched Bobby empty a paper cup. It was a perfectly reasonable question. Bobby only wished he had a reasonable answer.

'You remember that missing transient?' said Bobby, crushing the cup into a soggy ball. 'He wasn't alone. There are others, also missing. And there's a pattern . . .'

'No one's told me. Who identified it?'

'I did,' said Bobby. 'Call up the files and I'll talk you through.'

It was hard to know who was bluffing whom. There were a hundred things Lieutenant Que could say to Bobby and none of them would mean a thing to the man who sat on the other side of the lieutenant's desk, staring out of the window.

Outside too long. Bobby knew what the Captain said about him. He'd been working the streets so long he behaved like he belonged there. It wasn't a case of dress, speech, look or even personal hygiene, merely mindset.

So Bobby kept doing what he did. It was hard to know if he'd ever been as good as legend insisted. All the same, Bobby knew his intuition remained a cornerstone of the lieutenant's defence: it was either that or get rid of him. And the lieutenant wasn't in the business of getting rid of officers wounded in the line of duty, even when something had been shaken loose in the shooting and never put back.

'The pattern . . . You're certain of this?'

'No, not really.'

Bobby reckoned it was that, more than anything else, which convinced Lieutenant Que that he might be on to something. If Bobby was bluffing he'd have taken care to appear more certain. The element of doubt had to mean Bobby was worrying at a lead, whether he admitted it or not.

'Okay,' said Lieutenant Que. 'We're done here.'

They both heard the dismissal in his voice. Although it took Bobby a second or so to act on it. Pushing back his chair, Bobby flicked an inappropriately flippant salute and reached for the door. Actually, the salute was doubly flippant, since Bobby still wore jeans and a black T-shirt and regulations restricted salutes to officers in uniform.

On his way out of the station, Bobby stopped off at the restroom to splash water on his face and comb his hair into a slightly neater tangle. Sanchez came in after him.

'That bad, huh?'

Shrugging, Bobby dragged the comb through his hair one last time and slid the object into his back pocket. 'All he has to do is fire me, retire me or let me resign.'

'You really want that?'

'What do you think?' said Bobby.

CHAPTER 4

Saturday 7 February

The day after Bobby talked to Lieutenant Que was the day before he met the nine-tail fox. Having got up, Bobby dressed, checked in for roll-call, and went out to talk to those to whom he usually talked; the destitute, addicts, people who sold themselves because they'd long since sold everything else they possessed.

A day much like any other, until Bobby ran into Colonel Billy in front of Starbucks, just outside Chinatown gates. The sun was setting and it was near enough the end of Bobby's shift for Bobby to need a coffee. The homeless man had other ideas.

'Look,' said Bobby. 'It's on the wrong side . . .'

Colonel Billy nodded and waited, politely. Quite why the dread-locked man was waiting was hard to say. Bobby had explained he couldn't do what Colonel Billy wanted, which was come with him across the bridge. If it had been anybody other than the colonel, Bobby would already be walking away or threatening the vagrant with arrest.

There were nearly 10,000 homeless people in the city. Of these a third were regarded as chronically homeless and a hundred were hard-core recidivists. At the top of this pyramid squatted Colonel Billy, self-proclaimed Vietnam vet.

'It's out of my area,' said Bobby. 'Call the sheriff in Marin County.'

'I tried,' Colonel Billy said. He held one arm crooked, as if broken and then badly mended, nursing a space where his missing kitten should be. Bobby doubted if the man even realised he was doing it. 'They weren't interested.'

'What did they say . . . ?'

'Not much,' Colonel Billy admitted. 'They wanted my address.'

Bobby could see how this might be a problem. On rainy days

Colonel Billy could mostly be found curled up in an alcove inside the Stockton tunnel, while high summer saw him camping out at the Sutro Baths, that ruin to philanthropy, private money and public hygiene. It was the days in between which gave Colonel Billy and everyone else problems. The days when fog rolled in across the Bay and even the Coit Tower was lost under a ghostly mist that could drop the temperature twenty degrees in as many seconds.

No one quite knew what Colonel Billy saw when the fog came down but it sent him howling through the streets, fists flailing as he fought off ghosts and demons no one else could see. According to Colonel Billy, ghosts were the homeless of the spirit world, and he wasn't about to have them move in on his patch.

'What did you tell the sheriff's office?'

'That I didn't have an address.'

Bobby could guess what came next. 'What happened?'

'They hung up.' Which was only to be expected. An itinerant with a stolen phone card could be a dangerous nuisance, particularly if he believed he'd seen aliens or a marksman from the CIA was hunting him down.

'You want a coffee?'

'No.' The homeless man shook his head. 'I'll take a McDonald's.'

Colonel Billy put half of his Big Mac and a third of his fries in the side pocket of his combat jacket for later, chewing his way through the half of the bun he'd decided to eat. Bobby made do with a grande latte.

'Tell me again what you found . . .'

'A baby,' said Colonel Billy. 'It was murdered.'

'How do you know?'

The man with the tied-back dreads, ragged jacket and old army boots glared at him and for a moment Bobby could believe Colonel Billy was what he claimed. A veteran of one of the nastiest and most pointless colonial wars ever fought.

'I know a dead baby when I see one,' said the man.

'So you left it where it was?'

'No,' said Colonel Billy. 'I couldn't do that. I taped her head back to her body, put her in a plastic bag and left her at Louie's place. You know, out by China Basin.'

Bobby sighed. 'Let me radio Officer Sanchez.'

*

An evening like any other. The insane parrot posse was shrieking like drunken dolls from the branches of a blue gum eucalyptus on Telegraph Hill, which was what they did best; although their chatter barely disturbed the concentration of the girl in black pyjamas who practised Tai Chi on the steps that ran down from the Coit Tower. It took more than a flock of feral parrots to disturb Kris Zha when she was being stubborn.

A cellphone could do it, though.

'Shit.' Kris flipped open her Nokia to check caller information. She almost didn't answer. 'Don't tell me,' said Kris. 'You want me to tell Mom that you're not going to make the parade . . .'

'Something's come up.'

'Of course it has.'

Attending the street festival for Chinese New Year was part of the Zha family tradition; Ellen's attempt to respect that part of her daughter's heritage. At least it had been a tradition until Bobby stopped turning up. This would make the third year in a row. The first time Kris had been disappointed, the second resigned: if his daughter was now angry, Bobby reckoned that represented an acceptable learning curve.

'There's a dead baby,' he said. Regretting it the moment the words came out of his mouth. 'Well, maybe . . .' But his daughter didn't hear the revision.

'A dead baby? Okay,' Kris said, 'I'll tell Mom.'

Bobby closed his own phone.

A thousand would-be sleuths, mostly bankers, journalists and retired school teachers were hunting through the side streets of the Financial District for charity, with a list of sixteen clues clutched in their hands and the memory of Bogart's Sam Spade colouring how they approached their task.

To the south of Union Square a paper dragon was shaking its head, tossing and turning itself into a beast which would dance up Powell and along Post Street, as the first of 60,000 firecrackers rolled in a wave around the Square and broke against the walls of Macys and Saks Fifth Avenue.

Bobby Zha knew how it would be. Even Lieutenant Que would be there. Walking with eight men carrying the flag, glaring out at crowds five deep along Post Street, daring them not to clap. It would be how it had always been. How it was always going to be two weeks after the

19

start of Chinese New Year, when the big parade wound through the city to mark the end of celebrations. There'd been a time that Kris and Ellen would have stood together in the crowd holding hands, but Kris was too old for that these days and, as for his wife, who knew whose hand Ellen was holding . . . ?

Not his, certainly.

CHAPTER 5

Saturday 7 February

The clouds above China Basin were busy emptying themselves onto anyone stupid enough to be out on the docks; and, in the opinion of Pete Sanchez, you had to be pretty stupid to be anywhere at all with Colonel Billy. Worse than this, Colonel Billy had just decided to mention that his murdered baby had a tail.

'What kind of tail?' asked Bobby, wiping rain from his face. Vestigial throwbacks were rare, but the sergeant knew of at least one case where a family had smothered a girl born with webbed fingers and toes. He'd been five and the newborn was his cousin.

'Curly,' said Colonel Billy.

'This long?' Bobby asked, holding his hands an inch apart.

Colonel Billy shook his head. 'No,' he said. 'Much longer. Like a puppy.'

They were all stood on an old naval quay, south of the rusting cranes, with a north-easterly wind driving rain in from the Bay and twilight turning to darkness around them. Beneath the quay's sodden planks water lapped restlessly against concrete pilings and worried at ragged stumps of wood, all that remained of an earlier pier.

Creeping gentrification would change this area, but not yet, and quite possibly never here, because the cancerous concrete and broken wharves of Poon Quay looked like they would crumble beneath the waves rather than succumb.

This was Louie's territory, Louie being Colonel Billy's friend, when she wasn't being his enemy . . . Sometimes they were lovers, though it was hard to know where that came in the sequence.

Bound by the Bay on three sides, and cut off from the shore by enough missing planks to give pause to anyone not willing to edge along slippery joists, Poon Quay formed the area Louie called *my island*.

The building which gave the quay its name had been elegant once, even beautiful, in a strict utilitarian sort of way, with half pillars flanking its doorways and art deco plaster work framing each window. But someone had kicked holes in a wall painted to look like stone, leaving a savage wound now colonised by pigeons, who cocked their heads and stared suspiciously at the three men stood in front of them.

'Where's Louie?' Bobby demanded.

Colonel Billy shrugged, his traditional answer to most questions.

'Was she there when you left the baby?'

A shake of the head.

'Okay,' said Bobby. 'We'd better search the building again.'

A sign on the front read, *Ticket Office – Han Poon Shipping*. It was so faded that, if it was not for the Chinese characters below, Bobby wouldn't have been able to decipher what it said at all. A newer sign read Carlo's Café, although even this had peeled with age.

'We've searched it twice already,' said Pete Sanchez. He turned to Colonel Billy. 'What were you doing across the bridge anyway?'

'Me?' Colonel Billy gazed out at the sullen Bay, his head tipped slightly to the side like one of the pigeons behind him. 'I was looking.'

'For food . . .'

'Of course not.' The homeless man squeezed water from his dreadlocks with blackened fingers and sniffed dismissively. He could hear helicopters coming low over the water. A steady thud like too much blood to the head and the low bass rumble of Wagner. Although that might have been a film.

'You remember Claude?'

Bobby did. A small vagrant with a hacking cough who hid his unease behind dark glasses, a Red Sox hat and wispy beard.

'He's disappeared,' said Colonel Billy. 'And I know who took him.' Pulling a crumpled page from his jacket pocket, Colonel Billy unfolded it. Only to hunch over his prize as soon as rain began to splatter the page.

'Look. It's in the *National Enquirer* . . . "Werewolf on loose in Marin County".'

It was a joke, Bobby wanted to say. *Michael Jackson is a Martian. Two-headed dog found in Moscow. Aliens ate my hamster.* Instead he asked, 'Why did you bring the baby here?'

Colonel Billy thought about it, then thought about it some more, apparently oblivious to the rain running down his combat jacket and filling his torn sneakers. Looking down at the sodden boards on which they stood, he considered the point, then went back to watching the black water. After a minute, he remembered.

'It seemed like the right thing. I needed to see Louie anyway. She's looking for Lucifer.'

Sanchez snorted.

'My cat,' Colonel Billy said crossly. 'He's missing.'

'You know,' Sanchez said. 'Beatrice and I are meant to be watching *Ballo della Regina* tonight and then grabbing something to eat at Rubicon . . .'

'I'll finish up here,' said Bobby. 'You take the car.'

Officer Sanchez didn't even pretend to protest.

Colonel Billy stared mournfully around Poon's ticket office. 'It was here, *bic*,' he promised, falling back into combat slang, as he watched Bobby's torch sweep another empty shelf. 'Tiny like a newborn, with weird eyes. Like one of those hooch kids from a ville.' His accent was thick, a thousand-mile drawl issuing from the mouth of a white San Franciscan who'd only ever left the city once. The time he went to Washington searching for his name on the Vietnam wall.

Bobby Zha knew this, he'd had the call. Just as he'd checked with the military to see if Colonel Billy had done time in the Gulf or Iraq, instead of Vietnam as the man claimed.

'I was there,' Colonel Billy insisted.

'Where?'

'In the valleys when the NVA come down the Ho Chi Minh. I got my purple heart at *A Shu* . . .' A medal was pinned crudely to the pocket of Colonel Billy's jacket and flapped every time he bent forward to check for dead babies under a broken table or upend a soggy box. So far as Bobby knew, the medal was not even real.

'Billy . . .' Bobby Zha began to say and then decided not to bother. 'Of course you were,' he said, steering the man towards the door through which they'd entered. As he escorted the homeless man back towards the road, Bobby listened to stories of firefights and jungle trails, dead friends and wars lost, wondering how much of what Colonel Billy said he actually believed.

'You . . .' The shout came from a security guard near a small gatehouse, which had been deserted when Bobby, Officer Sanchez and Colonel Billy originally pulled up outside the link fence. The guard carried a maglight in one hand and a wireless in the other.

'What are you doing here?'

'Police,' said Bobby, stepping into the light. He flipped the badge he still wore on a cord around his neck. 'Official business . . . We're on our way out,' he added.

'I want to stay,' insisted Billy. 'Find that dead baby.'

'Well, you can't,' said Bobby. 'We're going.' Stopping a cab half a mile down the road, he got a ride to the edge of the Tenderloin, paid off the driver and tucked $20 into the open pocket of Colonel Billy's jacket, before walking him to the door of a hostel where Billy was known.

Bobby didn't wait to see if the man went inside.

CHAPTER 6

Sunday 8 February

'As a matter of interest,' said Pete Sanchez. 'Why did you tell the boss about Colonel Billy?' After a morning re-searching the ticket office and Poon Quay, plus an afternoon trying to hunt down Louie, Colonel Billy or anyone else who might know where they'd both gone, Sanchez had returned to the station to sign off, only to come right out again because Lieutenant Que now had something else for him to do. Sanchez could have got away with sounding resentful. Bobby was impressed that he merely sounded curious.

'A dead baby is a dead baby.'

'Billy Boy probably imagined it,' said Sanchez. 'I mean, he said it had a tail . . .'

'What if he just imagined the tail?'

Bobby caught the glance Sanchez threw him. And then the junior officer had his eyes back on the road. The raised expanse of the freeway was as empty as it ever was on a rainy Sunday evening; lights showed from houses below them, evidence of life in a city locked down by rain and thoughts of work next morning.

Up ahead was a yellow cab that had overtaken Officer Sanchez's SUV a second or so earlier. It had one of those arched rooftop signs, in this case advertising a steam beer Bobby barely recognised. He could remember when almost every cab in the city advertised either Basta Pasta or quick-fry sauces.

'How was the food at Rubicon?'

'Good,' said Pete Sanchez, sounding surprised Bobby could even ask. The chef at Rubicon was famous. Sanchez and his fiancée ate there so often Bobby wouldn't have been surprised to discover they had an account. Rubicon was where the beautiful people ate, and most of

Chinatown Station were still coming to terms with discovering that such a group included one of their member.

Pete Sanchez was third-generation Mexican/American and represented the future of policing. Off duty, he wore understated suits from Billy Blue, mentioned only occasionally his degree in criminology from Austin and dated the new mayor's niece. As a teenager he'd gone to Austin round-faced and bashful, only to return with cheekbones, perfect teeth and a shit-eating grin that had half of the Chinatown Station – the female half – smiling back.

Bobby Zha wore glasses, pre-worn jeans from Gap, thought Brooks Brothers shirts elegant and had married the only daughter of a Jewish dentist, who emigrated to Tel Aviv, leaving his daughter the dental practice, a house near Russian Hill and a passing comment that if her husband sold shrouds then people would stop dying. He also left the address of a good divorce lawyer. So far, Ellen had resisted that final piece of advice.

'Hang on,' said Sanchez, pulling round the cab and cutting up a motorbike for good measure.

'You know . . .' said Bobby, then decided not to bother; Sanchez had been born in a hurry, and something that looked like an upscale Humvee crossed with a smoked-glass statement on wheels suited Sanchez perfectly.

Of course, a year's worth of swapping his vehicle for something less gas-guzzling would improve the environment more than recycling plastic bottles for a century. Bobby decided not to mention this either. He only knew it because his daughter had taped a page from *Cosmo Girl!* to the fridge. It made Bobby glad his wife owned the Merc, otherwise he'd have felt obliged to justify himself or get cross. Ellen simply ripped the page down and binned it without comment. She was on her way out to the surgery and Bobby and Kris had been there when she did it.

'You think this call is for real?'

'Maybe.' Bobby shrugged. A break-in had been reported at a deserted warehouse behind Grant Avenue. The place was awaiting rebirth as apartments and the call came from a public phone box, no name given. It was property crime.

Everything about the call said it should be dealt with by uniforms from the night shift, but Lieutenant Que had sent Sanchez to get Bobby to drop the search for Colonel Billy. Bobby guessed it was the lieutenant's way of telling them the dead baby search was over.

So now he was headed back, with Pete Sanchez nodding along fiercely to some track from *Get Rich Or Die*, while enthusing about langoustine with garlic, lemon grass and shaved lime leaf. Things in the SFPD were changing. There were exams and job appraisal forms, review boards and seminars on how to relate to the city's different minorities.

Pretty strange, Bobby thought, given San Francisco had always been a city where the minorities made up the majority. That was one of the things he liked. Of course, when he started things had been different. The force had needed more ethnic officers and Bobby counted, his last name being Chinese.

'Off here,' said Bobby. 'Hang a left . . .'

'Down here?'

Glancing up at a half-lit sign, Bobby nodded. The name of the street was in Chinese and the sign had rusted at the corners where it was screwed to the wall.

'Halfway down,' said Bobby, 'then stop by the arch.'

'Okay . . .' Slinging his SUV next to an empty store, Sanchez flipped open his door and heeled it shut behind him, stretching lazily, like a man who'd driven far longer than the fifteen minutes he'd actually been at the steering wheel. Somehow his casually parked SUV managed to look both official and not worth noticing. Something to do with the angle at which it was parked.

'What?' demanded Sanchez.

Bobby shook his head. 'Nothing.'

'You armed . . . ?'

'Of course I'm armed,' said Bobby. Like most officers, he put on his gun in the morning and took it off at night. He didn't fetishise the thing or spend his weekends polishing it. And if he kept his gun in good condition, that was to make sure it worked.

A short alley opened onto an odd-shaped area and facing them was the warehouse they'd come to check; a jutting square of yellow brick that stole the middle from what had once been a large courtyard. A passage ran down its right side, a sliver of space left over from when the warehouse had been built fifty years before. This passage eventually led left, into a blind alley behind the warehouse, while also heading straight until it reached the road up to Stockton Street. Bobby knew, he'd played here as a child.

'Okay,' said Sanchez. 'How do you want to do this?'

'Go round the back,' Bobby said. The basic rules said you approached a suspect building quickly and quietly, preferably from an unexpected angle. So this was exactly what Sanchez did, taking advantage of both *cover* and *concealment* and staying out of the *line of sight* of the building's windows and darkened door. By the book, from the moment he left Bobby's side to the point he disappeared into the passage. The man was good, Bobby had to admit that.

This area of Chinatown had seen brothels, drug dens and sweat shops come and go. In the late 1920s, the courtyard had been used as a backdrop for *Manchu Demon*, one of the last silent films to star Lulu Kite. In the early 1990s, the warehouse they were investigating had provided space for travel agents, a friendly society and a firm which machine cut soapstone carvings.

Eighteen, nineteen, twenty . . . Bobby counted off under his breath, decided Sanchez had been given enough time to get into position and jogged after him. He found the young officer crouched behind an empty oil drum. The drum stank of wet embers and rotting food. It might not provide much protection against anybody inside, but it was what there was. Again, Sanchez had got it right.

And should someone be inside, they'd expect trouble to come from the front, where sliding doors had been ripped from their rail. That was Bobby's theory anyway.

'Try the handle,' Bobby said.

Moving fluidly, Sanchez ducked from behind his cover and made it to a narrow metal doorway which made up the building's rear exit, half disappearing into shadow. A second or so later Sergeant Zha joined him.

'Unlocked?'

Sanchez nodded.

It helped that the door was steel and thus provided an element of armour. Doorways were dangerous, so said the manual. They funnelled those entering and provided those inside with an easy target. There was even an equation to describe the situation, only Bobby had never really understood why that might be useful.

'Open when you're ready,' he said, but somehow Sanchez seemed more reluctant than Bobby expected. 'Hey,' said Bobby. 'No problem. You want me to do it?'

He might as well have slapped Sanchez, given the look he got in return. All the same, something seemed to resolve itself in the younger officer's head, because he gripped the handle, twisted it silently and nodded as he felt the door come free. 'All yours,' Sanchez said.

'On three,' said Bobby. *One, two . . .*

Bobby went through the door with his revolver drawn and swept the hollow darkness. Not a sound and not a movement. The only thing he could see was a sour flicker from a light through the entrance beyond.

'Clear,' he said.

And then, because Sanchez remained outside, Bobby said it again. Only this time he said it more loudly.

Nothing.

Scanning the echoing darkness, Bobby debated returning the way he'd entered and decided against. *Approach from an unexpected angle . . .* So, watched by the ghosts of his own childhood, he traversed the warehouse floor, gun held half up/half across his body, moving lightly for a man in his late thirties.

The sliding doors were wide open, and beyond the arch and across a side street, a woman was adjusting her curtains. Bobby noted this, as he noted most things, except for those he forced himself to ignore. Like the way his daughter barely bothered to hide the fact she was smoking.

As for Ellen . . .

Sergeant Bobby Zha stepped through the door and into the courtyard with anger at his wife and the thud of a Fifty Cent track he didn't even like looping in his head. And the last thing he thought before he stepped into a silenced bullet was . . .

Shit, who's that?

The concrete took so long to reach him that, when it got close, Bobby realised the stains he could see were not on the concrete, but hung like torn curtains between the world and the inside of his eyes. When the click came, Bobby realised it was a lock knife being opened.

'Hey,' said a voice, sounding aggravated. 'You can do that later.'

'What difference does it make?'

'I'm not ready.'

'Too bad . . .' Hands reached down and rolled Bobby over, not hard or rough but as if he wasn't really there. There was a yank as someone freed the back of his T-shirt, and then pain so vicious he pissed himself. Far beyond anything he remembered, it dwarfed the cold numbness in his chest.

That was when Bobby accepted that, yes, he had been shot. Only now something else was happening and it was infinitely worse.

'Stop him shaking.'

Hands gripped Bobby's ankles and pulled on his legs until they were both straight. 'Hurry it up then.'

Hot pain sliced apart the flesh below his ribs, hot fingers burrowing through torn meat as the screams trapped in Bobby's lungs strangled on the bubbles in his throat.

It took Bobby Zha two hours to die. Given that he'd been shot with a .38 slug through his lower lung and then had the slug cut out of his side, this was far longer than was reasonable. Although there were a few small mercies. The main one being that Bobby was unconscious by the time his assailant finally prised free the slug, having found it a good six inches from where he'd first started looking.

The slug was old-fashioned, jacketed over a soft-lead core and cut crudely at the point so that it spread on impact. If half the powder hadn't been taken out, the slug would have passed right through Bobby; but then, of course, there was a risk it might simply get lost somewhere in the darkness.

'Bobby . . . ?' Hands were shaking the darkness awake.

'Are you okay?'

Despite the stickiness in his throat and the hot pain that gnawed at his chest, Bobby almost smiled. That was Sanchez for you. *Of course I'm not fucking okay*, he wanted to say, but the words remained stuck in his head.

'Don't talk,' said Sanchez.

And Bobby Zha did smile then. Mostly because he couldn't have talked if his life depended on it, which it didn't. Bobby knew things had moved beyond that. His life was spread out in a puddle below him.

'I've called for help,' Sanchez said.

Bobby Zha tried to focus on the figure kneeling beside him. All he got was a blur and words that alternated between anxious and soothing. This wasn't how life was meant to end. So much undone.

'It's okay,' Bobby tried to say. Only the fog and darkness were rolling in again and by the time they cleared Sanchez was gone.

In his place was a fox.

The fox was pure white and carried its tail high and curled like flame over its back. Its eyes were red as coals, fierce with anger. White canines showed on either side of its mouth.

'*Jinwei hu*,' said Bobby.

The fox nodded, even though Bobby had only said the name in his head. Somewhere on Grant Avenue, a kid let off a string of firecrackers left over from the night before and the fox grinned.

That was when the man in the puddle of blood, lying just inside an empty building, half a block behind Stockton Street, knew that he'd been right. Sometimes it was better to be realistic than hopeful, and he was dying. Although he found the appearance of the celestial fox far more shocking than the thought of his death.

Death was just going to sleep and not bothering to wake, and it was years since Bobby had gone to bed with real joy at the thought of waking up again. His life had become a round of duty and compromise and Bobby wasn't even sure he could even pin when that began.

When their first baby died? The summer Ellen had an affair? The evening he refused to retire on medical grounds? The night he watched Ellen accept he'd lied about working late and she hadn't cared enough to call him on it? All of those were possible.

But *Jinwei hu*?

He'd been six when a teacher explained that spirits didn't really exist and Bobby could still remember his grandfather's rage when Bobby told the old man his stories were untrue.

'You can insult ghosts,' he told the boy, 'although this is dangerous, and you can ignore them, if you must, but you deny they exist at your peril.' Putting down his brush, he turned to the boy, face serious.

'There are three worlds,' he said. 'The world of the demons, the world of the gods and our world, they overlap like shadows in a wood. The *Jinwei hu* can move between these worlds as easily as you walk from room to room. If you call he will come, whether you want him to or not. And sometimes he will appear, without you even realising that you'd called.'

This was the answer Bobby carried to his teacher. Which led to a quarrel between Bobby's father and grandfather, in which Bobby's mother came up, as she always did. But the teacher had been wrong and his grandfather right.

The nine-tailed fox did exist.

The beast just stood there, squinting at him. So close that Bobby could smell its sour reek and feel breath on his face.

Bobby Zha . . .

What? demanded Bobby.

Then realised it might have been better to ask, *Why?*

The fox was telling him something important, but Bobby could no longer hear anything above firecrackers somewhere inside his head. And then he couldn't hear these either, because whiteness came rushing up to greet him.

CHAPTER 7
Stalingrad Winter 1942

The snow came to the boy's knees, certainly no deeper. The noise, which Misha thought was cannon fire, was actually an 82mm BM-8 Katyusha, known to the enemy as Stalin's Organ. A detail which mattered not to the boy. What mattered was the bike. This was almost new, which Misha counted as the first miracle. The second miracle was that the bike had fuel, and the third was its engine started with a single kick.

Had Misha known anything about bikes, he would have recognised the machine as a Soviet version of a side-valve BMW. Although now the Nazis had overrun Russia, this collaboration was never mentioned. Checking he had Professor Persikov's notebook, icon and Nagant revolver, Misha yanked the flat twin off its side stand, wheeled it round on the frozen mud and slung one leg across a broad saddle.

Only three gears were working, the transmission was crude and the oil so cold it felt as if the crankshaft was trying to stir treacle, Misha noticed none of this. He was on a working motorbike and heading out of Stalingrad. For once in his life, Misha was doing what he was told.

He'd passed five dead *hiwi*, collaborators hung from the windows of a ruined factory and was almost at the river bank before the sniper fired his first shot. The sniper was Russian and so was Misha.

It was one of those misunderstandings of war. Misha would have stopped to explain he was on official business, but he never got the chance. The sniper was crouched behind the chimney of a department store almost a mile away, and it was mere luck his bullet grazed the side of the boy's skull.

The sniper had little expectation of hitting his target. He'd been firing more to make a point than anything else. The point he'd been making was that this was Stalingrad.

You didn't run.

Wrestling his bike upright, Misha climbed back onto the saddle. He wasn't running and, besides, Stalingrad was saved. In rubble, starving and pocketed with rats grown fat on corpses, but saved. A million troops, 2000 tanks, 3000 heavy guns, and three Air Armies . . . Those were the figures Professor Persikov gave him. The fight was almost over. In eight weeks the German offensive had been turned around and the city encircled by Soviet troops.

It was not as if the rats remained fat. When no man's land shifted, whole warrens of sewers and ruins became free. That was when the vermin were caught, cooked and eaten. So now it was the rats who were running out of places to hide.

Anyway, Misha was on official business. He might only be thirteen but he wasn't stupid, he knew what happened to those who ran away, Russian or German. They got shot by their own side.

Misha had eaten rat. Mind you, he'd eaten many things, most of them strange; centipedes thick as his wrist, an anteater so scaly it took him a whole day to peel away its armour. The turtle had been good. The sturgeon should have been, but somehow it ended up tasting like mud. It was old and the professor said Misha should have soaked its flesh in water first, to make it sweet.

He ate it, though, the professor. By then the professor was dying and Misha wasn't sure he meant some of the things he said. They were coming for him, the professor said. That's why the city never gave up. Misha didn't believe this. The city fought almost to the last man because this was what the Boss told them to do. And he told them because, as everyone said, this was the city that bore his name.

Stalingrad.

No one would ever forget it.

The professor was of middle height and balding, with a small beard and long fingers, like a pianist. He wore suits that frayed at the edges and carried his spectacles in a leather case, which he kept in the top pocket of his coat. He taught Misha how to kill animals swiftly and gut them efficiently, but most of all he taught Misha how to cook what he'd killed.

After the sturgeon and the turtle, the armadillo and the centipede came capuchin, lemur and something with huge eyes, fat paws and a

Latin name Misha found impossible to pronounce. He cooked them all, in pans at first, fried with black pepper and lemon juice from a bottle. At least the professor said it was lemon juice, he mixed it himself in the lab. After a while, the oil ran out and the primus stove broke, so Misha boiled the meat, which was a great Russian tradition. And then a sniper broke in looking for morphine. She found nothing but the clay pot Misha used to cook. It got smashed when Professor Persikov's NKVD lieutenant shot the soldier for looting.

After that, Misha roasted his meat over an open fire. He'd peel away the skin, stuff a metal bar into the animal's anus or mouth and hold it to the flames until flesh blackened and blistered. The meat had to be white or dark, not red. The professor was very firm about this. After a while, Misha stopped bothering with this because the man was dying anyway.

Professor Persikov thought it very funny to be dying. Misha knew this because the man told him. Misha was never able to understand why.

'Irony . . .'

And then, of course, the professor had to try to explain to Misha what irony was. Since this seemed to involve opera, Chekhov and a man who wrote a book about a large black cat that walked, talked and smoked cigars in Moscow, Misha came away no wiser.

'You must leave.'

Looking out at the rubble of burnt houses beyond the broken wall, Misha wondered where the professor thought he should go.

Yanking the bike up a gear, Misha headed towards a fat white ribbon where the Volga had frozen. Autumn sleet had turned most of the track to mud and then the long winter had fixed the mud to stone. Broken walls on either side jagged from the ground like teeth, all that remained of a city.

They'd been shelled by German guns. They'd been shelled by Russian guns. And for one memorable week, when the snows were falling, they'd been shelled by both at once. One either became used to the noise or went mad, like the professor's previous assistant. The professor had wanted Misha to skin, fillet and cook the man. After all, Fedya was already dead and the professor could ill afford to lose another animal to the pot.

Back then there had been many animals, the primus stove still worked and the NKVD ordered to guard the cellar with their lives still had weapons and ammunition. So Misha refused. Also, he didn't understand then about the animals, how fast they died and how few, in real terms, the professor had left.

Misha could still remember the first time he was allowed through the steel door. The stink, this was the main thing he remembered. Fear had a very special smell, somewhere between stale sweat, urine and shit. When he mentioned this to the professor, the man smiled.

'That's sex,' he said.

A dog was strapped to a table, its legs tied at the front and back. Its tail had been nailed to the table top. When Misha bent down the dog bared its teeth at him.

'Seventy-three hours,' said the professor.

Misha nodded.

'My record's ninety-seven. That's for a dog. A cat lasted five days.'

The dog's body was held in place by a cradle made from wood. The head was separate, about seven inches away from the animal's severed neck and short plastic tubes ran from head to body, carrying blood. Misha tried very hard not to be sick.

'Come and look,' said the professor.

In another room, smaller and with no windows, a naked man was strapped to a bed, face up this time. A Nazi uniform lay bundled in the corner.

'You see this?' The professor pointed to a combat dressing taped across the dead man's stomach. 'He'd been shot. That's why he died so fast. I told them to find me someone fresh.'

Professor Persikov nodded in the general direction of the stairs. He must mean his soldiers, Misha realised.

'I'm allowed prisoners,' said the professor. 'Prisoners and criminals. That's our agreement. I keep working and the NKVD keep protecting me.' He smiled at the boy. 'You understand now why they brought you here?'

Misha did.

'Unfortunately,' said the Professor, 'you're too thin. The shock of operating would only kill you. What did you do to get arrested?'

'I stole food . . .'

A soldier had taken salami and a bottle of vodka from an old woman. Misha had followed the man to the ruins of a bakery and waited until he was too drunk to stand. Misha might have got away with stealing the salami, his mistake had been to go back for the vodka. How could he not? A salami by itself was riches almost beyond imagining. A salami and what was left of the vodka . . . ? He could have swapped it for enough bread or dry biscuits to feed himself and his sister for weeks.

'You have family?'

Misha shook his head.

'But you're from here. This is your city?'

'It's everybody's city,' said Misha, that was what the Boss had said. Stalingrad belonged to everyone. The whole country was watching its brave defenders. 'Can I ask you a question?'

The professor looked at Misha, then nodded.

'What are you trying to do?'

'You wouldn't understand . . .'

'I would,' said Misha. 'I'm very intelligent. Everybody says so. I can see you're cutting off their heads and then trying to stop them dying. I just don't know why.'

'It's a secret,' said Professor Persikov, and when Misha looked doubtful, he added, 'The Boss's secret.'

That Misha understood. The Boss knew things, the Boss did things, cruel things but it was a cruel world and if the Boss didn't do these things to save his country there would be no country left to save. It made sense that the Boss had secrets.

'I can help,' said Misha. 'I'm good with my hands. I'm clever. I can cook.'

'What can you cook?'

'Show me what you've got . . .'

The professor glanced at the dead German.

'Other than that,' said Misha. 'I can cook the dog when it dies. Or rats, I know how to cook rats.'

'Really?' said the professor. 'How about an armadillo . . .'

The laboratory was in a cellar behind what was left of the zoo. Misha didn't know Stalingrad had a zoo, and then it turned out that it didn't, not really. A few of the animals had belonged in the city, but most arrived on a train with the professor. Many had died since, in the bombings, and NKVD officers had been forced to shoot those who came scavenging after the corpses for food. Of course, the NKVD were now gone. The professor wasn't sure where.

Over the next few months, Misha had pieced together most of

Professor Persikov's story. How he'd been working in Leningrad, which he often called St Petersburg. As the war got worse, the professor moved and moved again. He'd had his own armoured train until some general stole it. Here was where Professor Persikov ended up. The professor, his animals, his files and an assistant, who drank surgical alcohol, slit his wrists with a scalpel, and then shot himself into the bargain.

'Through the brain,' Professor Persikov said bitterly. 'You're not going to shoot yourself, are you?'

'No,' said Misha.

The wolves had been released that morning, having grown too hungry and wild to be useful. Professor Persikov was working mainly with small animals now, cutting the heads from mice, fixing the tubes and timing how long they took to die.

'I worked with an elephant once.'

'What happened?'

'It died . . .' He caught the boy's look. 'Oh, they all die,' he said. 'I mean it died while I was still operating. By the time I'd finished severing its head from its body, the nervous system was already beyond saving. We fed its flesh to the hyenas. That was in Novgorod . . .'

When Misha nodded, Professor Persikov smiled. And Misha guessed the man knew he had no idea where that was.

'You know the story about the runaway goats?'

Misha didn't.

'A herd of goats were galloping down a road when they were stopped by the local police. "What have you done?" demanded the police.

' "Comrade Beria has ordered the arrest of all elephants."

' "But you're goats."

' "I know," said the goats. "But try telling that to the NKVD." '

After he'd finished cleaning out the cages, Misha checked the animals, fed those that needed food and gave them all fresh water. Their real food had long gone and so the professor had taken to feeding the animals to each other. He'd begun with the herbivores, for obvious reasons; then had Misha kill the larger carnivores to keep the smaller ones fed, this Misha did with an old Nagant 7.62 revolver.

So life passed.

The mortar attacks continued, the sound of small arms fire and the thud of tank shells became as familiar as the wind which threw snow into Misha's face and froze the dead like twisted logs of wood. All the while, the sky was busy with Nazi bombers. Until this too changed. And Soviet planes rode the cold blue, looking down on the ruins of a city which would, after all, remain theirs.

As Misha grew stronger, Professor Persikov grew weak. His cough, always bad, became worse, until the blood he used to spit discreetly into a handkerchief began to dribble down his chin. The linen handkerchiefs were gone, as were almost all of the animals, his guards, the wood that kept his fire burning and the fuel that powered his single generator.

'It's over,' he told Misha.

'The war?'

'This . . .' The professor gestured at his desk, a simple table pushed against a cellar wall. 'My research. No one else has my level of knowledge. It will all go to waste.'

'Give it to me,' said Misha. 'I'll give it to another professor.'

'Another . . . ?'

'There must be someone else.'

'At the Zoological Institute in Moscow,' said the professor. 'If he's still alive. The man's a fool, but not as stupid as most. I'll write down his name.'

'I should go to Moscow?'

The professor looked at Misha as if he was mad. 'Of course not,' he said, 'you go to the nearest general and say you have a message for the Boss. Then you give the general these . . .' Professor Persikov pointed to the notes on his desk. 'He will send it to the Boss. The Boss will know what to do.'

Misha didn't doubt this. It was an act of faith that the Boss always knew what to do. So Misha took the bike, which apparently belonged to a NKVD colonel, kick-started the machine and walked it in circles across frozen mud, before climbing into the saddle. The bike was easier to ride than Misha expected, its centre of gravity so low the machine practically glued itself to the ground. It was because Misha didn't know in which direction to find a general that he rode away from the gunfire, and it was this that got him shot.

Red on red. Someone had put a blanket of purple in front of the snow. Misha could feel the warmth on his face and under his collar. He wore a uniform because his own jacket had rotted under the arms from sweat and because Professor Persikov told him to wear new clothes. And he carried . . . Misha tried to remember the things he was meant to be carrying and what he was meant to say when he arrived.

It was important.

He would be rewarded if he succeeded and punished if he failed, Misha had never seen the professor so stern. Maybe it was like the man said, dying concentrated the mind.

'*You*,' said a voice, although it said it almost kindly.

Hands dragged the weight off his leg and lifted him to his feet, which was when Misha realised he was no longer riding his bike. He'd kept going after the shot, long after warmth began to drip from the graze along the side of his skull. It was dark like night, now. The voices distant. Someone let go of Misha's shoulder and caught him again when the boy began to fall.

'Got a message,' said Misha.

'From the colonel?'

'No . . . Professor Persikov.' People repeated the name around Misha. It didn't seem to be one they knew.

'Who's this message for?'

'Comrade Stalin,' said Misha.

In the darkness around him, someone began to laugh, then stopped.

CHAPTER 8
Monday 16 February

One eye open, the other shut. In the beginning there was the fox. Its breath was sour and its howl like feedback from a lead guitar. Sometimes its eye glared red, like sun seen through skin, and other times it burned sullen and yellow, like cheap electric light. Often, the mind suspended in darkness barely noticed the fox was there at all.

Which was fine, because it wasn't . . .

In the far corner of a dingy room was a television. It was cheap, five years old and tuned to some NY cable channel that ran heavy rotation of ancient MOR classics and a sprinkling of new songs that sounded like old ones.

On screen, guitarists outnumbered keyboards three to one, and a solitary drummer beat out 4/4 rhythm on real kit, instead of twiddling knobs on some drum machine. There was a preponderance of poodle cuts, broken only by a shaved head with extravagant goatee. Whichever station it was obviously still considered Evanescence Goth.

This didn't matter, as there were only three people in the room and they were all unconscious. All three were male. LivingSoul Inc also ran a ward for women, but that was at the other end of the green-painted corridor, behind frosted double doors. The newest male patient was thirteen, wired to an old-fashioned and rather clumsy life-support system. He'd been unconscious for two years and was expected to live another ten.

No one knew much about the twenty-five-year-old in the bed by the window. His parents visited weekly but spoke only Basque, which made it hard for the staff at LivingSoul to discover more than his name.

The oldest of the three was Robert Vanberg. He had black hair, cut badly. His skin was flawless, as befitted a man who'd never really lived and his face was thin, eyes deep-set. Obviously enough, these were shut.

Originally Robert had been housed at Upper West, one of five Mount Olive hospitals in New York and the most expensive of those actually located in Manhattan. Cost had not been an issue in 1978 when Robert Vanberg was admitted, following a crash between his parents' Volvo and an out-of-control truck hauling industrial waste on FDR Drive. The boy was not expected to live.

By the time it became obvious the injured seven-year-old had fallen into a coma and might live for another ten years, the trucking company's insurers had all but admitted liability. So money was put into trust with di Simion, Barchetta & Rosenberg, who made the arrangements for the boy's long-term care.

In the twenty-one years that passed between the accident and the death of Robert Vanberg's mother, she visited him every week, except for the last three, when she was in hospital herself. During the entire time, Edward Vanberg, the child's stepfather, visited him only once. A week before his wife's death, when he went to Mount Olive to sign papers releasing the boy into the care of another medical institution.

When Edward Vanberg died a year later he'd spent exactly half the fee he extracted from Silvio di Simion for assigning his unconscious stepson to a cheaper hospital on the Lower East Side. All of which explained why the man, who struggled awake in a hospital bed at 2.30 in the morning on Monday 16th February, six years after this, found himself in a ward overlooking the Hudson, rather than out over Central Park.

It didn't matter to him, of course. As yet, he still thought he was in San Francisco.

Guitar chords clashed and a boy snarled into a mic, only not so ferociously that anyone watching was likely to get upset. Meticulously torn clothes fluttered in the breeze and then the screen faded to black, before going live on some update about Britney Spears.

As a small child, Bobby had smuggled a stone into the local pool, wrapped both hands around it and jumped into the deep end, to see if he could touch the bottom. What he remembered most was the tightness in his lungs as he stood on the bottom, and the fear he might never regain the surface. Bobby Zha was still swimming towards the light, voices and electric guitars when he remembered he was dying, and then, as Bobby opened his eyes to a single overhead bulb, he realised he wasn't. Not unless hell ran on fifteen-watt light bulbs hanging from bare twisted flex.

'So,' said a voice, 'will Britney sign a new movie deal or not?'

'Hard to know,' someone else answered. 'Guess we'll just have to wait and see.'

There'd been an earlier voice, talking about other things. This voice used *Bobby* a lot, as if that might make the man slipping below the darkness suddenly change his mind.

'We're losing him . . .'

'You can't,' said Officer Sanchez.

'I'm sorry.' The speaker was male, professionally sympathetic, his words apparently tinged with the respect one emergency service pays another. 'There's nothing we can do.'

'*You must.*'

If Bobby hadn't known better, he'd have sworn Pete Sanchez was crying.

'The trauma's too widespread,' said the man, still sounding sympathetic. 'There's not enough time to operate.'

Bobby was standing outside himself. Actually, when he thought about it, he realised he was crouched like some wild animal, with a crumbling wall at his back and the night world before his eyes lit in very non-human colours.

Again, that light.

Letting go his memories of Officer Sanchez and the stranger, Bobby felt himself released from whatever held him by the wall. Instead he concentrated on a bulb which hung like a dying sun from a fraying length of flex. The light it gave was so sullen Bobby could see the bulb had writing around the bottom.

That was when he realised life was even stranger than he remembered. Without glasses Sergeant Bobby Zha couldn't read headlines on the *San Francisco Chronicle* from across the squad room. Even with his spectacles, his left eye was so weak he barely made it through last year's medical. Yet he could distinctly see lettering on the underside of the bulb.

After a while, Bobby realised it was the bulb itself which was important. So he turned his attention to this instead, concentrating for so long that his eyes began to water; on one hand the bulb was so dim he could read the maker's name written in a circle around the bottom, on the other, its light was bright enough to make his head hurt.

If this was a contradiction, it was just one of many.

Very slowly, Bobby began to move his hands, to see if he could feel bandages around his chest, but his left hand wouldn't move, and when he tried harder, hooks tore at skin all the way up his arm. So he stopped trying to move that hand and concentrated on his right instead. The same thing happened.

Weasels rip my flesh.

Something Colonel Billy used to repeat, over and over as he stared out at the combined elegance and squalor of San Francisco's Union Square. Bobby never had known what it meant, even back then. As he began to shake his head, something obscene grated inside his throat and the movement nearly choked him. He was fixed to the bed by wires and tubes.

For a moment, Bobby felt certain he was in a police hospital recovering from being shot, but then where were the police? What was with his new eyesight? And why were cobwebs strung like net between the ceiling and light flex?

A military hospital, maybe. Some establishment used to dealing with severe body trauma. There were places locally where wounded grunts were nursed back into something approaching health after their time in Iraq or Afghanistan. Perhaps he was in one of those . . .

Listening hard, Bobby considered the hum of life beyond his room. A car ground its gears. Children yelled. Nothing that sounded like shouted orders or the stamp of soldiers on parade. And the texture to the sound was wrong, almost muffled. Like someone had taken the city outside, filtered away the high notes and then decided to get rid of the bass notes as well.

Not a military base.

Maybe he was hallucinating, Bobby made himself consider that. Perhaps this was the final stages of death and his oxygen-starved cortex was constructing a world for him to inhabit for as long as what was left of his identity clung to life. This seemed an unusually complex thought for someone operating on the vestiges of their reptilian brain, so Bobby discarded that idea as well.

He was in a room and tied to a bed.

When you have eliminated the impossible, whatever remains, however improbable, must be the truth . . . His grandmother used to tell him that, but then she was English and in many ways as opaque to the world as Colonel Billy. Children's shouts, the clash of metal against stone. A seagull high and sudden, calling its loneliness to the skies. Bobby listened to them all, wondering at the muffled nature of the sounds, until at last he heard footsteps and then a voice.

'*Mierda, esta nieve*, it kills me . . .'

Another voice agreed, the door shut and the clatter of mops against a pail told Bobby that two people had entered the room. Bobby owed most of his Spanish to an officer he'd dated briefly during his second year on the force. It was only later he worked out that most of what she taught him was not fit for polite society. But all the same, *this snow* . . . In San Francisco?

Shit indeed.

The voices talked over him in their mixture of Spanish, Creole and something Bobby couldn't recognise, and by the time a white-haired man with a mop had slopped the floor under Bobby's bed, absent-mindedly checked the face of the coma patient over which he was bending and then gone back to wringing out his mop, Bobby had managed to get his mouth open.

'Where am I?'

That was what Bobby meant to say. Only he was trying to say it around a fat tube which obstructed his throat and his lips felt numb and his tongue was trapped beneath a plastic restraint. So what he actually said mostly resembled the gargle of a newborn baby.

A narrow beam of light reached through the patient's cornea and iris to illuminate the cones at the back of his eye. Whatever Dr Hamid saw, it satisfied him.

'That's good.'

'And his pupils react to light?'

The doctor grunted. He'd already been through this with Ms Rowat, but Sally Rowat was a hospital administrator so she needed everything repeated three times and preferably put in writing.

Ms Rowat sounded less pleased with the result than Dr Hamid.

'You're sure?'

Dr Hamid straightened up, adjusted his coat and turned to face the hospital administrator. 'Of course I'm sure . . . He's scoring four on the Glasgow Coma Scale and five on his motor response test . . . And I've little doubt that if you removed that tube he'd score at least four and probably five on verbal. Not only are his eyes reacting to light, which I would expect, they're following the movement of my torch, which I would not . . .'

The doctor glanced around at the ward with its peeling paint and scuffed floor, then turned his attention back to Ms Rowat. 'So I would suggest, very strongly, that I take that tube out of his mouth, while you go tell his family to prepare themselves for a shock.'

It was Ms Rowat's turn to grunt. While she was still considering the many ways in which this was a bad idea, Dr Hamid continued to check the patient. Heartbeat normal, lung function fine, the reactions were adequate and muscle tone no worse than one might expect from someone who'd been unconscious over twenty years. There was a lot to be said for electrotherapy, although he suspected LivingSoul Inc used it because it was cheaper than hiring a live physiotherapist for the seven coma patients they still had on site.

Hospital was really a bit of a misnomer where this place was concerned. LS House was more a parking lot for families who needed round-the-clock provision for members unlikely to be talking to them or anyone else any time soon. Dr Hamid knew exactly what was worrying Ms Rowat. The patient represented an eighth of the fees that kept the operation up and functioning. Losing a patient was probably the difference between keeping and losing her bonus.

'There've been no signs?' Dr Hamid felt he had to ask. He was on supply from an agency and his own boss was bound to require that information for the report.

'Not that I'm aware.' Sally Rowat shrugged. 'Dr Weyler might have known, but he's . . .' She left the rest of that sentence unsaid. There was something perverse about a man noted for pro-bono work on accident victims killing himself in a car crash, particularly when no other vehicle was involved.

Suicide had been mentioned, until his family began threatening to sue. Now it was officially a tragedy. His recent work among street children in Brazil a matter of public record.

'You must have proper notes.'

Ms Rowat flipped open her woefully thin file, making a mental note not to use Dr Hamid's agency again. 'I'm sure we have,' she said carefully. 'They're just not here at the moment.'

'Let me unhook him,' said Dr Hamid. And to the patient, he said, 'I'm going to free you up a little.' First Dr Hamid removed a saline drip from the patient's arm and then a glucose feed. The wrist on the other hand had only one feed, although the ceramic implant set into his flesh had room for three.

'We'll do the catheter later,' Dr Hamid said. He came from a culture where to strip a man in front of a female stranger was unthinkable, although he realised things were different here. 'Just let me remove these . . .' Reaching across, he unplugged wires attached to four transparent circles on the man's chest.

'Okay,' said Dr Hamid, 'that just leaves this.' He nodded towards the throat tube. 'I'm sorry, this isn't going to be fun.'

Gripping the tube, Dr Hamid twisted carefully so that it slid out of the man's mouth in one steady curl of plastic. 'I know,' he said, to the choking man. 'It's always horrid.' As a student in Algiers, Dr Hamid's professor had stressed time and again that it really didn't matter what you said to patients most of the time, so long as you said something and your voice was calm and confident.

'Still, it's done now . . .'

Dr Hamid looked at the name attached to the wall beside the bed. Robert Vanberg. There was a date underneath the name. He looked at that twice.

'Robert,' he said.

'Bobby,' said the man in the bed. There was a rawness to his voice and an expression of complex horror on his face, as if listening to himself speak was the most obscene thing that had ever happened.

'Robert . . .' Dr Hamid agreed, kneeling beside the bed so his face was close to his new patient. The eyes which stared back were those of a hunted animal.

'Where am I?'

'In hospital.' The doctor wanted to say more but he knew almost nothing of the patient's case. 'You were in . . .' He glanced at the woman standing back from the bed.

'A crash,' Ms Rowat said reluctantly. 'You were in a car crash.'

'Car,' said the patient, adding 'crash' a moment later. The words could have been a foreign language. 'Where am I?' he asked again.

'In hospital,' said Dr Hamid, catching the administrator's eye. Perhaps matters were not as straightforward as he'd thought.

'No,' said the man. 'Where *exactly* am I?'

'You're in LivingSoul House,' said Ms Rowat carefully.

'Which city?' asked the man.

CHAPTER 9

Monday 16 February

New York? Bobby Zha looked at the man watching him. Middle Eastern, maybe North African. The woman had Japanese in her blood but dressed in best WASP fashion, albeit cheaply. As a half Cantonese boy growing up on the Chinatown/North Beach border, Bobby had become good at reading faces.

'I need to ask you some questions,' said the doctor. 'Let's start at the beginning. Do you remember your name?'

Of course he did.

'Your full name is Robert Edward Charles Gore Vanberg,' said the man in the white coat. 'And I'm Dr Hamid.'

'Bobby,' said Bobby, more firmly this time.

'Must have been his childhood name,' said the woman. Papers rustled. 'No record of it here . . .'

'You were in a car accident,' the doctor added, 'when you were small.' He said the last bit after he glanced at something attached to the wall. 'In a minute, Ms Rowat is going to move you to somewhere brighter.'

The woman looked as if she might object.

So the doctor nodded to her, one of those discreet nods meant to signal everything and nothing and moved casually towards a window. After a second, the woman followed. Whatever he said was enough, because the woman looked slowly round the tatty ward as if seeing it through someone else's eyes, then nodded.

'He's safe to move, right?'

'Yes,' said Dr Hamid.

'I'll get the porters onto it.'

Pulling out a cellphone, Ms Rowat speed-dialled a number and gave whoever was on the other end a rapid list of orders. 'They're emptying a stock room' she said. And then Ms Rowat seemed to listen to what she'd just said and reached again for her phone. 'An office,' she told Dr Hamid. 'They'll free up an office overlooking the river.'

After Ms Rowat went to make some calls, Dr Hamid used her absence to remove the last remaining tubes from his patient's body. 'Okay,' he said. 'Let's get you moved.'

The man who came to collect Bobby was the one who'd left the ward at a run, dropping his mop and bucket, such was his hurry to fetch someone in authority. Only instead of overalls, this time Enrique Xavier wore a stained white coat and had a gold badge with the word *porter* cut into it below his name.

'Enrique's going to take you to another room,' said Dr Hamid. 'And then I'll come down to check you again. Ms Rowat has gone to call your trustees . . . The people who help look after you,' he added, speaking slowly, as if talking to a child. After a second, Bobby realised this was because the doctor believed he was speaking to a child, albeit one trapped in the body of a man.

'I'm in New York, right?' said Bobby.

He watched the doctor nod.

'And what is today's date?'

Dr Hamid blinked. 'The date?' he said slowly.

It was Bobby's turn to nod.

'Well,' said Dr Hamid. 'A long time has passed since the accident. So you mustn't be upset . . .' He sucked his teeth in an absent-minded sort of way, and sighed to himself. 'A long time,' Dr Hamid repeated. 'So long it's actually another century now, the twenty-first. So it's two thousand and . . .'

'Not the year,' said Bobby. 'The date.'

This was not the reaction Dr Hamid expected from a patient coming out of long-term coma, although not that many long-term coma patients ever surfaced, so data was limited. All the same . . .

'Come on,' said Bobby. 'What day is it?'

Localised obsession?

'Is it still February?'

Dr Hamid really looked at his patient then . . . And, in the background, the television began rerunning the Britney Spears interview, so Enrique changed channels without even glancing at the screen,

49

ending up with New York One and details of the snowstorm currently swamping the city.

'Yes,' admitted Dr Hamid, 'it's February.'

'And the date?'

'We'll talk about it later,' said Dr Hamid, wondering why he hadn't thought of that answer earlier. 'First we need to get you onto that stretcher.'

'Good idea,' Enrique said. 'She's not going to like it if we take too long. I'll roll this end,' he added, reaching for the patient's shoulders. 'Perhaps the doctor could help with your feet.'

Between them, the two men tipped Bobby onto his side, slid a stretcher beneath him and rolled him back, shuffling him into position like an old length of carpet.

'Okay,' said Dr Hamid. 'Let's get him onto the trolley.'

A moment later their patient was being lifted from his bed and the stretcher was balanced on the cross bars of a battered gurney. Neither seemed quite made for the other, so Enrique ended up steering with one hand and holding the stretcher in place with his other.

'Not far,' he said.

The lift stank and was unpainted. A single, recessed bulb lit walls that had once been polished metal, but were now too scuffed and battered to reveal more than mere ghosts of the three men's reflection. Enrique stood against one wall, the trolley and its patient next to him. Dr Hamid was in the opposite corner, he seemed to be holding his breath.

'Keep still,' Dr Hamid told his patient. 'I know you want to see things but wait a little longer.'

'I'm fine,' said Bobby. Maybe there was an echo in the lift or perhaps this was how his voice had always sounded. Either way, Bobby was pretty sure he'd seen all he needed to see . . . Certainly enough to know that this wasn't a normal hospital and, if the SFPD had him in hiding, the cover was deeper than any he'd seen or heard about before.

'I'm definitely in New York?'

Enrique glanced towards the doctor, asking permission to say something and when Dr Hamid nodded, Enrique smiled. It was a sad smile, from a man who'd seen most things and was still shocked to see someone come out of a long-term coma.

'Yes,' he said, 'you're in New York. That's where your parents used to live.' A half glance at Dr Hamid checked it was all right to mention this. 'You were very young, remember? There was a big truck . . .'

Bobby Zha shook his head.

'My sister works in the office,' explained Enrique. 'She keeps the accounts.' He was talking to the doctor.

'Tell me,' said Dr Hamid, switching his attention to Bobby. 'What do you remember?'

CHAPTER 10
Tuesday 17 February

The man who stood up to greet Robert Vanberg looked worried. It was a well-hidden worry that revealed itself only in a slight twitch in one eye and the way Silvio di Simion's gaze slid away from his client to alight on something in the far distance.

On the desk in front of Mr di Simion was a medical report written by Dr Hamid and counter-signed by Jamie Miles, after Ms Rowat from LivingSoul insisted a second opinion was necessary before Robert Vanberg could be allowed to discharge himself from the clinic.

Dr Miles had suggested Bobby begin to think of himself as Robert, since he was an adult now. The way the doctor said this let Bobby know the man didn't believe this was entirely true.

Of course, both Dr Hamid and Dr Miles believed their patient was Robert Vanberg, and when Bobby tried to say he might be someone else, Dr Hamid had looked so horrified Bobby found himself nodding along to the suggestion that he was still in shock.

Apparently coming out of a coma was difficult. To come out of a coma that had lasted six presidents and a couple of major wars . . . Dr Miles had been sympathetic. Such confusion was to be expected. The best thing Bobby could do was let himself be looked after for a week or two. If he didn't like LivingSoul, then he or Dr Hamid could always recommend somewhere . . .

Dr Miles also recommended a good psychiatrist. One who'd already worked with a recovered coma patient. The fact the man had apparently become famous by writing about this patient Bobby failed to find reassuring. All the same, he locked the name away at the back of his skull ready for use, should he need it when he finally discovered what the fuck was going on.

Which he would, because Bobby had already reached that agreement with himself.

'Mr Vanberg.'

'That's okay,' said his visitor. 'Call me Bobby.' He knew exactly why the lawyer was so worried. Bobby had been in enough interview rooms to know when lies were about to be told.

It was Tuesday morning and beyond the windows of di Simion, Barchetta & Rosenberg, the whole of Park Avenue was silently turning an elegant shade of white. The silence made the snow impressive. A storm of flakes and not a sound to let anyone know how thick that storm really was. Rain, now you could count on rain to make itself known, thought Bobby, but snow turned down the sound and put the streets into half focus.

'Are you all right?'

Bobby glanced back, delighted he'd accidentally held the silence long enough to force di Simion into asking the first question, only to realise it was real. The lawyer was still worried, but it was a different kind of worry.

'I'm fine,' said Bobby, listening to his words betray him.

It had taken twelve hours to talk himself out of the clinic and into the office of his trustees. And in that time he'd listened to each and every one of his own words and been shocked, time and again, not to recognise his own voice. As for his face, he had badly cut black hair, deep-set eyes and high cheekbones. It was a good face. He only wished it was his.

'It will take a while,' Silvio di Simion said.

'What will?'

'To adjust,' said the lawyer. He hesitated, as if searching for the right words. 'Look,' he said. 'I've talked to Dr Miles and the next few weeks are going to be difficult for you. That's just one reason why it might be better if you left your trustees with power of attorney . . .'

Silvio di Simion didn't mention that he'd also talked to Dr Hamid, Ms Rowat and a psychiatrist his firm kept on unofficial retainer, asking each about the possibility of having Robert Vanberg declared unfit. Silvio di Simion's position was simple and convincing, even to himself.

How could a boy of seven trapped in an adult body be expected to look after his own affairs? That question had resulted, the night before, in the arrival at LivingSoul House of Dr Jack Gates, one of Manhattan's most famous psychiatrists.

Dressed head to toe in Gap, Dr Gates looked as if he'd nipped out of the gym to buy a decaf skinny latte. From the clean but worn Nike Air Convertibles to the half-full bottle of Evian carried in one hand, everything about him said relaxed and easy. So much so, Bobby had searched for some kind of irony undercutting the look and decided, after a second and closer examination, that there wasn't any.

'So,' Dr Gates had asked, running one hand through sandy hair. 'How are you feeling?' His hair was going thin on top and Jack Gates had one of those faces which got worse with age. Men were born with two kinds of faces, at least they were according to Bobby's grandfather. Some were born pretty and aged badly, but most men grew into their faces. Bobby had been fifteen when he was told this and Ellen had just dumped him for a boy three years older.

'I'm good,' said Bobby, reaching for the remote. He hated people who didn't bother to introduce themselves. It took arrogance to assume others already knew who you were.

'What are you watching?'

'The news,' said Bobby, though that should have been self-evident. An Israeli tank was advancing along a dusty street into a hail of stones, although it was unclear whether those throwing were Palestinians or settlers, they just looked like children.

'You know who they are?'

'The soldiers are from Israel,' said Bobby. 'The kids are just kids. The reporter hasn't said yet whether we're in the Golan Heights or Gaza.' One of the things about living with Ellen was she didn't let you remain neutral about this stuff. How could she, when her own father had retired to Tel Aviv and taken her younger sister with him.

Bobby shook his head.

'It's the drugs,' said Jack Gates. 'They make you feel a little weird.' His glance returned to the screen. 'You understand this stuff?'

'Of course I don't,' said Bobby. 'There are probably three people in the world who understand Middle-Eastern politics and two of them are lying . . .' Bobby shrugged. 'Can I tell you the difference between Hamas and Shin Bet? Yes, of course I can. What do you think I've been listening to for the last few years . . .'

And they'd arrived at the problem.

To which Bobby had already supplied a solution, although not one that LivingSoul, Dr Miles or di Simion, Barchetta & Rosenberg liked. Actually, it was Enrique, the old man with the pail, who'd supplied the answer in the minutes before Bobby was moved to his new room, by flicking channels and replacing gossip about Britney Spears with a documentary on Rikers Island.

'That'll do,' he said. 'It's not as if they're really listening.'

Keep it simple and make it impossible to refute. That was the secret of a perfect alibi. So many suspects felt the need to disguise their lies with ever more complex window dressing. In the end it was minor inconsistencies that destroyed them.

Not a mistake Bobby Zha was about to make.

'I was,' said Bobby. 'I could hear the television.' A simple, irrefutable statement. Of course, it would have been easy to refute if the television had only just been introduced or had been broken for years. It was pure luck that neither of these were true.

'I always knew,' Enrique said.

'What?'

Enrique had smiled. 'That you were different.'

'Really?' Bobby tried to match the smile with one of his own. Although the muscles of his face felt frozen and his tongue was too large for his mouth. 'What kind of different?'

'Not so . . .' Enrique stopped, his smile turning to embarrassment.

'You can say it,' said Bobby.

'You know, not so dead. Some of the others . . .' The old man thought about it. 'No one would know they were alive if it didn't say so on the machines. And Dr Weyler, he knew you were different too.'

'Dr Weyler?'

'He came in three times a year to run tests . . . For nothing. He was famous.'

Bobby looked puzzled, blank and vaguely disbelieving . . . Between the three expressions it was possible to acquire significant leverage without even opening one's mouth. There were definitely times when it was best to stay silent, and this was one of them.

He'd seen the celestial fox and been killed. Those two facts were burnt into his memory. He should have woken in the afterlife or not at all. Instead he'd woken in New York, wearing someone else's body. Bobby could accept this had happened or admit he was insane. And if he refused to accept it had happened then he would become insane anyway. He knew this for a fact, because he could feel the weight of his own panic like water behind a glass dam, just waiting to crash in and drown this weakened body.

'This man, Dr Weyler, he's dead?'

'Killed himself in a car crash,' Enrique said. 'A terrible thing.'

'It happened here?'

Enrique shook his head and readjusted the curtains, his face turned away from the man in the bed. Although Bobby couldn't be sure he thought the old man might be crying. 'It happened a week ago.'

'Where?' said Bobby.

'San Francisco,' said Enrique. 'Everyone's still really upset.'

CHAPTER 11
Tuesday 17 February

'My file,' said Robert Vanberg. 'It's definitely missing?'

Silvio di Simion stared at the dishevelled man on the other side of his desk. The interview was not going the way Mr di Simion had expected and there was something unsettling, almost knowing, in the way his client kept returning to the same question. It was as if Mr Vanberg already knew the lawyer was lying.

'Yes,' said Mr di Simion. 'It's missing.'

The man on the other side of the desk smiled. A slightly disturbing smile that spoke of dark dreams and months, maybe even years, trapped in a limbo between life and death.

'There seem to be a lot of missing files,' said Bobby. 'My medical notes. Dr Weyler's own files on my case. Now last year's accounts for my trust.' Standing up from a chair that probably cost more than Enrique earned in a year, Bobby prowled the edges of Mr di Simion's office. Expensive paintings, a marble bust of Cicero, leather-bound legal books.

'I'm sure you won't mind,' said Bobby, 'but I've appointed Niffenger and Sutcliffe to look over the figures, when you find them. If you can't find them, then obviously they'll just have to reconstruct the accounts from scratch . . .'

Bobby had been nowhere near Niffenger and Sutcliffe. He had, however, heard them mentioned on the car radio on his way over. Something to do with a corporate fraud case involving a sub-group of a failed multinational, he hadn't been listening that closely. He'd been busy watching Sixth Avenue unravel a few yards at a time in a snow-blind canyon of concrete and glass.

'I'm not sure that's entirely necessary.'

Glancing back at the space on Mr di Simion's desk where the files should have been, Bobby shrugged. 'I do hope not,' he said.

The Vanberg settlement had been covered by a confidentiality clause, which was probably just as well. Had it been made public, it would have made history. The victim was seven, talented, intelligent and came from a family with good connections. The company that owned the truck was under investigation for everything from fraud to dumping toxic waste half a mile from a junior school. It was also on the point of being offloaded by its owners onto another company, which could strip the assets while claiming to be removed morally from all that had gone before. In the end, vast as it was, the Vanberg settlement became just another accounting cost.

There were three bank accounts. The first, exclusively for hospital bills, drew money from a second, which was a general account. Money for this came from a third. In this was a sum larger than every dollar Bobby had ever earned in all his years with the SFPD, added together, doubled and multiplied by the age of his daughter. It was, he knew, an impossibly ridiculous sum. He also knew that if Silvio di Simion was prepared to admit to holding this much money, then chances were di Simion, Barchetta and Rosenberg held substantially more.

Quite how Bobby knew this was difficult to say, but it turned on Mr di Simion's handshake. Not in the ordinary way of being weak, too brief or over firm, those markers that Sergeant Bobby Zha would have noticed without even knowing he'd noticed them, it was much stranger than that.

He'd shaken the man's hand on entering Mr di Simion's office and immediately felt anxiety overlaid with a deep bitterness that life could be this unfair. And it took Bobby a second to realise that those feelings were not his own, and another to understand they belonged to the elegant lawyer currently assuring Bobby that he was stunned but delighted by the recent turn of events.

'I presume,' Mr di Simion had said, 'you don't want any publicity?'

The man who'd been told he was Robert Vanberg looked at the man he'd been told was his personal lawyer.

'Coming out of a coma like that. It would be quite a story.' The lawyer had paused, watching for some response Bobby was obviously failing to provide.

'No matter . . .'

Pointing to the only armchair, Silvio di Simion suggested Bobby rest himself. Only then, did Mr di Simion walk around his own desk and settle himself into a leather and walnut recliner. It went without saying that the recliner put the lawyer higher than his client. Very little of what di Simion did was about putting his clients at ease.

'This story Jack Gates told me about you listening to the radio . . .'

'Television,' said Bobby. 'And it's not a story.' Looking round, Bobby's gaze settled on a copy of that day's *New York Times*, now lying discarded in a waste bin. 'Honk Kong Suisse,' he said, reading aloud a sub-head. 'That's the Harare money. Siphoned off from Zimbabwe's International Aid budget and hidden in Zurich . . .'

Silvio di Simion stared at him.

'It's taken Hans Zimmer three years to track it down.' Bobby named the German financier who led the hunt. The chances of anyone outside financial circles being interested in the story would have stayed slim if one of Mugabe's ex security chiefs hadn't tried to blow up Hans Zimmer in a Paris restaurant, killing a young American couple in the process. The woman's family came from the Bay Area and for a week both the *Chronicle* and *Examiner* covered little else.

'Of course,' said Bobby, 'Zimmer only got help from HKS because Chris Chinhoyi exploded that bomb on Rue Jacob. Without it, Zurich would still be denying all knowledge of the accounts.'

The meeting had gone downhill from there, though di Simion managed to keep his smile right up to the point Bobby demanded sight of all the paperwork for the Vanberg trust.

'You've really talked to Niffenger and Sutcliffe?'

Producing a small Nokia from his pocket, Bobby nodded. 'I called them on my way over . . .' The phone belonged to Enrique and the mere promise of its return had been enough to persuade the old porter to lend it to Bobby.

Silvio di Simion and Bobby went through a bundle of forms in near silence, the lawyer indicating points where the client needed to sign and Bobby reading every paragraph before signing *Robert Vanberg*, the signature strange and unsettling as it appeared on the paper beneath his hand.

It was only on the way out of the office that Bobby noticed the Persian carpet and wondered how much of di Simion, Barchetta and Rosenberg's undoubted elegance had been provided by the Vanberg trust . . .

'You okay to drive me to a bank?'

'Sure thing,' said Enrique, opening the passenger door of his battered Volvo, almost as if he was a real chauffeur. 'I'll keep the engine running until you need me,' said the old man with a grin. 'You have any trouble in there?' Dark eyes watched Bobby from the driver's mirror.

'Should I have done?'

The grin got wider.

Morgan Cabot had their headquarters in a sandstone-fronted building on Fifth Avenue, just south of Eighteenth Street. The sidewalk was icy and two cars across the road had been reduced to smooth bumps beneath drifting snow, but the lobby was warm. It was also paved in Italian marble and had original Art Deco lift doors and brass surrounds, although everything behind the doors had been updated or replaced. A discreetly uniformed guard began moving towards Bobby before he'd even had time to stamp compacted snow from his heels. Maybe it was the jacket that Enrique had found for him.

'Sir?'

Having seen himself in the mirror, Bobby could understand the man's uncertainty. The hospital haircut worn by Bobby had probably involved little more than Enrique trimming round his ears once a month. And the jacket came from a thrift store opposite LivingSoul. So far Bobby owed Enrique $58, plus whatever the old man wanted for acting as a driver.

'I'd like to see Mr Cabot.'

'Mr Cabot?'

'The younger,' said Bobby. 'I gather his father is still in the Bahamas.' This was something Silvio di Simion let slip when Bobby first mentioned the bank. Henry Cabot Senior was on vacation for the winter. It was only later that Mr di Simion admitted the man's son would probably be there.

'If you could tell him I'm here?'

Bobby Zha liked Henry Cabot Junior on sight. Since he'd have said a New York banker was probably the last person in the world with whom he'd have anything in common, the thought amused him. Young Mr Cabot was just that, young. He was also dressed in a suit that looked as if it came straight off the peg at Bergdorf Goodman, but was undoubtedly even more expensive.

In the days before . . . Shaking his head, Bobby cut dead that thought. In his early days, before he first made sergeant, Bobby had worked a couple of cases involving fraud, CEOs and banks at the height of the dot com bubble. That was one of the reasons he was surprised to find himself liking the man who stepped from the lift and walked confidently across the floor to greet him. The other was that the man had bothered to come down at all. Even Bobby had been expecting to be sent up to his office.

'Henry Cabot, Junior,' said the man.

'Robert Vanberg,' replied Bobby, shaking the hand he was offered. Bobby watched the young man blink, although whether at confirmation of the name or at the touch of static between their fingers was hard to say. Without another word, Bobby pulled di Simion's letter of release from his pocket and passed it across.

Henry Cabot skim-read it once, then read it again, more slowly. He looked at the di Simion, Barchetta & Rosenberg letterhead, ran his finger across the logo to confirm it was engraved and discreetly re-checked Silvio di Simion's signature.

'What surprises me,' said Henry Cabot, 'is that Silvio hasn't telephoned to tell me about this . . .'

Bobby's smile was sour. 'I expect,' he said, 'that Mr di Simion is still getting over the shock.'

'You'd better come up,' said Henry Cabot, then looked at the letter he still held and adjusted his words. 'That is . . . If you'd like to?'

Bobby Zha left Morgan Cabot with a cheque book in the name of Robert Vanberg, even though Henry Cabot admitted no one really used cheques any more. It was just that Morgan Cabot was that kind of bank. He also carried away a cheque guarantee card and a shiny black credit card that read *Morgan Cabot* on one side, in silver lettering. There was a chip built into the credit card and this was also black.

'Anything else you need,' said Henry Cabot, 'just call me.'

As if. Somewhere behind Bobby's eyes, someone was trying very hard not to panic and a bit of Bobby was still trying to work out if that someone was him. He'd reached a deal with himself in the car on the way over, sort out the financial stuff and deal with everything else later. So that's what he was doing.

Most of the Vanberg money was now safely deposited in an investment account paying one quarter above bank rate, with the rest in a current account that still contained more than Bobby could ever have imagined owning.

'Enrique . . .'

The old man grinned. He'd parked his battered Volvo estate against a snowdrift and was busy ignoring a taxi that wanted to fight past. 'Everything good?'

'Sure.' Bobby nodded.

'Where to now?' asked Enrique, when he was back in the driver's seat. A New York cop who'd been marching purposefully towards the Volvo hesitated, considered calling in the licence plate and decided not to bother.

'Close,' said Bobby.

Enrique shook his head. 'No,' he said. 'They're not going to book you. It would be bad luck . . .' He grinned again, white teeth showing in the driver's mirror. 'No one messes when the Spirits ride.'

Bobby was still considering this when Enrique pulled up outside Lord & Taylor. 'This should do,' he said.

'Do what?'

'For a suit,' said Enrique. He glanced at the jacket Bobby wore, then shrugged. 'That looks okay,' he said, 'but it came off a dead man. Although that probably wouldn't worry you.' He looked as if he might say something else, then shut his mouth with a snap, pushed open his door and walked round to let Bobby out of the car.

'I have to go now,' said Enrique. 'My shift is starting.'

'Wait . . .' Bobby reached into the side pocket of his jacket and took out an untidy bundle of $50 notes. He gave the man $500, thought about it and added $500 more. 'That's for the suit and driving me around.'

'It's too . . .'

'No, it's not,' said Bobby. 'I'm going to need you later.' Extracting the Nokia that Enrique had lent him, he offered it to the old man.

'Keep it,' Enrique said. 'Until you get a better one.'

The first thing Bobby bought in Lord & Taylor was a wallet into which he decanted the bulk of the notes he'd taken on account from Morgan Cabot. Then he headed for the tenth floor and men's clothing. Half an hour later, Bobby left the department store with three suits, five black T-shirts, two pairs of shoes, a rose gold Evidenza watch and a leather case stuffed with everything he'd bought, apart from one black T-shirt and the Paul Smith suit, which he decided to wear.

And the man who walked into a barber's on the corner of Sixth and

Thirty-seventh earned a smile from the receptionist and the offer of coffee and a newspaper from an overworked junior, who nevertheless found time to put some biscuits on a plate to go with the coffee.

More snow was expected. Moscow was demanding sight proof that refugee oligarch Gregory Osip really died when his yacht exploded off San Francisco. No one mentioned a coma patient on the Lower East Side come back from the dead.

The Croatian girl with the scissors said nothing about the state of Bobby's hair. Instead she waited until the junior had washed and rinsed it in warm water and then set about making something from the mess.

'Face lift?' she asked finally.

'What makes you say that?'

'Slight scarring,' she said. After that, she combed his hair more carefully and although she'd suggested cropping it, she left it long at the sides. Even so, when Bobby left, he still looked infinitely slicker than when he'd walk in.

Once his hair was cut and he was back on Sixth, Bobby hailed a cab and named a hotel he'd spotted in the style section of a paper, while drinking coffee and waiting for his hair to be cut. Money, clothes, hair and hotel. He was running out of tick boxes. Pretty soon his list would be done and he'd have to face the thing he'd been avoiding.

'Kris?'

'Yes.'

'It's Dad.'

'What . . . ?' His daughter sounded bemused.

'It's me,' said Bobby. 'It's Dad.'

'You're *sick*.' The insult came in a shout. A sound he remembered from her childhood, when arguing with Kris meant facing a pre-teen with fists balled on her hips. She'd been permanently furious ever since. McDonald's, killing whales, digging up unspoilt bits of Alaska. He had trouble keeping up with what was wrong in her world.

'Let me talk to . . .'

'*Who is this?*'

Bobby never got to ask Kris for Ellen, because Ellen was already on the line, demanding his name. In the background Bobby could hear Kris vomiting.

'It's me,' he insisted. 'It's Bobby.' A couple coming out of Hotel 60 Thompson stopped to stare at him, looking away when Bobby glared back. 'Ellen,' said Bobby. 'It's me.'

'My husband's dead,' she said.

You could always tell when Ellen had gone beyond anger into fury, because an iciness entered her voice. It was then one remembered the stories about her father's childhood in Warsaw and how her grandfather had taken the eyes from a Nazi lieutenant using only his thumbs.

The officer had raped Ellen's grandmother. A hundred hostages died in the reprisal.

'This call will be traced,' said Ellen. 'My husband was a police hero and I have friends in the SFPD. They will find you. But let me give you my own warning. If you ever upset my daughter again I will hunt you down myself . . .'

Bobby didn't doubt that she meant it. 'Ellen,' he said. 'It's . . .'

A click ended their conversation.

CHAPTER 12

Thursday 19 February

After the snow stopped falling and the runways had been cleared, Bobby caught the first flight out of New York for San Francisco. The hotels circling Kennedy Airport were full of families waiting for flights. So it took money and perseverance to find Bobby a seat, although it helped that Bobby wanted to fly business class and was willing to pay the first price offered. All he wanted was what everyone wanted, to get home. It was only as Bobby headed away from check-in that he realised his home might still be in San Francisco, but the house there was no longer his . . .

'Mr Vanberg?'

The voice matched the questioner's face, professionally pleasant and slightly watchful. As if a career catering for the whims of those elevated enough to use the Platinum Club Lounge at New York's JFK had trained Sharon Gold in the fine art of reading people's personalities.

Bobby knew her name because it was engraved into a small brooch on the lapel of her blue jacket. And it was engraved, not die struck or laser cut. He knew it was engraved because his eyesight was good enough to catch the slight scratching inside each letter where metal had been cut away.

'If you'd like to give me that?'

Looking from the woman to the briefcase he carried, Bobby shook his head. Quite apart from anything else, if Sharon Gold carried his case then she'd realise it was empty. Anyway, he really didn't see why she should have to carry his luggage just because he'd paid something stupid for his flight, especially since it was all of ten paces from the club door to the chair she was offering.

'Can I get you a drink?'

Silence.

'Mr Vanberg . . . ?'

'Sorry,' said Bobby. 'I was thinking.' He'd pulled Ellen's number from memory, surely that proved something? How could he have Bobby Zha's memories and not be Bobby Zha? . . . Only Sergeant Bobby Zha was dead. It said so in the *Chronicle*.

Police Hero To Be Buried Today.

The burial was to be in San Mateo county, and Lieutenant Que had donated a funeral plot he'd been saving for himself. The plot was high on the side of a hill, overlooking a garden of remembrance and the feng sui was perfect. It was in the paper Bobby had picked up on his way through the terminal.

'Mr Vanberg?'

'Water,' Bobby said.

When she returned Bobby made himself smile and say *thank you*, even though he'd have preferred his water without bubbles, ice or the slice of lemon that kept bumping against his lips like a stranger's kiss.

There was nothing wrong with the body he wore. Apart from the obvious, that it belonged to someone else. It had a full head of hair, winter blue eyes, near perfect teeth and skin that had barely seen sunlight in thirty years. He was tall, well dressed and rich.

'Anything else you'd like?' asked Sharon Gold.

When Bobby was seven he flew to Paris for Christmas. Not *the holiday season* or *the winter break* but *Christmas*. His mother's sister insisted on the word when talking to Bobby. According to Grandfather Lau, this was because she hoped to counteract the influences of Bobby's other family.

Helen Campbell never actually said this, although she mentioned the fact Bobby needed to understand all his cultures and that was how Grandfather Lau translated what she said.

Paris, until then, had been a series of postcards for Bobby, each showing a building or scene more improbable than the one before. Notre Dame's ugly balustrades, a skeletal monument to the ego of Gustave Eiffel, the sugar confection that was Sacré Coeur, smirking down on the city like some poisonous skull.

It was his father who explained the sights to Bobby, in the days before Johnny Zha got shot. He'd gone to university in Paris, a surprising number of Chinese students did, and that was where he met Liz and Helen. No one quite knew what happened, because Johnny was meant to be going out with Helen, but Liz and Johnny married once Liz got pregnant and they both moved to San Francisco. Bobby Zha was born on 18 May, his mother died less than a day later.

Helen stayed in her room on the edge of the Marais. She never quite learnt to speak French properly but living there was better than going back to the small town where she was born and in which she'd never felt at home. She told Bobby this the Christmas he came to stay with her.

She told him many things. Most beyond the understanding of a boy of seven. Although his mother had never really liked men, apparently she lacked the courage to make friends with women . . . Growing up in a market town did that to you apparently. Bobby wasn't sure why, but he nodded at what his aunt said all the same. And he could see why his mother originally came to Paris. So many of the women seemed to be friends.

His aunt laughed at this, messed his hair and took Bobby for a walk in the Tuileries Gardens. Almost everything they did was free. All her money had gone on his ticket and the cost of a lawyer.

Three weeks it had taken to reach an agreement. In the end she'd used blackmail, that was what Grandfather Lau said, blackmail and a lawyer. Even so, it took crying, shouting and long-distance silences every night for three weeks for Bobby's father to agree that Bobby could spend one holiday in Paris.

Johnny Zha told his father it was the threat of lawyers that finally changed his mind, because Grandfather Lau understood lawyers could be dangerous, but Johnny lied. It was the letter from a Parisian oncologist that did it.

After Christmas came Easter, and New York was suggested.

There were conditions, of course. Helen paid for everything from Bobby's flight and the cost of his hotel room to food, winter clothing and taxis both ways from Bobby's home to San Francisco airport. Added to which, she was to meet him at JFK and have a taxi waiting.

No using the subway, no sharing cabs with complete strangers.

Bobby's father had no problem with her using the bus. Grandfather Lau, however, wanted to make it as difficult as possible. And, because of this, Helen had to fly out from Paris to New York the day before Bobby was allowed to fly from San Francisco to meet her.

Everything was to turn on a telephone call. Until Johnny Zha heard from his ex-wife's sister that she was already at JFK, Grandfather Lau would not allow Bobby onto the New-York-bound plane. In the end, Helen Campbell waited for fifteen hours in the wasteland that was JFK Arrivals, and though she smiled when the boy came through the gates in the company of a Pan Am stewardess, exhaustion had bruised her eyes.

Bobby could remember very little of his time in New York. Even to a child in a new city the hotel had been concrete and depressing. Their room on the seventeenth floor looked across a side street to the windows of an office building beyond. Only rain falling in dark ribbons made any impression on the boy.

And while his aunt was at Duane Reade, buying chocolate and painkillers, Bobby threw open the window to their room and leant out as far as possible, bracing his heels under the edge of a bed, and balancing himself across an ugly air-conditioning unit until he was stretched out into the darkened air.

'Hey . . .' The voice behind him was frightened. 'What are you doing?'

'Nothing,' said Bobby, then saw in her face that this was not answer enough. 'Nothing bad,' he promised. 'I'm just trying to catch the rain . . .'

It was years before he understood why his answer made her cry.

At the end of their week in New York, they took a Carey bus back to the airport. It was meant to be a taxi because that was what she'd agreed with Grandfather Lau but most of her dollars were gone and she'd had to put room service on a second card when her first one wouldn't work.

Neither of them cried at the airport. Not even when a young stewardess with a badge announcing her name as Nancy turned him round at the gate so he could wave goodbye.

'You're a brave boy,' Nancy told him.

It was all the boy could do not to ask why. Instead he muttered something non-committal and waved half-heartedly, seeing, even from that distance, the hurt in his aunt's eyes as he turned away.

Turning back, Bobby waved harder, but he was too late. His aunt was already walking away, shoulders hunched around her loneliness and her feet dragging misery like a shadow.

'I'm sorry,' said Nancy, when Bobby tried to pull away. 'You have to come with me now.' Maybe she felt badly about dragging him through the gates like that, because she spent much of the flight bringing him chocolates stolen from business class . . .

'Okay,' Bobby said, when his father asked him how New York had been. This seemed to be the right answer, since it was the only question Johnny Zha asked. They said nothing in the car on the way home and Bobby went straight out to play with friends until bedtime. This seemed to be the right thing to do too.

Families were complicated. Grandfather Lau believed in a queen of heaven, as did Bobby's aunt. Only her queen looked nothing like the one prayed to by Grandfather Lau. Bobby wasn't sure what his father believed, maybe nothing, because when Bobby asked, his father smiled and said he left stuff like that to women and old men.

The sex was quick and almost brutal. At the end, when Sharon Gold was buttoning her blue jacket, having pulled her bra down over one heavy breast and tucked her white shirt into the band of her regulation skirt, Bobby stepped back and steadied himself against the restroom wall.

He was alive. A heart not his might hammer in a body stolen from a hospital dedicated to keeping the already dead in this world and out of the next, but he was alive and awake. He had just proved that to himself. The dead did not have sex.

And then Bobby remembered.

They did. At least they did if Grandfather Lau was to be believed. Sometimes ghosts didn't even know they were dead. You could live with one your entire life and, not only might you not know it, the ghost might not know it either. The worlds of ghosts, humans and gods could get messy where they overlapped. The best Bobby could say was that he felt alive. More alive than at anytime before he was dead.

'Are you all right?'

'I'm good,' said Bobby, making himself smile, just as he'd made himself thank her earlier for the water. 'You'll probably need these.' He watched impassively as Sharon climbed into her knickers. She was pretty, slightly beyond her best and beginning to be embarrassed, and he'd just used her to try to prove something that remained unproved.

'One last thing,' said Bobby. 'Can I have your number?' It was worth asking for the shock in her eyes.

'Sure . . .' Sharon scrabbled in her bag for a pen and only stopped scrabbling when Bobby reached inside his jacket and extracted a black and silver Mont Blanc. He'd filled it with red ink before leaving Lord and Taylor. It looked strange now, taking down the number she dictated, but red was lucky, his grandfather had always been very insistent about that. And Bobby needed whatever luck he could get.

'What about your number?'

'Ahh . . .' Fishing out his new phone, Bobby pushed a couple of buttons and read off the digits. 'It's new,' he said, seeing the question in her face. 'So I don't know it yet.'

He didn't feel proud of giving her the wrong number and since he was only one digit out and that was in the area code there was a good chance she'd be able to call him anyway, assuming she could be bothered to look it up.

'Keep it,' Bobby said, when she tried to hand back the pen. 'It's not really my style.'

Sharon Gold looked doubtful at this, as well she might. Bobby had been equipped head to toe by a dresser from Lord Taylor and there was not a single thing in the ensemble which was out of place. From the crocodile-strapped gold Evidenza to the Italian leather shoes he looked . . .

Like someone else, Bobby thought sourly. Whoever that was. He also looked like a Fifth Avenue dummy come to life. Bobby knew this from watching the windows on Fifth on his way out of Manhattan.

'What time's your flight?'

She asked it with such formality that they both laughed, and Bobby leant forward to kiss her lightly on the lips.

'You know,' Sharon Gold told him. 'The sex . . . I don't often do stuff like that.'

'You never do stuff like that.'

'How do you know?'

'It's in your eyes,' said Bobby, because anything else would have been too complicated. 'And for the record, nor do I . . .' Although, in his case, Bobby was talking about that final kiss.

On his way out to the Boeing 757, Bobby smelt his fingers. Something he'd been unable to stop himself doing since his teens. His hands were thin, ring-less and totally unscarred, his fingers long. Not the hands of a police officer.

All he could smell was restroom soap. And while it was true that his pen was gone, he could have lost that anywhere. At CompUSA where he signed for an iPod he'd probably never use. At the duty free, where he'd bought a litre of European vodka only to abandon it in the men's restroom.

A missing pen meant nothing.

Not when his fingers smelt of soap and his head was beginning to piece together old bits of film that felt awfully like Sharon Gold's memories. And maybe that was so much shit. Maybe he was what he thought he was. A dead man in a borrowed body.

Bobby sighed.

CHAPTER 13
Thursday 19 February

Half of Bobby's childhood seemed to have taken place on planes. San Francisco to New York. New York to Paris. Paris to San Francisco. Juggling families, trying to slip through gaps between the loyalties that threatened to crush him.

Aged eleven, on a hot October afternoon, Bobby watched a couple ignore each other for the time it took a plane to travel from San Francisco to New York. Two children sat in the seats between them, buffers against a silence that was already frosting as the plane accelerated along the runway.

One of the children was a girl, maybe a year older than Bobby. The boy was younger, and took most of the anger on himself, largely by refusing to sit quietly with his head buried in a comic. The boy's eyes were dark with worry, while those of his sister were flat and experienced beyond her years . . .

In New York, after he landed, Bobby introduced himself to his grandmother, a woman he'd never met, and hugged her warmly, not giving himself time to recall Grandfather Lau's words of warning. And when Elizabeth Campbell asked him, that evening, if Bobby didn't find life hard without a mother, Bobby remembered the man with the check shirt and the woman in dark glasses sitting silent, with their children trapped between them, and shook his head.

She'd been surprised at that.

Almost as surprised as she was that Bobby could eat with a fork and spoke English as well as she did, though their accents varied and he used words like *gasoline* when she used *petrol*. Something his grandmother found odd and Bobby thought obvious, since the distance from San Francisco to London was almost half way round the world, so the very fact they even spoke the same language counted as a miracle.

At a cathedral on Fifth Avenue, his grandmother taught him to light candles for his mother and his aunt. Mostly, it seemed to Bobby, because she felt she should, rather than because it came naturally or she thought it would do him good.

And they walked round the edge of Central Park – talking obliquely about Aunt Helen, death and Bobby's future – until both agreed they were too hot to walk further. So she showed Bobby how to hail a yellow cab and they rode back to the Algonquin Hotel, where the walls of the lobby were dark wood and each chair so deep it seemed to have its own gravity. Whatever the temperature outside, the lobby was always warm and rich with the scent of coffee, polish, leather and cigars.

'Madame,' said a black man wearing a top hat, and Bobby remembered not to laugh. The carpet gave him little electric shocks and their waiter had to have everything repeated three times before he could understand Elizabeth Campbell's accent, but when the tray finally arrived, Bobby's grandmother had ordered tea for both of them, extra orange juice for Bobby and cookies still hot from the oven.

'That's Matilda,' said his grandmother, pointing to an elderly cat that suddenly appeared under the feet of those standing by the front desk.

'Really?' said Bobby. 'How do you know?' He was pretty sure his grandmother had never been to New York before.

'She's famous,' the old woman said. 'You can buy postcards.'

So began the strangest week of Bobby's childhood. A week that was to end as it began, over a cup of tea in the foyer of the Algonquin, while Matilda sat on their cases and all three waited for the cab that was to take Bobby to the airport.

'We need to talk,' said Bobby's grandmother, settling back into her seat, only to lean forward again, face narrowing with intensity.

'What do we need to talk about?'

'You,' said his grandmother.

The boy sighed. Grandfather Lau had told him to expect something like this. Although the old man had been careful not to specify exactly what *this* might be. 'Expect everything,' he told the boy.

'Do you like where you're living?'

Bobby nodded, without actually thinking about it.

'I mean, really?'

The basement was small but Bobby knew families who lived in

places much smaller. It could be damp, because a buried stream ran under the floor and the noise from lorries unloading vegetables into the warehouse behind sometimes kept him awake but it belonged to Grandfather Lau and there were only two of them now, Bobby and his grandfather, though others came and went.

Bobby slept at the back on a settee and his grandfather had the room at the front. That was where the old man kept his brushes, ink stone and sheets of hand-made paper, the only luxury he allowed himself. Alongside the ink stone lay a button that fell from the jacket of Madame Chiang herself. He'd been young then, handsome and brave. She told him to keep the button and keep it he had.

As a child, in the aftermath of the 1906 earthquake, Grandfather Lau had also been in the very meeting when Look Tin Eli, manager of Living Prosperity, decided to use the foreigners against themselves. Europeans had long come to Chinatown for prostitutes or opium and been followed by those who only wanted to look. This could be turned into something useful, something exotic enough to stop certain city fathers stealing the land.

So began Look Tin Eli's campaign to *add* Chinese decoration to those buildings still standing and ensure all new offices and shops, whether designed by Western architects or not, included their share of green roofs, golden dragons and carved doors. Chinatown's otherness became its protection. Although it was not until later that the Dragon Gate was erected where Grant Street crossed with Bush Street. By then Chinatown, still peopled mainly with immigrants from the province of Guangdong, had grown used to seeing banks and post offices given decoration better suited to a pavilion in Beijing's Forbidden City.

'What are you thinking?'

Bobby blinked. 'About Canton,' he said, reaching for his cup of tea. It was cold.

'You've never been there.'

'I've never been to England either.'

His grandmother sighed. 'I always knew this was going to be difficult,' she said, pinging the bell for someone's attention.

'You want me to come and live with you,' said Bobby.

'How do you know that?'

Bobby thought about his new clothes, the squeaky shoes and afternoon tea and the way this woman made herself ask questions to which she knew she wouldn't like the answer.

'It's obvious,' he said.

'Excuse me . . . Mr Vanberg?'

The voice was polite and so soft that had Bobby really been sleeping it would not have woken him. He guessed that was the point. Opening his eyes just as the blonde woman began to turn away, Bobby nodded.

'Oh,' she said, 'I'm sorry. I thought you were . . .' She offered him a menu with one hand, while using her other to steady herself lightly against the back of his seat. The plane was still passing over flat lands. At the moment it was suburbs and laid out roads but Bobby guessed a city would come next.

'Where are we?'

'About halfway,' she said.

'Then what's that city?'

She leant across, her breasts shifting slightly beneath the cotton of her blouse as she peered through his window. 'I'm not sure,' she said. 'I can find out for you . . .'

And before Bobby could stop her she was gone.

'Someone's asking the captain,' she said, when she returned. 'Would you like some lunch?'

The menu offered salmon, chicken or lamb. Nothing there to worry Hindus, Moslems or Jews. Behind him, in economy, flight attendants were pulling ready-made meals from a trolley, but a couple of lines at the bottom of his menu told Bobby that his meal could be prepared at any time during the flight except immediately after take off or less than half an hour before landing.

'Chicken,' said Bobby, choosing his wife's default dish. It broke few rules and couldn't be cooked in its mother's milk and such things mattered to Ellen, just as they'd mattered to him, for a while. Although they hadn't mattered so much to Ellen until her father left for Tel Aviv and Ellen refused to emigrate with him.

'You should make her go,' he told Bobby. 'You'll get a good job. Israel needs policemen.'

'I'm not stopping her,' promised Bobby, but the old man left San Francisco refusing to believe that and went to his grave still refusing.

Shaking his head at the offer of wine, Bobby watched the flight attendant walk away, her hips swinging beneath the blue material of her skirt. He drank still mineral water, ate the chicken, left most of his mustard mash and was lost in memories of his first meeting with Ellen before the stewardess had time to collect his tray . . .

CHAPTER 14

New York, mid 1980s

It was late autumn, which in New York seemed to mean warm rain and the tail end of Hurricane Edward, which ripped apart houses from Havana to Atlanta but was content with merely shredding awnings by the time it reached the city. Unfortunately, the storm it brought was severe enough to keep a dozen planes on the ground. In one of those planes, a thirteen-year-old boy folded an English newspaper, stuffed the paper into the pocket of a seat in front and shut his eyes.

The plane had been lined up for two hours and the captain had just announced it would be at least another two hours before the first of the line was cleared for take-off, apparently they were eleventh and a request to ground control for permission to disembark had just been refused.

Everyone was bored. The men were cross about the wait, the women silent and tight lipped and only one person was being noisy. A girl across the aisle in a pink angora sweater and spectacles.

'I'm bored.'

'*Ellen . . . !*'

'Well, I am. Why can't we get off?'

For all that her tone itself was childish, the voice was filled with a very adult anger. Opening his eyes, Bobby glanced across, willing to be impressed.

'What are you looking at?'

The girl's face was framed by a shock of black curls and she wore black jeans, Nike trainers and that pink sweater, which was already too tight. It was the last year she wore her hair long, although that was how Bobby always thought of her, if he shut his eyes and summoned up her face.

77

Bobby was on his way back to San Francisco, having changed planes in New York. Maybe it was because his grandmother had died, maybe because he found saying goodbye to London harder than he expected, but the flight across the Atlantic had left his manners as raw as his nerves. In the restroom earlier, he'd trapped himself in a cycle of soaping one hand with the other, over and over again, something he hadn't done for years.

'I'm looking at you,' he said, before adding, 'Obviously enough.'

'Well, don't.' The girl scowled.

Over the course of the next half hour, Bobby watched in his window as her reflection glanced at him five times, and when, on the sixth, he stared back, she rolled her eyes in disgust and pointedly looked away.

Bobby grinned and Ellen didn't like that either. He knew this, because she'd actually kept watching him out of one eye.

'You know,' said the man next to her, 'it's okay if you want to sit with your friend for a while.'

'Hey, thanks Dad . . .' Ellen's reply was loaded with more meaning than Bobby could filter.

'You don't have to,' Bobby said.

'Of course I don't *have* to.' Ellen's voice was sharp. 'Although Dad would like it if I did.'

Again, that sour weight of unspoken anger.

'They just got married,' Ellen explained. She was climbing over Bobby's legs as she said this, her rucksack having been thrown onto the empty window seat next to him. He'd offered to shift across but Ellen told him not to bother.

'Married?'

'Yeah. *Zey vant to be alone.*' This was said with a heavy European accent and another roll of her eyes. When Bobby's expression remained blank, she sighed and he guessed he'd failed some kind of test. 'How old are you?'

'Fifteen,' said Bobby.

'You don't look it.'

'Well, how old are you then?'

'Fifteen.'

Bobby almost said, *you don't look it either*. But she did. Ellen's hair was pulled back behind a tortoiseshell comb that looked both expensive and adult. She wore lipstick and eyeliner, enough to be seen in the artificial twilight of a night time plane.

Settling herself into the window seat, Ellen yanked the safety strap across her hips, then pulled a face. 'Must have been a twig,' she said, seeing Bobby notice.

'Probably a kid,' said Bobby.

Ellen smiled. 'You using this?'

Bobby wasn't, so Ellen flipped up their armrest and settled back, turning slightly towards him. He didn't know it then, but what she saw was black hair, cut cheaply, wide cheekbones and dark, weird-shaped eyes. As she said later, she'd seen better and kissed worse.

Over the next ten minutes, as the captain repeated his apologies and the lights went lower, Ellen and Bobby watched her father reach for his new wife's hand. After that, the two adults sank into their seats and the woman rested her head on Mr Goodman's shoulders. A while later, the couple pulled a blue blanket over themselves and snuggled down, eyes shut.

'It's so embarrassing,' said Ellen. 'They've been like this for weeks. They were like it at the airport. It's indecent.'

'Are you meant to call her Mom?'

Ellen shook her head. 'I'm spared that. She said I should call her Janice.'

'That's cool.'

'We're Jewish,' said Ellen, as if that explained everything. Looking at the serious-faced boy sat beside her, she said, 'How about you?'

Bobby shrugged.

They talked, Ellen cried. And as she cried, Ellen rested her forehead against his and then, when her tears became too much, wiped them away by burying her face in Bobby's neck: until he turned her head slightly, both then looking to see if her father had noticed their kiss.

That was what Bobby took away from five hours on the runway and what bound him to Ellen through the years that came after, the taste of her tears and the oily, almost animal smell of her hair. It was dark beyond the glass, water glistening on blacktop. The lights of distant buildings were stars, spots of light that flickered in the rain. Sleep had overtaken most people and the presence of the cabin crew had been reduced to a mutter of conversation from the back.

'Hey,' whispered Ellen. When Bobby said nothing, she looked again and realised he was asleep, now curled up, with his cheek flat against the material of his seat. Beyond Bobby, across the aisle, she could see Janice and her father, cocooned under their blanket.

Bloody-mindedness, and the fact she couldn't be bothered to stretch up and switch off the little vent busy blowing air onto her face, made Ellen reach behind her, extract the sealed blanket that had been pressing against her back and rip off its plastic cover.

Having tossed the plastic into the well at her feet, Ellen flicked out the blanket and let it settle across herself and the boy beside her; then she turned round to face the window, shuffled backwards slightly and let nature take over.

'Okay?' asked Bobby.

Ellen said nothing, although she opened her eyes and shut them again, having satisfied herself that the plane was lit only by the light of a single man who stubbornly kept reading his magazine. The plane had taken off, finally. A trolley of meals that almost no one wanted had been walked down the aisle, then tidied away. The lights were down and Bobby was curled up behind her. All it took was for Ellen to move her arm slightly when Bobby reached round.

Because this seemed safest, Bobby rested his hand on Ellen's stomach. Only to feel her lift his fingers, placing them firmly against the underside of one breast. Bobby almost asked if that was okay, but stopped himself in time.

A minute later, Bobby was cupping the whole breast, prepared to swear he could feel Ellen's nipple through pink angora and the cotton of her bra beneath. That was when he dropped his hand to Ellen's belt, taking care not to touch her tummy on the way down.

Too fast.

Although Ellen let his fingers lie there, when he tried to undo the buckle of her belt, she stopped him. Their tussle was silent and restrained. Both aware not just of the others dozing around them but also of Ellen's father across the aisle behind them. Ellen was stronger than Bobby expected, and she was pulling at his thumb with her whole hand, while he still needed to use that thumb and his fingers to unbuckle her belt.

Okay, he said finally, *you win* . . . Although he didn't say this aloud.

After defeat, came disengagement and Bobby fully expected the girl to have nothing more to do with him, which only showed how little he then knew of such things. Or maybe he'd just underestimated how angry she was with her father.

'Sorry,' said Ellen, once she'd turned to face him. 'But that's not allowed. I promised my mother.'

What? Bobby wanted to whisper. *What did you promise?* He was wondering how much room that promise allowed for negotiation. Instead, Bobby said, 'That's okay.'

Ellen's smile was amused. Later, she said, 'You know what it means when people kiss like this?'

'Of course I do,' said Bobby wondering.

'Yeah,' she said. 'I thought you did.'

Ellen undid her own bra, reaching behind her and flipping a hook that Bobby had been fumbling. 'Always tricky,' she said, her words taking the sting from the matter-of-fact way she'd pushed his hand aside.

'There,' said Ellen. 'That's better.'

Bobby wanted to tell Ellen that she was the first girl he'd ever touched, and yet, instinctively, he knew this would be a really dumb move. It had occurred to him that Ellen might believe what he said. She really thought he was fifteen.

They got married seven years, two break-ups and a couple of other lovers later. Ellen was pregnant with the child they lost.

PART 2

CHAPTER 15

Saturday 21 February

Contractors had taken three bulldozers and scooped out half of a hill, removing rock and flattening small valleys until the site looked as smooth and soulless as a golf course. Orange tape still sealed off the new area and would remain in place while sprinkler systems fed recently seeded grass. Only when this had grown, been mowed, rolled and tended could the new lawns be planted with what was meant to be planted there.

Bodies.

So now a handful of marble statues stood lonely on their plinths, amid a sea of reddish earth and thin scabs of new grass. They were elegant and tasteful statues, mostly women draped with robes that suggested hips and breasts without ever revealing them. The men were stern faced, with curled beards and the blank eyes of dead Roman emperors.

'Classy,' said the cab driver, drawing to a halt on a road above the cemetery.

The man in the back of the taxi said nothing. He barely noticed the improvements about which the managers of Remembrance Park were so proud. He was too busy watching a tall man in the dress uniform of an SFPD lieutenant reciting words beneath the upturned bowl of an open sky.

Prayer, eulogy or brief speech of farewell. If the man hadn't known better, he'd have thought Lieutenant Que meant it.

Opening his door, the man stepped out of the cab and stood, one hand shading his eyes from light reflecting off chipped marble, that stuff some cemeteries use to keep down weeds and hide the fact few families bother to tend their plots once the ceremony is over and the cars have all gone home.

An earlier manager had planted eucalyptus and Monterey pine and cypress along the crest of a hill behind him, breaking up the San Mateo horizon and giving Remembrance Park an almost rural edge. Dried leaves crackled underfoot as the man turned back and peeled off a handful of fifties. The driver had been reluctant to come out this far, until money persuaded him . . .

The leaves beneath the passenger's feet were long, slightly curved like paper sickles and the tree from which they'd fallen had long scars on its trunk, where strips of bark had peeled back to reveal grey beneath.

Those trees were everywhere in San Francisco. In fact, he'd seen identical trees his entire life, and it shocked him to realise he had no idea what they were actually called.

'You want me to wait?'

'What . . . ?' The passenger looked from his driver to the bundle of notes in that man's hand. He knew what his driver thought of the mayor, which was good. And what he thought of the previous administration, which was far less so. He'd heard about the driver's time in Vietnam and done the maths, catching sight of the man's grey hair and ravaged face, to work out that, yes, he could be for real.

'It's okay,' said the passenger. 'I can find my own way back.'

'You're the boss.' The driver glanced down at the uniforms gathered around an open grave, then put his Cadillac into reverse, ready to back up the way he'd come. 'Someone you know?'

'Yeah,' said the passenger. 'Something like that.'

Dead leaves gave way to scrub and then to lawns that sloped down to wide white gates and a distant sea. The open grave was closer to the trees than the gate, so most mourners leant slightly backwards to compensate for the hill.

Only the Rabbi and Lieutenant Que leant forward, since they stood on the far side of the grave, with their backs to the sea. This meant they were the only ones able to see the man in the Armani suit walk down towards the group around the grave.

'So,' thought the man, 'I can still be seen . . .'

It was a ridiculous thing to think, but nothing sensible seemed worth thinking, because nothing sensible made sense. In fact, nothing really made sense, sensible or not.

Although that could have been the pain in his head.

Or being dead.

Perhaps both.

The Rabbi nodded, without breaking his train of thought or the prayer that issued in easy tones from his mouth. Lieutenant Que just stared. And in that stare Bobby knew his clothes had been costed, his haircut noted and his dark glasses regarded with disapproval.

Bobby nodded to the Rabbi in return. And then nodded to Lieutenant Que. All the same, he remained roughly five paces behind the others, which gave him enough height to look over their heads and out across the ocean. Ellen, Kris and Officer Sanchez stood together in a tight little knot, with a blonde woman stood slightly to one side. Beatrice de la Paix had her hand trailing, as if she needed Sanchez to reach for it and reassure her. Sanchez, however, was staring rigidly ahead.

'And now we recite *El Maleh Rachamin* . . .' Since the Rabbi was the only one to continue talking, Bobby decided he'd been talking about himself in the plural. Words began to fill the afternoon air, solemn and serious; only to be broken by a high sob.

It was Kris.

As Bobby began to step forward, Ellen turned. Whatever Ellen said to her daughter wasn't enough, because the sobs grew louder and Bobby saw Lieutenant Que glance at Ellen who nodded, folding Kris in her arms.

For a second it seemed that Kris would fight the comfort being offered, but then she stopped struggling.

'It's okay.' The lieutenant's words came clear across the open slash of grave. 'You're doing really well.'

'No, I'm not,' said Kris, her words mostly lost in Ellen's shoulder. And as Bobby watched, Officer Sanchez reached out to grip Ellen's hand, only once and hard. Whatever he said was too low to be heard and Bobby saw Kris tense, suddenly aware she no longer had her mother's full attention . . .

It was turning out to be a day of surprises. Having checked in at the Hotel Triton, Bobby had detoured to 850 Bryant just long enough to check if it was true about Bobby Zha's funeral. The look he got from the Hispanic sheriff operating the metal detector told him all he needed to know.

'When's it happening?'

Deputy Molina checked her watch, the way some people instinctively do when asked the day or some question about the future, only Deputy Molina meant it, Bobby realised. She was checking to see if he was too late.

'Pretty much now,' the deputy said.

'I thought it would take longer,' said Bobby, the words leaving a sour taste in his mouth. 'What about the autopsy?'

'That's done. The body's been released for burial.' Deputy Molina shrugged, looked round and leant a little closer. 'The wife was making a fuss. Apparently he should have been buried the next day. A religious thing . . .' The deputy said it like she'd personally taken one of the calls. And Bobby could imagine his wife on the line, laying down Judaic law. But for him . . . ?

'Well, Ellen's Jewish,' he agreed. Bobby stumbled over Ellen's own name but Deputy Molina was already shrugging. Her attention on a line of visitors building up behind Bobby. All waiting to get through the metal detector.

'The problem is,' said Bobby. 'I'm still here.'

The deputy looked up, with an expression that said, *Don't I just know it.*

'You a friend of Sergeant Zha . . . ?' She'd already noticed the man didn't wear uniform and a second glance told her his suit was too good for a plain-clothes officer. He looked more like a member of the Mayor's mob, too slick for his own good.

'Yeah,' said Bobby. 'One of the last.'

A scowl on the woman's face begged to disagree and the weird thing was, even looking again, Bobby couldn't remember noticing her before, much less having banged uglies.

She gave him an address and Bobby gave her a smile. Only by then she'd gone back to waving visitors through the arch of her metal detector.

'I'm Lieutenant Que,' said the elderly Chinese officer, offering his hand. His grip was firm and unthreatening. A sign that he'd long since moved beyond having to prove himself to strangers. Brown eyes swept over Bobby, stumbling again at the dark glasses.

'Migraine,' said Bobby.

A sense of loss. Somewhat unexpected. A sense of loss and a weariness so deep it reached to bone.

Lieutenant Que was a man who wore his age well, and only the liver spots scarring his hands and a slight trembling in his shake showed that age and illness continued to take their toll.

As always his uniform was immaculate, but then this was a man who had slept with his trousers folded beneath his mattress as a young officer because he could not afford an iron. The little money he earned had kept his mother, father, three sisters and one cousin in food.

Having given his name, Lieutenant Que waited for the man opposite to do the same. Not least, because the lieutenant had never seen him before and yet the man walked among the departing mourners as if he belonged there.

'Vanberg,' Bobby said. 'Robert Vanberg.' He meant to say the surname as one word but stumbled in the middle and heard Lieutenant Que repeat it back to him as two.

'You knew Bobby Zha, Mr Van Berg?'

Of course I fucking did, Bobby wanted to shout. *It's me. Don't you get it?*

Instead Bobby stared over the lieutenant's shoulder to where Kris stood next to Ellen, who was locked in close conversation with Sanchez. Seeing his gaze, Lieutenant Que turned and nodded.

'Ellen Zha,' he said. 'And Kris, their daughter . . .'

She's never been Ellen Zha in her life, thought Bobby. It's always been Goodman. That was how she was born and how she intends to die. *I should know.*

'Zha?'

Lieutenant Que nodded, reappraising. Killers came back to haunt funerals so frequently, they might as well have been ghosts themselves.

'I thought Ellen still used Goodman?' said Bobby, and watched the lieutenant relax slightly.

'Their daughter's taken it hard,' said Lieutenant Que. 'She quarrelled with her father the day before. About half an hour prior to last week's Chinese parade. He called while the kid was practising . . .'

'Tai Chi,' said Bobby, without thinking. 'I heard,' Bobby added, when the lieutenant stared at him.

'No,' said Lieutenant Que, 'you didn't. The only people who know that are Ellen, the kid and me . . .'

'And Officer Sanchez.'

The lieutenant looked almost puzzled. 'Why would Pete Sanchez know?'

'I thought . . .' Bobby hesitated. 'Didn't Bobby tell Sanchez on the drive back from the docks? Before they went to investigate that warehouse.'

'Sergeant Zha was by himself,' said Lieutenant Que. 'And we're still trying to work out what he was doing in a building behind Grant Street in the first place. So if you know . . .' The elderly officer's gaze took in Bobby's elegant suit and East Coast haircut.

Bobby wanted to say, I don't get it. I thought you told us to go there. Instead he stared from the lieutenant to where Sanchez stood, back to both of them, his arm now around Kris, consoling Bobby's daughter.

'What aren't you telling me?' said the lieutenant.

As grins went, Bobby's could have stripped humanity from a skull. 'You know,' said Bobby. 'You can't begin to imagine what I'm not telling you.'

Turning to walk away, he headed towards the little group around Officer Sanchez, but the lieutenant caught Bobby up and somehow managed to steer him towards the open grave.

'He was one of my best officers,' Lieutenant Que said. 'So if you know how this happened then tell me.'

'One of your best . . .'

'What?' said the lieutenant. 'Why are you shaking your head?'

'That wasn't what I heard,' said Bobby. And then he made the mistake of looking down at the coffin. White lacquer, with three distinct humps in the lid. A traditional Chinese model of a type he hadn't seen for thirty years. The kind his father had been buried in.

A handful of earth smeared its glossy surface. It was like looking in the mirror and finding nothing on the other side.

'You all right?' asked Lieutenant Que.

'No,' said Bobby. 'I think it's fair to say I'm anything but . . .' He shook his head, trying to clear it of sirens, darkness and the red-eyed silhouette of a nine-tailed fox. 'You saw the body yourself?'

'I identified it.'

'Ellen didn't come down?'

'No,' said the lieutenant. 'There's no way I was going to let her see Bobby looking like that. It would destroy her.'

'A gun shot,' Bobby said, 'knife wounds to the back. I'd have thought the face was pretty clean.' *I'm not having this conversation*, he thought. *I'm not here standing on the edge of my own grave.* Looking up, Bobby found Lieutenant Que staring at him.

'What now?' said Bobby.

'They smashed in his head,' the lieutenant said flatly. 'Crushed it with something crude like a sledgehammer. Shattered his skull into small fragments and spread his brains across the concrete. We're still looking for the weapon. I made the match based on a scar on his shoulder and two crushed toes.'

'The trapdoor,' said Bobby, feeling sick. 'At Janice's house.'

Lieutenant Que's stare darkened to a scowl. 'Why would the Feds know details like that?'

The feds?

It had to be his suit, Bobby decided. 'There's nothing I don't know about Bobby Zha,' he told Lieutenant Que, watching the lieutenant think that one through.

Ellen's father and Janice lasted six years, which was something of a personal record for both of them. After Janice moved out of Russian Hill, she took to inviting Ellen to stay at her new place above an Italian restaurant in North Beach. Her apartment had a ladder up to a flat roof, where Janice made bowls on a potter's wheel she worked with pedals. At the time Ellen had just started seeing Bobby again and that was the summer he grew his hair into a ponytail and took to going everywhere barefoot. Between them, a gust of wind and the trapdoor almost cost Bobby his toes.

'Sir . . . Excuse me, sir.' Materialising at Lieutenant Que's elbow, Sanchez said, 'It's probably time to go.' Bobby got the feeling those *sirs* were for his benefit. Looking from the grave to Lieutenant Que and then at Bobby, Sanchez kept his gaze direct and slightly hostile.

'You knew Sergeant Zha?'

'Oh yes,' said Lieutenant Que, before Bobby could answer. 'He knew the man right enough.' And with that the lieutenant walked away.

Bobby got a lift with Inspector Otomo from Central. He wasn't sure what Otomo was doing there since they'd never even liked each other and Otomo had a very obvious habit of only making close friends with officers whose families had originally been Japanese. But the inspector was brilliant at ripping data from disks their owners considered safely trashed and had once extracted a school project for Kris from her broken laptop, solely, it seemed, for the challenge.

He discovered what Inspector Otomo was doing when the man stopped to allow Beatrice to catch up. Beatrice was quarter Japanese and her mother was Commissioner of something or other important.

'That's kind,' said Beatrice, when Bobby reached for Otomo's car door. There were women at Bryant Street who'd have ripped his head off for even thinking they wanted a car door opening but Beatrice wasn't SFPD. She didn't have a job or need one. She was just . . .

'Beatrice de la Paix,' said Inspector Otomo. He looked at Bobby, waiting for the man to introduce himself.

'Robert Van Berg.'

The blonde woman nodded, his name barely registered. She had bags under her eyes from lack of sleep and if Bobby, from where he stood on the far side of the door, could smell gin on her breath, then there was little chance it had escaped Inspector Otomo either.

So sad, cold like ice and hollow as a cave. Lonely eyes stared from way back in the darkness.

'You want me to drop you somewhere?' Inspector Otomo asked.

'Better not,' said Beatrice. 'Pete wants me there.'

The inspector looked as if he might have something to say about that; but whatever it was, he left it unspoken. Instead, the inspector waited for Bobby to climb into the back seat beside Beatrice and then shut the door for him.

Interesting, Bobby decided.

'You local?' Inspector Otomo asked.

'I flew in from New York.'

'For the funeral?'

Bobby nodded, realised the man wasn't looking in his mirror and leant forward, until he was close enough to see dandruff dusting the shoulders of Otomo's suit. 'Yeah,' Bobby said. 'It wasn't an event I could miss.' That was a joke, he told himself, staring at the roadside so neither Beatrice or the inspector could see the terror in his eyes.

He wondered if Beatrice knew she was holding his hand.

92

CHAPTER 16

Saturday 21 February

Slinging his BMW onto a sidewalk outside Filipacchi's, Inspector Otomo stuck an SFPD notice on the dash. All of the windows in the SUV were smoked but it was still possible to read the card and anyway Traffic would be too discreet to book a car parked up outside Filipacchi's.

Anyone might be driving.

'You know this place?' asked Inspector Otomo.

'I've head of it.'

Filipacchi's was in an alley off Columbus Avenue, on what had once been the front line between Chinatown and the Italian communities of North Beach. That Chinatown had won that particular battle was obvious. Where Italian cafés and delicatessens once stood there were now Chinese restaurants, supermarkets and grocers, their fruit and vegetables spilling out onto sidewalks that filled with tourists each summer.

A watering hole for Central and Chinatown, Filipacchi's was one of the last of the old-style bars. Its survival helped by two things, the fact it occupied the far end of a narrow alley where few visitors dared wander and its status as first choice for after-work drinking to three generations of SFPD officers. Most of those who drank there believed the rules, that differences of rank and race were left at the door. Neither was quite true. Something Bobby Zha had realised the moment he walked through the door as a fresh-faced recruit.

Sergeants who shouldn't have done more than tell him to move out of their way shook hands or, at the very least, nodded vaguely. And then one of the other recruits asked him his name and a second later put two and two together and worked out where they'd heard the name before. His father had been a *dai lo* for the Deep River Tong.

'That's Lieutenant Que,' said the inspector. 'Bobby's first boss.' Bobby was holding the door open for Beatrice when Inspector Otomo said this.

'You know,' said Beatrice. 'Bobby was like a son to him.'

Bobby nodded. 'So I've heard.'

Following Beatrice into the dark interior that was Filipacchi's trademark, Bobby looked round, missing the noise and tight fug of regulars who usually filled the place. Then he realised everyone was there, just standing quietly and wearing uniforms or dark suits.

Tony had polished the brass along the edge of the bar and swept the floor, he'd even wiped down the front window. Rows of fat Chianti bottles were already open and bottles of Soave, anorexic and pale green, stood behind glass in a chill cabinet that hadn't been there the last time Bobby used the place. A plastic box filled with ice held the Anchor and Black Diamond, which was pretty classy for Tony who usually used metal gash cans to hold the beer at parties.

'Everyone here?' asked Lieutenant Que, as someone pushed a glass into Beatrice's hand and gave Inspector Otomo a bottle of Black Diamond. Bobby was waved towards the bar where a single white wine and a couple of glasses of red still remained from the earlier lines.

'Well?'

Half a dozen uniforms immediately nodded. Only Officer Sanchez looked round, did a quick scan of the bar and a rapid head count and then agreed.

'Okay then. We've had the speeches and the piper, the service and the funeral itself . . . Not to mention this morning's press conference. That was the official stuff. This is to remember a fellow officer. We have Ellen and Kris with us and they'll be staying for as long as they want, although I understand they have to go elsewhere later.'

Bobby saw the look Kris flicked her mother, who frowned slightly, stilling the question.

'To Sergeant Bobby Zha,' said Lieutenant Que. 'A good officer.'

Glasses were raised and voices called back the name.

'I'm going to keep this short.' The lieutenant's voice tried to be matter of fact but was betrayed by its hollowness. 'Bobby Zha was a stout heart, an honest partner, an excellent husband and a better father. Many of you know that he came from a family who . . .'

The lieutenant paused, collected his thoughts.

'Who did not necessarily approve of his decision to join the SFPD.' He caught someone's eye and nodded. 'You're right. Just as my family did not necessarily approve of mine. In spite of this, Bobby did his job quietly and well. A lot of you used to wonder exactly what it was he did all day . . .'

A second pause, intentional this time. 'And there were times when I used to wonder that myself.'

Their laughter was unforced and a couple of Chinatown officers found themselves nodding. Sergeant Zha was notorious for his poor time-keeping and inability to file forms. There were those, usually the ones young enough to remember their handful of psychology lessons from the Academy, who used words like *pathological*.

This wasn't, if Bobby remembered rightly, usually seen as a good thing. Mind you, they also had no idea how hard he found it to stay untidy. A hairline crack in his armour and he'd have been rearranging the entire Chinatown station house and filing paperwork alphabetically by date, within categories.

'Most of you know Ellen,' said the lieutenant. 'She's asked to say a few words of her own. So here she is . . .'

One of the uniforms began to clap, then faltered and stopped when he realised that no one else was doing the same. The man was from Traffic and apart from the fact Bobby had once borrowed a car without asking, he wasn't really sure why the man was there.

'For those of you who don't know me,' said Ellen. 'I'm Ellen Zha and this is my daughter.'

'Hi . . .' Kris looked up from under darkened eyes, tried to smile and then lowered her gaze, as if searching the floor for something she'd dropped. For once his daughter didn't need black eyeliner to make her face drawn and haggard. Real grief had given her the hollows that several months of wearing Goth makeup only hinted at.

He was seeing too much, watching too closely. The lieutenant and Officer Sanchez had both noticed his interest in the two women, so alike and yet so different, now holding the floor.

What would happen if Bobby joined them? If he stepped out from behind Inspector Otomo and joined his loving wife and dutiful daughter, those members of an ideal family he never even knew he had . . .

Bobby could imagine it. Ellen's anger and the outrage of Lieutenant Que. What he couldn't imagine was anyone believing him. The lieutenant would know the old myths, the *Chuanqi* tales of wandering ghosts and fox spirits but for him that's all they were, old myths. That was all they'd been for Bobby until a week ago.

Until this.

'I can still remember when we first met . . .'

He was missing Ellen's speech, Bobby realised. If such a term could be used for the stumbling words that outlined her past happiness and how blighted life would be now that Bobby was dead. All of which came as something of a surprise to Bobby, since the last time they'd spoken it was to argue about who got Kris should they divorce. That was the day he got shot, the morning after he'd missed the Chinese parade for the third year in a row, and the conversation came after a bout of swift and violent sex, when they rolled off each other and accepted what they already knew. Disappointment created fractures that even raw sex couldn't mend.

'. . . we sat and talked as all the grown-ups around us slept.'

That was one way of putting it.

'And as we were landing Bobby asked for my number. It was three months before he called.'

It was two, and Bobby had finally phoned because Ellen refused to answer his letters. Those single pages he struggled over for days in an attempt to make them appear effortless. Cartoon faces that looked like they'd just been dashed off, band logos and punchlines taken from other people's T-shirts. He should have known it wasn't going to work when Ellen took the scrawls at face value and never once bothered to read between his achingly careful lines.

'Okay . . .' said Ellen. 'I want to thank you for your support. Kris and I have to go now. Try to rebuild our lives. It's not going to be easy.'

'God, she's brave,' whispered Inspector Otomo. 'I can't begin to imagine what it must be like.'

'No,' said Bobby. 'I don't imagine you can.'

As they watched, Ellen looked down to locate her bag and smiled bravely when Beatrice picked it up for her. Opening her bag, Ellen double-checked she'd got her house keys and then did that little thing she always did, of turning sideways to slip through a crowd, even though the gap between Beatrice and Officer Sanchez was wide enough.

That was when Sanchez put his hand on Ellen's elbow. The tiniest touch, barely noticeable, but it had the effect of slowing Ellen, while she listened intently to whatever Sanchez had to say. Kris had already begun to shake her head when Sanchez stepped around her and said something to Lieutenant Que, who nodded.

'I'll be back in about ten minutes,' said Sanchez.

'Take your time,' the lieutenant told him. If Lieutenant Que said this loud enough for Bobby to hear, it was only because Bobby had taken a step towards Sanchez the moment he put his hand on Ellen's arm.

'Ah,' said Lieutenant Que, 'Robert Van Berg.'

Ellen paused politely.

'A good friend of Bobby's, apparently . . .'

There was no flicker of a reaction in Ellen's eyes and why should there have been? The name meant nothing.

'I knew him well,' said Bobby. 'Not quite the same thing.'

'Glad you could make it,' Ellen said, holding out her hand.

Bobby shook. He shook hands with his own wife and felt absolutely nothing. No little jump of static or cold frisson. The only thing he noticed was that Ellen's wedding ring was back on her finger and so was her engagement ring, a cheap hoop of white gold inset with an opal, bought from a jewellery boutique on Union Square, a place that opened and shut the summer they agreed to get married.

He tried to remember the last time she'd bothered to wear it.

'I'd better go,' she said, and with this Ellen turned away, her daughter following after like a reluctant shadow. Whatever Beatrice was about to say got cut off by a look from Sanchez.

'Later,' he told her.

Everyone agreed that it was a tragedy. Everyone wondered what Bobby had been doing alone in a deserted building behind Grant Street. A number of officers, fingers wrapped round their second or third drink, made a point of swearing Bobby to secrecy and then telling him how upset Sanchez was not to have been there.

'He blames himself. Stupid I know . . .'

'And Sergeant Zha was definitely alone?'

Oh yes, they agreed. And no, there were no leads yet to the murderer. Although, obviously, the Chief herself had made solving this one a priority. No, things weren't looking good in that direction.

So Bobby did what he would have done if this was his case. Which it was, when he thought about it. At least that's what he told himself. So he was dead, he'd just attended his own funeral and he was about to face another night of not knowing, as he went to sleep, whether he'd ever wake up again. It was still a case, with people to interview and alibis to check. All other thoughts and possibilities Bobby pushed away.

He made a trip to the bar for a glass of Soave, positioned himself on the edge of a couple of groups, and then carried the glass to where Beatrice waited, still locked in stilted conversation with Inspector Otomo and the man from Traffic whose car Bobby had borrowed.

'You look like you need this.'

'Thanks,' said Beatrice, swallowing most of the wine.

She drank the next glass equally fast, matching Bobby for speed, only he was drinking diet Coke. The glass after that she sipped endlessly and repeatedly, the way a child sucks on its dummy, only to appear surprised when her wine was gone. By then Filipacchi's was almost empty and Beatrice was among a hard-core grouped in a corner.

'Where's the lieutenant?'

'Settling the tab,' said Inspector Otomo, nodding at the zinc and mahogany bar. As Bobby watched, Lieutenant Que pocketed his wallet, shook hands with Tony Filipacchi and headed for the restrooms beyond.

'Time to go,' said Bobby.

Beatrice nodded.

'You want a lift?' she asked him.

All the guy from Traffic could come up with was, 'You probably shouldn't drive.'

'She's not going to,' said Bobby. 'I've got a car.'

So he had. During one of his own trips to the restroom, he'd called a contact in Bay Side, introduced himself as an old friend of Bobby Zha and checked what the man had in government blue. He'd settled for a Lincoln town car and a driver, suit not uniform. The initial contract was for a week and Bobby paid in advance, sat in a stall, trousers round his ankles as he read off the number from his Morgan Cabot credit card.

'What about my Porsche?' demanded Beatrice.

'Where is it?'

She named a steel mesh and razor wire car lot two blocks away that would be already locked for the night. 'Collect it in the morning,' said Bobby. 'When you're feeling better.' And putting his arm out so

Beatrice had something on which to steady herself, Bobby walked her towards the door and his car.

The night was too dark to face alone.

CHAPTER 17

Saturday 21 February

Even dead, it seemed Bobby Zha's name could produce results. The limousine was almost new, its windows slightly smoked and its chrome bright enough to sparkle beneath a street light on Columbus Avenue.

'Latif?'

'That's me, sir . . .'

The man stood next to a long and very blue Lincoln. His aubergine skin almost as rich as the leather used for the car's interior and his charcoal grey suit had been matched to a red silk tie and hand-sewn shoes, although what Bobby really noticed was that Latif wore two watches, one on each wrist, in gold and silver.

'Call me Mr Van Berg,' said Bobby.

'Sure thing,' Latif said, then glanced over his client's shoulder. 'Is Madame coming with us?'

'That a problem . . . ?'

'Only if she throws up on my seats.'

The man's reply was polite but firm. Limousine companies nation-wide got used to being treated as suppliers of everything from brothels to moving crack dens, although the situation in San Francisco was nothing like as bad as LA or New York. Anyway, that wasn't the problem, Latif's uncle was in the business of supplying moving brothels and knew a man who could provide the whores and crack, if necessary. That was how Bobby knew him.

'If she vomits,' said Bobby, 'don't bother trying to get the leather cleaned. I'll have the seats replaced.'

Latif thought about that, then smiled. 'You're the boss.'

Only at the last minute did Bobby remember to ask Beatrice where she lived, rather than just giving the address of Sanchez's place in

Richmond. Bobby was glad he did. When he asked where she wanted to go Beatrice reeled off an address in Pacific Heights, one which was unknown to him.

'That's where you live?'

'My parents' place,' said Beatrice.

It was one of those wood-framed houses faced with board and painted in white and pink, with an absurd octagonal tower that rose from one corner and looked down from its highest window on the lights of the university. A twisted cypress stood in silhouette next to the tower. This part of the city was full of such houses, places thrown together in a matter of weeks using local wood, and now selling for millions if they ever made it onto the open market at all.

'Give me ten minutes,' Bobby told Latif, as the driver opened his door. In the event, when Bobby checked on the car in the small hours before dawn, Latif was still leant against the hood, watching Beatrice's house. Bobby found that oddly reassuring. Mind you, right up to the point it went beyond being relevant, Bobby pretended to himself that he didn't intend to stay, merely ask Beatrice some questions and then leave. It was Beatrice who persuaded him otherwise. A touch of her hand and again that little spark.

So lonely, so cold.

'Call me Bea,' she insisted. So Bobby did.

They were still stood just inside the front door. At the entrance to a white-painted hall hung with elderly mirrors and a couple of dingy oil paintings that were probably priceless. One showed a Christ and the other a woman, both with the straight noses and dark eyes of a French aristocrat.

'My grandmother,' said Bea. 'She came from Paris to marry my grandfather.'

A long Persian rug ran the length of the hallway. It had been worn to the thinness of pancake but still looked more valuable than anything Bobby had ever owned. This was what old money looked like, he realised. Tarnished silver frames and ruined carpets, a room full of dark paintings that honoured the dead or showed landscapes and cities long since lost to history.

Money smelt like cabbage and old wax.

'You want a drink?'

Bobby looked at Bea de la Paix. A woman somewhere in her

twenties, with eyes ten years older and a smile borrowed from the face of a troubled child. 'You've probably had enough,' he said.

Bea pouted.

If she'd scowled or sworn or demanded he get her a whisky, Bobby might have asked his questions and left; but the look which went with her pout said Bea knew exactly what she was doing.

'Go on,' she said. 'Help yourself.'

The decanters were in the drawing room. And looking round the lowest level of the octagonal tower, Bobby counted off three oil paintings and then glanced at the furniture, much of which was a Japanese interpretation of Art Deco. He'd got used to doing this during investigations, because sometimes a room could tell you more about a family than those who lived in it.

'Osaka via Paris,' said a voice behind him. Bea was talking about her grandfather.

Bobby put two fingers of whisky in a glass and splashed with water from a carafe. 'Here.'

'Pour one for yourself,' said Bea. 'While I deal with the curtains . . .' She paused. 'Did you really know Sergeant Zha?'

'Yeah,' said Bobby. 'Pretty well.'

'What did you think of him?' Curtains done, Bea flopped into a chair to take off her shoes, flashing stocking as she did so.

'He was okay,' said Bobby finally.

Bea tossed her shoes onto a carved table. 'No,' she said, 'Believe me. He was a shit.' They sat in silence after that, Beatrice slowly sipped her whisky into ice and emptiness, while Bobby thought about what she'd said and the viciousness with which she said it.

'What kind of shit?' he asked eventually.

CHAPTER 18
Saturday 21 February

Bobby went to her room because she asked him, and Bea asked him because the idea of burglars frightened her. At least, that's what she said.

'Unlikely,' Bobby told her. He'd seen the alarm system she deactivated on entering the house, just as he'd noted the release code from the dance of her fingers across a tiny keypad.

She made him look in all the upstairs rooms, beginning with the bathroom and ending with the attic. For good measure, he checked a cupboard in her room, the walk-in wardrobe in her parent's suite and a large airing closet on the landing that held a childhood's worth of old towels and sheets.

'Thank you,' she said.

Her own was tiny and tucked under the eaves. A single teddy bear sat on a narrow bed, beneath a neatly framed poster advertising a band that had split years before. A pink rug covered wooden boards and a glass Madonna rested next to blue china horses on a single shelf. There were no books.

'I'd better go,' said Bobby, wondering what he'd do if she agreed. He could recognise a sanctuary when he saw one. As easily as he could recognise somewhere he shouldn't be . . .

'Stay,' said Bea. 'You're nice.'

'And you're engaged to Officer Sanchez.'

'Yeah,' she said. 'And in case you missed it, Pete's busy consoling the unhappy widow.' Patting her mattress, Bea indicated that Bobby should sit.

'Do you mean that how I think you mean it?'

'Depends,' said Bea. 'On what you think I mean.' Her frown had a vague, unfocused look, as if trying to work out why he was scowling. 'You don't mind, do you?'

'About Ellen?'

'No, this . . .' Pulling open a cupboard to reveal a small closet, with lavatory and basin, Bea hooked up her dress. She pissed with the door open and her knickers round her ankles. The knickers were black, to match her stockings.

'Not worth putting these back on,' she said, kicking them into a corner. She looked round for her drink and Bobby watched her realise she'd left it downstairs. 'You can get me a new one later,' she said.

'Let me get it now,' Bobby suggested. Who knew, maybe he'd find the strength on his way downstairs to keep walking . . .

'No,' said Bea, turning her back on him. 'I'm going to need help with this.'

The dress was Dolce & Gabbana, which probably explained why it looked like a child's nightie, and there was only one button, a small freshwater pearl that fitted through a loop at the back of the neck. The bra was skin-tone, almost sheer, lacked shoulder straps and seemed to have no function apart from covering Bea's nipples. It certainly made no difference to the upturned shape of her breasts.

The stockings came next.

Bea hung Bobby's jacket on a wooden hanger, even though she'd kicked her own clothes into a small heap on the floor. And then, wearing only suspenders, she left the room, head up and shoulders back, exhibiting the iron self-control of the very drunk. When she returned it was with a second hanger.

'For your trousers.'

Around them, walls creaked as the heat of the day was lost to the night and wooden timbers twisted and shrank. A police car lit up the distance, its siren rising out of silent streets. A thud, steady as a drum, filled Bobby's head, getting louder and louder until he realised it was the sound of his own heart.

After a while, Bea and Bobby added the creak of her bed to all the other noises. It creaked when Bobby swung his legs up over the side, and it creaked again when Bea climbed on top of him and reached down to position Bobby against her; it creaked as Bea began to lower herself, and it creaked as she rode him, her back arched and her gaze lost in the cracks of a cobwebbed ceiling.

It was doubtful Bea even heard the grinding of her bed frame or remembered who lay beneath her, she looked so isolated up there. A woman hoping to get lost inside herself and never quite managing it, despite jagged cries that saw her collapse across him, in a sprawl of suspenders, quivering legs and long blonde hair.

'You been with Pete Sanchez long?' That wasn't quite how Bobby intended to begin this conversation, but those were the words which came out of his mouth. Bea's suspenders had gone the way of everything else, an omelette had been made and eaten, and they were back in bed.

Raising her head from the pillow, Bea said, 'Why . . . You jealous?'

Her bed wasn't really big enough for Bea, never mind for both of them and the way it was positioned against a wall meant Bobby lay half on/half off, his back to the open door.

'No. Not really.'

'That's usually the reason men ask . . .' Bea was matter of fact, as if this was unqualifiably true, so maybe it was. Her PhD was in sexual politics, one of the things that made her relationship with Sanchez so interesting; another was a ring of bruises around her upper wrists. So far, both of them had been too polite to mention those.

'I just wondered,' said Bobby.

Actually, he knew it was at least a year because he'd seen a photograph in the *Chronicle*. Some charity affair where Bea stood next to her mother, with Pete Sanchez to one side. Bobby only remembered because Ellen had taken Kris.

'It's been a while,' Bea said suddenly, long after Bobby thought that particular conversation was over.

'Really?'

'Yes, really,' said Bea, and what crinkled her eyes in the half light bore no resemblance to a smile.

'So finish it.'

'You don't know Pete Sanchez.'

Slinging his legs over the side of the bed, Bobby pulled a sheet around him. Her room was lit by a small onyx and ormolu lamp. The ceiling sloped along one side, one of the window panes was cracked and cobwebs decorated the far corner of the ceiling.

'Pio Emilio Sanchez,' he recited. 'Otherwise known as Pete, Peter and Dirty Bastard, for obvious reasons. Born sixth September. In his third year as a SFPD officer. MA and PhD from Austin. Good connections. Well liked. Ambitious and occasionally ruthless. His father worked in a grocery store south of Market until last year . . .'

'Pete told me his father owned that store.'

Bobby shook his head and waited for Bea to join the dots, which she'd already begun to do, because he could see questions forming behind her eyes.

'How do you know this stuff?' she said.

'It's my job.'

Her laugh was hard and bitter. 'And there I was thinking you just wanted my body.'

'I did,' said Bobby, reaching out and wondering how he'd known she would flinch. 'Still do,' he said. 'I also want to know why you gave Sanchez an alibi for the night of Sunday eighth February . . .'

'An alibi for when?' Bea looked puzzled, not scared or shifty, just puzzled.

'The night Sergeant Zha was shot.'

Blowing out her breath, Bea rolled onto her back to stare at the cracked ceiling, she seemed to be thinking. 'I don't get it,' she said finally.

'What's to get?'

'Why you think Pete would need an alibi. Why you think he wasn't here.' Bea glanced round the room, realising what she'd said. 'Not actually here,' she said. 'No one comes here. We were at my flat in SoMa. That's south of . . .'

'Market Street,' said Bobby, 'I know. I heard Officer Sanchez helped you find it.' He wanted to get a feel for what linked this woman to Pete Sanchez. Although it was obvious what tied Sanchez to her. If Bobby had to guess, he'd say it was her surname, her family money and the fact sex with Bea felt like an advertisement for some miraculous 12-step pelvic-floor exercise plan.

Bea scowled. 'Can we please stop talking about Pete?'

'He was with you that night?'

'Yes,' Bea said firmly.

'Okay,' said Bobby, rolling her over and kneeling her up. 'We'll stop.' He'd made a pass at Bea once, months ago. Bea had slapped him but she hadn't told Sanchez. Looking at a bruise on her lower back, Bobby began to understand why.

He entered her slowly, hands gripping Bea's hips to hold her steady, and in a narrow mirror on her wardrobe door, a man Bobby barely recognised did the same. Both man and reflection held themselves against the buttocks of their partner, savoured the moment and then pulled away again, watching each other.

Positioning himself against the girl, who now had her forehead against a pillow, the man in the mirror reached down to hold her open and eased himself inside. Bobby grinned. Bea was all the things he'd ever wanted from such an encounter.

Pulling out, Bobby separated her thin buttocks so he could watch Bea's anus open and see her vulva glisten as he slid out of her. He liked it so much he entered again and again, watching Bea in the mirror, her pout utterly unconscious and completely private. Each stroke took him further, until all Bobby wanted was to let go and drive himself deep into her body.

Instead, he pulled back.

'Do it properly,' she said.

So Bobby did. The first thrust knocked the breath from her lungs and left her open mouthed and open eyed, her privacy discarded. The second wrenched a whimper from her throat and then Bobby was pounding against her. In the mirror, a woman pushed back, trying to stop herself being ground into the wall. Her breasts were swinging frantically, her mouth open and her eyes closed.

'Grip the bars,' Bobby told her.

'What?'

He repeated it, saw her puzzlement and realised he'd been speaking Cantonese.

'The bars,' he said. 'Hold them.'

So she did. Steadying herself against her own slight weight and thrusts that still threatened to drive her up the creaking bed. (Later, Bobby discovered she'd gripped so hard her nails had cut perfect half circles into the palm of each hand.) Sex felt good, if different. Then Bobby realised it was different. He was in a different body, one he'd been wearing as carelessly as his discarded suit, and it was okay, at least the woman on the bed and the woman in the mirror seemed to think so.

'Shit,' Bea said, when she was finally able to say anything at all.

'Yeah,' agreed Bobby. That was all he said for several minutes, while his breath steadied and his heart came back from the edge of what felt like cardiac arrest.

He'd left slight bruises on her hips and a slap mark across one buttock, earlier payback for biting him, not just the once, or even twice but three times, each bite overlapping another, like some Japanese sports logo cut into his shoulder. But it was only when Bea stood up and promptly had to sit down again, legs trembling beneath her, that she began to grin. Her grin lasted as long as it took her to reach the tiny lavatory and squat.

'Fuck,' she said. 'That stings.'

Sleep came slowly. All the same, Bobby slept, curled up behind Bea, one arm wrapped across her stomach to hold the woman in place. He liked the sound of her breathing and the feel of her ribs as they rose and fell, hiding her lungs and protecting her heart. She wore her life easily, as he'd once worn his.

Bobby was still worrying that sleep would never come and, if it did, he would never wake, when he awoke to the yowl of a cat.

'Meet Hero,' said Bea.

Bobby nodded to a black tom, who'd turned slightly at the sound of its own name and now regarded the stranger with as much interest as he might have shown an unfamiliar chair.

'I'll feed you in a moment,' promised Bea. She smiled as the cat flopped off the bed, stalked across her room's narrow floor and took up guard beside the door.

'That's what I'm doing here,' she said. 'Cat-sitting while my parents are away.'

'When are they due back?'

'Fairly soon.'

Washing the frying pan and plates from the night before, Bobby put them back where he'd found them and wiped down a bread board he'd used to cut a sourdough loaf.

'God,' said Bea, sounding almost impressed. 'You're domesticated.'

Looking round the kitchen, Bobby considered explaining the difference between being domesticated and making oneself invisible and decided not to bother. Her sheets were already spinning in circles inside a washing machine in the pantry, so he guessed she knew something about that anyway.

'Be seeing you,' said Bobby. 'Or not,' he added, walking across the kitchen to where she stood. 'If that works better . . .' Leaning forward, he kissed Bea very carefully on her brow.

'One thing,' she said.

Bobby stopped.

'Last night,' said Bea. 'What language were you speaking?'

CHAPTER 19
Sunday 22 February

The morning wind was chilly and the sky above the city was pale but blue, ready to deepen later. Church bells rang in the distance and the air coming in through Latif's limousine window smelt of salt and a batch of croissant baking in a nearby oven.

Patisserie Milano, read an old wooden sign, neatly eliding two cultures.

A woman with a chrome and plastic stroller was jogging along the edge of Van Ness Avenue, her toddler wrapped in red Oshkosh sweater and bobble hat. It was hard to know which of them looked more bored.

'I know,' said Bobby. 'Let's get some breakfast on the way.'

Latif grunted something non-committal, but slowed down anyway. 'You got somewhere in mind?'

'Café de la Presse.' Bobby told him. 'At Grant and Bush.'

Nodding, Latif turned his blue Lincoln off Van Ness and a few minutes later found them heading down Powell, behind a cable car filled with cleaners and kitchen staff. The tourists would take over later, hanging off the sides and riding the line for fun rather than because they had somewhere to go.

The actual cables that ran beneath the roads had broken once, reducing this part of the city to a weird and unhealthy silence. When the cable started up again and the area regained its rumble, people had come out onto the streets to cheer. Bobby could still remember it.

'We're here,' said Latif.

'What do you want?'

'Grande latte, a croissant and a cinnamon roll for later. Don't let them heat the pastries.' Latif glanced at Bobby, to check that last comment was okay.

'I won't,' said Bobby.

The Café de la Presse was opposite the Chinatown Gates and had its entrance on a corner, so everyone leaving the café had to check both ways. A crack kid with bare stomach was sat on the sidewalk, panhandling.

'Spare some change?'

Bobby gave the girl a couple of coins. He was inside the café before he stopped to wonder why he hadn't given her more. Turning round, he went back.

'You need anything to eat?'

'No . . . Not really hungry.'

Peeling off a $5 note, Bobby held it up. 'You know where I can find Colonel Billy?' Washed out eyes watched the note, then slid between Bobby's hand and his face. 'Here,' said Bobby, handing it over. 'It's yours. Now tell me. You know where I can find Colonel Billy?'

The kid shook her head.

'See if you can find out,' he said. Having given his breakfast order at the take-out counter in the café, Bobby disappeared through the restaurant at the back, using a short passage that joined it to the Hotel Triton next door.

It took Bobby less than a minute to reach his room, another minute to mess up his bed and the same again for a chrome-lined Otis to deliver him to the foyer, managing all three before the punk track that had been starting when he first climbed in even finished playing.

Two guitars and a drum machine, something French.

Bobby nodded to the woman behind the desk, who nodded back faux casual. 'Forgot this,' he said, holding up his case.

She smiled.

At the counter in the café, Bobby collected his order and went through the rack of newspapers that gave the Café de la Presse its name. A *New York Times*, a *San Francisco Chronicle*, *The Times* from London, something French and something German. Bobby didn't speak either language, at least not well enough to read *Le Matin* or *Dei Zeitt*, but it would muddle his scent if anyone came asking.

Hero buried.

His funeral made page three in the *Chronicle*, at least the official ceremony did. There was a small photograph of Ellen, with a caption which said she'd asked that the actual burial be private. In the circumstances, the Chief had agreed.

A larger photograph showed Bobby's coffin, draped with a flag, being watched over by four uniformed officers, Lieutenant Que was one of them and Pete Sanchez another. For reasons unknown to Bobby, the man from Traffic was a third and in the best traditions of the new SFPD, the fourth officer was female. The woman who'd driven Natalie Persikov out to the house that day. Apparently her name was Felicidad Valdez.

A think piece covered previous shootings of sheriffs, marshals and SFPD officers, going back to the Gold Rush. On the letters page, someone bemoaned the fact that San Francisco had become as dangerous as New York, while an academic from SFU pointed out that, based on crimes per thousand, the city was actually safer than it had ever been. It was a final reference to his murder that interested Bobby the most. A small photograph on the Op Ed page announced that Sergeant Bobby Zha was rumoured to have been working undercover at the time of his death.

It asked what the city was not being told.

'Interesting?' asked Latif.

'You could say that.'

Latif was pulling onto the Golden Gate Bridge at the time, other cars overtaking as the Lincoln moved slowly enough to draw glares and the occasional flash of a headlight. Bobby wanted to see if he remembered anything from his original conversation with Colonel Billy, although that wasn't what he told his driver. He told Latif that he wanted to see the view.

'My Dad worked on this bridge,' Latif said suddenly.

'He helped build it?'

Latif laughed. 'How old do you think I am?' Between them, he and Bobby were sorting out the rules. Latif had already worked out that Bobby didn't want just a driver, someone to call him sir and deliver him places in silence.

'He was one of the solder men . . . My Dad used to go round soldering little clasps onto all the manhole covers to stop people using them to climb through to the underside.'

'People really used to do that?'

'Sure,' said Latif. 'Still do.'

On one side of the bridge spread the Pacific, slate grey and seemingly endless; on the other side the Bay was a childish blue. Just looking from grey to blue made Bobby wonder how early explorers could have imagined the landlocked bay was actually ocean. Maybe, when the first ships found themselves sailing between headlands, the bay was still alive. A wilderness where animals far outnumbered humans in their scattered huts.

No longer.

Bobby could feel the difference like an ache. Now the Bay was where the Pacific came to die. Wrapped around with so many buildings it became a ghost of itself, an imitation of what had once been.

'You all right?' Latif asked.

'Sure,' said Bobby. 'Just thinking.'

They left the blue Lincoln in the park at Vista Point, in the shadow of a cypress. Built tastefully from stone and wood, the Visitor Centre still looked what it was, a couple of restrooms, with additional storerooms locked behind thick metal doors. A bank of information boards described the plants, birds and animals that visitors might expect to see.

In the men's lavatory, Bobby washed the last of Bea from his fingers, watching cold water swirl in small circles until a man and his son at the next basin caught Bobby's eye, then hurriedly looked away. As soon as both were gone, Bobby splashed water on his face and rinsed her taste from his mouth.

'Any breakfast left?'

'Sure . . .' Latif handed across the paper bag. 'That's it?' he said, when Bobby took an espresso.

'It's enough,' said Bobby. 'I'll be back in about an hour.'

'Right you are.' Looking at the Rolex on his right wrist, Latif checked it against the Omega on his left, adjusting the second watch to agree with the first.

'What?' asked Bobby, catching the man smile.

'Nothing.' Latif sat back against a fence and stared at the cars, one eye on where he'd left the Lincoln. 'Just wondering if that hour was likely to be flexible? I mean, last night you said you'd be gone for ten minutes . . .'

'If I'm not back in two hours,' said Bobby, 'come looking for me.'

'You really mean that?'

Bobby nodded, watching Latif think it through.

'Okay,' said Latif. 'First things first . . . You got a gun?'

The armoury was in the boot of the Lincoln under a square of carpet.

Someone had done a neat job of sinking a gun safe through sheet steel and welding it into place, although the numerical lock of the lid probably made it unwise for anyone to rely on grabbing a gun in a hurry.

'Take your pick.'

Bobby chose a Sig Sauer, with black plastic grip.

'Interesting choice,' said Latif.

'Not as interesting as the fact you stock it.' Standard for the US Secret Service, best known for guarding the President and slightly less well known for their fight against corporate fraud, the Sig Sauer P229 was also gun of choice for FBI field agents and half the police departments across America. One big advantage it had over the earlier P228 was choice of calibre. As if to prove the fact, the gun in the Lincoln's boot came with two barrels.

Bobby chose .357.

'Need a holster?'

'No,' said Bobby, as he put the gun together, snapped in a clip and pushed the weapon into the back of his waist band. 'I'll be fine like this.'

Across the bridge, Beatrice de la Paix took her sheets from the dryer and checked that they were completely dry. She kept her single bed because it was the only place she felt really safe. Although it was probably fairer to say she kept the room, because anything bigger than a single bed would have required her to change floors.

There was a three-room suite on the second floor, built the summer she went to Italy. It was a secret, her fifteenth-birthday present.

Of course, she'd been delighted, throwing her arms around her father and kissing her mother on the cheek. Masako de la Paix not being a woman one threw arms around. Yet somehow the planned move from one floor to another never came. It was a couple of years before Boaz de la Paix realised his daughter had no intention of changing rooms at all.

Having made sure her bottom sheet was completely dry, Bea checked that it was properly clean. Years of use and Bea's refusal to let her mother replace the sheet had produced a square of cotton so worn that light showed through.

'It'll do,' said Bea. She was talking to the cat.

A minute to make her bed and another to tidy her room. The bear went on the pillow, with its back to the wall. A water glass she'd stolen from summer school in Rome was put upside down on a saucer, ready for next time. Her Moroccan slippers went under the bed.

Bea wasn't stupid. She knew that arranging this room had nothing to do with making it neat or tidy. It was a primitive form of magic, based around a belief that life would be less dangerous if only one kept to the rules.

The kitchen was clean, the sink had been wiped down and the coffee pot was in the process of being dried when Bea saw her father's Cadillac pull up in the drive.

'How was it?' she asked.

Sometimes, with her mother, asking first was the only way of getting a word into the conversation. Tuning out an endless litany about bad roads and poor restaurants, Bea watched her father.

Five, four, three, two . . .

'It was fine,' he said, his voice cutting through his wife's complaints. 'A bit tiring for your mother, but still good.' Boaz de la Paix had a face stolen from a Medici portrait, all nose, beard and sunken eyes. If he appeared to stare down at those to whom he talked, this was only because his body was so thin it exaggerated his height.

He was one of those men who'd finally grown into confidence with middle age, the awkwardness of his adolescence and early adulthood replaced by a gravitas made all the more effective by careful use of silence. Psychiatrists have to have psychiatrists, and Bea's tutor had explained the use of silence to her, around the time he suggested Bea should stop being quite so besotted with her father.

'More to the point,' said Boaz. 'How was the funeral?'

'Sad,' said Bea, because that was what you said about funerals.

Her father nodded sagely.

'Who went?' Masako demanded.

The suitcases Bea helped carry upstairs were made from pigskin. There had been those who said her grandfather was originally Jewish, not that they had anything against Jews, of course. Bea sometimes wondered if her father's very public purchase of Marlene Dietrich's hand-made cases had been in response to that rumour, and whether it meant the suggestion was true or not.

'You know,' said Boaz. He was wrestling a huge case out across the landing, his pale eyes carefully not on his daughter. 'You can always come to me if you're in trouble.'

115

'If I'm what . . . ?'

'If you have problems.' Dumping the heavy case at his bedroom door, he stepped back to look at his daughter. 'If you're not happy . . .'

Boaz stopped himself.

'That was a stupid thing to say,' he said. 'Of course you're not happy. Any fool can see that . . . There must be a way I can help.'

'I'm fine,' said Bea.

They walked back to the car together, Boaz collecting the only remaining case and a small vanity box, while Bea stood and watched. 'Are you going to stay for lunch?'

'No.' Bea shook her head. 'I'm not hungry.'

'Well,' said her father. 'Say goodbye to your mother and then drop in to see me, I'll be in my study.' Bea liked his white-painted study, with its old furniture and leather chairs so ancient they smelt of nothing but dust and polish. She'd always liked it in there, always felt safe.

'I'll do that,' Bea said.

'Oh, and Beatrice . . .'

She turned to find her father looking half embarrassed at the bruises around her upper wrists.

'You might want to wear longer sleeves.'

CHAPTER 20

Sunday 22 February

From the northern end of the Golden Gate Bridge it is possible to see Horseshoe Bay, with its concrete storm brakes and crumbling jetties. And if one stands at the chain-link fence at Vista Point and looks south, one can see Lime Point Lighthouse, a white block of buildings a poet described as looking like a small night club picked up and put down next to the waves.

Because the bridge is organised so pedestrians keep to a walkway on the Bay side and bicyclists use a path on the other side, at least during daylight, those who walk the full length of the bridge tend to remember looking down on a black roof at the Marin County edge of the rocks.

This is the lighthouse.

There is a smaller building on the Pacific side of the bridge, just out of sight. It was built in January 1942 as part of a plan to guard against a Japanese attack on San Francisco. Quite what use a small hanger built into a clifftop would be in guarding a net seven miles long and 7000 tons in weight was hard to say. Maybe it was merely an observation post, Bobby never really knew. What he did know was that Colonel Billy sometimes used the building as his winter base.

'You there . . .'

The voice on the other end sounded surprised. 'Of course I'm here,' said Latif, then paused. 'Why? You need back up?'

'Not yet,' said Bobby.

The route under the bridge and along the edge of the low cliffs that gave Marin County its signature profile was little more than a rough path, decorated with crushed foam cups and slicks of dog shit. Halfway along, Bobby got a prickling at the back of his neck.

Nobody.

Stepping into the shade of a fir tree, Bobby let his eyes readjust to the shadows and took another look. After a couple of seconds he found the source of his discomfort. A man with a notebook was crouched a hundred paces away, writing something in pencil.

Fair hair, heavy jacket and stout boots. A pair of binoculars hung on a leather strap around his neck. Greenland's *Plant Guide to California* protruded from his jacket pocket.

'Franciscan paintbrush,' he said when Bobby passed, nodding to a spiky bush with reddish needle-like leaves. 'It's early . . . And there's a strand of sticky monkey just about to flower if you're interested.' The man indicated an area behind him and Bobby realised he meant the whole hillside.

'That's good,' said Bobby.

He was the last person Bobby saw, until Latif came looking an hour or so later and found Bobby knelt over the body of Colonel Billy. A broken door stood open behind Bobby and, through the doorway, Colonel Billy's few possessions could be seen strewn across the floor of the ruin.

'You need help burying him?'

When Bobby looked up, Latif was shocked to realise his employer had vomit stains on his suit.

'I don't get it,' said Latif. 'If it upsets you that much, why kill him?'

'I didn't,' said Bobby. 'He was dead when I got here.'

Inside the ruined house, endless roll-ups littered the dirt. Plastic bags had been emptied, old newspapers, magazines and clothes thrown everywhere. A bottle of cheap brandy lay on its side, the concrete beneath smelling very slightly of alcohol, which meant it might have been knocked over a while back, maybe in a fight. Looking round at the chaos, Bobby almost chose this as the most likely of several possibilities. If not for the fact Colonel Billy's face was completely unmarked and the only damage to his hands looked like scratches from . . .

'See if you can find his cat,' said Bobby.

'Where do you suggest I start?'

'With tuna.'

After Latif went back to Vista Point to collect his car, Bobby carried Colonel Billy into the sunlight, found himself a spot not overlooked from any of the trails and began to cut off the man's rags, using a lock knife borrowed from Latif.

Bobby knew what he expected to find.

The dead body stank before Bobby went to work and by the time he'd unlaced the combat boots and cut off Levis and cavalry jacket, hacked his way through a check shirt, two layers of vest and sliced away underwear that might once have been white, the stink was far worse. Some of it was that inevitable corruption, which begins within minutes of death and had obviously been going on for much longer, but some came from the filth coating the man's body.

Colonel Billy wore his dirt like armour, each layer of grime another filter against the world. Bobby had lost count of the number of dead bodies he'd seen. You didn't serve with the SFPD without seeing your share, and working Vice and among the homeless meant you got to see quite a few other officers' shares as well.

All the same, he found it hard to look at the colonel dispassionately.

There'd been nights when Bobby stood under a shower for hours at a time and still came out of the locker room with death coating every hair on his head and clotted like blood to the inside of his nose. It had been worse in the early days and, Bobby told himself, he hardly noticed it now . . .

Except he did.

The corpse in front of him was barely ripe compared to others he'd seen working the homeless detail, and yet not vomiting took all Bobby's will. Something had definitely changed. A statement so absurd Bobby pushed it to the back of his skull and focused his attention on the naked body in front of him.

He'd deal with his own death some other time.

Colonel Billy was too young to have fought in Vietnam, that much was obvious. The upper arms now revealed were unlined and his wrists lacked age spots. His body hair had still to go white. Lividity had already painted Colonel Billy's fingertips and the underside of his arms near black, and blood had pooled along his side, where gravity had dragged it towards the ground. His face, when Bobby rolled the colonel over again, looked almost camouflaged, so dark was the mottling to his nose and mouth.

Around Colonel Billy's neck hung a pair of cheap dog tags on a thin chain. One of the tags was merely battered, while the other had been rolled into the form of a tube and pinched at both ends.

Colonel Benjamin Black, read the battered tag.

A number followed, though it looked like no military reference Bobby had ever seen. The back of the tag read *GI Joe*, followed by a copyright symbol and the name of a manufacturer. Colonel Billy had scratched his rank, name and number into a tag given away free with a child's toy, using a pin from the look of things.

Tearing off a square of newspaper, Bobby dropped the tags and chain into the middle, folding the edges in on themselves in the way a crime scene tek had once shown him. Evidence bags were better, but Bobby was SFPD, he could work with what he'd got.

There were no wounds to the front of the body, no side wounds and nothing at the back. Tissue damage could be seen along the edge of one finger, but as the tearing was only skin deep and revealed teeth marks it was possible to discount human causes. Colonel Billy's body showed no signs of injury, certainly nothing serious enough to lead to death, leaving Bobby with the possibility that the homeless man might simply have died.

It happened. In fact, it happened all the time.

All the same . . .

Something didn't make sense, because there were footprints scuffed in the concrete of Colonel Billy's hut and at the start of the path that led back towards Vista Point. Not one set of prints but half a dozen, same boots, different trips. Not the colonel's combat boots either, but something fancier. Stout boots of the kind a hiker might wear. And Colonel Billy wasn't the kind of person to share his space with anyone.

Except maybe Louie, and then only rarely.

Crouching beside the bundle of clothes he'd taken from Colonel Billy's body, Bobby began to go through them. There were rips in the colonel's jacket and tears in his shirt. Sweat had eaten into the underarms of both and age had rotted what sweat could not reach. As he held them up, Bobby tried to match the holes in one with tears in another. Nothing looked likely until he reached the left underarm of the cavalry jacket.

The smallest rip through which light could still fit. And it matched a tiny tear in the shirt. Returning to the body, Bobby rolled Colonel Billy over. Rigor was long gone and his arm moved freely, too freely, as if the muscles beneath the skin had already begun to deliquesce.

There was a third cut, just visible though the matted hair beneath Colonel Billy's arm. An unusually thin stiletto could have done it, maybe a length of sharpened wire. Under the arm and straight through to the heart.

Bobby had his proof, Colonel Billy had been killed. What he imagined he was going to do with it was another matter.

The patch pockets of the colonel's jacket were empty, as were the side pockets of his jeans. A ticket for the Hyde Powell cable car was in the back, but since Bobby couldn't imagine the colonel being allowed on board, never mind buying a ticket, he guessed the man must have found it and liked the colour. A half-empty packet of Marlboros was tied into the tails of his check shirt and its breast pocket contained . . .

The needle shocked Bobby out of his list making.

'Are you carrying a point?'

Before beginning to search a suspect, that was practically the first question any SFPD officer asked. And officers had been known to go easy on anyone who volunteered in advance that his pockets or clothes contained a needle. No one needed the grief. Getting spiked by a hypodermic meant six months of AIDs tests and enforced counselling.

Only this was not that kind of needle.

Turning the stickpin over in his hand, Bobby saw a simple pair of wings, a motto and the name of a regiment for anyone who still needed further clues. It looked real.

After he'd worked his way through Colonel Billy's clothing and checked the bottom of every plastic shopping bag, which produced nothing but a soiled T-shirt, a cheap sleeping bag and a pamphlet from Jews for Jesus, Bobby turned to the combat boots. He'd been running the search as if the man was alive and standing there in front of him. Bobby only grasped that when he realised he'd left Colonel Billy's boots for last.

They stank. If the clothes smelt and the body was beginning to get high, then the boots stank and had that slimy feel inside from years of unbroken wear. All the same, Bobby found what he was looking for in the toe of the second boot. A twist of cellophane wrapped around a dozen misshapen lumps of crack.

Unwrapping the rocks, Bobby upended an empty tuna can that Colonel Billy had used to make a drinking saucer and shook the last drops onto the floor of the hut. Heating the bottom with Colonel Billy's plastic lighter, Bobby dropped a crystal onto the blackening metal.

Smoke rose into the air.

'Come on,' he said. 'I know you're out there.'

*

121

When Latif finally got back, Bobby was sat against a tree staring at the darkness visible through the hut's open door. He seemed to be lost in thought.

'Shit,' said Latif, seeing the naked body lying in full view.

Holding up one hand, Bobby whispered, 'Wait.'

Smoke had thinned to nothing and the can was almost cold by the time a fist-sized bundle of fur lurched out of the door and halted abruptly at the sight of Latif.

'Lucifer, this is Latif.

'Latif . . . Lucifer.'

The kitten ate the tuna straight from the tin, tearing pink flesh with tiny teeth and scooping flakes with his claws.

'Is that smell what I think it is?'

Bobby nodded. 'Cat's been like this since it was born. It took Colonel Billy two days to work out what was wrong. He reckoned the kitten was born addicted because its mother came from a squat in the Castro. All that smoke in the air . . .'

'So your man and his cat shared their crack?'

'No,' said Bobby. 'It wasn't like that. Colonel Billy was clean. He bought drugs strictly for his cat . . .' Bobby's smile was sour. 'You ever tried pinning a rap on someone buying crack for an animal?'

'You knew this man?'

'Yeah,' said Bobby. 'I knew him.'

Latif looked puzzled. 'I thought you came from out of town?'

'Well, in his way, so did Colonel Billy.'

According to every official report, Colonel Billy was born and raised, and had remained, in San Francisco. He might talk the talk of Tet and offensives, Hueys and napalm in the morning, but his insanity was officially home-grown. Colonel Billy's version was very different, as was Louie's, but then Louie and Colonel Billy had been lovers and Louie believed in everything from ley lines to Area 51. She'd been in Iraq, a sniper, or so she said. Mind you, she didn't say this until after she met Colonel Billy and he told her about Tet.

And Bobby's own version? Because he'd need one. Being Sergeant Bobby Zha wasn't practical in a city where half the population had read about his death or seen it reported on TV, and where those who apparently counted themselves as his friends were probably still nursing hangovers from yesterday's wake.

'What are you planning to do with the cat?'

'Keep it,' said Bobby. The colonel and Bobby had a deal. If anything happened then Bobby took care of Lucifer. As promises went, it was a small price for having Colonel Billy act as Sergeant's Zha's eyes and ears on the streets. In San Francisco the homeless weren't just a problem. They were an embarrassment to a city so gilded it was happy to look down on New York. Much of Bobby's old job had been about keeping them from becoming more embarrassing still.

'It's just an animal,' said Latif.

'Yeah,' said Bobby. 'Aren't we all . . .'

They laid Colonel Billy to rest under a pile of rocks and hid the mound with brush taken from a nearby thorn bush. Burying him properly was out of the question, the ground around the hut being mostly rock and the earth skin deep. All the same, Bobby scraped out as much of a trench as he could.

With luck, the stones would keep off anything bigger than a coyote, while the *Danger* signs and barbed wire circling the old lookout should be enough to do the same for humans, most of them anyway. The Colonel Billys of the world would always find their way here.

As Latif pulled up outside Hotel Triton, he clicked a switch to unlock his car's doors and kill a satellite alarm. That way, his uncle would know this was a legitimate stop and no one was in danger. The Lincoln was almost new and GHS positioning was the least of its capabilities. 'You sure?' he said. 'You want to book me for a month. But I'm only needed when you call?'

Bobby nodded.

'In that case . . .'

If Latif's client wanted time to himself that was his business. It was still only 10.30 on Sunday morning. The city was walking out to warm weather and news of five more military deaths in Iraq, unrest in Haiti and reports that an American journalist, shot in Red Square after publishing a list of companies owned by the late Gregory Osip, had apparently fallen prey to Chechen muggers. Moscow's Chief of Police could announce this for a fact.

The muggers had confessed.

CHAPTER 21
Sunday 22 February

Strangely enough, it was the cat who decided to change hotels. That is, Bobby took Lucifer into the Triton tucked inside his jacket, ran the animal up to his room through an elevator-induced barrage of New York punk and put the cat on his bed while he checked no one had entered the room.

A *leave me alone* sign still hung from his door and his suitcase was precisely aligned with a crack in the floor of the cupboard, the drawers of his desk remained exactly one quarter inch open. Bobby was just wondering who he expected to have ransacked his possessions when he noticed the sheets. Some one had stripped them back and then replaced them, managing only a close approximation of the mess Bobby had made that morning.

Which begged some pretty weird questions.

'Wait,' said Bobby.

The cat ignored him.

And when Bobby ignored the cat, its mewling got louder and louder until eventually it seemed impossible that an animal so small could make such noise. That was when Bobby realised Lucifer needed another hit.

'Oh shit . . .' He wasn't used to this. The edges of Colonel Billy's lighter heated up so fast Bobby seared his fingers on the wheel. And then he dropped the tuna tin, because that also burnt his fingers. Which made two burns this time and two from the time before.

He was going to need practice.

It felt weird to be heating base for a kitten, but Bobby needed the silence and Lucifer was hardly to blame. All the same, the stink was a little too obvious for his liking. When he'd made his calls, Bobby was going to have to find somewhere a little more anonymous. So maybe the decision to move was his and Lucifer just supplied the reason. Bobby thought about that, decided it was probably true.

Having locked the cat in the lavatory with the smoking tuna tin, Bobby used the silence to dial Washington. It was Sunday, so the offices were staffed but no one was that interested in talking to him. In all, it took three calls and half a dozen transfers from one department to another before he even reached the right office.

'What's the number?' The voice on the other end was abrupt.

Bobby read out the digits scratched onto Colonel Billy's dog tag.

'And where did you come across this?'

'On a dog tag,' said Bobby, and was rewarded with absolute silence.

Someone would be tracing the line as they spoke. That was okay. So far as the Triton knew, Bobby was due to fly back to New York in three days' time; that's what he told them anyway, which meant that was what they'd tell whoever came looking.

'A tag . . .'

Bobby got the distinct feeling the man at the Pentagon was talking to himself, but he answered all the same. 'That's right,' Bobby said. 'I can give you a name as well, if you want.'

'A name . . . ?'

They'd be shouting at someone to hurry up with the trace by now. Maybe having been transferred internally so many times between departments meant tracing would take longer or wasn't even possible, Bobby didn't know. He'd always been able to rely on teks for that kind of thing.

'And where did you find the tags?'

It was a good question. Almost as good as asking Bobby his name, how he'd known which department to call (he hadn't), and from where was he calling . . . Bobby had liked the correctness of that sentence construction, but had refused to answer all the same.

Where had he found them?

Life was a series of tipping points, mostly invisible. The right answer to the wrong question. The wrong action at the right time. Most people could draw a map of their life in all its glory of wrong turns and roads which lead back to where they started.

'Are you still there?'

'Yes,' said Bobby, half wondering how long he'd kept the man waiting. 'I found it on a body,' he said.

Obviously enough, the man wanted to know where.

Bobby sighed. 'We've been through this. You tell me who he was and maybe I'll tell you where to find him. He did exist, then?' Bobby added almost as an afterthought.

'What do you mean?'

'Colonel Billy . . .'

Another silence, not so impatient, more puzzled. 'I'm not sure I understand the question. And I'm not sure I understand why you keep calling the man Billy.'

'It was the name he used.'

'You knew him?'

Bobby thought about that. 'Yes,' he said finally. 'The man was a friend.'

Something in that statement changed the attitude of the officer on the other end of the line; or perhaps the change was more cynical than this and tracing the call had failed after all. Whatever, the man announced that it might be good if the caller talked to someone senior, there was a click as the connection was transferred, and then another voice came on the line.

'This is General Charles Greenburg,' said the voice. 'I'm at home. You've been talking to my ADC . . .'

'General,' said Bobby.

'You know Colonel Billy?' The general stumbled over the name. It was obvious that they were trying very hard to keep Bobby on the line and at some point they'd have started recording the conversation, unless, of course, every call to that office was recorded as a matter of course.

'I knew him,' Bobby said, remembering the body he'd buried that morning. 'As I said, he's dead.'

'How did he die?'

'Hunger, drugs, too many years on the streets . . . Any or all of those. It was a miracle Colonel Billy survived as long as he did.'

'Are you saying what I think you're saying?'

'I don't know,' said Bobby. 'The Colonel Billy I knew was a vagrant with a recent arrest for buying crack . . .'

Bobby decided not to mention the cat.

'. . . now he's dead. No one will be doing an autopsy and I doubt if anyone other than me will even notice he's gone.'

'*Other than you?*'

Bobby probably shouldn't have said that.

'And so now the colonel's dead . . . How does that make you feel?'

It was, in retrospect, an odd question.

'Responsible,' said Bobby.

'Ahh, yes,' announced the voice on the other end. 'Join the club.'

CHAPTER 22

Sunday 22/Monday 23 February

Bobby made two further telephone calls that afternoon. Although he made them from a hotel near the airport, where he'd booked in for one night only, having mentioned a flight to Paris in the morning.

The first he made to the wrong person at Inter-departmental Liaison at 850 Bryant St, to announce that a Mr Robert Van Berg would be arriving sometime the next day and should be given all possible help. The second was to Sol Mancini, an engraver who'd retired to a Spanish villa near the corner of Marina and Cervantes, just ahead of a police swoop that retired his colleagues to much less comfortable surroundings. Mr Mancini was unhappy about meeting Bobby so early in the morning, but became happier when Bobby mentioned the sums of money likely to be involved.

'You know what I hate about this place?'

Glancing round, Bobby saw a vast room that overlooked a long row of yachts, most costing more than a house. Sol Mancini's living area was up a flight of stairs and had once been two bedrooms and a bathroom, before Mediterranean arches were knocked into the walls and the house inverted, so its owner could sleep in a basement room at the back, one reinforced with concrete and guarded by a steel door.

Some of his old friends were less than happy about the timing of Sol Mancini's retirement.

'What do you hate?' said Bobby.

'Them.' Sol gestured towards the window, his mouth twisted in distaste.

'The yachts . . . ?'

'Hate yachts? Of course I don't hate yachts. I've got one.' He singled out a single black hull, which stood amid the white like a mutant gull.

'It's them I hate.' He meant the early-morning runners, power walkers and middle-aged men on racing bikes.

'Every fucking morning,' said Sol. 'They're out there in those stupid clothes, jogging up to the field and back again. And if you think they're annoying, you should see the ones on skates. Idiots.'

Wheeling his bulk in a circle, Sol turned his attention to Bobby. 'Who did you say you were?'

'I didn't.'

'But you know . . .' The man mentioned a long-retired attorney. This was the name Bobby had used to get through the door. Although it was flattery about Sol Mancini's skills that got Bobby up to this room.

'Yes,' said Bobby. 'We've helped each other out now and then.'

Corruption is a sucker plant, that was what the lieutenant always used to say. It takes root and spreads, is weeded out and breaks through again, sometimes years later. All it takes is one officer to go on the pad. One of the reasons Bobby had remained in the force was that, whatever else he did, he never did that.

Putting $10,000 on the table, Bobby stood back so Sol Mancini could shuffle forward, spread the notes and peel one from near the top, one from near the bottom and another from somewhere around the middle, taking all three notes over to the window and holding them up to the light, one after another.

'Bulletproof?'

Sol tapped the glass. 'This? What do you think . . . ?'

Whatever Sol was looking for he found, because he returned the notes to the pile on the table.

'Nice,' said Bobby, nodding at the object. 'Antique?'

It was hideous, with legs curved into the shape of naked dryads and a Bacchus face at each corner. The marble top was so white it looked as if it had been bleached.

'Kingdom of the Two Sicilies,' said Sol. 'I swapped it for a Tiepolo sketch years ago.'

'Someone got a bargain.'

'True enough.' Sol nodded, still pleased with himself. 'Let me fix some coffee . . .'

This was an honour indeed. The old man waddled over to a desk and slapped a small bell loudly. 'Venetian,' he said, 'late eighteenth century.' A few minutes later, a bird-like woman appeared at the top of the stairs, her head wrapped in a blue scarf.

'*Caffè*,' demanded Sol.

She grinned, said something in a language unknown to Bobby, turning back to add something that left Sol frowning.

'I found her in Addis Ababa,' Sol said. 'In nineteen thirty-eight, it's a long story.' Sol sighed. 'Probably should have left her there.'

'What did she say?' Bobby asked. It was the right question, Bobby knew this when Sol hesitated.

'That you were dangerous.'

Bobby shook his head. 'No,' he said, 'what did she actually say?'

'That people like you get people like me killed, because you're dead already. She could see this in your eyes . . .' The fat man laughed. 'Ignore her,' he said. 'She gets like that.'

So pale was the coffee that it was almost golden. It tasted like warm grass mixed with cardamom. That was how coffee was meant to taste, Theodora informed him through Sol, when Bobby looked surprised. Americans didn't know how to make coffee. Arabs didn't know how to make coffee. Italians didn't know how to make coffee . . .

Sol gave up translating the list after Italians.

Coffee was meant to be scented. Sipped from tiny glasses and not mixed with milk and served in paper buckets topped with foam.

When the glasses were empty and Theodora nothing but an angry clatter of pans downstairs, Sol sat back in a truly hideous Napoleon III chair and looked at Bobby. 'This is like I was told, right? Occasionally someone would come to ask for my help . . . It counts as a favour.'

Bobby stared back. Since his bundle of $100 notes lay on top of Sol's Two Sicilies table, it took him a second or so to work out what the old man meant.

Witness protection?

The Mafia?

Who exactly had helped Sol into safe retirement? Not that it really mattered. 'Yes,' Bobby said. 'We have friends in common.'

'Good,' said Sol. 'You'd better tell me what you want.'

They worked it out between them. A layer of identity with another layer behind. Robert Van Berg became an FBI agent, complete with ID card, Virginia driver's licence and a swipe key to get him into the garage at Langley . . . A gun licence and a LP53 allowing him to carry a gun across state lines completed this part of the plan.

'How long will that take?'

Sol thought about it. 'I can do you convincing by this afternoon for the ID card, the rest tomorrow . . . Or,' he paused, 'I can do you special. Something to worry everyone. It'll take slightly longer and it will cost more.'

'The special.'

'Come on,' the fat man said. 'You're meant to ask me how much.'

'That doesn't really matter,' said Bobby.

'Of course it does.' Sol looked really unhappy. 'Ask me,' he said. 'I don't need the bad luck and I like sleeping at nights.' That was when Bobby got it. The only people who didn't worry about how much something was going to cost in Sol's world were those who didn't intend to pay.

'I'll give you 20,000 dollars for the first skin, another 20,000 for the second and an additional 10,000 dollars for the third. And everything you do for me is better than convincing.'

Sol smiled.

'What's more,' Bobby said. 'I need the lot by tomorrow night.' And he watched Sol's smile turn into a grin.

'25,000 dollars each.'

They settled on $60,000 for three separate layers of identity and both accepted without mentioning it that the original $10,000 was to be the cost of Bobby's introduction to Sol.

'So what do you want for your back-up identity?'

Bobby dictated a number to Sol.

'That's a Washington area code.'

'Yeah.'

'Is the number real?'

'Oh yes,' said Bobby, remembering General Greenburg. 'It's real. Although you wouldn't want to ring it to find out who is on the other end . . .'

At Sol's suggestion, the second ID card contained three items. Bobby's name, the telephone number, which was that of the last department Bobby had called before being transferred to the office of the general, and an American Eagle. The eagle Sol took from a dollar bill and came ready-weighted with so much cultural baggage that Bobby found himself impressed before the card was even roughed out on Sol's computer screen.

The laptop would be destroyed, Sol had already explained this. The disk wiped to NSA standards, reformatted, filled with junk and then fed over an industrial magnet. Three separate layers of identity meant three new Sony laptops, the additional cost being added to his bill.

The final item was to be a single letter on 80 gsm weave, contained in an envelope of similar weight. By the time this reached Bobby it would be signed by the President and franked with White House markings.

'I need something for now,' said Bobby.

'Such as?' Sol looked amused.

'What have you got?'

Bobby hadn't known the CIA carried flip-up shields and, chances were, they didn't. As an SFPD officer he'd had the occasional and traditionally uncomfortable experience of working with suits from the FBI. This translated as being patronised, disregarded and ordered about by people with no real authority over you. The CIA were outside Bobby's area of experience.

'Is this real?' Bobby asked.

'Who can tell?' said Sol with a smile. 'That's what should make you happy. Who around here can tell . . . ?'

The office of Inter-departmental Liaison was on the third floor of 850 Bryant, which also housed the offices of the DA. It could only be reached by the single bank of four escalators that served SFPD HQ. The office was small, because almost all of the offices were small, but it was freshly painted in hospital green and the matching carpet was almost new.

'Robert Van Berg,' said Bobby.

A uniform looked up, dark eyes irritated. She was Pacific Asian, like many of the newer staff at Bryant Street and she wore a uniform so smart it must have been freshly cleaned.

'I'm sorry?' Something about the way Officer Li said this conveyed the information that she was anything but apologetic. Her visitor had arrived five minutes before she was due to go off shift. A fact that was entirely intentional on Bobby's part.

'I'm expected . . .'

Officer Li shuffled notes on her desk. 'Not by me, sir.'

'Then we have a problem,' said Bobby. 'Because I was there when my office made the call . . .' He leant forward and took the papers from her hand. And he did this with such utter confidence in his right to read her notes that Officer Li sat there open mouthed.

'Is your Chief here?' Since Bobby had just seen her get out of the lift as he was getting in, he certainly hoped not. 'Perhaps you could check . . .'

When Sandra Li put down the phone it was hard to tell who was more relieved. Officer Li to escape having to explain why she suddenly needed to put a meeting in the Chief's diary or Bobby, who'd had to gamble that the Chief really was on her way out of the building.

The difference was that Bobby could see the relief in Officer Li's face; while she just saw a tall man in an expensive suit blocking her doorway.

'How about Lieutenant Que?'

'The lieutenant's not based here. He works out of Chinatown Station on Grant Street.'

'Really?' Agent Van Berg did a good impression of looking embarrassed. 'That could explain it . . . If you could call ahead for me?'

'Of course.' Officer's Li's nod was decisive. 'I'll do it now.' She gathered up her pens, slung a lipstick and compact into her handbag and reached for the phone. 'Who shall I say?'

'Robert Van Berg,' said Bobby. Palming his badge, he put it on the desk in front of her and then removed it before she had time to pick it up for herself. Small, enamel, shield shaped with the words CIA in gold lettering. God knows where Sol Mancini had found it.

'You're with the Agency?' Officer Li's voice was pitched somewhere between awe and revulsion.

Bobby smiled. And as she had cards on her desk announcing that Officer Li represented Inter-departmental Liaison, he took one.

The lieutenant wasn't in either. There was a chance he was on his way to some meeting to be addressed by the Chief but Bobby was willing to bet he was on his way home. Monday was the day Lieutenant Que logged off early. The day he visited the Kong Chow temple and dropped by the Six Companies to pay his respects to childhood friends. Tea time would find the man playing mah-jong for dollar bills in some smoky basement behind Stockton. Lieutenant Que was a model officer, husband and member of Richmond society for six days of the week. The other day was today.

'Agent Van Berg,' said Officer Valdez.

It was the uniform who'd been carrying Bobby's coffin in the photograph. She looked like she was trying to remember where she'd seen him before.

'Filipacchi's,' he said. 'The wake.'

'Ahh. That's right . . . I had a call from Bryant Street.'

'Officer Li,' said Bobby, 'Inter-departmental Liaison.'

Officer Valdez nodded. 'Perhaps you could tell me how we can help? Officer Li wasn't entirely clear on that.'

'Of course. It's about the Natalie Persikov case . . .'

CHAPTER 23

Tuesday 24 February

The girl behind the desk at the Marriott Airport Hotel waved them goodbye and the woman on the door radioed for a complimentary car. She pocketed the $10 bill Bobby gave her and tickled Lucifer briefly under his chin, raising the kitten to a sullen purr.

'See you next time.'

This was probably just something they said, decided Bobby as his shuttle slid into the late morning traffic and headed for the airport. He was tempted to skip this bit and suggest the shuttle driver dropped him at the nearest taxi rank, saving Bobby time and a worthless trip out to Departures. The downside of this was that changing his destination from airport to city was odd enough to make the driver talk, or at least remember.

So Bobby sat in the back with the kitten and listened to the man's opinions on everything from the last election to the chaos in the middle east.

'They let cats fly now?' the man asked finally, heaving Bobby's case onto the sidewalk.

'Sure, provided you're willing to pay.'

'That's life.'

Six hours after his shuttle pulled away, Bobby wandered out of Arrivals, haggled a price with a Mexican taxi driver and took a ride back to Grant and Columbus, entering Chinatown from the north. In the gap between arriving in his original shuttle and climbing into the back of the taxi, Bobby had decided to check his luggage into a nearer airport hotel, arrange it neatly in a wardrobe and crumple the bed to make it look like he'd slept at least one night there. Anyone who came after him looking for a pattern would waste days trying to join up all the dots.

Having showered, Bobby shaved, dressed, took a nap and changed his clothes. He also fired up some base for Lucifer, using a metal ashtray from his room. An open can of tuna and upturned pot plant did as food bowl and dirt tray.

Bobby was running on instinct.

At least that was what Bobby thought, until he was sat in the back of the taxi and realised this wasn't what he was doing at all. He was using memories, folk tales and fragments of something far deeper. Conversations overheard as a child between his grandfather and the old man's friends. Stories about hiding among villagers from the spies of enemy warlords. Layering identities and creating false truths to be given up only under torture.

The idea of multiple names was sanctioned by time and the spirits. Did not Tin How, Queen of Heaven and guardian of those who crossed the sea to California also go by the name Ma-Tsu, at least among the people of Fujian and Guangdong? And Guan Di, so divided he carried a sword in one hand and a book in the other, did he not manifest as patron saint to both poets and soldiers, gangsters, prostitutes and the police?

As a child, Bobby had understood little of what was being said. All he knew was that the heroes had lost. They'd overthrown an emperor, carved out a republic from the middle kingdom and seen it stolen away by criminals in the name of all those the heroes had thought they were representing.

It was only later Bobby put names to the figures who wandered in and out of his grandfather's stories and finally understood why old women dipped their heads and men stepped back when his grandfather walked by. The old man had been someone once. And the leader his grandfather had met while still a boy was Sun Yat-sen, the man who overthrew the Manchu emperor, using money raised in San Francisco's Chinatown.

The fairy tales were real.

In the front of the limousine the driver was on the phone to his lawyer, complaining about some ticket his son had been given by the police. 'That's not a limousine,' he was saying crossly. 'It's a private car. Yes, I know it's registered in my name. It used to be a limousine . . .'

Whatever the lawyer said wasn't sufficient because the Mexican growled something about calling back and banged his phone back into its cradle.

'Hey,' he said. 'You come from round here?' Taking Bobby's silence as answer enough, the man launched into a description of traffic law in San Francisco, the unforgiving nature of the SFPD and the fact a single unpaid ticket could get you cuffed and carted away if you got stopped again.

'Can you believe that?'

Bobby paid the man off outside the last of the Italian delicatessens on Columbus and walked south, following a crowd of German tourists. It was weird seeing Chinatown through fresh eyes. Twenty-two blocks of prime San Francisco real estate, prettied up with green tiles, gold leaf and red paint. The centre of a world to which he didn't belong and from which he'd never quite been able to separate himself.

There were shops he'd visited as a child and restaurants to which he'd taken early girlfriends, the handful of teenagers he'd dated in the gaps between seeing Ellen. The names and facades changed and so did the chefs but the locations remained and the food was the same.

The daughter of a fishmonger, the niece of an accountant, Bobby could count those years off in cheap jade rings bought from tourist shops and uneasy meals in upstairs cafés where a dozen old men watched their every move.

So why was he here?

A question so large Bobby had to break it into small pieces before he could bring himself to consider the fragments. He was here, in China-town, because he was looking for somewhere to stay. Obviously enough, a whole heap of questions were backed up behind that choice and Bobby intended to ignore all of them.

He had a hotel, but was still looking for somewhere central because he needed a base from which to investigate two crimes. The death of a burglar in Tamsin Steps and the shooting of a SFPD officer. The two crimes might be linked or they might be entirely separate, Bobby had his own opinions on that.

He was investigating the crimes because one of the deaths had been his. A fact so absurd Bobby glossed over it swiftly. Except, of course, he'd been glossing over this fact for the best part of seven days and it was time he stopped. Either he was back from the dead, or he had someone else's memories; the alternative was that he was insane, which was his preferred solution.

All this still ignored the real question. Not why was he standing outside a redbrick warehouse currently awaiting redevelopment, because he knew the answer to that one. And not, how did he think he could get the Natalie Persikov investigation reopened without getting himself arrested or sectioned, to which he still didn't have an answer . . .

But, why was . . . why was he here? Now.

Alive and himself.

Most people got through their entire existences without scratching the shiny surface of that question – and they were alive to start with. Someone must know. His grandfather would have done.

'Hey,' said a woman. 'You're crying.'

Looking up from his table, Bobby saw a woman standing over him. *Hispanic, probably in her early twenties, full breasts under a blue shirt and a waist already beginning to spread over her regulation belt.*

Wasn't that how he remembered her? She'd thrown a coat over her uniform and had her SFPD jacket stuffed in a bag.

'Is this a bad time?'

Considering he'd just got himself from Columbus Avenue, via Stockton Street to Café Claude to keep a meeting he'd forgotten he had . . . Yeah, you could say that. Under one arm Officer Valdez carried a fat envelope, sealed at both ends and wrapped in tape.

'That what I think it is?'

Officer Valdez nodded.

'All the papers?'

'Everything I could find . . .' She paused, realised that Bobby might think the pause significant and scowled. 'We haven't kept anything back,' she said. 'This is what there was.'

'And you've taken copies . . .' He'd been very insistent about that. The originals were to be left in the files.

Officer Valdez nodded, slightly impatient.

'Thank you,' said Bobby.

When Officer Valdez smiled she dropped five years. Which was a bit of a problem as she looked about twenty to begin with. 'Happy to help,' she said, the terrifying thing was she meant it.

'What?' said Officer Valdez.

Bobby shrugged.

'Come on,' said the officer, 'you can't just look at me like that and shake your head. If I did something wrong, tell me . . .'

'You didn't,' said Bobby. Slitting the envelope, he shook the

138

contents onto the table and shuffled his way through the first three forms. A witness statement from the couple across the road, Natalie's original confession and a report from the first officer to reach the scene.

'These are great,' Bobby said.

'Good . . .' Officer Valdez waited and then waited some more, puzzled now rather than impatient. 'Aren't you going to ask me to sit?' she asked finally.

Bobby looked at her.

'You invited me to supper. You're supposed to ask me to sit.' She glanced round at the crowded bar. Café Claude's customers were young and professional, media mostly, with a slipstream of allied trades. A handful of them were watching the plumpish officer stand awkwardly by Bobby's table, obviously torn between politeness and a desire to go.

'Here,' said Bobby, standing to pull back a chair.

Kicking the bag containing her jacket into a corner, Felicidad Valdez sat. Their table was next to a window, overlooking a cluster of tables in the alley. All either could see of the customers outside was the back of half a dozen heads, and hands carrying duck breast towards unseen mouths.

'Wouldn't have thought this was your kind of place.'

'No?' Bobby smiled. 'What kind of place would that be?'

'Somewhere less trendy,' said Officer Valdez, 'more confident. Listen to them . . .'

A girl laughed as her neighbour repeated a comment that hadn't been funny the first time round. Someone started humming to drown a third repetition and the only man in the party started talking over the top of that.

'Nobody needs to talk that loud,' Officer Valdez said.

They ate at Café de la Presse in the bistro at the front. It was full of French expats, English tourists and a group of philosophy majors arguing the nature of being and non-being at great length and in sentences where the only understandable words were limited to simple verbs and the indefinite article.

A woman in the other corner – out of town haircut, son and daughter in tow – was stating in short simple sentences her continuing shock at the Monica Lewinsky story. 'I know it was a long time ago, but I still can't get over how she threw that internship away. It was so bad for everyone else. And she could have made fantastic contacts.'

'Yes,' said Officer Valdez, 'this is more what I had in mind.'

A bit of Bobby wanted to say the only reason they were here was because Café de la Presse was the first place he'd seen after they left the last place, but he didn't because he needed Officer Valdez's help and she was far more intelligent than she pretended and she'd know he was lying. He'd chosen Café de la Presse because it was the kind of place that she'd have expected him to choose.

He ate fois gras for similar reasons and she forgave him. Although she made sure he knew she was vegetarian. Around the time Bobby finished his fois gras he remembered to ask her first name.

'Felicidad. My friends call me Flic . . .'

'That what your boyfriend calls you?'

'I don't . . .' She stopped, put down her glass of sauvignon blanc and smiled. 'Very slick.' It took Bobby a second to understand what she was saying.

After they spilled out onto Bush Street he offered to get her a taxi.

'I can get my own.'

Bobby sighed. 'I meant, pay for it.'

'Are you always this much of a gentleman?'

'No,' said Bobby, 'almost never. I just thought it's late, it looks like it might rain and you probably need to get home . . .'

What was more, he really meant it.

CHAPTER 24

Wednesday 25 February

She was sweet and beautiful and cried a little because she'd shared a bed on the first date and she didn't do stuff like that. So Bobby kissed her forehead, wrapped her in his arms and told her it didn't matter because he knew that anyway. They were in a room off Union Square which Bobby had booked when it became clear Flic had no intention of taking that taxi.

She had no intention of having sex either, although Bobby realised this before she did. So they kissed and undressed each other rather less than Bobby would have liked. By the time dawn arrived, Flic had removed everything except her knickers and was curled against Bobby. Another night gone. Another day of waking to find himself still alive. His heart mirroring the beat of a woman he held in his arms.

'You okay?' he asked.

'Sure.' She snuggled against him. 'Why wouldn't I be?'

He'd slept like that, although it would be more accurate to say Flic slept like this, because Bobby had spent most of his time watching darkness slide away to reveal the room.

> *A brother, younger*
> *Priests, prayers, her mother*
> *Someone dead.*

The tiny bursts of static were getting weaker by the day and Bobby found it hard to know how much of what he felt was real, how much he was making up to fill the gaps in the silence between her breathing. All the same, each new sliver of memory felt like static. A tiny spark of understanding that burnt his skin. And, when sunlight finally revealed all it could and Bobby's arm had passed through stiffness and pins and needles into absolute numbness, he felt the woman beside him stir.

'You sleeping?' said Flic.

'No.' Bobby shook his head.

'Just wondered. You mind if I take a shower?'

He didn't.

Reaching for a hotel robe, Flic crossed the room and Bobby heard the bathroom door lock. Water fired up and ten minutes went by and then another ten.

'Can I ask you something?'

Opening his eyes, Bobby blinked. The bathroom door was open and clouds of steam billowed out. So thick was the fug from the shower that Bobby could barely see the bathroom's wall. Flic was standing at the foot of the bed, only now she was dressed in uniform.

'Sure,' he said. 'Fire away.'

'Why are we here . . . ?'

His confusion over her question went a long way towards smoothing out the anger in Flic's voice and left her almost smiling. Apparently she found it funny that he thought she might be asking him one of life's great questions.

'You mean, why are we *here*?' Bobby glanced around him.

'Yes,' said Flic.

'We needed a room . . .'

'Maybe I'm just being paranoid,' she said, 'but I thought per-haps . . .'

And then Bobby got it. 'My hotel's out at the airport,' he said. 'This seemed simpler. That's the only reason.'

'Really?'

'Yes, of course.'

'You're based at SFO?' Flic didn't add, *are you nuts*? Although she might as well have done. It was fifteen miles from the airport to the city centre and who needed the commuting time? . . . Also, why stay at SFO when there had to be ten good hotels within a stone's throw from Union Square, like this one for a start.

'I was at the Triton,' admitted Bobby, 'but I changed hotels yester-day. Took my luggage and stuff out to the airport.'

'This is an Agency thing, right?'

'Something like that . . . You off now?'

Officer Valdez frowned at him. It was a very pretty frown, at least Bobby thought so. 'The uniform,' he said, 'the fact you're dressed.'

'You were sleeping,' said Flic. 'Well, you appeared to be. I thought you might be pretending . . .'

They got coffee in a small café off Mission. By then Bobby had established that it was Officer Valdez's day off, her mother had established that Felicidad was working all night and Bobby had to endure a difficult and embarrassing chat with Mrs Valdez while Flic took a totally unnecessary shower at her mother's suggestion, to freshen up.

'Espresso,' said Bobby, when asked what he wanted for breakfast.

Flic ate tomato, bread and thin slices of a hard goats' cheese imported from Spain, washed down with mugs of milky coffee and two glasses of freshly squeezed orange juice.

'Sex makes me hungry,' she added, then blushed when Bobby raised his eyebrows. To judge from her next comment, it also made her thoughtful. 'I don't suppose this is for real?'

'It's not forever,' said Bobby. 'If that's what you mean.'

'Well, at least you're honest.' Flic's bark of laughter almost hid the hurt in her voice. 'I wasn't asking, *Is this forever?* I meant more, *Are we going anywhere?* Though I guess you've answered that . . .'

Putting down his coffee, Bobby shuffled his chair closer to the table, so he could reach Officer Valdez's hand. He didn't do anything so crude as actually try to take it, just touched the back of her wrist with one finger, feeling a flicker of unhappiness jump between them.

'Things are complicated,' he said. 'I may not be around for long.'

As Flic sat there and thought over what he'd just said, Bobby took in the café with its fading posters of Madrid and battered furniture. To get there, they'd had to cut down a narrow passage behind Valencia Street and skirt the back of a machine shop, where angle grinders sparked against twisted metal and broken cars were bullied back to something approaching health. The only other people in the café were an old man reading a Spanish language newspaper and a woman behind the counter who was doing her best not to stare at them.

'You used to come here as a child,' said Bobby, suddenly making sense of something. 'And you used to cut round the back of that garage as a kid. This is your turf . . .' He was touched and a little surprised. She was trusting him with something she valued more than her body. Memories from childhood.

'How did you know?'

'Intuition, I guess.' Nodding to the woman behind the bar, Bobby signalled for another espresso. 'You want anything?'

'No,' said Flic, 'but since you paid last night I'll take the check.' There was something so final in her voice that Bobby realised he was about to be consigned to a file labelled *mistakes*.

'I want to show you something,' he said. 'But I need to explain something first, because I don't want you hurt.'

Flic nodded, doing a good job of not looking at his face.

'Last night was great,' said Bobby. 'I like you and we're good together in bed . . .' He kept his voice low, only too aware the chrome espresso machine had stopped its hissing and the owner had emerged from behind the counter. The woman said something to Flic in Spanish so rapid Bobby only caught the word *Felicidad* and then found himself lost in a scatter-gun conversation that only finished when the woman stamped back to her post.

'She doesn't see me enough,' said Flic. She tried for a smile but it went missing from her eyes. 'She thinks I should come home more often. She thinks I spend too much time at work and not enough time with my mother.'

'And do you?'

'Depends on your point of view,' said Flic.

He could leave it there, or he could return to what he'd been saying and Bobby could see in the eyes of the woman opposite which she would prefer. He'd humiliated Flic and stood on the edge of patronising her. Now would be a really good time to say goodbye.

'It's not long term,' said Bobby, wondering at his own stupidity, 'because I can't guarantee being around.' In the last fifteen years he'd screwed his way through half a dozen SFPD officers who should know better, most of the girls from Zil's Kabaret and a host of strangers who'd made no more impression on his life than he'd made on theirs. Yet here he was justifying his behaviour to some girl he would have regarded at any other time as little more than one-night stand.

Life was weird, but the side effects of getting killed were weirder.

'We could still have stayed in touch.'

'No,' said Bobby, 'you're missing the point. *I might not be here.* In the long term I can't guarantee being around.'

'Shit,' said Flic, as she sat back in her seat and stared off at a wall.

'*You can't guarantee* . . . How can I be so fucking dumb?' When she looked back there were tears in her eyes and she gave Bobby a smile he understood was totally undeserved.

CHAPTER 25

Wednesday 25 February

'Isn't this a bit morbid?' asked Flic, peering out of a basement window. 'I mean, that's where . . .' She was right, about the warehouse at least.

It was.

Standing on tiptoes, Flic nodded towards yellow brick. Beyond the edge of the warehouse could be seen a section of courtyard. Someone had tried to make the courtyard more Chinese by bolting a pagoda-like frill around its walls at the top. The whole of this fake edging was made from pressed tin that age and rain had weathered to the blackness of old slate, and part of it had come away from the courtyard wall to tilt at an angle, held precariously by rusting bolts on one end.

According to Bobby, the basement was damp because a river ran directly beneath its floor. This was good luck. Living space took up most of Bobby's new apartment, while a small bedroom could be found at the back. A bathroom off the side was smaller still. A narrow sash window stretched from floor to ceiling, with a white-painted radiator blocking what little of the bottom was not blocked by the bed. A small fridge acted as table to an elderly microwave and a single ceiling light worked from a switch near the door. There was no desk or table or wardrobe.

To reach the apartment they used a freight elevator, the kind with a sliding grill that could not be opened until the car had stopped. Their alternative was a narrow flight of steps, but these were blocked by a wrought-iron door with a rusting padlock and Bobby was still waiting for a copy of the key.

'Okay,' said Flic, 'so this is not just about that.' Her nod took in the alley, someone's ankles and the rattle of a wheelbarrow, but they both knew she meant the warehouse where Sergeant Zha had died.

'No,' said Bobby, 'it's not just about *that.*'

He was almost telling the truth.

A smile spread across Flic's face. 'You're saying this is your area,' she said. 'You grew up in Chinatown.'

'Yes. Something like that.' He was saying he grew up in this room. A place he'd massively overpaid a waiter from Golden Rose Dim Sum to vacate. 'It's a long story.'

While Bobby tipped the contents of the Natalie Persikov file onto the mattress and began to sift his way through statements and CSI reports, Flic went shopping for things she thought Bobby might need. Soap, sheets, bottled water, fruit, fig newtons, condoms . . . She didn't ask what he wanted and as she unpacked the bags, put apples in a bowl and placed the condoms discreetly on top of the lavatory, she didn't comment on what she'd bought.

'Okay,' Flic said, 'that's done.' She glanced at the pile of paper on the bed. 'Any point me asking how it's going?'

'Slowly,' said Bobby. 'I'm not quite sure what I'm after. Maybe you can help. How did the kid seem to you that morning you ran Natalie out to the house . . . What?' he asked, shaken by the expression on Flic's face.

'How do you know about that?'

Good question.

'Sergeant Zha mentioned it,' said Bobby. 'I didn't remember at first, but then when we met at Filipacchi's . . .'

'Sergeant Zha didn't know my name.' Flic's voice was entirely matter of fact.

'Yes he did,' said Bobby. 'He asked Lieutenant Que. You ran Natalie out to the house on Tamsin Steps. How did the girl seem to you?'

'Scared,' said Flic, professionalism winning out over doubt. 'Locked down and very scared.'

'And afterwards?'

'Upset, like she'd failed some test. She sat in the back with her arms wrapped tight around her knees, scowling. That child was furious with herself.'

'How do you know?' asked Bobby.

'Because I've got a younger brother,' said Flic. 'One brother and two older sisters. I know what fury looks like. Can I ask a question?'

'Can you . . .' Bobby looked surprised. 'Why on earth not?'

'Because you're Agency,' said Flic, setting the last of five oranges on top of the apples. 'I'm not sure what I'm allowed to ask. I thought this case was done and dusted.'

'I'm with you so far,' said Bobby.

'And there are some people, important people, who think the family court's suggestion that Natalie undergo therapy is already too much. So I'm wondering what is the Agency's interest in this?' Flic half smiled. 'Now's when you tell me you can't talk about that, right? It's something to do with security.'

'Suppose Natalie really is innocent,' said Bobby. 'Who shot the burglar?'

'Her grandfather . . . ?'

'He's blind.'

'Burglars can make a lot of noise. Dr Persikov probably wouldn't have too much trouble aiming.'

'The dead man was still outside the window.'

'Where does it say that?'

Bobby flicked through the statements and then flicked through them again. He knew it was true. He'd seen tiny slivers of glass in the flowerbed where the bullet exploded through the window. 'Look,' said Bobby, pulling out an early sketch made by some tek in CSI.

Flic frowned. 'But the officer's statement . . .' She came over to the bed and began sorting through the papers, then stopped, suddenly embarrassed by her own actions. 'I read a couple of the reports,' she admitted.

'A couple?'

'Okay,' she said, 'I read everything from cover to cover. I was trying to work out the Agency's angle. I'd have thought this was FBI or Homeland Security at the most.'

'Take a look at the man who was shot,' said Bobby, his mind on other things. He was still trying to work out why the reports conflicted with what he knew he'd seen on the ground.

'Russian,' said Flic, shuffling paper. 'Ahh . . .' It was unlikely to be his real name, but a man called Andrei Tarkov had flown into SFO two days before the shooting. As with everyone entering the US on a Russian passport, Andrei Tarkov had been both fingerprinted and photographed. This information finally reached Central Station the morning after the Natalie Persikov case was closed.

'Russian intelligence?'

'Only if they're very careless,' said Bobby. 'And Putin doesn't strike me as a careless man. All the same, Tarkov wasn't just robbing that house.'

'So what was he doing?'

'I don't know,' Bobby said. 'That's the big question.'

They ate at a dim sum place on Grant where Bobby surprised Flic and shocked himself by ordering in fluent Cantonese. Luckily, his accent belonged to his grandfather and was so out of date the waiter, newly arrived from Hong Kong, treated Bobby with respect but not as a local.

'Wow,' said Flic, 'where did you learn that?'

'At CIA school,' said Bobby, then watched Flic Valdez try to work out if he was joking. Everything Bobby told her would get fed back in confidences to her friends and, whatever she intended, from there would make its way to Lieutenant Que, maybe even the Chief. Lies becoming truth by mere repetition. It was the action of a shit and Bobby wasn't that, except that he was and apparently always had been.

This was what he'd learnt the previous night when Flic was dropping off to sleep and tiredness and satiety had rendered her truths simple. 'Sergeant Zha was a shit,' Flic said. 'I only found out after he died. No one's allowed to say that now, but everybody knows it.'

'How did you find out?' Bobby felt he had to ask.

'I was upset,' said Flic. 'Someone told me not to bother and then explained why. You know he was taking bribes?'

'*No he wasn't.*'

'Hey,' said Flic, 'you don't have to bite my head off.'

'Sergeant Zha was not on the pad,' said Bobby. 'Never once.'

'There are other ways of taking bribes,' Flic said crossly. 'You know he used Zil's Kabaret as his own personal brothel? Alphonse daVilla was getting busted by Vice every week and suddenly Vice get told he's on some semi-official list of protected sources . . . Hell, most of the men didn't even know there was a protected sources list.'

There wasn't.

Bobby had made the list up, backdated the thing and signed it with the lieutenant's signature before filing it. When Lieutenant Que finally worked out what was going on he simply announced the list was abolished, without ever mentioning he hadn't authorised it in the first place.

Added to which, Bobby did get information out of daVilla. The lieutenant knew this. Why else would he have covered for Bobby?

'It wasn't meant to be a big deal,' said Flic, sounding almost apologetic. 'I was just saying, you know . . . I only met him the once and he seemed quite cute.'

'I'm not sure cute's the right word,' said Bobby, and felt Flic sit up so she could see his face in the light which filtered through their hotel window.

'How well did you know him?' she asked.

'Honestly?'

'Yes,' Flic said.

'Obviously not as well as I thought.'

Flic had fallen asleep after that, leaving Bobby to his thoughts and a dead arm as she slept away the hours and he counted off the seconds and the memories . . .

'What are you thinking now?' asked Flic, as Bobby lifted *char siu bao* from a revolving plate and put it in his bowl. Some of the cafés off the main drag had trouble getting their heads around the concept of vegetarian. Flic was coping by taking out the barbequed pork and arranging it around the edge of her side plate.

'About Natalie Persikov and Bobby Zha and that kind of stuff.'

'You really think they're linked . . . ?'

'Don't you?'

'No one's mentioned it.'

'No,' said Bobby. 'The idea doesn't seem to have occurred to anybody. Doesn't that strike you as strange?'

CHAPTER 26

Friday 27 February

Having collected the kitten from his room at the airport hotel, Bobby fed it another can of tuna, fired up the last of the base, gave the animal milk from a saucer and decided it was time he found Lucifer another home.

It took Bobby a day and a half to track down Limping Louie. He began with all the obvious places like the chess tables outside Betterbuy Shoes where Fifty Street met Market and the homeless encampment around the fountain in front of City Hall, and then Bobby worked his way through the less likely to places that were frankly absurd.

Colonel Billy's sometime lover was finally run to ground under a boardwalk near the yacht marina on South Beach. The self-proclaimed poet had built herself a shack out of canvas, ripped-open carrier bags and wood a couple of paces from the edge of the water.

'What happens when the tide gets high?'

'I get wet.' The woman looked at Bobby, considered his clothes. 'You police?'

'Something like that . . . I want to talk about Colonel Billy.'

'Ain't seen him,' said Louie. 'That's the truth. Ain't seen him for days, maybe weeks. Things like that get hard to remember.'

'He's dead,' Bobby said, pulling the kitten from his pocket as proof. 'I need someone to look after Lucifer.'

'You kill Billy?'

Bobby shook his head.

'You sure about that . . . ?'

'Quite sure,' said Bobby, 'I didn't kill him but you're right, someone did.' Handing over the kitten, he added a new wrap of crack that turned out to be several wraps all tied up together.

'Not my thing,' said Louie, 'You got the wrong girl.'

'It's not for you,' Bobby said. 'That's for him . . .' He indicated the cat. 'I got you this.' Bobby gave Louie a tub of fresh fruit salad from Wintergreen and a bottle of mineral water, still vaguely chilled. 'Forgot that little spoon thing,' he apologised.

'I'll manage.'

They sat on the boardwalk above Louie's camp and watched joggers on South Beach, while Louie ate her way through the fruit salad, starting with grapes, followed by red watermelon and finally, when she'd finished spitting pips politely into her hand, by green cubes of honeydew. After that, Louie drank most of the mineral water, reserving the last inch to rinse out her mouth and spit over her fingers.

'You'd better tell me what you want.'

'I want you to look after Lucifer,' said Bobby.

'That all?'

'No,' admitted Bobby. 'I also want to talk about Colonel Billy. And there's more,' he added. 'Colonel Billy used to keep his eyes and ears open on the street for a friend of mine.'

'That policeman,' said Louie. 'He's dead too.' She tipped her head onto one side to look at Bobby suspiciously. 'Do I see a pattern here?'

'I'm not sure,' said Bobby. 'Do you?'

Louie laughed. 'Hell,' she said, 'I see a pattern in everything. That's one of my problems . . .'

When Bobby left it was with a handful of promises, although it was hard to know how much value to put on any of them. Maybe the one about looking after Lucifer. About one in five of San Francisco's street people owned animals; which meant 1500 animals living rough, providing company, love and warmth to those who couldn't find such things anywhere else. And Bobby had known street rapes and murders, maimings, beatings and enough theft to keep an entire station busy for a year, but he could count on a couple of hands the number of times he'd seen one street person hurt another's animal.

Louie would look after the kitten and feed it even on the occasions she had no food of her own, that was how it worked. She'd even buy it crack, at least in the short term, while she worked out the best way to wean the animal off drugs. Louie had a very strict code about stuff like that. So strict it prevented Louie from taking her own meds.

Two paper fans for a dollar . . . A plastic sword, more samurai than

Chinese. Enough jade to weigh down an empress, some of it quite good. Bronze cash, probably fake, but still scratched, battered and thick with verdigris. Netsuke of cats, dogs, dragons and every sexual position under the sun, including a pair of coupling samurai, one of them looking very surprised indeed.

The shops on both sides of Grant Street were thick with tourists stopping to examine window displays or sorting through baskets of knick-knacks on the sidewalk. Such had been the background to Bobby's childhood and he still found it as reassuring as it was irritating. All the same Bobby was glad when he reached the entrance to Golden Rose Dim Sum.

The waiter who served him last time showed Bobby to a table. Its location was better than the table he'd been given before. A red banner at his back proclaimed the new year and exhorted luck for all. The man brought green tea without being asked and wondered aloud if he should leave the other table setting or remove the bowl, cup and chopsticks . . .

'Remove them,' said Bobby, reaching into his pocket for a phone. Flic already had his number in her mobile's address book, she must have done, because when Flic answered she already knew who was on the other end and she sounded excited.

'People are talking about you.'

'Really,' said Bobby. 'Is that a good thing?'

'You came up at a meeting.'

'They let you into meetings now . . . ?'

There was a brief silence from the other end while Flic worked out whether or not to be offended. *You need to be more careful,* Bobby told himself.

'No,' admitted Flic, 'but I heard . . . Believe me, I heard. Apparently Sergeant Sanchez was asking the lieutenant about you.'

Sergeant? That was quick.

'And what was *Sergeant* Sanchez asking?'

'Whether we should be keeping an eye on you . . .' Flic paused. 'I'm not sure I should be telling you this.'

'But you are.'

'Oh, it gets better. Sanchez thought it might be useful if someone got close to you. So I got the gig.'

'Why?' asked Bobby.

'. . . I'm single,' Flic said finally. 'I'm young and I'm female, in case you missed that bit. I'm also the person you first talked to when you came by the station to look at the Persikov files.'

'So what are you meant to be doing now?'

'Engineering a meeting. Except I've just discovered you checked out of your airport hotel, so I'm checking with all the airlines to see if you took a flight to New York or Washington. I've got a feeling I'm probably going to draw a blank . . .'

Flic was enjoying herself far too much, this much was obvious and she was putting her job in danger. Bobby ran through all the reasons why Flic might do that and didn't like any of them.

'I'm going to call Lieutenant Que,' said Bobby. 'And tell him I changed hotels to something even closer to SFO, because I had face-to-facers all day with colleagues flying in and then taking a flight home. After my last meeting this afternoon, I'll be relocating to Union Square, but I'll keep my room at the SFO Hyatt because I may need to do another meeting at short notice.'

'Yeah,' said Flic. 'That sounds convincing.'

Shit, thought Bobby. He hadn't exactly been asking for her approval. All the same . . .

They ran into each other in the lobby of the Mandarin Oriental. Bobby was sitting at a side table reading the foreign news section of the *Washington Post* when Flic stepped out of the lift with an officer he vaguely recognised from Traffic. Both women were done up to the nines and beyond, long dresses cut low and made almost decent by silk shawls thrown casually over bare shoulders.

Bobby saw at least one half of a couple get his knuckles rapped for looking a little too obviously. If this was Flic's answer to his throwaway, *Why you?* then Bobby stood very publicly corrected. At least half a dozen men watched as he stood up and walked over to the two women.

'*Yes?*'

'It's okay,' said Flic, 'I know him.' She didn't sound very enthusiastic, merely matter of fact and slightly bored, as if work had suddenly intruded on her evening out. 'How are you?'

'All the better for seeing you,' said Bobby, and heard the other woman groan. 'I mean it,' he told Flic. 'I've been wanting to thank you for collecting together all that stuff on the Persikov case. Perhaps I could buy you a drink?'

'Perhaps you could,' said Flic. 'We'll have champagne.'

The other woman grinned.

'Sure,' said Bobby. 'Tell me where you're eating and I'll have a bottle sent to your table.'

'The Mandarin Lounge,' said Flic.

'I'll fix it.'

'Well,' said the other, 'at least he has style.' The woman stopped Bobby from leaving with a touch to his shoulder and looked him up and down, as if having trouble pricing his suit, shoes and watch.

'This is Katerina.' Said Flic.

Bobby offered his hand and winced as she shook. The woman had a grip to crack walnuts and a grin that split her face to reveal a childhood's worth of successful cosmetic dentistry.

'Call me Kate.'

'Robert Van Berg,' said Bobby. 'I'm over here from New York.'

'NYPD?'

'No.' Bobby shook his head.

'Didn't think so. Not with those clothes.' He'd been wrong, Katerina Liatos knew exactly how much his suit had cost, and was now waiting for him to tell her what he did. Bobby let her wait.

In the end, the two women invited him to share their table. Ordering Krug as promised, Bobby made polite conversation about the spectacular view from the window, the fact the Transam Pyramid was only four blocks away and why the designer had managed to have a huge Chinese good luck sign worked into the lobby floor in black marble. And around the time they finished the bottle, he stood up from the table, nodded to both of them and went to find the restrooms.

Kate was gone by the time he got back. 'She remembered something she needed to do,' said Flic.

'In that dress?'

'Apparently you made it obvious you fancied me. So Kate decided to give us some space.'

'I thought I was really good,' said Bobby, 'about talking to both of you, and I asked all the right questions.'

'Yeah,' Flic said, 'but you only listened to my answers. Women tend to notice that kind of thing . . .' Flic shrugged. 'She'll get over it. All the same, she told me to be careful. She's met men like you before.'

'I doubt it,' said Bobby.

In the end he and Flic shared chicken focaccia at their table, having danced uneasily around the question of whether they wanted to eat at all. Bobby ate the grilled chicken and Flic ate bits of focaccia and picked her way through at least half the paprika fries.

'What now?' said Flic.

'I'm going to get you a taxi.'

She looked at him.

'One, I'm a perfect gentleman. And two, do you really think we can go back to that hotel on Union Square without someone finding out about earlier . . .'

'What about your apartment?' said Flic, then blushed. Each was taking it for granted the other wanted to spend the night and she wasn't used to that level of self-exposure.

'If we go there, the lieutenant will know neither of us spent the night at my hotel. So what did we do?'

'We might have booked a room,' Flic said with a shrug.

'You're right,' said Bobby, 'we might. Always assuming you want Lieutenant Que to think of you as someone who books into hotels with targets.'

'Only certain targets,' Flic said, but she let Bobby order her a taxi and pecked him lightly on both cheeks, before climbing into a cab to be driven away without looking back.

CHAPTER 27
Monday 1 March

The school on Runyon Drive had been built in 1875 to educate the sons of the newly rich, and San Francisco in the late 1870s was a city firmly divided into the newly rich and those still desperate to join them. The great days of the gold rush were gone and sailing clippers no longer beached on the Bay shore, remaining there to rot as whole crews abandoned their watch to go in search of riches.

Great faith had been placed in the transcontinental railroad and its ability to open San Francisco to the culture, sophistication and elegance of the East Coast. In the event, the railroad brought only disaster. Cheap goods flooded the city, putting whole neighbourhoods out of work. The track layers, mostly Chinese, thousands of whom had been injured, died in blasting accidents or burnt out their lives as indentured labour, found themselves blamed for the city's plight. Laws were passed banning the men from marrying. While Chinatown itself was owned by whites, who rented out rooms at extortionate rents to those not allowed to live anywhere else.

That was what Bobby had been told by Grandfather Lau, to whom such things mattered. It was 1872 before a Chinese man was allowed to testify in court against anyone white and far longer before the repeal of anti-naturalisation laws gave him the vote.

The first Chinese boy to go to the school on Runyon Drive was Bobby's father, who went for the last two years of his formal education, and there were teachers still at the school who regarded this as a mistake. In the year Bobby's daughter was born, the principal suggested Runyon Drive go co-educational and less than thirty per cent of the parents objected, which was how Kris got to follow in her grandfather's footsteps.

She'd been on the brink of losing her scholarship for the last eighteen months and Ellen had been due to attend a meeting with the principal set for two days after Bobby was shot. If what he'd overheard at his own wake was true, Bobby's death had bought Kris another term. Hypocritical or not, part of him hoped she was going to use it wisely.

This hope was slight and what Bobby saw when he neared the school gates made it slighter still. Kris was on the sidewalk, dressed in black jersey, black jeans and exploding black hair, very carefully not getting in anyone's way as she tried to hand leaflets to those going to school. A security guard from a private firm was stood five paces away, talking intently into his radio.

'Yeah,' he said, 'she's here again. No, she's not blocking anyone's way . . .'

At this, Kris looked round and smiled, briefly grateful that the security guard was being fair. She was big on fair. That was why she was stood outside the gate of her own school trying to hand anti-vivisection leaflets to pupils, the occasional, embarrassed-looking father and the kind of mothers who reserved their mink for Aspen and Europe.

It was an expensive school and Bobby certainly couldn't have sent Kris there on his salary. You needed $88,000 just to live in the city, rather than south or across the Bay, that was the figure the newspapers always quoted anyway.

'Can I help you, sir?'

The security guard was smiling when Bobby looked up. One of those professional smiles that get taught in Public Relations 101. Bobby knew how it went, you could kick shit out of the idiot who shot your partner, but you had to keep calling him *sir*, even when you had your hands round his throat.

'I don't know,' said Bobby. 'Can you?'

That always used to wind him up and it also seemed to work for the security guard, because a certain tightness manifested around his eyes.

'This is a private school,' the man said heavily.

There were so many things wrong with that statement Bobby barely knew where to begin, even admitting a certain accuracy to the central fact. All the same . . . Bobby opened his mouth to explain the laws governing access to city owned sidewalks and decided not to bother.

'ID,' he said.

The man blinked.

'Presumably you're carrying ID?'

Despite himself, George nodded. The man undoubtedly had another name but it didn't make it onto his tag.

Bobby held out his hand.

Gregos Georgiou was 43, lived in San Mateo and had worked for SecureGuard for the last five years. He looked a lot younger in his photograph.

'Ex cop?'

'Kansas,' said Georgiou, 'apparently my skills weren't transferable . . .' The story would be a little less straightforward than this because it always was. Every life history was a simplification of things unsaid. He'd have been on the take, sleeping with his boss's wife or a little too ready to pull a gun.

Something grubby. Someone like him.

'She giving you trouble?' Bobby nodded towards the girl by the gate, who was steadfastly refusing to admit defeat as pupil after pupil politely refused her leaflet. It was a very well-behaved school, with one obvious exception.

'Not really. I'm here because I am, if that makes sense. I've been here every morning for the last three years. It doesn't cost the school much and it keeps that lot happy.' Georgiou meant the string of women climbing back into SUVs. 'At least, it doesn't cost much in relation to the cost of sending a kid here. You any idea how much that is?'

'Yeah,' said Bobby, but he was wrong. The figure Gregos Georgiou quoted was three thousand dollars higher than Bobby remembered. Georgiou would know, because security guards did. They were like post boys. The only people in any corporation who actually knew what was going on were the CEO and the guy in the post room.

'Hang on,' said Bobby. 'I want to talk to her.'

Kris handed him one of her leaflets with a scowl.

'How about smiling,' suggested Bobby. 'You might get more business.'

The first thing he'd said to his daughter in three weeks and it was an instruction. Bobby winced. Of course, Kris didn't know he was her father but she knew the tone.

She scowled harder.

'You want me to hand some out?'

'I want you to . . .' Kris never did say what she wanted him to do, because in the second before she told Bobby to fuck off she realised the man was serious. 'Here,' she said, thrusting a pile at him. 'You take that side. Don't be surprised when they ignore you.'

'It's a school project,' Bobby told the next woman to climb from an SUV. 'A combination of role play and creative investment.'

'Really?' said the woman, turning the leaflet over and skimming the conclusion. She shrugged. 'Whatever . . .'

On the way back to her BMW, she said something to another mother who laughed. When she got to the gate she took the leaflet Kris offered, folded it in two and stuffed it into her bag. The man following after did the same, taking a leaflet from Kris's hands almost before she was ready.

'Nice work,' the man said. To judge from his chinos, jacket and wire-framed glasses he was probably talking about the typography. Over the course of the next five minutes Kris and Bobby handed out all of her leaflets and then it was time for Kris to go in. She'd been planning to refuse until her leaflets were gone, but they were, so she was stuck . . .

'How did that happen?'

Bobby told her.

'*You shit.*' The words were practically hissed at him, and she did that thing with her face, where she closed down to a scowl and hard cold eyes. He'd seen it in her mother and there were days when he'd got up, looked in some bathroom mirror and seen it in himself.

'Think about it,' said Bobby. 'Did you want those idiots to take one or not? If this is about you, then whether they do or not doesn't matter. If it's about . . .' He skimmed a leaflet. 'Seal culling in Canada, using rabbits in cosmetic testing, and Alecrce . . .' He stopped.

'Trees,' said Kris, with a sigh. 'In Chile. They're endangered.'

'Well,' said Bobby. 'If it's about that. Then you've just got rid of all your leaflets, which is little short of a miracle. Who knows, one in ten might actually bother to read the thing.'

Kris was on the edge of relenting. Not sure if she was still angry, not sure if she was being had. Pretty much standard for someone of her age.

'I should go in,' she said, and Bobby only just restrained himself from telling her that *yes, she should.*

Have a good day, he wanted to add. *See you later. Work hard* . . . All the things he'd given up saying around the time they gave up talking to each other. It wasn't Kris's fault she had her mother's face.

'I'm Robert Van Berg,' he said. 'I used to know your father.'

Kris shook.

Sadness. Anger. A lot of emotions to which she had not yet put names.

'Here,' Bobby told the security guard, 'you might learn something.' He stuffed the last of his leaflets into the man's pocket and turned to go, then thought better of it. 'You got time for a coffee . . . ?'

'So, you're a private detective?' The man on the other side of a café table looked interested. 'How does that pay . . . ?' Glancing at Bobby's rose gold Longines Evidenza, the man shook his head. 'Silly question. You need a local licence to operate here?'

'Supposedly,' said Bobby. The state of California had reciprocal PI arrangements with Texas and Arizona, but not with New York or anywhere useful. 'That is, if I was doing this openly . . . Do you remember a shooting at Tamsin Steps? A burglar . . .'

'Sure,' said Georgiou. 'The kid goes to that school.' He stopped to think about this, putting things together. 'Okay, now I get it. You're investigating the Persikovs . . .'

'The man's family are suing.'

'Dr Persikov?'

'No,' said Bobby, putting down his mug. 'The guy who died . . .' Gregos Georgiou looked suitably outraged. 'I'm working for Dr Persikov's insurance company,' Bobby added. 'That's why I need to talk to the girl.'

'The old man's granddaughter . . . ? I don't get it,' said Georgiou. 'Why not just ask the old man?'

'Because he doesn't know I'm here. The insurance company want to know how Natalie Persikov will stand up in court if that's what it comes to . . .'

'She's just a kid.'

'Just a kid at the centre of a fifty-million-dollar lawsuit,' said Bobby. He held up his cup to signal that they both needed more coffee and picked at the edge of his cookie. The café was in North Beach proper. A place of Italian delis and restaurants full of old men still eating breakfast at eleven in the morning. Cafés where the coffee came in two sizes, large, which came in a glass pot, and small, which was very small indeed and hissed its way out of an old Faema coffee machine.

'That's confidential, obviously.'

'Sure, I understand. You also used to be a cop, right . . . ?' The security guard saw Bobby's face and put up his hands, half joking and

161

half serious. 'Hey,' he said, 'no big deal. Shit happens . . . And it arrives wearing a uniform. You want a lift somewhere?'

That was Georgiou's way of saying he needed to get home.

'End of a shift, right?' said Bobby.

'Eight hours of rounds and then the school . . . You want that lift?'

Bobby didn't, but he wanted the man's number and wasn't yet sure Georgiou was ready to hand it over. So he took the lift anyway. Georgiou's car was a Ford, same model as the last issue for the SFPD, only instead of black and white with *emergency 911* in white out of black along the trunk, it was white and blue, with *SecureGuard* and a number. His uniform was also a close approximation. Blue jacket and trousers, peaked cap and heavy belt. The handcuffs were in the right place and the wireless hanging from its holster looked like heavy-duty issue. Even the shield on his chest was enamel.

When did it happen, Bobby wondered. When had the world become a culture of copies?

CHAPTER 28
Monday 1 March

The tall man wearing a dark suit walked carefully, as if his shoes were still new. Actually, he was probably little more than six foot but the crowd on Stockton Street were mostly Chinese and the assassin was shorter than almost everyone around him.

This was not a good height. The ideal assassin was average in every way, from weight to hair colour, skin tone and voice. Ivan Ivanovich could pass without comment on the streets of Irkutsk, where Soviet exiles had once made up a third of the population. But here in San Francisco, the small man with wide shoulders and sandy hair stood out, mainly because Ivanovich looked so impressed by everything on sale in the shops.

Ivanovich was not really an assassin, at least not yet. And his name was not really Ivan Ivanovich, but the man was fed up having to spell out his real name to foreigners and fake passports were surprisingly cheap in the US, not to mention really rather good. For a country obsessed with security they could be astonishingly bad at it.

Tall, good suit, slight limp as if one foot was blistered. What else could he tell about Robert Van Berg merely by looking? No ring, so he was probably unmarried. Expensive watch, at which he kept glancing. So either Mr Van Berg was late for a meeting or time was running out on him.

The watch was gold, had a pearl face and was undoubtedly real. Ivan knew about watches because they were used as currency in his business. It was surprisingly easy to walk through customs with $50,000 on one's wrist, when the same amount in used notes set alarm bells ringing.

He'd spent much of his time crossing borders. In the beginning he'd been carrying drugs. A mule, as disposable as the plastic suitcases in which he carted his merchandise. He'd progressed since then, through laser sights and even yellow cake to bank details and encrypted data, carried in battered laptops where the guts of each machine far exceeded the value of its tatty casing.

Each step was a promotion, a sign of the *oblast*'s faith in his efficiency, although the change of direction had been Ivan's own choice. Ivanovich was always amazed by how little the West knew about the *Komitet*. There had been two choices back in 1990, but only one of these paid. So most of those who'd trained to protect the USSR realigned their loyalties. They still worked for the same people, only now those people were buying and selling Siberia and stripping away from Russia's infrastructure things the country hadn't even realised were assets.

Whole cities emptied as the young moved out and the old were left with no electricity or transport, and what was the point of being allowed to buy a house if the city itself was dying? In Northern Siberia a whole town could be bought for the price of a good German car. Ivanovich took work where he could find it.

That work had brought him here.

The man Ivanovich was following stopped to talk to a young man who sold name translations to tourists on Grant Avenue. So, Robert Van Berg spoke Chinese, Ivanovich wondered if his boss knew that. The conversation was brief, the Chinese boy shaking his head and smiling.

And then Robert Van Berg moved off again, dodging around a fat German couple who'd stopped to look at some examples of the boy's work. Ivanovich liked Chinatown, probably because it reminded him of home. Almost everything not nailed down looked for sale, if only one could find the right person to sell it to you.

In Irkutsk ten paces behind a target would be far too close but Chinatown was so thick with tourists and locals, both doing their irritated best to avoid each other, that he might as well have been invisible.

'You sure you're up to this?'

Ivanovich's boss had been standing beneath a tree when she asked this. Ivanovich wasn't good on American trees but it had sickle-like leaves and bark that peeled back like burnt skin.

'I'm sure.'

'Okay then, if you really are . . .' The boss had nodded, mostly to herself, and reached inside her jacket. A Browning HiPower, new from the look of it. Ivanovich dropped out the clip and counted the bullets, then pulled the slide to find a slug already chambered and looked up at his boss's smiling face.

'Very wise.'

Ivanovich tried to return the smile. With the boss, it was hard to know what she was thinking and his dropping out that clip had been instinctive. Everybody knew of a case of someone in the *Organizatsiya* being given a gun and told to kill. Only the gun was loaded with a couple of bullets at most and the killer went down under a hail of fire from the opposition. One of the nastiest cases had been in St Petersburg, where the boy was given one real bullet and seven blanks. He died still thinking he could fight his way out of there.

'One to the heart, another to the back of the neck?'

As if he had to ask.

Those trained under the *Komitet* kept to the old rules, and those who came after tried to live up to the past, although things were changing again. Things had been changing ever since the colonel came to power. Just before that happened, the colonel had been asked about his aims and the man had smiled, that quiet smile few in the West knew how to read.

According to him, a group of operatives dispatched to work undercover in the Russian government was about to complete its first mission.

All the Western journalists had laughed and the colonel had laughed also, then gone ahead and appointed ex-KGB officers to many positions of power. The *Komitet* was reborn from its ashes. Only then did those who thought about such things realise that half its original members had left to become criminal.

No wonder the boss looked unhappy.

Ivan Ivanovich was in San Francisco to repay someone else's debt. That was how the *Organizatsiya* worked. Everything was currency and the oligarchs were under attack from the little man in the Kremlin with his love of judo, neat endings and paperwork. Quite how this related to the suit cutting down an alley in front of him Ivanovich wasn't sure. Maybe it didn't relate, that was possible.

A few seconds later, Ivanovich stopped. There were two reasons why he was suddenly unhappy, the most obvious of which was that he'd been here before, twenty-two days earlier. On a Sunday night when he'd gone some way towards earning the boss's respect.

The other reason was that the alley was empty. That is, it was heaped with builder's sand, wheelbarrows and piles of breeze blocks, a metal fire escape was folded on the far wall, above head height, and washing on a cross wire flapped in a sullen breeze, but the man was gone.

To Ivanovich's right was a smaller alley, leading nowhere. A handful of faded signs spoke of shops that had long closed, although the only sign in English was printed onto glass and was obviously new. It also featured French, German and Japanese.

Mystic Sauna – all types available.

Ivan Ivanovich grunted. Ringing a bell as the sign instructed, he pulled open the door and found himself facing an empty lift. *Girls* announced a note taped next to the number five, so this was the button Ivanovich pushed. Stepping into the lift, Ivanovich dropped to his knees and waited, while the cage rose through empty floors with Zen-like slowness. He felt less exposed that way and anyone peering through the windows in the outer doors would be less likely to see him. The cage itself had mesh on all four sides and was held together only by its iron frame, which was the colour of old lead and greased with years of neglect.

'Hello, sir.' A thin face and a wide smile. Tourist-friendly red cheongsam with black trousers. 'Delighted you are visiting us.' Her eyes were as empty as the welcome.

Ivanovich grunted, got off his knees.

'If you would come this way . . .' She indicated an open door with a single table beyond. Someone had piled magazines onto the table so the room looked like a doctor's waiting room.

'Is my friend already here?' Ivanovich's words came out louder than he'd intended and the woman's posture changed. She thought he was drunk, Ivanovich decided.

'We're all your friends here.'

'No,' said Ivanovich. 'I was meeting a friend from New York. He's wearing a suit and carrying a paper. I saw him come this way.'

The woman juggled her problems.

Ivanovich was a client, this was good. What was less good was his obvious nervousness and the fact he believed a friend was already here. 'No one here but you,' she said. 'Your friend will come soon.'

Things went downhill from there.

In the end the madame decided it might be best to let the stranger see for himself, since this was all he asked and because he kept putting one hand in his pocket. In her experience, when men did this it was because that was where they kept their courage, in the form of some weapon or other.

'Come with me,' she said, putting command into her voice.

There were five tiny stalls, a bathroom and the reception room he'd already seen. A girl sat on a stool in each of the cubicles. And though each looked up when the door opened, something about the madame's face kept their own expressions blank and carefully under control. All but one wore variations on knickers and bra. The one who didn't wore a thong and was shaving her bikini line when Ivanovich entered the stall.

'See,' said the madame.

As flies to wanton boys, the gods are just and kill us for their . . . No, that was wrong. His daughter had acted in *Lear* one term (Runyon Drive was that kind of school), but it was still wrong. The phrase he needed was, *dog to its vomit*. Although whether he was the dog or vomit only the next few minutes would tell.

From the small window of his basement kitchen, Robert Van Berg watched the man leave Mystic Sauna, turn a full circle and fix his attention on a dumpster out of sight against the alley wall. It had to be the dumpster that interested him, because there was nothing else but a couple of balconies and one end of a washing line.

Being able to look up at Mystic Sauna had appalled Flic so much, when she first inspected Bobby's kitchen, that she'd kept returning to look. Which, as Bobby pointed out, slightly undermined her outrage.

Robert Vanberg . . . Bobby Zha . . . Bobby Van Berg? He was going to have to sort that out in his head, Bobby decided, but first . . .

'You looking for me?'

The thickset man swung round so fast he almost tripped.

Amateur, thought Bobby. *Quietly done or not, he should have heard me shut the basement door.* Maybe it *was* just a mugging after all.

Although there had to be a thousand better targets out there, slopping around in jeans and shirts, pockets full of cash and heads full of preconceptions. The man was staring at Bobby, checking his face. Someone had shown this man a photograph and that worried Bobby, because he couldn't remember one being taken. Which meant someone had trailed him and they'd been good.

'Yes,' said Bobby. 'You've got the right man.'

At the window of Mystic Sauna, a thin woman in a red cheongsam looked down into the alley, considered the two men and casually yanked down a blind. Whatever happened next she'd remember nothing, Bobby could bet his life on that and probably just had.

'Come on,' Bobby said, 'let's get this over with.'

'I'm sorry?' The man sounded puzzled. His accent was thick, but his words perfectly clear. Pushing back heavy blond hair, he stared around him. 'I'm lost,' he said, 'perhaps you can help?'

Bobby knew that voice.

'What difference does it make?'

'I'm not ready.'

'Too bad.'

Remembering the words, Bobby could almost feel fingers dig into the flesh of his back, searching for a bullet. In total, he'd faced five people who wanted him dead, not including this man, the one who finally succeeded. One had burned with hatred, another regarded him with icy contempt. The rest had been drunk or drugged, suicidal and fuzzy-headed with anger. He'd killed the first two and got away with overpowering the other three.

Civilians misunderstood. They thought cops went in, solved crimes and moved on. It didn't work like that. Cops went in, got fucked over by the shit they were investigating and dragged it behind them like a length of slime. When the slime finally got too sticky to let them walk down the street, the brass handed out desk jobs or put you on something easy and insubstantial, like handling the homeless.

And standing in front of this man, the thing that really made Bobby angry was not being shot, but how he'd felt about dying. He'd gone out in an agony of failed breaths, drowning in his own blood from a sucking chest wound – *and he hadn't even minded.*

The fight back, the panic had been at a primal level, his body struggling to continue its existence. That wasn't him, Bobby had been the small boy in the corner watching the fox.

'I've got some questions,' said Bobby, extracting his Agency badge and flipping it, blue enamel and a white star within a circle. 'You can start by telling me who sent you . . .'

But the man had no intention of answering. That flicker, the sideways look, a sudden stiffening of the shoulders when he should have been composing himself and considering what to say, all of them betrayed him. When Ivan Ivanovich reached for his holster, Bobby's good intentions drifted like smoke.

It was almost too easy.

Pivoting to slam a forearm into the man's throat, Bobby unwound equally fast, crashing an elbow into the side of Ivan Ivanovich's head, then kicked out one of the man's knees as he fell. Although unnecessary, the elbow strike was a kindness. It meant Ivan Ivanovich was already unconscious when Bobby stamped on his neck.

Removing the gun from the man's holster, Bobby sighed. A HiPower, full clip and one in the chamber. The gun that had killed the burglar at the house on Tamsin Steps. Either someone was being clever, or they were very careless indeed. Alternatively, they'd actually expected this man to succeed.

And why not?

Since when was some incomer from New York going to register a tail in the crowded chaos of San Francisco's Chinatown? Dragging the man deeper into the blind alley, Bobby hefted him into the dumpster, then scuffed the ground with a square of cardboard to remove his own footprints.

He kept the gun.

CHAPTER 29

Tuesday 2 March

'Someone was looking for you.'

The girl on the early evening shift at the SFI Best Western sounded embarrassed. She was pretty in an overblown way, her hair teased into a complicated mess and enough of her breasts were on show to catch Bobby's eye.

'Man or woman?' Bobby asked.

'A man,' Disirée said, shuffled pages of her magazine, then stopped on the edge of saying something else.

'Go on,' said Bobby.

'Probably police.'

'In uniform?'

Disirée shook her head. 'No,' she said. 'Just the way he talked. You know, how you sometimes get that feeling?'

Looking at the black girl with her watchful eyes and copy of a Toni Morrison novel half tucked under her magazine on the counter, Bobby nodded. He reckoned she'd know because Disirée had turned knowing into an art form.

Every time he dropped back to the airport hotel, she checked how he was doing, whether everything was okay. It was how she coped with the boredom of her job. Making mental notes, writing the script to other people's lives and smiling sweetly when she asked, *everything okay with your bill?* (Which translated as, *those are your porn films, aren't they . . . ?*)

'The man leave a message?'

'No,' said Disirée. 'Just wanted to know when you were likely to be back.'

Bobby raised his eyebrows and Disirée smiled. 'I said you'd only just gone out.'

'Thanks,' said Bobby. Without realising it, the girl had just provided him with an alibi.

'That's okay,' she said.

Peeling a $100 note from his wallet, Bobby slid it between the pages of her upturned magazine. He was watched by Disirée as he did so, although it was hard to tell from the twisted smile on her face whether she was offended or amused.

'Can you describe him?'

'Old,' said Disirée, who looked barely older than Kris. 'Chinese looking . . .'

Bobby held up his hand to stop her. 'About so tall,' he said, indicating someone of roughly his height. 'And thin, with a small beard . . .'

The girl on the other side of the counter began nodding before he got to the bit about the beard.

'You're right,' said Bobby. 'He's an SFPD lieutenant.'

'Someone you know?'

Bobby smiled and scanned the lobby of the airport hotel. Sheet glass and cheap marble, wooden chairs bought in bulk and three mid-Westerners stood guard over their suitcases. No one who looked like a tail.

'Yeah,' said Bobby. 'You could say that.'

Bobby rang the lieutenant's number from memory, using the house phone in the lobby. Disirée had gone back to her paperback, although Bobby guessed she was keeping half an ear on his conversation.

'You were looking for me?'

'How the . . .'

Listening to Lieutenant Que fight down his urge to ask: 1) how Bobby knew who he was and, 2) where he got the lieutenant's home number, Bobby actually felt sorry for the old man, which had to be a first. He'd felt exasperated often enough and sometimes come close to hating this living memory of his childhood, but pity was something else.

'I recognised you from the description,' said Bobby. 'We met in Filipacchi's after the funeral, remember?' He couldn't bring himself to say which funeral.

'And the number?'

'I got that from your office.'

'Did you?' Lieutenant Que's voice went soft. 'I don't suppose you got the name of the officer who gave it?'

'No,' said Bobby. 'I don't think I did.'

'Surprise me.'

Now the lieutenant would waste most of tomorrow trying to discover who'd been stupid enough to give out his home number. And one would have to be pretty stupid to give out Lieutenant Que's home number, particularly to some stranger who called the station house.

'I think we should meet,' said Bobby.

'Why?'

'Because I'm not sure we can have this conversation on the phone.'

'*I don't want a conversation,*' said Lieutenant Que. 'This doesn't merit a conversation.'

Anger, thought Bobby, barely held in check. 'What do you think I've done?' he asked. It seemed an obvious question.

'*What do I . . . ?*'

It was like listening to someone slam on the brakes and Lieutenant Que didn't do that, not where work was concerned. (His personal life was another matter. Most of the station had no idea the man was married and had been for thirty-five years.)

'You went by Katherine Zha's school this morning.'

'Sure,' said Bobby. 'I helped Kit hand out leaflets about evil Canadians who club baby seals and rotten capitalists cutting up puppies . . . You'd be surprised how many leaflets you can shift if you claim it's a school project.'

Utter silence rewarded Bobby, although it took him longer than it should to realise why. He'd called the girl Kit. No one called her Kit but her parents and the kid had trouble enough taking it then.

'Whatever you're investigating,' said the lieutenant, 'it has nothing to do with *Katherine* Zha.'

'She goes to the same school as Natalie Persikov. And who said I was investigating anything?'

That earned Bobby another silence.

'Okay,' said the lieutenant, 'you're right. We should meet. I'll come out to your hotel.'

'No,' said Bobby. 'It can wait until tomorrow. I'm due to have supper with a friend.'

The bike that delivered Flic to the Chinatown gates was a Harley V-Rod, pearl paint and two-tone fenders in shades of designer grey. The tiny screen wrapped around the chrome headlight was smoked in matching shades, running dark to light, like expensive sunglasses.

Fat chrome exhausts hung low on one side. Since much of San Francisco reflected a city plan arbitrarily imposed on inconvenient valleys and hills, the ground clearance this allowed was undoubtedly a victory of style over common sense.

The rider wore a full-face helmet with mirrored visor. As he drove off he turned to stare at Bobby. It was a hard stare. The kind he was meant to notice . . .

'Friend of yours?'

Flic looked round, saw Bobby and smiled. 'Sergeant Sanchez,' she said, 'that's his promotion present.'

'To himself?'

'From his girlfriend's parents . . .' Catching Bobby's expression, Flic nodded. 'Yeah, I know,' she said. 'Some present.'

A bribe or a perverse warning, Bobby wondered. Keep your nose clean, stay away from the widow, don't be nasty to our girl . . . 'Pretty impressive,' he agreed, but he was remembering the bruises on Bea's wrists. 'You mind going via the apartment?' Bobby asked.

Maybe there was something strange in his voice. Whatever, Flic glanced back. 'Are you all right?' she said.

'I'm not sure. There's just something I need to check.'

The alley behind the warehouse was taped off with police tape and the madame from Mystic Sauna was sitting on her doorstep, cutting open live scallops with a tiny knife and tossing shells onto the dirt. She barely glanced up to watch them go past.

'Shit,' said Flic. 'You probably didn't hear.'

'Hear what?'

'There was a fatal mugging right here. It got called in this morning by a Canadian tourist . . .'

'A what?'

'Canadian,' said Flic. 'It took a while to get the story. Apparently the woman was desperate for a piss and too nervous to go into one of the cafés. So she went behind the dumpster and then decided to be neat and get rid of her tissue. Bad choice . . . Apparently she's still being sedated.'

'What makes you think it was a mugging?'

'No wallet and no watch. The guy's pockets had been turned inside out. Someone had stolen his shoes. That sounds like a mugging to me.' Flic said this with all the confidence of someone who'd done twenty-eight weeks at the Academy and four months on the street.

She thought he'd brought her back to fuck, Bobby could feel her disquiet. The sense she'd somehow overestimated him. *We're not there yet*, her expression said. Proprieties had to be upheld and rituals observed. It wasn't the eating out that mattered to her so much as the time spent talking. Investment in who they might become.

He never used to know this stuff.

'You sure you're okay?' Flic said.

'Headache,' said Bobby, disappearing into his bathroom. Splashing his face in cold water, Bobby rinsed out his mouth and stared in the mirror. He still had the same slightly spiky black hair, the deep-set eyes, the high cheekbones. It remained the face of a stranger.

'Here, drink this,' Flic said, when he came out. She was holding a cup.

'Where did you get that?'

'On Stockton Street. Along with a kettle . . .'

Reaching for the cup, Bobby used its contents to wash down three di-hydrocodeine, wincing as green tea burnt his throat.

'Those things are addictive,' Flic said.

'Yeah,' said Bobby, 'I know.' There'd been days before the fox when Bobby's first action on waking was to wash down a handful of ibuprofen with his coffee. Now he was letting himself go almost blind with pain before he even reached for prescription pain-killers, it was beyond weird . . .

After a while, Bobby became aware that the sky outside had grown dark between one thought and another. Lights had come on behind the sign for Mystic Sauna and postRock could be heard from a cellar bar at his end of the alley. Three naked girls were sharing a spliff across the alley, five floors up and two sheets of glass away.

'How long?' said Bobby.

Flic knew instantly what he was asking. 'About an hour,' she said. 'Maybe a little more.'

'I'm sorry.'

'Don't be.' Standing up from the kitchen's only chair, Flic walked over to the window and wrapped her arms around him. 'Do you want to talk about it?'

'About what?'

'My dad was a cop,' she said. 'After he died, my mother would close down like that for hours. Completely blind to the world . . .' Her eyes when Bobby met them were soft with sorrow. 'Who was it?' said Flic. 'Who did you lose?'

She would have gone to bed with him then, for all the wrong reasons. So Bobby stepped away from her and stretched, feeling his spine catch and the muscles in his shoulders creak.

'There was a guy I knew . . .'

'What happened?'

Buttoning his jacket, Bobby shrugged. 'That's what I'm about to find out. I'll see you at Aqua in an hour.'

He was gone before Flic had time to protest.

Mystic Sauna was much as Bobby imagined. An old Otis, greasy with age. A reception room that looked as if it came from central casting. A handful of cubicles hacked out of factory space. Cheap sauna, cheap posters, a shower room for the girls. Customers were supposed to ring the bell but Bobby wasn't a customer. The woman in the red cheongsam was waiting for him at the top, wearing a smile so tight it was probably strangling her.

Flipping his shield, Bobby pushed past and began opening random doors. 'Police,' he told the first three men he met. They got up, dressed and left without complaint.

'Any other customers?'

When the madame looked blank, Bobby asked again, in Cantonese. It was only later he worked out what was odd about her eyes. Not their darkness, nor their flatness, but the fact she never once blinked, although her eyebrows rose at his sudden and unexpected fluency.

'Well?' Bobby demanded.

She shook her head.

'Good,' said Bobby. 'Because I'm here to talk to you about a crime.'

'We saw nothing,' she said. 'I was out buying provisions. My girls were working. No one saw anything. You can ask them . . .'

Yes, thought Bobby, *I bet I can*. He glanced along the landing, watching faces disappear behind cubicle doors. 'You stripped the

175

body,' he said, and before the madame could answer, he added, 'You were seen.'

Now was when things could fall apart.

Not you, he almost corrected, *your girls*. Only Bobby realised in time that this was unlikely. However scared of her they might be, the madame still wouldn't trust her staff not to keep something valuable.

'You were seen,' Bobby repeated.

When the madame returned it was with a wad of notes, mostly twenties; which told Bobby all he needed to know about the sauna's clientele. 'Here,' she said, trying to thrust the cash into his hands.

'I don't want your money,' said Bobby. 'I'm here to get answers about a crime.'

There are a dozen clues when someone is guilty, although older SFPD officers put the number at fifteen. An inability to keep still, a reluctance to meet another person's eyes and a change in the tone of voice when lying are just three of the most common. The madame exhibited no such signs. Bobby, on the other hand, was obviously as guilty as hell.

'I saw nothing,' insisted the madame, voice flat.

That was when Bobby realised his problem. She'd seen him. Small wonder the woman was admitting nothing. 'You stripped the body,' he insisted, 'took the watch, wallet and shoes.'

'There was no watch,' the woman said. 'No watch and no wallet.'

Okay, that bit Bobby believed.

'So why take his shoes?'

For a moment it looked as if the woman might actually answer, instead she shrugged. 'I know nothing about any shoes.'

She was small, bird-like, with wide cheekbones and a face that had aged better than her hands, which had crêped like the skin around her neck. Younger than Lieutenant Que by a generation, Bobby guessed, although the lieutenant undoubtedly knew her. The lieutenant knew most people in Chinatown.

'I don't care about the shoes,' said Bobby. 'If there was a wallet, then fine, keep it . . . I'm here to talk to you about another crime, something that happened out there three weeks ago.'

So slight was her smile that Bobby almost missed her approval of the way he'd played his moves. Pulling out his wallet, Bobby gave the woman $500, then took out the same again, thumbing the five notes into a fan.

'Last month,' he said, 'a police officer got shot in the warehouse down there. I want to know what you saw, either before or afterwards.'

'Nothing,' said the woman, her eyes on the notes in Bobby's hands. She sounded so regretful that Bobby believed her.

'A pity,' he said. 'I was hoping to find out what really happened.'

'Ahh . . .' The madame considered the money on offer, nodded to herself and shut the door between reception and the cubicles. 'This I know,' she said. 'It was about drugs. One of my girls heard two people arguing.'

Drugs? thought Bobby, although what he said was, 'People?'

'Men . . . *laowai.*'

Foreigners, people like him.

'This policeman and someone else. They were speaking Spanish . . .'

Bobby was about to shake his head when the woman added, 'One of them was fat.'

'She saw them?'

'Only the fat one. He wanted paying for his drugs.'

'Which drugs?' said Bobby.

'The crystal meth they found next to the dead officer . . .'

It took another $500 for the madame to agree to let him question the girl, and a further $20 to persuade the girl to put her clothes on first.

CHAPTER 30

Tuesday 2 March

Flic and Bobby ate at Aqua on California Street, because this way they could be seen and eating somewhere so obviously expensive made statements about how seriously Bobby took dining out with Flic.

That was what he told Flic anyway. Her response was that Lieutenant Que would merely decide CIA agents were overpaid or had more money than sense. Actually, Bobby's real reason was more complicated. Aqua was where Pete Sanchez sometimes took Bea for dinner and Bobby knew the way Sanchez's mind worked . . . The fact Bobby had taken Flic there would offend the man.

'Come on,' said Bobby. 'How bad can it be?'

In the event Flic needn't have worried. Aqua might be a salmon-pink temple to high cuisine and fresh seafood, but their waiter was completely unfazed by Flic's request for steamed vegetables and nothing cooked in stock.

Bobby ate scallops with haricots verts, hazelnuts and mustard sauce, followed by halibut with morel mushrooms. At least that's what it said on the menu, once all the adjectives had been filleted. Flic ate peppers, carrots and asparagus, arranged on a plate with such precision the dispatcher obviously had a fine-arts degree.

The restaurant was elegant, Flic was beautiful and Bobby had drunk more Sauvignon Blanc than was good for him. He had money, expensive clothes and the ability to indulge himself, by taking over the basement behind Stockton Street for a start. In an hour or two, he'd roll into bed with Flic, proprietaries observed. It was a life, his . . . It was even a life Bobby liked, but was it what he was in San Francisco to do? Assuming, of course, he was back here to do something.

That assumption could be divided into two parts.

Carefully cutting a scallop down the middle, Bobby wiped one half across his plate and scooped up the last of the mustard sauce. For his own part, he wanted to find out who'd ordered him killed and how drugs came to be involved. This could be wrapped around in a tattered flag and called his need for the truth. Only the real truth was that Bobby wanted to find out who gave the order and put a bullet through their brains. There was, however, a second part to all this.

What if he was there for another reason?

'Are you religious?'

'Am I what . . . ?' Flic looked up from her chilled glass of Grgich Hills. 'I was christened,' she said. 'My mother has a photo of me taking first communion. I'll probably get married in a church . . .' Flic hesitated, aware that might be revealing too much. 'I'd say not,' she said finally, 'but I'd probably be lying. How about you?'

'I don't know,' said Bobby. 'Can you have ghosts without God?'

'You believe in ghosts?' Flic's tone was surprised. 'That's odd,' she said. 'You don't strike me as the type.'

'I'm not,' said Bobby, 'but I saw one once.'

Putting down her wine, Flic thought better of it and reached for the bottle in a silver bucket beside their table. A waiter materialised before her fingers could even touch glass.

'Thank you,' said Flic, only Bobby saw the roll of her eyes.

'About the ghost . . .' she prompted, when the man had gone. 'Whose was it? It's okay,' she added, seeing Bobby hesitate. 'You can tell me.'

'I saw a fox,' said Bobby. 'Just standing there on the edge of the darkness watching me . . .' He'd drunk too much and this was probably a conversation to be avoided, but he had to tell someone. 'It was huge.'

'A fox?' Flic sounded thoughtful.

Bobby nodded.

'What makes you think it was a ghost?'

Emptying his own glass, Bobby leant over and took hers. 'It had nine tails,' he said, 'and it spoke to me.'

That was when Flic surprised him. Instead of laughing or looking for the door, she asked, 'Why does that make it a ghost?'

So Bobby found himself explaining about celestial foxes, ghosts, spirit worlds and their powers . . . *'At the age of fifty a fox can change to a woman. At a hundred to a beautiful girl or daemon lover. At a thousand it can talk to heaven and becomes celestial . . . a nine-tailed fox.'*

'Someone taught you that,' said Flic.

'Yeah.' Bobby nodded. 'My grandfather.'

'And he was interested in Chinese culture?'

He saw himself then through her eyes. It wasn't just the Armani suit she saw or his elegantly cut if slightly messy hair. When Flic looked at him she saw, without even noticing, the shape of his eyes and the bleached parchment of his skin.

'My grandfather was Chinese.'

'Really?' said Flic.

Bobby sighed.

She had full breasts that over-spilled his hands and nipples darker than the darkest honey. Her skin was soft and unblemished and taut with youth and life unlived. And when he dragged his mouth down the soft curve of her belly and buried his face between her thighs, she twisted her fingers into his hair and yanked him against her.

The memory traces were fainter now, if they were there at all, if they'd ever been there. The sense of other mouths, other beds, couplings almost forgotten or guiltily remembered. Salt and tears, sweat, the animal smell of unwashed hair. Some things were universal.

'Shit,' she said, when it was over and Bobby had crawled the length of her body to reach her mouth. 'I'm sorry.'

He was impressed that she didn't mind her own taste.

'About what?'

Handing him a tiny mirror, Flic angled her bedside lamp so Bobby could take a look. His mouth was swollen and his bottom lip had split slightly. When he thought about it, the underside of his tongue was raw where it had scraped his lower teeth.

'Insatiable,' said Bobby, and Flic looked embarrassed. 'That was a compliment,' he said.

They were in her bedroom in a Victorian house on Valencia Street. One of those narrow-fronted buildings where everything from the walls to the decoration over the windows had been made from wood and then painted to look like stone. The front door was up a series of steps and set back into shadow. While they'd stood there, Flic still fumbling in her bag for a key and the taxi disappearing behind them, Bobby had checked that his being there really was okay.

'It's fine,' insisted Flic. 'My mother's staying with her sister.' She led him up the stairs and into her room, leaving Bobby there while she went back to lock the door. 'My brother's downstairs,' she said. 'Asleep on the settee . . . So we'll have to be quiet.'

'If you're sure.'

'Look,' said Flic, 'don't worry. We'll be gone long before Felipe wakes.' She was almost right.

As dawn lit the streets outside, Flic rolled out of bed and padded naked across cheap carpet, opening her door a fraction. The only other person awake was sprawled naked on the bed behind her, watching her hips swing and buttocks move.

A few minutes later Flic was back. 'I left the lavatory unflushed,' she said. 'Hope that's okay.'

He washed quickly, splashing water over his face, rinsing out his mouth and then guiltily refilled the basin to wash his prick and balls, soaping them so quickly he splashed water on the tiles and had to mop up with loo paper. Dropping the sodden paper onto the sheet Flic had left discreetly floating on top of the pan, Bobby pissed away a night's worth of waiting to be allowed to use her bathroom and flushed.

It was on his way out that he walked straight into a thirteen-year-old Hispanic boy wearing a black eye and a Harley-Davidson T-shirt, which was one item of clothing more than Bobby.

'Shit,' said the boy, then grinned through his own broken lips. 'Double shit . . .' Looking at Bobby, he shook his head. 'I wouldn't have believed it.' Quite what Felipe wouldn't believe was left unsaid because the boy stepped around the visitor and locked himself in the bathroom. Bobby was almost at Flic's door when the loo flushed again and Felipe banged his way out the bathroom rather louder than was necessary. It sounded as if he was whistling.

'Tell me you didn't,' Flic said.

Bobby tried to look guilty.

'Shit,' said Flic, sounding very like her brother. 'Life's not going to be worth living.'

'He's going to tell your mother?'

'Are you joking? He's going to take me for everything I've got and then some . . .' Pulling on her SFPD jacket, Flic left Bobby to his shirt and trousers and wandered away to repair as much damage as she could. Whatever Flic said, her brother did not reappear.

'Don't you dare look back,' said Flic, as Bobby and she turned the

181

corner at the bottom of the steps and found themselves on Mission Street, but it was too late. Bobby already had and was now wondering whether or not he should wave to the boy grinning at him from a downstairs window.

'Weird,' said Bobby. 'I'd have thought he'd be angry and protective. I would have been if I was that age and you were my sister.'

'You don't get it,' Flic said. 'I *never* do stuff like this. And I spend my life telling Felipe not to do it either.' She shook her head and lengthened her stride, as if leaving the Mission district behind her might make the problem go away.

'How about we get some coffee?'

'Not sure I have time,' said Flic, as she reached into her pocket and checked her phone for messages. 'I mean it,' she added, catching his expression. 'I'm on early shift.'

'Good,' said Bobby, 'I'll come with you.'

CHAPTER 31

Wednesday 3 March

And that was where Sergeant Sanchez found Bobby. Crouched over a computer screen as Bobby ran down lists of missing people, a pile of post-it notes building up on the desk beside him. A dozen names had been scrawled into a cheap notebook and half of them crossed out again. Lines led from Colonel Billy to Bobby Zha and Louie's friend, the vagrant who vanished three months earlier.

A second window had been opened on the screen, revealing scant details of the crash involving neurosurgeon Dr Charles Weyler, bi-coastal celebrity, fund raiser for charity, and tragic suicide, the morning after Sergeant Zha was killed.

The photographs showed a fresh-faced man in his thirties and a crumpled Lexus, burnt out and blackened to bare metal. There was no other vehicle involved. The Lexus just went off Highway 280, hit a pillar head-on and burst into flames.

A quick and dirty search on Google had pulled up the press release issued by his family. This mentioned a children's charity in Sao Paulo, name unspecified. So far Bobby had called five of them and none had even heard of the man. Wherever Dr Weyler had spent his last few months, it looked like being somewhere else.

'How did you get into our system?' demanded Sanchez.

'The usual way . . .'

'Using whose login?'

'Que's,' said Bobby. 'It's got supervisor privileges.' He said this as if that should be obvious. Despite himself, Sergeant Sanchez glanced again at the notebook, seeing his own name circled heavily. A post-it note to the left of Lieutenant Que's keyboard gave the last five dates on which Colonel Billy had been arrested. A pile of sticky yellow squares to the other side listed the CSI teks who'd worked the shooting at Tamsin Steps. A printer in the corner of the office was churning out copies of the coroner's report on the late Sergeant Zha.

One shot, probably subsonic, no powder stippling so fired from at least three feet away, alternatively the weapon was silenced. A knife cut to the lower back, clean sharp margins and no bruising, which meant the blade was sharp. Fragments of supraorbital bone, brains . . . It was impossible to say if the victim had been dead when his skull was crushed. No signs of drugs or alcohol.

This was a translation, obviously enough. A translation Bobby made without even knowing he'd made it. He just ingested the jargon and looked for meaning behind the words.

'What exactly are you investigating?' Sergeant Sanchez asked heavily.

'Tamsin Steps.'

'Yeah,' said the sergeant. 'That's what I've been told. I'm just not sure I believe you . . .' He sat in the seat across the desk, leant forward and stared intently at the man in Lieutenant Que's chair.

Bobby returned to his screen.

'You're meant to say, *why not?*' said Sergeant Sanchez. 'Then you get to lie to me a bit and I decide whether to pretend to believe you . . . Alternatively we just call CIA HQ at Langley.'

'Go ahead,' said Bobby. He pushed the desk phone across to Sanchez and reeled off a number for the Truman Building. 'Alternatively, I can dial direct if you'd rather?'

'I know you're not CIA,' the sergeant said flatly.

'So . . . ?' Bobby kept his own voice equally bored. 'Who said I was?'

'You did.'

Bobby shook his head.

'You told Officer Valdez you were with the Agency . . . I called our contacts man and he talked to someone at inter-departmental Langley. They said they'd never heard of you.'

'Of course they haven't.' Returning to the screen, Bobby keyed his way into the SFPD database and pulled up the file on his own shooting. 'Tell me about the crystal meth found next to Bobby Zha's body,' he told Sergeant Sanchez, steeling himself not to wince at the word.

'Tell you about . . . ?'

'Did Lieutenant Que send it to forensics?' Bobby glanced at the other man. 'No,' he said. 'I didn't think so. He doesn't seem to have mentioned it in his official report either. As for your report . . .'

Crouched at the stranger's shoulder, Sergeant Sanchez watched page after page of his own statement scroll up the screen, details of how he'd said goodbye to Sergeant Zha at the end of that night's shift and gone home, assuming the other officer was doing the same. How the first he knew of his partner's death was a call from Lieutenant Que much later that night.

'We heard you were there,' said Bobby. 'And kept hold of his hand while he bled to death.' Bobby nodded at the words still scrolling up the screen. 'We don't think it happened like *this* at all . . .'

'Wish to God I had been there.'

On the other side of Lieutenant Que's window, officers from the morning shift drifted past, glancing faux casually through the glass, while Flic sat quietly, and the woman opposite her stood up for the third time to peer through the glass.

'You do?'

'He was a good man,' said Sanchez. 'A good officer. No one deserves to die alone like that . . .'

'If he did,' said Bobby. He would have said more, but the office door crashed open to reveal Lieutenant Que, and all of the morning shift behind him suddenly looked busy.

'Sergeant Sanchez was just showing me . . .'

'I'm showing him nothing,' said Sanchez. 'He was in here when I arrived . . .'

Bobby shrugged. He hoped it was an elegant, who-gives-a-shit shrug. And from the sudden tightness around Lieutenant Que's eyes, it looked like his hopes might have been answered.

'Out,' said Lieutenant Que.

Sergeant Sanchez stood back to make space. The expression on his face unpleasantly close to a smirk.

'*I meant you.*'

'Me?'

Bobby and the lieutenant watched Sergeant Pio Sanchez leave the room, shutting the door very quietly behind him, and silence was never good where Sanchez was concerned. No one looked up as the sergeant walked to his desk, pulled out his chair and sat down, carefully straightening the sign that read, *Lead, follow or get out of the way.*

'Okay,' said Lieutenant Que. 'Let's start with who you really are . . .'

Bobby shook his head. 'No,' he said, 'let's not. Start with who you think I am and we'll take it from there.'

Digging into his pockets, Lieutenant Que found his cigarettes and shook one from the packet, lighting it with a thin brass lighter. In doing so he broke so many SFPD regulations that Bobby could only stare.

'I don't know,' said the lieutenant. 'You tell Officer Valdez you're with the Agency. The security guard at Katherine Zha's school thinks you're a PI from New York. Without actually saying it, you leave a desk officer at 850 Bryant thinking you're with the FBI. And I've just run your name through the NSA system and you know what I got?'

'No,' said Bobby.

'A Robert Van Berg exists all right. Well, spelt as one word. Only he's locked down in some hospital on Manhattan's lower east side, either unconscious or gibbering. The manager was unwilling to say which.'

'There has to be more than one Robert Van Berg,' said Bobby.

'Three in Manhattan alone,' said Lieutenant Que. 'Another two in New Jersey. Fifty-four in total in the New York State area, but only one of them with your date of birth, and he was hospitalised as a child in a car accident.'

'Truck accident,' said Bobby. 'It was a truck on Roosevelt Drive. Killed his parents, injured the boy and the driver of the truck walked away unhurt. The insurance company paid out a record sum in exchange for confidentiality.'

Lieutenant Que glared at Bobby. 'Are you saying that's you?'

'If it's not,' said Bobby, 'I've got real problems.' He nodded to the report of Bobby Zha's death still visible on the lieutenant's computer screen. 'What can you tell me about that?'

'Why would I tell you anything?'

'Because you're about to retire,' said Bobby, oblivious to the lieutenant's sudden stillness. 'And you don't want to end your career with me going to the *Chronicle* with stories about missing drugs and dead officers. Besides, you don't really believe that pile of shit either.' Double-clicking *print*, Bobby watched a cheap laser printer in the corner begin to spit out Sergeant Sanchez's testimony.

'Do you need me to point out the holes,' asked Bobby, 'or have you already tripped over them yourself?'

Lieutenant Que stood right behind Bobby, until Bobby realised he was meant to be getting up to give the lieutenant his seat back. Once this was established, the lieutenant suggested that Bobby give him the testimony and then Lieutenant Que sat back and smoked three Lucky Strike in a row, dragging each almost to the filter and using the first two to light the one that came after.

'Tell me why it matters,' Lieutenant Que said finally.

'*Why it . . . ?*'

'Zha was a shit,' said the lieutenant. 'And whatever he was actually doing when he got himself killed, it's pretty much guaranteed to make us look bad. Why would I want to dig it up?' He stopped, looked at Bobby. 'Fuck,' he said, 'you're from Internal Affairs.'

'No.' Bobby shook his head. 'Not that.'

'What then?'

'Tell me about Sergeant Zha,' said Bobby. 'Then maybe I'll tell you about myself. It matters,' he added quietly, when Lieutenant Que looked doubtful. 'And, believe me, I need someone I can talk to about this.'

'Okay . . .' The lieutenant sat back, considered something for a moment and then shrugged, tapping the last cigarette from his packet. 'His grandfather was one of the Tong leaders, back in the days when that mattered . . . Yeah I know.' The lieutenant caught Bobby's frown. 'There are still gangs and crime families but things have changed. We've got Columbians, Vietnamese, the Russian mafia. It's all crack and heroin now.'

'What was it before?' Bobby asked, though he knew the answer as well as the old man sat opposite. He'd seen new girls appear on the streets, their prices falling as fast as their looks faded and gravity and hard living dragged their bodies south.

'Whores,' said the lieutenant. He didn't use the word *prostitute* or *call girl*, it was as if CAYOTE had never happened. But then the lieutenant was remembering the days before trade unions for sex workers even existed, Bobby could see it in his face.

'Was it really better?'

'Oh yes,' said Lieutenant Que. 'I think it was. Old man Zha was clever. He paid off City Hall and gave money from the brothels to the temples and political parties. He never started a gang war he couldn't win or made a promise he didn't keep. You can carve out quite an empire on those two things alone.'

'You sound like you admired him.'

'He was a murderous bastard who knifed his own brother and married off his sister to a creditor twenty years older.'

'Which doesn't really answer the question.'

'Okay,' said the lieutenant, 'I admired him. He was the last member of the Zha family with any guts or sense. His son was a monster and his grandson . . .' Lieutenant Que hesitated. 'It began after Bobby's father died . . .'

'Yeah,' said Bobby, 'I know about that.'

The lieutenant shook his head. 'I very much doubt it,' he said. 'There were maybe three people who knew exactly what happened, now there's me.'

'All the same . . .' Shrugging away the rest of that sentence, Bobby leant across and took the printout from Lieutenant Que's fingers, turning it sideways so they could both read what it said. 'Let's talk about this,' he said.

CHAPTER 32

Wednesday 3 March

He'd been warned off, politely and firmly. In a way that spoke of decades of authority taken completely for granted, both by the person who wielded that authority and those around him. But it was why he'd been warned off that impressed Bobby most. The lieutenant had paid him the respect of actually rereading Sergeant Sanchez's statement before sitting back to stare at his visitor.

'Shot full of holes,' agreed Lieutenant Que, 'but it could be argued Sanchez was in shock at the death of his partner.'

'They were together for a matter of weeks. I doubt if Sanchez even liked the man.'

'All the same . . .'

Bobby glanced at the lieutenant, aware that he was seeing him through a stranger's eyes. The office was small, little more than a glass box in the corner of a bigger room. Green paint covered the wall behind the lieutenant's head, a bubble of air separating a fat patch of it from the bare brick behind. Faces and foxes hidden in a shape logic said had to be random. It was like looking at the moon as a sleepy child and seeing the things that mostly poets and madmen see.

'Why did you pair them?' he asked.

'Pragmatism,' said Lieutenant Que. 'I had Zha, and then I had one officer foisted on me by the top brass. Unfortunately, he came complete with raging ambition, close political contacts and a willingness to cut corners.' Catching Bobby's surprise, Lieutenant Que smiled sourly. 'You've probably heard that he fills out forms and gets his paperwork done on time.'

Heard from Flic, presumably.

'Whatever anyone might say about the new SFPD, that's still not

189

enough; and his manner is way too smooth. You know what I mean . . .'

Bobby did. He was just surprised the lieutenant had noticed.

'Zha was different. The man couldn't do paperwork to save his life and looked so at home on Market he might as well have lived there. Not the kind of officer anyone wants hanging around when the Chief is due. Sanchez said he wanted to spend time on the street, so I put him with Zha to avoid having to put him with anyone else.'

That made sense.

'About the drugs that were found . . .'

For a second it looked as if Lieutenant Que was about to deny that there had been any drugs, then he shrugged. 'Crystal meth,' he said, 'pretty crude. My guess is that Sergeant Zha was trying to sell the stuff.'

'Where did he get it?'

The lieutenant stabbed out his cigarette. 'Your guess is as good as mine,' he said. 'I've got a theory,' he added, punching a button on his desk. 'Although not about that.' Lieutenant Que waited for a sour-faced woman to slouch her way into his office. 'Coffee,' ordered Lieutenant Que.

The woman grunted.

'My sister,' said the lieutenant, once his secretary had gone. 'She's less than happy about the fact she's going to lose her job.'

'Why would that happen?' asked Bobby.

'You said it yourself. I'm about to retire.'

Bobby took his coffee black, mainly because Sergeant Zha used to take his with milk. Bobby was working on points of difference. Life beyond the window had returned to normal and many of those who'd been watching were now on patrol, while most of those who remained had lost interest the moment the coffee appeared, since fireworks were obviously off today's menu. Only Sergeant Sanchez and Flic retained their interest, a fact made clear by their stubborn refusal even to glance in that direction.

'Look,' said the lieutenant. 'I'd appreciate some honesty.'

It sounded like the kind of thing he'd heard on Oprah, only Bobby found it hard to imagine the lieutenant watching chat shows, and from what he knew about Lieutenant Que's personal life, time not spent with his wife, playing mah-jong or paying respects at the Hong Chow temple went on SFPD working parties and committees. He wondered if the old man was worried about how he'd fill those gaps.

'Sure,' Bobby said. 'If I can answer honestly I will.'

He was rewarded with a sour smile.

'Why are you here?'

'To be honest,' said Bobby. 'I don't know. I'm still working that out.'

The lieutenant stared at him. An old man with bags beneath his eyes and a jaw line weakened by loosely hanging skin. The splashes, liver spots and carcinoma scars on the back of his hands seemed worse than Bobby remembered. Lieutenant Que only had to look in the mirror to know that he was dying. It wasn't the thought of her brother's retirement or the threat to her job which made his sister so grumpy.

'*You don't know?*'

Bobby sighed. 'At it's simplest,' he said. 'I guess I'm here to find out what really happened at Tamsin Steps in early February. I know the case has been closed, that Natalie Persikov is receiving therapy and that a lot of people would rather this was all let well alone, but I still need to know why a man like Michael Persikov would let a child take that rap . . .'

'Misha,' Lieutenant Que said, 'not Michael. And he's letting her take the rap because he's afraid.'

'You know that for a fact?'

Tired eyes stared back. 'I don't need to,' said the lieutenant. 'I can count on one hand the things that motivate crime. Misha Persikov has more money than he can spend. You've seen that little house of his . . .'

This was, Bobby felt, an important point for the lieutenant, on a number of levels; although it was hard to say why and the house on Tamsin Steps hardly counted as little. 'I've seen it,' he said.

'You know that Russian mafia boss wanted to buy it, contents and all? He flew into SFO to negotiate direct with Dr Persikov.'

'Osip bought White Drop.' Bobby named a villa cut into the cliffs south of Fort Point Rocks. Five years back, its sale had made all the major papers, *New York Times* and *Washington Post* included. As well as being one of the world's richest men, the late Gregory Osip was also one of the meanest. Along with Byzantine art and Renaissance silver, there was a rumour he'd collected used wrapping paper, rubber bands and string. The price he paid for White Drop made it one of the most expensive houses in America.

'Only after Persikov refused to sell. Dr Persikov could leave Natalie nothing but that house and she'd still be fixed for life . . . No,' the lieutenant said, 'money means little to the man. Sex? He's been impotent since the second prostate operation. I knew his last mistress,' the lieutenant added, as if this explained his depth of knowledge. 'Not money and not sex, that leaves power, which he already has, or fear . . .'

'Of what?'

'The man escaped from Stalingrad. So I doubt if he's afraid for himself . . .'

'Natalie.' They both said it together.

'She's all he has left,' said the lieutenant. 'His son died in a car crash twelve years ago and – since the court case – he no longer talks to his daughter-in-law. She was drunk,' he added, 'also driving. Her only excuse was to be less drunk than Persikov's son.'

'And the court case?'

'Irena Persikov was pregnant at the time of his death. After the birth, Misha Persikov fought Irena for custody of Natalie.'

'Harsh,' said Bobby.

The lieutenant nodded. 'He's not a nice man. You probably need to remember that. Tens of thousands died during the siege of Stalingrad, from starvation, cold and disease. When the Soviets finally fought their way into the city, Dr Persikov demanded to be taken to the nearest general and was on his way to Moscow within the hour. He was thirteen years old. He makes no secret of this. In fact,' said Lieutenant Que, 'I'd say he's pretty proud of it.'

'So how did he end up in the US?'

'Ahh,' said the lieutenant. 'I was hoping you might know.'

'One last question,' said Bobby. 'What do you know about the accident that killed Doctor Charles Weyler?'

'It wasn't an accident.'

'You sure of that?'

'Not my area. But according to Traffic the Lexus was almost new, the tyres were good and the vehicle had working ABS brakes. There were no skid marks on the road and no signs of braking.' Downing the last of his coffee, Lieutenant Que smiled, a sour smile that thinned his lips and barely reached his eyes. 'As far as I'm concerned, that makes it murder or suicide.'

'Can you get me the file?'

'Maybe,' he said, 'but first let's talk about other things. Like the fact Bobby Zha was working for you. Am I right?'

Bobby raised his eyebrows, in the circumstances it seemed the safest thing to do.

'You know too much about us,' said Lieutenant Que. 'All that stuff about Sergeant Sanchez. There's another point. A lot of things only begin to make sense if Zha *was* working for you, because he sure as fuck didn't seem to be working for anybody else . . .'

'You really didn't like him, did you?'

'Not by the end,' said Lieutenant Que. 'All the same, he had a way with kids and bums that got through to them. You had to give Zha that. I've got another question.'

'Ask it,' said Bobby.

'If you're not Agency, what are you?'

A ghost, Bobby wanted to say. He wanted to lean forward and say, 'I'm Zha.' But common sense choked the words in his throat – and he didn't feel like a ghost. Sweat trickled under his arms and beaded beneath his hairline, one heel still hurt from his new shoes. Flic's smell could be found on his fingers, from where he'd used the urinals earlier. His heart was tight in his chest and his head hurt. It was a very human feeling.

'I'm Robert Van Berg,' said Bobby, seeing tightness reclaim the lieutenant's eyes.

'For real,' Bobby added. 'LivingSoul said what they were told to say. You could fly to New York and all they would do is show you an empty bed.'

'You could have had the body moved.'

'No.' Bobby drained the last of his own coffee. 'Van Berg is right here,' he said, 'sitting in front of you.' Reaching into his pocket, Bobby pulled out an envelope and hesitated. It was his hesitation which convinced Lieutenant Que that he was about to get the truth.

'You might as well,' said the lieutenant, holding out one hand.

Bobby gave him Sol Mancini's masterpiece.

'Oh shit . . .' The words were soft, utterly unconscious. The officer in front of Bobby read the sheet of paper, reread it and then very carefully folded the letter in three along its original creases and gave it back. Letters from the president tended to have that effect on people, even fake ones . . .

'What do you want from me?'

'Cooperation,' said Bobby. 'Access to your files. And there's something else.' It was his turn to fix the man on the other side of the desk with a look. 'I want you to tell Dr Persikov why I'm here.'

'You want me to tell him about the letter?'

'Of course not. I want you to tell Misha Persikov that the investigation into the death of Sergeant Zha is to be given highest priority. And while you're at it, mention that the case involving his granddaughter is about to be reopened.'

'About Officer Valdez,' said Lieutenant Que.

'Yes?' Glancing back at the lieutenant, Bobby frowned. 'What about Flic?'

'Are you using her to get access to this station? Because if you are, I'll give you whatever access you want. Hell.' The lieutenant nodded toward the envelope now safely back in Bobby's pocket. 'After that, I'm hardly likely to do anything else. It's just if you *are* using Valdez . . .'

'Then stop,' said Bobby.

Lieutenant Que nodded.

CHAPTER 33

Wednesday 3 March

'How dare you talk to Lieutenant Que about me?'

'I had no choice,' said Bobby, glancing at the officer who sat opposite, cap on the bench beside her, muffin untouched on her plate. 'The lieutenant seemed to think I was using you . . .'

'You were,' said Flic.

'No,' said Bobby. 'I wasn't.'

'Look,' said Flic, 'you're here to investigate the death of Sergeant Zha. The lieutenant told us about it after you left. Everyone's to give you total cooperation. He wanted to talk to me afterwards, alone . . . You lied. You're not really with the Agency at all.'

Bobby sighed. 'What did he say?'

Flic said nothing.

'He gave you some orders . . .'

'Suggestions,' said Flic, her voice bitter. 'Full cooperation at the station. Stay away from you outside. I don't think taking that advice is going to be much of a problem.'

Green eyes, made brighter by unspilled tears.

'I took you home,' she said, this was what upset her most. 'I took you back to Valencia Street. Sergeant Sanchez told me you were dangerous.'

'Did he now?'

'*How can you?*' said Flic, loud enough to make a tourist couple at the next table slip sideways in their chairs and stare across.

'How can I what?'

'Sit there looking quizzical. I don't think this is funny . . .'

Starbucks was Flic's best offer, after Bobby refused to have their conversation on a sidewalk outside the Chinatown Station and Flic

195

refused to go anywhere except the nearest franchise. So now they sat with slowly cooling espresso and latte between them.

'I don't think it's funny either.'

'You know what,' said Flic, pushing back her chair. 'I don't believe you. And it wouldn't surprise me if you were married.'

She looked very young walking away. A uniform wrapped around a young woman still carrying the emotional fragility of someone far younger. Bobby could remember when he'd felt that raw in the face of life's cruelty. Remembering it didn't make him feel any better.

Bobby left Starbucks to a round of scowls, led mainly by the tourist couple at the next table. In fact, when he got up to make for the door the woman actually hissed, like she was on some television programme.

'You know nothing,' said Bobby.

'Hey,' said her husband. 'That's enough.' He made to stand and Bobby stepped forward. This, combined with the woman suddenly grabbing her husband's shirt, left the tourist half rising from a red plastic bench.

'I'll call the cops,' said the man's wife.

'I am the fucking cops,' Bobby told them. He felt better after that, although this only lasted until he made it onto Bush Street and then he felt . . .

A long time ago, Bobby's aunt had given him a picture of a man standing on a bridge. It was valuable, she told him. A lithograph from the second run, he wasn't to damage the thing. In this picture, the man was holding his hands to his ears and had his mouth wide open.

Almost nobody he showed understood the picture. Ellen took one look at it, clasped her hands over her ears and yelled so loud that Janice ran up two flights of steps without stopping.

'Edvard Munch,' Janice said, when her breath was back. 'Norwegian. A genius but neurotic . . . And you really shouldn't shout like that.' The Goodmans were a very civilised family.

Only the man on the bridge was not screaming. It was the world around him which screamed, that was why the man had his hands clamped over his ears, to keep out the noise. That was how Bobby felt standing outside Starbucks. As if the sound of cars, trams, tourists and city had been magnified until it shook his body like a window rattled by a passing truck.

Without even thinking about it, Bobby cut between a group of Midwesterners and started up Bush Street towards Stockton, head down and shoes slapping the city in its face. In at a door beside the post office, up three floors and out into a small lobby cluttered with broken carvings and the remains of an old cupboard. A hand-written sign beside the next door read, *No photographs*.

In the twenty-five years since Bobby last visited this place, the gilt on the biggest statue had crazed and faded and the old women who knelt before the altar now looked younger. A boy, hair gelled and a chain looped from belt to pocket, knelt beside one of the old women, his hands filled with sticks of burning joss. A girl in one corner fed hell banknotes to the temple furnace, *cash* to ensure prosperity for her family in the afterlife.

Nobody so much as glanced at Bobby, which was pretty impressive given he was obviously a tourist or from out of town. Gabbling his prayers with all the swiftness and thoughtlessness of a child, Bobby reached the last word, only to begin again, more slowly.

He still found the basic idea of prayer hard to believe. And yet, he'd lain there on the concrete, not a mile from here, while a nine-tailed fox slunk out of the darkness, eyes burning in the night and breath sour on Bobby's face as the world whimpered itself into smoke around him.

Self pity, Bobby told himself.

Weakness.

He could hear his grandfather's voice. The clipped tones of a man who wore his pride like armour, even after age and politics and a changing city had done their best to cut that pride away.

'Are you all right?' It was one of the old women.

Bobby nodded, surprised that anyone here would talk to him. Such places were regarded as private and he was a stranger.

'You sure?'

'Prayers for my grandfather,' said Bobby.

'Ahh . . . I understand.' She spoke with the accent of someone who'd arrived from Canton as a child. Next to her stood the boy with the haircut and chains, his feet shuffling in incense ash which drifted across the floor, stirred by the wind from an open balcony behind him.

'Duty,' said Bobby. He said it in Chinese, the voice of his grandfather still echoing in his head, then he remembered to be polite. 'Thank you.'

She nodded and would have left it there. The boy, however, was looking at Bobby with new interest.

'You expecting trouble?'

He'd had the same sixth sense at that age. An ability to read signs and a taste for the unusual. 'No,' said Bobby. 'Why?'

'Because someone's following you,' said the boy.

A couple of quick questions later and Bobby had established that a tall man in jeans, T-shirt and black jacket was waiting on the street below, pretending to read a magazine. Asked why he thought the man was waiting for Bobby, the boy indicated his grandmother with a grin and asked if Bobby really thought the man was waiting for her.

The boy, his grandmother or Bobby, those were the options. The temple was almost empty, its bundles of paper money burnt and the man behind a table in the corner with a sign in three languages reading *offerings* had gone, along with everyone else Bobby remembered having been there the last time he looked.

'Where did everyone go?'

'They left.' The old woman looked puzzled.

Looking down, Bobby realised that ash dusted his fingers and the stubby handful of sticks he held had grown cold.

'How long have I been kneeling here?'

'An hour.'

'She wouldn't leave until she knew you were alive,' said the boy. 'And she wouldn't let me prod you to check.' Glancing at his grandmother with an expression halfway between exasperation and fondness, the boy shrugged. 'So we waited,' he said. 'Until you began to cry. That was when she asked if you were okay . . .'

'And the man outside?'

'No one stands on the corner for an hour looking at a magazine . . .'

It was Sergeant Sanchez. The black coat was actually dark blue. A blazer from Brooks Brothers matched with Banana Republic jeans and brown boots. He might be trying to look inconspicuous but Sanchez stood like a police officer. Besides this was his area, in or out of uniform his face was known.

'I need you to do something for me,' Bobby said.

The boy looked at him.

'You know someone who organises funerals?'

A stare, growing wider. Despite himself, the boy nodded.

'Here,' said Bobby, 'I'll make a list.' Pulling a notebook from his pocket, he tore out a page and scrawled down half a dozen items. 'I need these,' said Bobby, and before the boy could object or claim to be too busy Bobby dipped into his jacket to extract his wallet.

'Keep the change,' he said, handing over a $500 note.

The boy would haggle for all he was worth. In fact, he'd probably stop at a store to break the $500 into lower denominations and then claim to have only a fraction of the cash he actually carried. This had nothing to do with being Chinese in origin or living in Chinatown, where haggling was a way of life. It was to do with his age and the fact he got to keep whatever was left. Bobby had been the same.

'All of these?'

'Yes,' said Bobby, 'but the item which really matters is the last.'

The boy showed the list to his grandmother who raised her eyebrows, then shrugged. 'Who really knows what you need in the afterlife?' she said.

By the time the boy returned, clutching half a dozen carrier bags, Bobby had long since made a call to Latif, asking the car to meet him at Chinatown gates as soon as was possible, and Sergeant Sanchez had given up with the magazine and was openly leant against the wall, tapping his watch.

'Got it all,' said the boy.

'Thank you.'

'You don't want to check?'

'No.' Bobby shook his head. 'I'm sure it's all there.'

He walked passed Sergeant Sanchez without breaking stride and climbed into the dark blue limo pulling up outside the gates, tossing carriers bags onto the seat beside him. Those that wouldn't fit, Bobby stacked up next to the driver.

'I thought you'd forgotten about me,' said Latif.

'Saving you.' Bobby's voice was dry. He liked the young black driver but they both knew the man wasn't there from choice. Debts could be a complicated business.

'Where to . . . ?'

When Bobby told Latif, all the driver allowed himself was the slightest glance in the mirror.

'You heard me,' said Bobby.

The cemetery was quiet. A dozen or more white banners flapped from posts near the entrance, although whether they were for a burial still to happen or one now gone was impossible to tell. An old man with a trowel was weeding a grave next to the road, completely oblivious to the limousine that rolled past.

'Over there.'

199

The plot looked different when approached from the main gates. On the best part of the hill, with perfect sight lines and flowering bushes already dropping white petals onto the grass.

When Bobby was seven, Lieutenant Que killed Bobby's father with a single shot that left the boy splattered with blood. One had to be very drunk to take a child on a robbery and more than drunk to use the child as a hostage when the heist went wrong. Even Grandfather Lau accepted that Que had no choice. All the same, the killing must have weighed heavily on the lieutenant. Nothing else could justify the expense or effort he must have put into securing this site.

'Wait here.'

About to say something, Latif saw Bobby's face and nodded. 'Okay,' he said. 'Call me if you need me . . .'

They both knew he was referring to the bike. A third of the way out to the cemetery, with the traffic thinning as they left the edges of the city behind, Latif had mentioned that a Harley was following them and Bobby told him not to worry.

Just as he'd promised Latif it would, the V-Rod peeled off before the cemetery gates and was now parked under the trees on the upper road. Sanchez would have field glasses with him, probably Zeiss. He was a man who kept his toys exclusive. When this bit of the plan was done, Bobby was going to buy some toys of his own, starting with a bike even bigger than the one belonging to Sanchez.

He grinned.

SERGEANT BOBBY ZHA
husband, father and officer
A good man . . .

Bobby began with the hell banknotes, large denomination, because hell banknotes were always large denomination. What was the point of burning small notes when no one knew what things cost on the other side? After the notes, Bobby picked up the car, making sure he held it so Sanchez could get a good look at what he was about to burn.

The kid had done him proud. Made from rice-paper and split bamboo, the car was quite obviously an SFPD cruiser, spray-painted in regulation colours and with a uniformed driver inside. It went up in a single burst of flame. Good luck, if his grandfather was to be believed. A speed boat, a pavilion of a kind found only on the Chinese mainland

and a carriage with horses, each horse having a flowing paper mane and shredded paper tail.

One after another, Bobby burnt them beside his grave.

And when all he had left was ash and a ring of scorched grass, he reached for his final offering. Everything else had been taken off the shelf, although the car had required modifying. This was special. The revolver was chunky, heavy and old-fashioned enough to make Bobby wonder about the age of the man who wove and bent the thin slivers of bamboo, before doping rice paper over the newly made frame. Old enough to think of handguns as large and cumbersome.

Bobby thought the weapon might be a copy of a copy of a Russian-made version of the Kriegsmarine. So many levels of history were rolled up inside that, he consigned the thought to the flames along with the gun. It burnt well, and Bobby only let go of the handle when it became obvious his alternative was to burn his fingers as well.

'All done,' said Bobby, although he was uncertain to whom he talked. To what was left of himself? Buried inside a white coffin with a domed lid, old style . . . Or whatever he actually was, demon or human or merely *Gui Hún*, one of those transmigrated souls about which the old men used to talk.

'Take me back,' Bobby told Latif.

So Latif rolled the Cadillac in a huge circle in one of the empty parking lots and headed home, the Harley always five cars behind them. 'Was that last offering what I think it was?'

Bobby nodded.

'Can I ask you a question?' asked Latif, having thought about it.

'Sure. Ask away.'

'Do you believe that shit? Or are you just winding up the guy on the bike behind us? If you don't mind me asking . . .'

'Winding him up,' said Bobby, then stopped, considering. 'Maybe both,' he admitted. 'There's some pretty weird shit around.'

'And that gun was for the dead guy?'

'Yeah.'

'Well, you forgot to include ammunition.' Latif's grin in the mirror was merciless. 'And you should have made the gun an Uzi.'

CHAPTER 34
Thursday 4 March

COP KILLER CONFESSES

In a surprise move SFPD officers yesterday arrested Carlos Nero, a resident of the Mission District and a man known to the police on a number of previous occasions. 'We were acting on a tip-off,' admitted Captain Kravitz. A spokesperson from the mayor's office said that for once the police seemed to have acted swiftly.

'HE'S INNOCENT!'

Carlos Nero's wife insists her husband is the victim of police brutality. 'He was with me that night. No way would he confess . . .' While speaking to the *Chronicle* a spokesperson at Mission Station let slip that Amparah Chico, mother of Carlos Nero's children, was in a rehabilitation programme for heroin offenders. 'We understand her pain,' he said.

FAMILY REFUSE TO COMMENT

'They're delighted at the arrest,' says close family friend Sergeant Pete Sanchez, 'but Ellen and Katherine Zha just want to be allowed to get on with their lives . . .'

A whole world of meaning could be hiding in the spaces between those final dots. Crunching the paper in two, Bobby tossed it into a bin and kept walking. He already knew the words by heart and could summon up their position on the *Chronicle*'s front page simply by shutting his eyes. His day had begun badly and seemed ready to get worse.

'Kris,' he said, 'don't . . .'

'I've got to go. Mom says I'm not to talk to you.' The house phone went down with a crash and Bobby could picture Kris standing in the book room, still glaring at the machine. Only Bobby called it *the book room*, Ellen called it *my library*.

The house had been a present from Ellen's father. Actually, it had been a tax dodge, an attempt to avoid Israeli tax – but the cancer was too far developed and the old man had found himself dying before all the paperwork could be filed. It was hard to say who was more pissed off, Ellen's father or the US accountant who'd been trying to get the old man to tax plan ever since he emigrated.

Bobby sighed. Flic was either out, in a meeting or unable to come to the phone; and the officer policing Flic's calls had come as close as he dared to telling Bobby to stop bothering her. Whatever she'd told the man, he now regarded Bobby Van Berg as a grade A shit.

In the end Bobby put in a call to Lieutenant Que, waited for the old man to agree to take his call and proceeded to lie in his teeth. 'There were four bags of crystal meth,' he said. 'You want to tell me what happened to the other three?'

'Four bags . . . ?'

'Check it,' said Bobby. 'Have you got any objection if I talk to Carlos Nero?'

'*Nero*, you want to talk to him?'

'That's what I said.'

The lieutenant sat at his desk and drummed fingers on battered wood. Felicidad Valdez, who had all the makings of a good officer, had spent most of the last five hours dashing into the women's restroom, only to come out five minutes later with her eyes red and water splashes still on her face. Staying away from Robert Van Berg didn't seem to be doing the trick.

Sergeant Sanchez had failed to make a meeting at 850 Bryant and only called in sick when the meeting was halfway done. Ellen Zha had just contacted the station house to say her daughter was getting silent telephone calls and she needed Lieutenant Que's help to get a new number by the end of the day.

The *Chronicle* was demanding to know the real story behind the corpse found in a dumpster at the back of a sauna in Chinatown, and a crack whore with the face of a grandmother and the body of a child had started turning up at the station, kitten in tow, with the names of street people she claimed had gone missing.

Somehow Robert Van Berg was behind all of this . . . Lieutenant Que couldn't get that idea out of his head. 'Why do you want to see Carlos Nero?'

'He shot Bobby Zha, right?'

'Yes,' said Lieutenant Que. 'He shot Sergeant Zha.'

'You really believe that?'

'What's to believe? He confessed.'

'So he did,' said Bobby. 'And what a confession it is. *I was looking for a place to hide drugs when Sergeant Zha came into the deserted warehouse behind me. It was dark and I thought it was someone come to steal my drugs . . . I bought the gun from a black man in Fillimore I met in a bar.*

'I'm going to go see him anyway,' said Bobby. 'I was being polite.'

The hell you were.

Bobby could practically hear the effort it took Lieutenant Que to swallow his words. The lieutenant knew when games were being played and he didn't like them being played on his pitch, particularly when the other side was unwilling to explain the rules.

'I'll fix it for you,' said Lieutenant Que. 'And I'll send a car.' Easing himself to his feet, the lieutenant walked over to the door of his office and looked out at a suddenly silent room. She was in the corner, having swapped desks.

'Valdez,' he said.

Flic drove in silence and she drove very carefully, using her mirrors a lot and signalling well in advance before every turn. And when she spoke to Bobby, which was a total of three times, she called him *sir*. It was hard to tell whether the anger behind her silence was aimed at Bobby or at herself. Whatever the lieutenant had hoped to achieve by ordering Flic to drive Bobby Van Berg out to the pen where Carlos Nero was being held, it probably wasn't this.

'I'll wait,' Flic said, drawing up next to a cruiser from the sheriff's department. A fat man behind the wheel made little pretence of not staring as she clambered out to open Bobby's door.

'No need,' said Bobby.

Shark Fillimore: bail posted. 24-hour bonds.

Bill Sams – Attorney-at-Law. Advice Always Available.

There were half a dozen taxis dropping off families and lawyers and if the worst came to the worst Bobby would get a ride with the fat man eating donuts.

'I'll wait.'

You don't have to do this . . .

The words went unsaid. Instead Bobby nodded, as if that was fine with him, straightened his coat, brushed dust from a sleeve and went inside to meet the man facing life for a murder Bobby knew damn well he didn't commit.

Carlos Nero was everything his confession suggested. A small man so far out of his depth he barely realised he was swimming. Too vain to crop his thinning hair, Carlos had gone the other route and left it long at the back. In a certain light and when he held his head in a certain way, Carlos Nero probably got away with it. Under the halogen strips of the visitors' room, he looked what he was; a thirty-something ex-pimp fighting a losing battle with age.

On the wall behind Nero's head was a poster, ripped across one corner and taped back together. Visitors were responsible for keeping their children under control at all times, anyone wearing gang colours would be denied the privilege of visiting, appropriate kissing, embracing and handshakes would be permitted between family members only and within the bounds of good taste.

'Why did you do it?'

On the other side of smeared glass, the small man settled into a plastic chair and leant forward, so his mouth was near the microphone. A sheriff's deputy stood hard-eyed and resentful in the doorway behind him.

'I've already told you. He came in while I was looking for somewhere . . .'

'No,' said Bobby. 'I mean, why did you lie?'

The small man went very still.

He had bad teeth, sallow skin and the look of a chain smoker who suddenly finds himself being held in a non-smoking facility. Although nicotine withdrawal was the least of Carlos Nero's problems. Someone had recently stamped the man's glasses into the side of his face, leaving an unmistakable bruise that ran from the corner of one eye to his ear. Cop killing was a bad way to make friends.

'I don't understand.'

'Why,' said Bobby, 'confess to something you didn't do?' There were a number of ways a man could react to that question. With hope or anger, contempt or bemusement.

Carlos Nero looked scared.

'I did it,' he said, voice tight. 'You've got my confession . . .'

'Absolutely worthless,' said Bobby. 'A child could have done better.' Actually, now he thought about it, a child had. Only Natalie Persikov had confessed to a different murder and she hadn't done that either.

'Look,' said Carlos Nero. 'I was searching for a place to hide drugs when Sergeant Zha came into the deserted warehouse behind me. It was dark and I thought it was someone come to steal the drugs . . .'

Bobby clapped.

'What?' said the man.

'Nearly perfect,' said Bobby. 'Only the confession says *looking* rather than *searching* and *my drugs* not *the drugs*. Otherwise pretty impressive. Did some one write it out for you? Or did you just sit opposite the man and practise it word for word?'

'*I've got kids.*' This was said in little more than a whisper. A statement of truth, a defence and also a plea, both Bobby and the man speaking understood that.

'How many?'

'Five . . .' Carlos Nero shrugged. 'I'm Catholic,' he added, although the small crucifix around his neck already made that obvious.

So's Flic, Bobby wanted to reply. Which hadn't stopped her demanding he wear a condom. 'I'll do you a deal,' said Bobby. For all he knew every word he was saying was being recorded. If so, then so much the better.

'I don't want to get out.'

'That's not what I'm offering.'

When Carlos Nero smiled, it was with the sour look of someone who expects the worst because that way anything else feels better. 'Okay,' he said, 'what *are* you offering?'

'Security.'

Carlos Nero shook his head. 'Even you can't give me that.'

'It's not for you,' said Bobby.

The deal was simple. Bobby would buy the house in which Amparah Chico and Nero's two youngest children currently lived and would then give it to her, wrapped up in enough trust lawyers to make sure she was unable to sell the property.

'You've already talked to my woman?'

Bobby shook his head.

'I just wondered how . . .' And then Carlos Nero realised his record undoubtedly included details about domestic disturbances. 'She can't help it,' Carlos said. 'Life's been pretty hard.' What impressed Bobby most about the small man on the other side of the screen was that Carlos already understood he was beyond help.

'And in return?'

'You give me a name.'

If the deal was simple, turning it into something acceptable to both of them was much more complicated. On his first run through, Carlos Nero span off into a story about how Sergeant Zha was on the take and Carlos got fed up with paying out and decided to save himself money. There was no name. Carlos had killed Zha, it was only his reasons that were hidden.

When Bobby refused to believe this, Carlos announced it was true, but actually he'd been paid to kill Zha by . . . Carlos named a small-time dealer Bobby knew had moved out of the area a month or so before. Only, this man was psycho, so admitting this in court was more than Carlos's life was worth. He used those words.

More than my life is worth.

'Try again,' said Bobby.

Flat eyes stared through filthy glass. 'What does it matter?' said Carlos Nero. 'Everybody knows that cop was dirty.' Sitting back in his chair, Carlos folded his arms. 'Maybe this was a bad idea . . .'

'Whatever,' said Bobby. 'Maybe I just go tell everybody about how helpful you've been.'

The eyes were not so flat now, the panic a little less well hidden. He'd be sweating trickles of fear under his arms, cheap plastic sticking to his buttocks and the back of his thighs.

'Let's make this simple,' Bobby said. 'I was there when Sergeant Zha died. That's the truth. I was there and you weren't . . . So why take the fall?'

'We've been through this,' said Carlos. 'I have children and I have a wife . . .' He hesitated on the edge of saying more. 'And Amparah owes people money,' he added reluctantly. 'Somebody called that debt in.'

'Who?'

'I don't know.' Carlos Nero held up his hand before Bobby had time to complain or refuse to believe him. 'I got a script. If I do well, then Amparah is fine, the kids too. If I do badly . . .' He didn't need to finish that sentence. 'I was doing okay until you came along.'

'You're still doing okay,' Bobby told him. 'All you have to do now is tell me who originally held Amparah's debt and we're done.'

'That's it?'

Bobby nodded.

Looking around the room, Carlos took in the cracked paint, strip lights and shuttered windows, then asked a question to which he already knew the answer. 'Whatever happens, I'm gone, aren't I?'

'Pretty much.'

'What about Amparah and my kids?'

'You did what you were told to do. It might be enough.'

'I need more than that. If I give you the name you've got to promise me they'll be okay . . .' It was a typical March for San Francisco, mid afternoon, slightly windy and cloudy overhead and Carlos Nero was sweating like it was high summer in Death Valley.

'Okay,' said Bobby, 'here's what we do.'

He picked up Amparah on his way out. She was the Hispanic woman in jeans and crop top sitting on an orange chair in the waiting area, browsing an eight-month-old copy of *National Enquirer*.

'Amparah Chico?'

She looked up and saw a policeman, maybe a lawyer. Not someone who worked office at the jail because his suit was smart and his shoes were expensive. Amparah had cleaned house for a family in Pacific Heights. She knew what money looked like close up.

'Carlos asked me to run you home . . .'

Her eyes went from doubtful to expressionless. 'I was meant to see him,' she said, her voice matching the emptiness in her eyes.

'I know,' said Bobby.

He led Amparah out to the car and watched her face harden when she saw the SFPD cruiser. Which was nothing to what happened to Flic's expression when she saw Bobby with Amparah.

'Where to?' Flic asked. This time round she let Bobby handle the doors, waiting impassively as he indicated that Amparah should sit in the back and then slid himself in beside the woman.

Bobby gave Flic an address just off Valencia Street, a little too far south to be an entirely safe neighbourhood for anyone but those born there. 'Are the children at home?' he asked Amparah.

'At school. I hope.'

Which was something. 'You needn't wait,' Bobby told Flic, and she didn't, dropping them on the corner of a dusty street. 228 Alicant Street was old, weather-beaten into a shadow of its original self and ripe for renovation. The prettification of the Mission District would eventually swallow up even here but until then the cluster of roads around St Bartholomao remained at the heart of an old working-class Hispanic neighbourhood.

Amparah led him up stone steps and reached into a pocket for her keys. The first opened a wrought-iron gate which closed off the small porch, the second undid the front door and the third unlocked a steel grill blocking the passage beyond. All of which might have made some sense if the house had been built from brick, concrete or stone. Although, even then, a carefully placed charge could chop out a door in a matter of seconds. In a wooden house that was over a hundred years old, steel gates made no sense at all. A child with a sledgehammer could have smashed his way through any of the walls in the time it took Amparah to unlock her doors.

'I don't have much money . . .'

'You don't . . . ?' Bobby looked at the woman standing there in front of him. 'Why would I want money?'

Silence greeted this remark. 'What did Carlos promise you?' she asked finally. From the look on her face Amparah obviously thought she knew.

'He promised me nothing,' said Bobby. 'I promised him to look after you . . .' Pulling out his wallet, Bobby peeled off a handful of $20 notes. 'I can't stop you buying heroin.'

Sad eyes looked back. 'I can't stop me buying heroin either,' Amparah said.

He left the dollar bills on a table in the kitchen and went upstairs by himself. The gun was exactly where Carlos Nero said it would be, in his youngest girl's bedroom under a floorboard covered by a Winnie the Pooh mat. The gun was old, it was cheap and it looked like it had been old before Carlos ever acquired the thing. A .22 revolver with the barrel sawn crudely to a stub. Barely anyone bothered with a calibre that slight these days. Even the gang kids in Fillimore turned their noses up at anything less than a thirty-eight.

As Carlos had promised, it was tied in an oiled cloth and the bullets were in a battered cardboard box wrapped up with the gun. Maybe fifty bullets in total. Bobby took both gun and box. Being careful not to get his fingerprints on the gun he carried it downstairs.

'Carlos has a pair of black gloves.'

She got them without being asked. 'Here,' said Amparah, 'I don't want them back.'

'You won't get them back,' said Bobby.

CHAPTER 35

Thursday 4 March

Wearing jeans, boots and his favourite T-shirt, the one with a winged logo across the chest and 'Life looks better from the back of a Harley' on the reverse, Felipe Valdez walked the long way round to Calpe Park, where he was due to meet Luis and Pedro.

Felipe told himself he went this way because the route let him avoid tourists and the evening crowds and he was right, it was faster and the narrow alleys through which he cut were almost deserted, a fact that worried him not at all. Although Felipe had another reason. Five days before, he'd lost a fight to Juan daVilla, nephew to Alphonse. The other boy was both a year younger and a head shorter than Felipe, but he travelled with an entourage who stole freely from the shops Alphonse daVilla had already taxed.

Losing to Juan daVilla was easy because Felipe just stood there and let the smaller boy knock him down. At the end of the fight, when Juan had stopped kicking him, Felipe simply stood up again and walked away.

Juan hated that.

Other boys fought back. Landing the occasional blow, they doggedly struggled to their feet only to be knocked over again. Juan walked away from those fights believing he'd earned his victory and that he really was the toughest kid to prowl the streets around Calpe Park. Felipe never allowed him that pleasure. In refusing to fight back, Felipe made clear that Juan won his fights only because Alphonse daVilla controlled this area of Mission. If not for your uncle, Felipe's actions said.

If not for your uncle . . .

Luis and Pedro Vicente were cross with Felipe because they felt he should have fought back and – in one of those absurdities Felipe was beginning to recognise – he'd ended up hitting his closest friend as the result of refusing to fight an enemy. So now Felipe took the long route, because he needed to avoid the Vicente house; Luis might have forgiven him but the same could not be said for Luis' father.

Because Felipe took a slightly different route, he passed the Bike Café. The place had another name and was one of three such cafés in the Mission District, though definitely the roughest. Originally, the café had been a brothel, but sometime before Felipe was born it became a meeting place for local bikers. After complaints to the SFPD, the madame applied for a catering licence, the whores became waitresses and the Bike Café became legit. It wasn't quite what the neighbours had in mind.

A couple of sportsters stood on an area of blacktop, carved out of what had once been garden. Next to them was something that looked like an old-school Bonneville, but was actually a Japanese copy. An Intruder and a huge black Yamaha with a tank that flowed into the seat stood on the other side. And beyond that was a bike Felipe had never seen before. Huge and red, with three down pipes and a fat radiator positioned face on, like a battering ram against the wind.

His sister hated Felipe's passion for bikes but he could have had worse ambitions. Luis already owned a gun and Pedro was busy saving up for one. The Harleys were low end, 883cc models, the new ones with rubber engine mounts to stop riders getting jaw-ache from all that shuddering, and the Yamaha was elegant; but it was the red Triumph Rocket III that Felipe stopped to admire.

And it was while he was walking around it, trying to guess its cubic capacity, that Felipe glanced up and found himself staring through an open door into the face of the piece of shit he'd seen creeping out of his sister's bedroom two days before.

Red eyes, tears, shouting, sullen silences. His sister was hurting and it hadn't taken Felipe long to work out the reason. At first Felipe was just going to glare, because Flic wasn't the kind of person who took well to others interfering in her life, especially not brothers, mothers or anyone else who might count as family. Then Felipe decided his sister was his sister and something had to be done. So he forgot the Rocket III and marched inside, stopping by the first table.

If the mug in front of the man had been full, Felipe would have thrown it in his face, turned on his heels and stamped out again.

Unfortunately, it was empty and the piece of shit's blankness suggested he had no idea who Felipe was at all.

'*Me cago en usted* . . .' Felipe expected anger or outrage, something fierce that would make Felipe want to step back but fight inside to stand his ground, instead the man looked irritated.

'Go away,' he said. Nothing more. Just that simple command.

'Didn't you hear me?' Felipe said. 'You're . . .'

'Yeah,' said the man. 'I'm a shit. Tell me something I don't know.' He looked behind him to check if anyone was listening and then leant forward. 'Fuck off,' he said quietly. 'Now, before anyone notices you.'

'I'm not afraid of them.' Sitting himself, Felipe nodded contemptuously to a group of bikers crowded around a table at the back, any one of whom he'd happily have crossed Calpe Park to avoid.

'It's not them I'm worried about,' said Bobby. He'd recognised Felipe and knew exactly why he was so furious. In his place, Bobby would have felt the same. He just needed the kid to be somewhere else and fast.

'Look,' said Bobby. 'I really like Flic. The last thing I wanted to do was hurt her.'

'Maybe not,' Felipe said, 'but it didn't stop you.'

A whole world of truth was wrapped up in that simple complaint, Bobby realised. When had it ever stopped him? 'Now is not a good time to talk about this,' he said. 'If you want to meet me later.' Bobby shrugged. 'You can take a swing or we can work something out, but I need you to leave . . .'

'Before I go,' said Felipe, his gaze following that of Bobby around the shabby café. Three women, two men on seats at the back. A retired whore behind the counter. 'Tell me why now isn't a good time.'

'Because I'm expecting someone.'

The boy nodded – thought about this – and intended to answer, *but they're not expecting you, right?* Only that was when things got complicated, because a heavyset man who'd been threading his way between bikes in the parking lot suddenly appeared in the café doorway.

'*You*,' he hissed, but by then Felipe was back on his feet.

'Senor daVilla.'

'You insult Juan,' said the man. 'He tells me. You think you're too good to fight him. So you stand there and let him bitch-slap you, like you're some woman . . .'

Alphonse daVilla did not sound happy.

'No,' said Felipe, 'I don't think that.'

At the rear of the café, one of the men began to grin and a Hispanic girl in leathers nudged him with an elbow and shook her head. The elderly woman behind the counter took a look at Senor daVilla advancing towards the boy and stepped into the kitchen. Felipe's sister was SFPD and there were some things it was just better not to see.

'*Leave it.*'

Perhaps the man didn't hear or maybe he just found it hard to believe Bobby's suggestion was addressed to him. Either way, Alphonse daVilla kept moving towards Felipe.

'*I said leave it.*'

He heard that time.

Slipping a gun from his pocket, Alphonse daVilla reversed the weapon so he could use its handle as a cosh and changed direction.

'Watch out,' shouted Felipe, although this was unnecessary.

While Senor daVilla's arm was still rising and his knuckles whitening around the gun, the man he intended to cosh twisted in his seat, drew back one heel and kicked out the fat man's knee.

It was simple, elegant and very effective and Bobby had never quite believed his father's description of *wet balloons* to describe cartilage rupturing until he heard Senor daVilla's leg collapse under him.

'Leave,' Bobby told Felipe.

He did.

Stamping hard on the hand with the gun, Bobby heard fingers break in the drawn breath between screams. He could have kicked the injured man in the ribs and cracked a few but Bobby wasn't ready for that yet. So instead he knelt to take the gun from daVilla's ruined hand, putting the muzzle against the man's remaining good knee.

'Remember me?'

Almost without thinking, daVilla began to shake his head.

'No,' said Bobby, 'that's right. You wouldn't . . .'

Hard eyes glared into his own. Hard, furious and almost bug-eyed with outrage, but also, behind it all, a little scared. 'You're going to die,' said Alphonse daVilla. 'In agony . . .'

Was that how he'd looked? Bobby wondered. Did he say something like that to the man who walked up to him? Had there even been someone who walked up to him at the end . . . ? It got harder to remember each day. Harder to remember and harder to believe.

'Okay,' said Bobby, voice soft. 'We'll start with a simple question. Who told you to set up Carlos Nero?'

Alphonse daVilla's face twisted. 'That's what this is about?' he said. 'I tell you, as of now, that man is dead.'

'You're probably right.'

Bobby pulled the trigger and felt the automatic jerk beneath his fingers. Recoil, the thing Natalie Persikov couldn't remember. The fact the muzzle was tight against daVilla's knee kept the gun from jumping too much.

Broken flesh. Shattered bone.

Hot gasses following the bullet would rip a star-shaped wound into the man's skin. That was how the hospital would know the gun had been pressing flesh. There would be scorching to the cloth and maybe a burn ring overlaying the gas wound.

'I'll ask you again,' said Bobby, moving the gun to daVilla's hip. 'Who . . .'

A sliver of the man probably still wanted to kill Bobby and shit on his corpse but most of daVilla was trying to crawl away across the café floor. Grabbing one ankle, Bobby dragged the man back and watched daVilla curl around himself to protect his soft organs from attack. Instinct was a wonderful thing, even a thousand years after gunpowder rendered that particular action pointless.

'Don't,' whimpered Alphonse daVilla, which was when Bobby realised he had a gun to the man's head.

'True enough,' he said. 'I'm not finished.' Bending over the man, Bobby turned daVilla's face until the man had no choice but stare into his attacker's eyes.

'You'll tell me eventually,' said Bobby. He was right.

After Bobby stood up, the woman with the leather jacket moved in, and though Bobby didn't wait to find out why she felt she had that right, Bobby could hear Alphonse daVilla's screams right up to the point he pushed the electric start on his Rocket III.

CHAPTER 36

Thursday 4 March

'Officer Valdez is looking for you . . .' The old man sitting on the bed stood up as Bobby opened the door and waved Bobby into his own room.

'Lieutenant.'

'You went out to the pound this afternoon?'

It look Bobby a moment to realise Lieutenant Que meant the holding jail south of the Creek. 'You know I did,' he said. 'You fixed it.'

'You went to the jail?'

Bobby nodded. And when the lieutenant repeated his question Bobby realised that nodding wasn't enough, so he replied properly.

'Yes,' said Bobby. 'I went to the jail.'

'Why did you go?'

Given the format of formal question requiring audible answers, Lieutenant Que should have had a tape recorder on top of the little fridge beside him. Bobby's fridge, because he'd been waiting for Bobby in the basement behind Stockton Street. Unless, of course, the lieutenant was wearing a wire.

Bobby considered this possibility and rejected it. What use would a wire be against a man Lieutenant Que believed to be connected to US intelligence at the highest levels?

'I went to interview Carlos Nero about his part in the murder of Sergeant Bobby Zha. In particular, about why he confessed to a crime he quite obviously didn't commit.'

The lieutenant scowled at that. 'And what did he tell you?'

'Nothing,' said Bobby.

'He refused to talk?'

'Not at all. Carlos told me repeatedly how he'd been looking for a place to hide drugs when Sergeant Zha came into the deserted warehouse. How he panicked and shot the man before he realised he was an SFPD officer. It's neat,' said Bobby. 'It even gets round the problem of you guys finding the crystal meth.'

'But you didn't believe him?'

'Of course not.'

Abandoning where he stood at the end of the bed, Lieutenant Que walked slowly across to the single window. Its glass was fly-specked and filthy but not so filthy he couldn't see the courtyard beyond the corner of the warehouse where Bobby had died. Shops had come and gone since the lieutenant was a small child. None of them lasting more than a few years.

'You know what happened out there?'

Of course Bobby did. They weren't talking about the death of Sergeant Zha or even the recent fatality from a mugging, so called. History overlaid that courtyard as it overlaid everything, events stacked up like shadows behind each other, ripples that spread through time until they became invisible or merely forgotten. Unseen currents that dragged at events from beneath the world's surface.

'I had no choice,' said the lieutenant. 'It was kill Zha's father or have him kill the kid.'

Bobby nodded, his father had been drunk and his father had been stupid. Even for a man famed for shitting on his own doorstep, trying to rob the herbalists opposite had been extreme.

'I need to know something,' said Lieutenant Que. 'What did you say to Carlos Nero?'

'Ask him,' said Bobby, then understood why that was impossible. No one would ever be able to ask Carlos Nero anything again, or threaten him or tell him to burn out his life in prison because the alternative was his wife got hurt, badly.

'Murdered?'

Some questions need to be asked, even when they don't . . .

'No. Slashed his wrists with a blade from a two-blade disposable swapped for a watch. Did more damage to his fingers breaking the razor than he did opening a vein.' Lieutenant Que sounded disgusted. 'And he left a note,' added the lieutenant. 'Would you like to guess what it said?'

'He was looking for somewhere to hide drugs when an SFPD officer came into the deserted warehouse. He didn't know it was an officer. He cannot face the guilt or life in prison and so . . .'

'Yes.' The lieutenant nodded. 'All this Carlos Nero swears on his soul.' Turning his back on the window, the man cast a slow gaze over the ugly room. One bed, on which Bobby now sat, a shabby table, a rug that had been tatty long before it got scarred with cigarette burns.

'Is this where you brought Felicidad?'

Not a question Bobby expected the man to ask, but he nodded all the same. 'One of the places.'

'I don't think you understand how badly you've hurt her . . .'

'No, probably not.' Bobby was coming to the conclusion he had little idea of how badly he'd hurt a lot of people over the years, starting with Ellen and Kris and going on from there. The missed parades and forgotten anniversaries. All the whores taken in payment for looking the other way. All the nights he forgot to come home.

'It wasn't intentional,' said Bobby, did that count against the total?

'Look at this from my point of view . . .' Lieutenant Que turned to the window, then turned back again, the room was too small for both of them, he didn't like the view outside and he felt caged and irritated. He'd passed the problem of Robert Van Berg up the line and had it handed back with a note saying there was no problem. So far as the SFPD was concerned, until officially told otherwise, the man was a tourist. Nothing more. He should be treated as such and left. Quite what that meant went unspecified, but *well alone* would probably cover it.

'You go see Carlos Nero and he kills himself twenty minutes later, just long enough to lacerate his fingers ripping open a razor and write a final confession; we know he did it in that order, because his blood's all over the paper.'

Lieutenant Que sucked his teeth.

'I discover you've turned a waiter out of his apartment so you can live opposite a brothel we've been watching for three months. It is, of course, entirely coincidence that this was the childhood home of the man whose death you're apparently investigating. And then, guess what, just after you move in some tourist finds a body in the alley over there. No labels in the clothes, no watch, no wallet and no shoes. The trousers were Russian. Although you probably knew that.'

Actually, Bobby hadn't.

'I send someone to tell Carlos Nero's wife that her husband is dead . . .' Lieutenant Que caught Bobby's glance and shrugged, half ruefully. 'Okay, so I send Felicidad, only Amparah is already gone. She's packed one bag, taken her two youngest out of school and left town for a couple of months.'

He waited for Bobby to look up.

'You know why?'

'No,' said Bobby. 'But you're going to tell me.'

'She told the school her husband was dead. You want to tell me how Mrs Nero knew that . . . ?'

Because she was a bright woman trapped in a bad habit, with more kids than she could look after and a petty thief for a husband. A man who, at the point of his death, had the guts to take a fall without telling his wife why. That was the thing about life. Even the simplest statistic could be as cruel as any opera.

'How would I know?' Bobby said.

'I look after my officers,' said Lieutenant Que. 'You need to understand that. I don't take kindly to graft or men on the pad, but I protect my own. That's how things were done in the SFPD when I started and that's how I do things still. The old-fashioned way.'

Bobby nodded. 'I hear what you're saying.'

'Good, because Officer Valdez was on her way back from Mission when she drove by Calpe Park. Her brother was there with two friends. He was the one on his knees in tears. Apparently he'd just seen a local pimp get shot by one of the man's ex-girls. Guess whose name Felipe mentioned as a witness. You want to tell me what the fuck is going on?'

'No,' said Bobby. 'I don't.'

'Want to tell me why?'

'You won't believe it.'

'At least tell me this,' said the lieutenant, 'because I'm taking this a bit personally. What's the Chinatown connection?'

Bobby looked at him.

'It's a simple enough question,' Lieutenant Que said. 'You've got a hotel out at SFO but you're holed up here. You spend your mornings in cafés on Stockton and your evenings at the Buddha Cocktail Lounge. You've been seen coming out of the Kong Chow temple. You speak Cantonese, for heaven's sake. Tell me, maybe I can help.'

Lieutenant Que spoke the truth, Bobby knew that. There were two Chinatowns, existing in parallel and overlapping only occasionally. In one of them tourists came searching for the unusual. In the other, a hundred thousand people got on with their lives while struggling with the conflict between earning a living and being left in peace.

There probably wasn't a family in the area that didn't owe Lieutenant Que a debt or their friendship, and he had access to people in alleys and courtyards that most officers at 850 Bryant barely knew existed. In some strange way, the lieutenant had inherited the web of connections and responsibilities once wielded and worked by Bobby's own grandfather.

'There's no mystery,' said Bobby. 'I'm just trying to think myself into the mind of Sergeant Zha.'

'That's it?'

'It's enough.' Had Bobby been the lieutenant, he wouldn't have believed him either.

CHAPTER 37
Friday 5 March

It was amazing how much could fit into two plastic carrier bags if the contents were packed carefully enough. The small wok Bobby had bought went at the bottom of one, with a half-empty packet of rice and an untouched bag of thread noodles on top of that, while peppers, onions and a string of dried mushrooms took up the rest of the space.

His other bag contained a cotton sheet Flic had purchased for $5. It was meant to replace the one left behind when the waiter moved out and wrapped into its centre was the automatic Bobby had taken from Alphonse daVilla, the .22 Saturday Night Special found under a Winnie the Pooh carpet in Carlos Nero's house and the Colt he'd recovered from the alley.

A fine collection of weapons, all owned by people lately dead; which was either excellent forward planning or the kind of coincidence he'd been trying to sell to Lieutenant Que last night, right up to the point the elderly officer let himself out of the door, with a parting comment that if Robert Van Berg really wanted to discover what had made Sergeant Zha tick, he was looking in the wrong place. He should be talking to homeless people on the streets.

On top of the sheet went two bowls, a pair of bamboo chopsticks Bobby had taken from a dim sum café less than a hundred paces away and two cheap Mexican glasses, the kind with a bluish tinge and bubbles in the side.

And it was the two Mexican glasses which fell from the bags and smashed when Flic punched him. Which was fair enough, because she'd been the one to buy them in the first place.

Bobby rolled, found his feet and began to rise. Straight into another punch. Flic didn't slap, she punched like a man, from the hips, aiming at a point six inches behind her target.

'Moron,' said Flic.

Grant Avenue came to a halt, at least that stretch of it just inside the gates, as early-morning tourists and people on their way to work stopped to stare. Stepping back, Bobby watched the uniformed woman step towards him, shoulders already swivelling, and he kept watching as her elbow pulled back, spotting in her eyes the point at which she decided to throw her third punch.

He caught it on his forearm, swivelled round to snatch her fist out of the air and twisted, carrying Flic's arm behind her back. Using the pain, he moved his attacker two paces towards the wall.

If Flic hadn't been so angry, she'd never have let it happen. Mind you, if she hadn't been so angry she'd never have been caught trying to beat up someone who looked like a civilian.

'I'm going to let go,' said Bobby, releasing her wrist and stepping swiftly back. A coachload of tourists had gathered round to watch, which was good, because they now hid most of what was happening. 'Family trouble,' Bobby said, and one of the men translated for the others. It said something of their expectations of San Francisco that this explanation was accepted without question.

'Excuse me,' Bobby added, watching the group part to let him through. Flic and he walked under the gate in silence.

'Was it supposed to impress me?' asked Flic. 'Some dumb pimp picks on my brother so you beat the creep to pulp. Am I meant to be grateful?' She halted on the far side of the road, the family behind Flic flowing around her, their irritation silenced by the sight of Flic's uniform.

'You want to give me one reason why we shouldn't arrest you?'

Flic was four months into the job, he loved that *We* . . . 'I can give you three,' said Bobby. 'One, you'd have done it already. Two, what makes you think it was about impressing you? And three, that wasn't some dumb pimp. That was Alphonse daVilla and he was alive when I left the café . . .'

'It wasn't about Felipe?'

'No,' said Bobby. 'I'm sorry if you thought it was.'

'He's thirteen,' said Flic. 'You know his friend carries a gun? And he's fourteen. What am I meant to do about that?' She was talking to herself, mostly. 'Felipe said he was in a café with you.'

Flic paused, aware how unlikely that sounded.

'You were in the café together,' she amended.

'He came in,' Bobby said, 'to tell me I was a shit for mistreating you. If I'd had any coffee left, he'd have thrown it in my face.' Felipe had left this bit out, Bobby could read that in Flic's expression. It made him wonder what else Felipe might have forgotten to mention.

'I was waiting for Alphonse daVilla,' said Bobby, his voice matter of fact. 'He has a coffee, buys industrial quantities of meth from the bikers and uses one of the whores if he's not in a hurry. All this Carlos Nero told me.'

'The man who killed Sergeant Zha?'

'No,' said Bobby, 'he was innocent.'

Flic looked shocked. 'So what really happened in the café?'

'Alphonse came in,' said Bobby. 'Began picking on Felipe. I told him to stop.'

'But not because he was picking on Felipe . . .'

'No,' Bobby said. 'We had business. Alphonse daVilla fixed for Carlos Nero to confess to the Zha murder.' Bobby had Flic's full attention now.

'Go on,' said Flic.

'I wanted to know who fixed daVilla,' said Bobby. 'And for the record that whore didn't kill Alphonse, the man was already dead. Only he wasn't as bright as Carlos Nero so he didn't know it yet.'

Half a dozen questions jostled their way across Flic's face, but when she spoke it was to ask about Carlos Nero. 'DaVilla threatened him, right?'

'Threatened Amparah. She used to work for daVilla.'

'One of his whores?'

'Not at first.' It had taken Bobby a while to remember. 'She started out at Zil's, stripping. When Amparah began turning tricks for herself daVilla gave her the usual options, get her bits resculpted with a box cutter or start working for him.'

Flic's blink served to remind Bobby that she still saw the world as a kinder place. 'Before Carlos Nero could marry Amparah, he had to buy out her contract,' said Bobby. '10,000 dollars. Only by then Amparah was addicted to crack and Nero had to help her clean up . . .'

'He got her off crack?'

'Onto heroin.'

'That's an improvement?'

'Yeah,' said Bobby. 'Believe me, that's an improvement . . .'

Although most of what Bobby had actually said sounded less clear than this, because Flic's first punch had caught his lip and Bobby was taking time out every few minutes to spit blood into a tissue. He was only glad she'd failed to hit an eye or his nose.

'You need ice,' she said.

'I need a lot of things,' said Bobby, then stopped.

'What?'

'That was glib.' He shrugged. 'I'm sorry.'

Stepping forward, Flic wiped blood from his lip and stood back, examining her thumb as if she might, at any point, be asked to write answers on what such things meant. 'I don't get you,' she said.

'What's to get? Alphonse daVilla set up Carlos Nero, who killed himself. Before Alphonse daVilla got killed he told me a couple of things I needed to know.'

'And you're not going to tell me what those were?'

'No,' said Bobby. 'I don't think I am.'

It was with regret, but without surprise that he watched Flic walk away. A flash of blue that finally lost itself in the early morning crowd.

CHAPTER 38
Monday 8 March

The next three days passed in a blur of administration and petty detail. The kind of stuff Bobby Zha used to hate beyond reason and Bobby Van Berg found himself able to do, albeit resentfully. He found a house to rent on Russian Hill, checked himself and his bags out of the hotel near to the International Terminal at SFO and began shopping for icons.

The file on Dr Weyler arrived by bike. The officer who brought it gave Bobby the briefest nod and a cold stare, so Bobby guessed the man had heard all about Flic Valdez. Spreading a handful of photo-copies out on his desk, Bobby started to make notes. Charles Weyler's body appeared clear of drugs and alcohol. The roadworthiness of his Lexus seemed good. A heart attack could not be ruled out, but looked unlikely. Crash damage and the fire which followed made it hard to answer these points with anything approaching conviction.

The bank statements were altogether more concrete. In the seven years since Charles Weyler resigned his professorship and stood down as CEO of a biotech company, with the aim of simplifying his life and devoting himself to good works, $150,000 a month had been paid into his account.

'Henry, hi. It's Robert Vanberg.'

Bobby listened to Henry Cabot Junior struggle to put a face to the name and realised it was still crack of dawn in New York. Probably not what Henry Cabot had in mind when he gave Bobby his home number.

'Sure,' said Bobby. 'Everything's fine. I just wondered if you could help me with something else . . .'

The trust paying into Charles Weyler's account was based in Liechtenstein. It originally had links with an Istanbul drug family but had, supposedly, been taken over by a rival sometime in the late nineties.

'Any way you can find out who?'

Henry Cabot Junior promised to try, while explaining apologetically, that, if called on it, he'd have to deny all the things he'd just said.

With a laugh, Bobby clicked shut his phone and turned to the next piece of paper, a list of operating equipment supplied by a medical company in Canada. The company had given Dr Weyler a hefty discount, on the basis that he was working for charity.

In between checking files, moving house and searching for icons, Bobby visited the market on Stockton, near Columbus and Broadway to buy a turtle, which he released into the sea in payment of a very old debt. He also found time to walk out to Calpe Park and make his apologies to Felipe, explaining that the fight with Alphonse daVilla had nothing to do with the boy and everything to do with a case Bobby was investigating for the White House.

'You're with the Secret Service?'

'No.' Bobby shook his head.

'FBI?'

'Not that either.'

'Who then?'

'Can't tell you,' said Bobby.

'. . . because then you'd have to kill me.' Felipe grinned at his own punchline and nodded. For someone who'd watched a man get hurt only four days earlier he was remarkably chilled. Bobby had been the same. When his father died he cried himself stupid for a day, retreated into silence for a week and then barely thought about it again for the rest of that year.

'I'm sorry,' Bobby said. 'Things went out of control. And, for what it's worth, I never meant to hurt your sister.'

'Hey.' Felipe shuffled in his shoes. 'That's cool.'

Bobby was embarrassing the boy just by being there, and both he and Felipe were acutely aware of the other two boys, watching from a broken bench fifty paces away. One of them was on his phone, the other pretending to read a comic and glancing repeatedly in Felipe's direction.

'Which one's got the gun?'

'Shit . . .' said Felipe. 'I should never have told Flic about that.'

'So why did you?'

'Because she was giving me grief about school. I was, like, it could be so much worse . . .'

It took a couple of minutes but Bobby finally got Felipe to describe the gun. Revolver, blue steel, plastic grip . . . They dealt with the basic stuff first, only getting on to calibre and make when Felipe ran out of less important things to say about the weapon.

'Okay,' said Bobby. 'I'm off.' Thrusting out his hand, Bobby waited, and after a second's hesitation Felipe shook. On his way out of Calpe Park, Bobby stopped by the bench with the two boys.

'That Colt thirty-eight,' he said. 'It was used to kill someone. Which means it's on file. Get arrested for so much as firing that thing at a door and the SFPD will pin a homicide on you . . . You might want to think about that.'

He walked away without looking back.

Artworks come with a provenance, sometimes simply a photocopied entry from an art book or encyclopaedia, at other times a sworn statement that a painting or statue had been in a family for a century or had been bought at auction so many years before. Reputations were lost, millionaires bankrupted and galleries and auction houses closed for faking or not bothering to check such things. False provenance was second only to false attribution in the list of sins an art expert could commit.

In the three days Bobby spent shopping for icons he discovered two facts, one, there were a staggeringly large number of art galleries in San Francisco and two, their owners were depressingly honest. All of the icons at which he looked were immaculately provenanced, many with sales records or ownership details going back more than a century.

All of which explained Bobby's relief when someone finally mentioned Ibrahim Nasra, adding the name of the gallery and the fact the man was a crook. Since this was what Bobby had been relying on, he was delighted. Alphonse daVilla had got Ibrahim Nasra's name wrong, maybe through panic or maybe he'd just misheard what was said and he'd only had one part of the name in any case. *Abraham*, with no clue as to whether that came second or first.

'How d'you do it?' demanded Flic.

Bobby was stood outside Midas Imperial in Jackson Square, which wasn't actually a square at all but half a dozen city blocks taking their name from Jackson Street. A surfeit of financial buildings was messing with his phone signal but he could still hear the doubt in Flic's voice.

Midas Imperial was shut, and not just shut, but locked down behind a metal grill. Unopened post had built up behind a glass door and a sour stink could be detected if you got down on your knees and lifted the letter box.

Bobby knew, he'd tried.

'How did I do what?'

'Felipe said you came by Calpe Park. How did you get Luis to give up his gun?'

What did you do to that poor boy? This was the subtext to Flic's question. She barely bothered to keep it out of her voice.

'I told Luis the gun was probably on file as a murder weapon and the first time he fired it forensics would nail him for everything not solved.'

'Shit,' said Flic.

'I've seen it happen,' said Bobby. 'You want to do me a favour?'

Silence said Flic didn't or at the very least was unsure. 'Depends what it is,' she said finally.

Making his apologies to Felipe had been simpler; but then, in many ways, the boy had much less to forgive. With Flic it was different. Bobby woke each morning with the taste of her nipples in his mouth and fell asleep to the memory of her anger and tears.

He wouldn't have forgiven him either. 'I need a door opening,' said Bobby.

'Call a locksmith.'

'It's more complicated than that . . .' When Flic refused to rise to the bait, Bobby explained anyway. 'I think someone's been killed.'

When the squad car turned into the alley off Jackson Street, Flic was driving and though she stalked round to the passenger door without even glancing in Bobby's direction, something about the way she held her head said she knew he was watching.

Sergeant Sanchez's smile was brief. 'You want to tell me what's going on?'

'Ibrahim Nasra,' said Bobby, nodding to the pile of letters building up on the wrong side of the glass. 'I think he's dead.'

'That's your evidence?'

Lifting the flap on the letter box, Bobby indicated that the sergeant should check for himself. To give Sanchez credit, the man dropped onto his heels and pressed his nose to the slot.

It was always the same. Five locks down one side, two hinges the other, without a single deadlock top or bottom to keep the hinged edge secure. 'Stand back,' Sergeant Sanchez ordered.

Having cut his way through the grill, Sanchez put the jump plate of a ram against the weaker edge of the door. A dull thud and one of the hinges broke. Another punch of steel and the door went down, fresh air from the street competing with stale air from the gallery inside. The fresh air lost.

'Shit,' said Flic.

'And the rest,' Bobby agreed.

'I'm going to call this in,' said Sanchez. 'You go ahead.' He was talking to Flic. So shoulders back and head still held high, Flic strode into the gallery, because that's what Midas Imperial really was.

The sign outside might say *General Antiques* but most of Ibrahim Nasra's stock hung on walls or stood on plinths. In one corner was a bronze dancer by Degas, although Flic only recognised this from a birthday card from an ex-boyfriend. The row of Dali etchings she recognised from a magazine. None of the objects in the gallery had a price, so she guessed that told her all she needed to know about what things were likely to cost.

'*Flic* . . .'

Turning at the call, she found Bobby holding an icon. A sullen Virgin with the Christ squashed onto her lap. 'What?' Flic demanded.

'You okay?'

She wasn't sure why he expected an answer to that one.

After four hours rigor sets in, sphincters have already loosened and the body has been losing heat at a rate of about 1.5 degrees Fahrenheit an hour. After twenty-four hours the corpse reaches room temperature, head and neck turn greenish-red and a definite smell of rotting meat can be detected. After three days, gas from bacteria causes fist-sized blisters under the skin, the body begins to swell noticeably and fluid leeches from any available combination of anus, mouth and vagina.

The body behind the inner door had been dead for at least three days. What would have been ugly under any circumstances was made both uglier and better by the fact Ibrahim Nasra's throat had been cut from ear to ear; uglier since the man's head lolled back with an extra mouth and better because the gash helped release gas from the stomach and had partially drained the cadaver of blood.

Any standing orders about not contaminating a crime scene were rendered redundant the moment Flic tried to catch her own vomit between cupped hands and only succeeded in spreading it over much of the carpeted floor around her.

'Wait there,' said Bobby.

When he returned it was with a packing sheet from an empty crate. Wrapping the cloth around Flic, he walked her back to the office doorway.

'I'll mark the area,' he said. 'You get yourself cleaned up.'

For a second it looked as if Flic might object but then she shrugged, looked down at the cloth and headed for the women's restrooms in the gallery behind her.

'Check there's nothing unusual in there first,' said Bobby. His only answer was a slammed door.

'You know . . .' The voice from outside sounded almost amused. 'If I didn't know better, I'd think you thought you were the ranking officer around here.'

'I am,' said Bobby. 'Feel free to call Lieutenant Que if you want that confirmed.' Turning his back before Sanchez could answer, Bobby pulled a felt tip from his jacket and drew black circles around the vomit. It helped that those bits of carpet not glazed with blood or sticky with vomit were still white.

Ibrahim Nasra had been tall and thickset, young enough for his beard to be black and old enough to have grey at the temples. Whoever had cut his throat had not been interested in robbery, because quite apart from the Dali etchings and Degas bronze in the room behind them, a ruby still sat cabochon-style in a ring around one constricted finger, while the Rolex digging into swollen flesh on the man's wrist was rose gold and almost new.

To complete the tableau, an old and jewelled Tibetan dagger sat on the desk in front of him, its blade three sided and pitted with rust and blood.

'Well,' said Sanchez, from the doorway. 'He didn't cut his throat with that.'

'*He* didn't cut his throat with anything,' Bobby said, holding his breath and bending as close as he dared to the dead man.

A jagged rip had opened the victim's throat and that took force. A man intent on death might find the courage to slash his own throat with a blade sharpened to razor-like fineness, although many began to cut and then failed along with their courage. To drag a blunt spike through

230

Dublin City Public Libaries
Ballyfermot Library
Borrower Receipt

Customer name: O'Leary, Charles

Title: Shutter man / Richard Montanari.
ID: DCPL1000006203
Due: 29-01-18

Title: Killing ways / Alex Barclay.
ID: DCPL0000872854
Due: 29-01-18

Title: The redeemers / Ace Atkins.
ID: DCPL1000002550
Due: 29-01-18

Title: The broken places / Ace Atkins.
ID: DCPL0000811696
Due: 29-01-18

Title: 9tail fox / Jon Courtenay Grimwood.
ID: 05750761518008
Due: 29-01-18

Total items: 5
08/01/2018 12:44
Checked out: 6
Overdue: 0
Hold requests: 0
Ready for pickup: 0

Items that you already have on loan

Title: Paradise valley / C.J. Box.
ID: DCPL1000041943
Due: 29-01-18

Thank you for using the self service system.
You can visit us online at
www.dublincitylibraries.ie

living flesh took more determination than anyone not utterly insane possessed.

No sign of forced entry and the shop was locked, the paintings seemed to be in place and yet a dead art dealer sat in his own leather chair, rendering the air so foul his entire gallery would need expert attention from one of the three firms in San Francisco who cleaned up after homicides.

Swelling split Ibrahim's skin on both sides of the watch strap but, from what Bobby could see, there was no sign of defensive cuts to the fingers or web of flesh between fingers and thumb, no hesitation cuts either, on the man's wrist or neck. Ibrahim Nasra had not expected his visitor to attack and this was not a suicide, that was Bobby's opinion anyway. There were people who knew this stuff better than him. Without thinking about it, Bobby dialled Chinatown Station, pulling the CSI number from memory.

'Yeah, hi . . . It's Bobby. We've got us a murder scene.'

And then, all too aware that Sergeant Sanchez was frozen beside him, Bobby paused, and as someone barked '*What?*', Bobby watched Sanchez force himself to unfreeze. When the sergeant turned, it was with a smile and a nod which said, *It's okay, I didn't hear that.*

His eyes said something very different.

'It's Robert Van Berg,' said Bobby. 'I'm at Midas International behind Jackson with Sergeant Sanchez and Officer Valdez.' Bobby wanted Sanchez to hear the formality in Bobby's voice and pull back that thought. The one Bobby had seen cross his face.

'Sergeant Sanchez has asked me to call for a crime team.'

'Okay. Has anything been touched?'

Bobby knew what the dispatcher was asking, the usual. Has anybody stamped their way through the evidence, picked up a murder weapon or ground cigarette ends into the carpet next to the corpse?

'Officer Valdez vomited . . .'

Silence, then, 'It's that bad?'

I've seen worse, Bobby was about to say, but restrained himself. It might be true but it was also glib and Flic's reputation was on the line. Say the wrong thing and she'd get ripped to shreds back at the station.

'We're talking a full steam clean.'

The teks did what teks do, photographing the room from several angles and making sketches of the desk and chair in relation to the only door and a window with bars across it. They wore masks and breathed only through their mouths, working as fast as decency and efficiency allowed.

It was a shitty job, often literally, and Bobby wouldn't have done it for the world. After the site photographs were taken and sketches made, the team moved on to the body, starting with shots that showed its position in the chair, then close-ups of the Tibetan dagger, Ibrahim Nasra's fingers, blood splatter patterns and finally the gash across his throat, only then did the senior tek allow Ibrahim's body to be removed.

What remained of the gallery owner would be stripped and examined in minute detail, with photographs taken of any unusual mark or tear on his torn and blistered skin. At this stage it was often hard to determine between acts of violence and the corrupting work of nature.

An autopsy would formally establish the cause of death, confirming or overturning initial suspicions. Although it was already obvious from the splatter pattern across the desk and white carpet beyond that Ibrahim's throat had been cut from behind.

After the body was removed, teks began searching the office for clues, dividing the floor into a grid on paper and combing each square individually. Another technician began fingerprinting.

Sergeant Sanchez, Flic and Bobby were forgotten. Control of the scene had passed to the teks who crawled over the gallery with the loosely worn intensity of true professionals. Blood, corruption and death was their world, but most of them would never even fire a weapon in anger. It was a situation Bobby envied.

A Matisse nude hung on the wall behind Flic and she had one knee resting against the plinth that held the Degas dancer, but Bobby doubted if she was aware of either. One of the teks had wrapped a silver space blanket around her, official recognition that this was a tough crime scene, which meant she'd get less grief than usual for losing her lunch.

'Let me take you home.'

Flic shook her head.

'You're no good to anybody here. I'll ask the sergeant to release you.' Bobby hesitated. 'How come you arrived with Sanchez anyway?'

'He was in with the lieutenant when I went to mention your call.'

'Yeah,' said Bobby. 'Of course.'

He stopped a taxi outside Chase Manhattan and gave the driver

Flic's address in Mission. She'd done a good job of removing most of the vomit in the restroom but by the time Bobby and Flic arrived at Valencia Street, the driver was wrinkling his nose and casting glances at his mirror.

'Take a shower,' Bobby told Flic, helping her out of the cab. 'Rinse your hair and skin, then rinse them again. Put your shirt through a hot wash and take your uniform here . . .' Pulling a pen from his jacket, Bobby scrawled the address of a dry cleaners onto the back of a restaurant card and gave it to Flic. 'They'll know what to do.'

'How do you know about them?'

Good question. 'I've been fully briefed,' said Bobby.

'Yeah, right.' Flic's smile was sad.

At the front door, Bobby nodded. His way of saying she should go inside now.

'Are you going back to the crime scene?'

Any chance Bobby had of answering ended when the door in front of him opened and a small woman glared out. Whatever the woman had been about to say died to a scowl when she saw Bobby.

'*Senora Valdez.*'

The woman's nod was abrupt.

'Your daughter needs a bath, a warm drink and sleep.' Stepping back, Bobby steered Flic through the door and saw something between surprise and sour amusement light the old woman's face.

'She's hurt?'

'Officer Valdez has been assisting at a crime scene. It was ugly.'

The woman glanced at Flic, who looked away.

'It's Flic's job,' said Bobby.

'My daughter, Officer Valdez, Flic . . .' Mrs Valdez looked closely at the man standing next to her daughter. 'What did you say your job was?'

'*Ma . . . !*'

'You going to be okay?' Bobby asked.

Flic nodded. 'I'll have a shower, bag up my clothes.'

'And try to get some sleep,' said Bobby. 'One last thing.' He paused, wondering how to frame it. 'I meant what I said about us talking. Can I call you tomorrow?'

After a moment's thought, Flic nodded to that too.

CHAPTER 39

Tuesday 9 March

Early next morning Bobby walked down to the school on Runyon Drive to see if Kris was still handing out leaflets at the gate.

She wasn't.

A dozen SUVs drew up and decanted neatly uniformed children onto the sidewalk under the gaze of their mothers and Gregos Georgiou, the security guard Bobby had talked to the week before. When Kris finally arrived, it was on foot and the gate was in the process of being shut. On the other side, pupils were filing through an arch in near silence. Runyon Drive was proud of producing more than mere results. Bobby's father had hated the place.

'Can't talk,' Kris said.

'I know.' Bobby gestured at the teacher waiting impatiently. 'You're late.'

Kris's mouth twisted. 'No,' she said. 'Not that. I mean I'm not meant to talk to you at all.'

'Who said?'

'Ellen . . .' Kris was the only girl Bobby knew who called her mother by her first name. Weird as it seemed, Ellen liked it.

'Did your mother say why?'

The teacher was moving towards them now, irritation turning to concern as she noticed that Bobby had his hand on Kris's arm, holding her in place.

'It matters,' Bobby said. 'We need to talk about your dad.'

'Pete Sanchez doesn't think you knew Dad at all,' said Kris. 'He told Ellen, but I overheard . . .'

It was horrifying just how much damage a child with sensitive ears and a soft tread could do to herself listening at doors. They'd seen a child psychologist about it once and she'd said Kris needed to be included in what was going on; given some of the shit that was happening, neither Ellen nor Bobby thought that a particularly good idea.

'Believe me,' said Bobby. 'I knew him as well as anyone.' Letting go of Kris's wrist just as the teacher reached them, Bobby gave Kris a card with his phone number and new address scrawled on the back. 'Call me,' he said. 'Any time.'

'Is there a problem?'

Bobby looked at the woman. Confident clothes, confident hair, nervous eyes. 'No,' he said. 'Everything's just dandy.'

Kris smiled.

Despite its hills, San Francisco was a city made for walking. A city where winter meant a mere dip in temperature and trees never really withered to reveal hard choices beneath. No snow simplified the skyline or reduced traffic to a halt, only the fogs, which could roll in off the Pacific and drop the temperature by twenty degrees in half as many minutes gave San Francisco's weather any edge at all. The city had history, location and climate on its side – and yet the place still felt temporary.

Having been destroyed in one earthquake, the city had seen its freeways ripped down in another and was busy awaiting a third; for all its climate, beauty and obvious affluence everyone living here existed on the edge of permanent uncertainty. Obvious really, Bobby realised.

Nothing personal.

The Begley House was wood-framed and grey-painted, an octagonal turret set in the left corner to match the turret on the right corner of the house behind. It had been built for Theodore Begley, a sugar importer and tobacco merchant whose father was one of the few to realise what damage the transcontinental railway would do to trade in the city. While others celebrated the hammering of the final spike, Theodore's father was busy buying up factories on the East Coast, ready to undercut not only himself but also his friends.

The house his son built had a huge hall, reception room and dining room, seven bedrooms, two bathrooms and a small garden cut into Tamsin Hill and supported with field stone walls. Almost all of the original fixtures were still in place and this had been reflected in the rental price. So no one at the real estate office was that surprised to receive notification of interest from New York. What did surprise them was the speed at which Morgan Cabot wanted to close the deal.

A glossy brochure produced by the agents stressed location and history, the fact Begley House could be found in almost every guide-book, along with the story of how it survived not only the 1905 earth-quake but the devastating fire which followed, a blaze so spectacular that Mrs Thomas Begley took her family on a picnic just to watch.

The man who climbed the wooden steps to the front door of Begley House and unlocked a seven-lever Chubb had rented the place for an entirely different reason. The house backed onto Tamsin Steps, and would have been within sight of Dr Persikov's house, had it been permissible to cut down a couple of trees originally planted by Mrs Thomas Begley to protect her privacy.

In renting the house, Bobby suspected he was also making a state-ment, and at some point, when he had more time, he'd have to work out just what that statement was trying to say. Meanwhile, two carrier bags of junk, a couple of empty suitcases and a delivery of groceries from Dean & Deluca represented Bobby's total attempt to take posses-sion of the house.

A coffee, shower and blueberry muffin later, Bobby cut through the terraced area itemised as a courtyard in the particulars for Begley House and reached a rusting gate. The gate locked off a path that ran from the house through to Tamsin Steps, the result of Thomas Begley's decision to retain a narrow strip of land when selling the bulk of his garden for use as a building plot in 1928.

If the particulars were to be believed, the gate was all that remained of the original wrought iron commissioned by Theodore Begley at the behest of his wife. They were very complete particulars, but then Begley House was a very expensive property, even for this area of San Francisco.

The hinges creaked less than Bobby expected when he unlocked the gate using a key he'd found in the pantry. He knew it was the right key because a brown cardboard label was attached, reading, *garden gate*. The writing had faded and was somewhere between elegant and spidery.

Pushing his way through undergrowth, Bobby found himself skirting the edge of Dr Persikov's garden, and from there it was a quick squeeze between rose bushes to enter the garden itself. White-painted walls and tall wooden shutters. Someone had replanted the flower bed beneath the dining-room window that Bobby remembered only as mud and glass. A bench had been moved and hedges cut back.

No clues remained that this had been the site of a killing.

'Can I help you?'

The woman's voice was raw and though the words were polite enough, her eyes said, *what do you want?*

It was Ozzie, the gardener Bobby had seen raking up leaves when Flic brought Natalie out to the house so the child could show Bobby how she'd held the gun. The one she'd barely been able to lift, but somehow managed to fire three times without breaking her wrists.

'I've recently moved in next door . . .'

Silence.

'So I thought I'd pay my respects to Dr Persikov.' It was an old-fashioned way of putting it, but something about the silence and the rose garden made this place timeless.

'He's not home.'

'Okay,' said Bobby. 'I'll come back later.'

'He doesn't see anyone.'

As Bobby turned to go, the woman stepped in front of him. 'It might be best if you went the other way,' she said, nodding towards Tamsin Steps.

The rest of that afternoon Bobby wasted on paperwork. However, since almost everything he did was on screen, this was probably no longer the right way to describe it.

Having logged in to Morgan Cabot, Bobby shuffled money between accounts, switching $3,000,000 from deposit to current. He paid off everything on his Amex, cancelled the card and ordered a new one from a rival bank, then he got on line to Niffenger and Sutcliffe to draw up a will. It was very simple and this simplicity was cowardice not strength. He'd have liked to work out what he really wanted to happen if he suddenly didn't wake one morning or his body went back to the mindless sinew and muscle it had been before he had inhabited it.

Only every attempt to work this out resulted in such a blinding headache that in the end Bobby left everything he possessed to Kit. No reasons and no explanations. The last thing he wanted was his will overturned in the name of insanity.

It was late when Bobby returned to the iron gate, all but one of the lights were out in the Persikov house and someone had padlocked his gate from the other side. Bobby wasted a few seconds wondering if this was a warning and then decided to treat it as a challenge instead.

Either the cutters he found were not nearly as rusty as they looked or the lock was cheap, because one snip dropped a now-useless chunk of metal into the leaves at Bobby's feet. Dr Persikov's house was now in total darkness. Not even a single light to break the intricate black of its fretwork silhouette. In fact, the whole place could have been cut and pasted onto a cheap poster of the city at night.

'Get a grip,' Bobby told himself. Only the voice in his head sounded like his grandfather.

'While you're there,' said Bobby. 'Tell me about the *Jinwei hu*. Was the fox real?'

His grandfather shut up after that.

How had the burglar entered the rose garden? Entering from Tamsin Steps would mean using the wrought-iron gate at the front. Obviously enough, it had been open that time Bobby walked into the garden after talking to Natalie. Which was fine, but Dr Persikov's statement said it had been securely locked on the afternoon of the killing.

This way then? The Begley House had been empty. SecureGuard had been employed to protect the property but it would have been easy enough to work out the times of day their driver came by. Turning around, Bobby went back to his own gate and began re-walking the path as he tried to think himself into the head of the burglar. Russian, at least his mask had been. So was the man Bobby killed in the alley behind Stockton Street, at least his trousers were; everything came down to recognising the right pattern.

The walk took him along the path, through the only gap in the hedge and out into Dr Persikov's garden, where he found himself facing the blank emptiness of the dining-room window. This had to be the way the burglar had come.

At the side of the house a ground-level hatch was padlocked through clasps that looked new. Chances were, it opened onto a coal chute leading to a cellar, but unlike the lock on the gate between gardens this one was well made and the clasp heavy.

Leaving his cutters behind a tree, Bobby went in through a window; although mindful of what had happened to the last person to try to enter that way, he stood back as he broke the window lock and took care to remain out of sight. It probably helped that the window Bobby chose was in the attic. To get there, he climbed the sycamore behind which he left the cutters, edged his way along a branch and dropped onto a walkway that ran round the top of the house. That Bobby could still get into buildings as easily as when he'd been a child was a source of obscure pride.

Dust and ashes, dead and done with . . .

A heavy-busted but headless mannequin confronted him and behind her a thinner sister, with another beyond that skinny enough to be adolescent. A lifetime of ageing captured in rotting canvas, horsehair and twine. Leather boxes along one wall made shelves for smaller boxes and random junk; the wheel of an old bicycle, an empty aquarium, a hat box labelled *Steffl – Vienna*.

Everything touched by Bobby's torch looked abandoned and there were dust planets enough in the air to make him want to sneeze. Creeping towards a thin sliver of light, Bobby knelt, then lowered himself onto his stomach. The floor on which he lay consisted of planking put down over joists, but it was through a crack in the lath and plaster under this that Bobby looked into the room below. And having looked, he swiftly glanced away.

The sight of Natalie Persikov in a nightdress made Bobby feel intrusive enough. Worse still was the fact that the child was on her knees at the edge of her bed, praying. Silent words twisted her lips and the whole weight of the world seemed to rest on her bony shoulders. She didn't look like a child coping surprisingly well with unexpected trauma (the verdict of a court-appointed psychiatrist). She looked like a child staring into the open door of hell.

Steps led down from the attic and Bobby trod these carefully, although he knew, just from the look on the child's face, how deep Natalie was in her own misery. It would take more than his silent tread on the steps to free her.

The bathroom next to her room was in darkness. A child's collection of soaps and bottles arranged neatly in a line. Next door to this was a guest room, empty except for a china doll sat against a pillow, legs to the front and arms crossed neatly.

At the other end of Natalie Persikov's landing were more bedrooms. Bobby checked these quietly, because the old slept badly and sometimes so did the young, and while he knew the girl was still awake, he was guessing midnight would be enough to see the old man asleep in bed. And so the house revealed itself slowly, in tiny pools of light: a snatch of tapestry in the beam of a pencil torch; a painting of a large woman in Victorian clothes; a grandfather clock on a half landing, its numbers faded to memories of themselves and its tick irritated and slightly erratic.

About halfway down the stairs Bobby met the bit of the house he remembered. Although, obviously enough, back then he'd been coming at it from a different direction, much like everything else really.

So what did he hope to achieve?

He'd spent the past few days stirring up a hornets' nest, upsetting Sanchez, getting in the old man's face and making himself worse than unpopular with Flic, whose only sin was to have allowed herself to like him.

And what was his answer?

There was the problem, because Bobby didn't have one. What he had was what he'd always had, a small knot at the centre of his gut to tell him Tamsin Steps was what mattered and the kid on her knees, praying to a God he personally doubted was real, held the key to what went on.

Somewhere in this ossified shrine to privilege had to be the reason Ibrahim Nasra died, his cut throat and open bowels testament to someone's anger. As did the reason why Natalie Persikov was lost in tears and prayer, Carlos Nero was dead, and Lucifer the crack cat had lost his owner, protector and dealer all in one go. Add to that the reason Bobby got shot through the guts, and for all Bobby knew, the reason he woke in the body of Robert Vanberg.

Snapping on his torch, Bobby lit hardwood floor at his feet and began to push open a door.

'Come in.'

The voice was enough to make Bobby hesitate.

'You can turn on a lamp,' said the voice. 'If you wish.' A silhouette sat at one end of the dining table, backlit by city lights breaking through uncurtained windows. It didn't get up, although its head turned towards Bobby as he stepped into the room.

'The switch is on the side.'

Flicking on his torch, Bobby swept the area to find the lamp in question. As he did so, his beam caught the silver of an icon on the wall above the lamp, Virgin with Christ – only it wasn't, was it? Instead of the sullen Madonna which had been there on Bobby's previous visit there was a Christos, eyes raised to heaven. The silver frame, however, looked identical.

'What?' demanded the silhouette.

As Bobby's torch switched from frame to table, it caught the ruined face of the old man sat in a tall wooden chair. White bearded and stern, tragic with lines and leavened with a twist to the lips and a half turn to the head, it looked as if Dr Persikov was listening intently.

Which it turned out he was.

The man's eyes had been cooked to the white of lightly boiled egg, with no pupils that Bobby could see. Although his hearing obviously remained acute, because he was following the footsteps, as Bobby walked from the small sideboard where he'd found the lamp, around the long dining table to where the man sat at its head, his chair pulled back from the edge. A notebook stood open in front of the doctor, while a pencil lay to one side.

Bobby wondered whether to mention that this pencil had been worn down to the wood, then decided the old man probably knew and, besides, it didn't really matter. He was hardly about to read back whatever he'd been scratching into a blank page.

'You're Misha Persikov?' asked Bobby, already knowing the answer.

'What do you think . . . ?'

It was fear not anger that put sharpness into the old man's voice. Fear kept resolutely in check.

'I knew you'd come,' he said.

'You did?'

'Have you any idea how many years I've been waiting?'

Bobby said nothing and the old man snorted, his disgust sharpening his courage.

'Of course you haven't. It's just another job to you. Another mess cleaned up with the minimum of fuss. I'll say that for the little colonel. He keeps things neat. The best in his line always were bookkeepers. You should have seen Beria . . .'

The old man sat back in his seat and raised his head. His face when he turned it to Bobby was magnificently defiant.

'Do it then,' he said. 'Do it cleanly and then leave. At least give me that.'

'What about the girl?'

Utter stillness. 'Which girl?' said Dr Persikov finally.

'The one in her room upstairs.'

'If you've hurt her . . .'

'Natalie's praying,' said Bobby. 'On her bare knees, in tears, like

241

her life depended on it. You want to tell me what she's praying for?'

'*You ask me that?*'

'Yes,' Bobby said. 'I ask you that.'

'Have you no imagination, no soul? How do you think it feels to be a child and kill someone?' A hollow look had entered the old man's face. 'God knows, I'm not the one to talk about what should or should not be forgiven; and I can forgive your colonel almost anything,' said Dr Persikov. 'Even sending a second person to murder me. But never that.'

'Not what?' Bobby said.

'Forcing Natalie to kill. I would rather you'd succeeded the first time than she be forced to live with that.'

It took five minutes for Bobby to persuade Dr Persikov that he was not there to murder the old man and even then, from the half turn to the head and the way Dr Persikov's body stiffened every time Bobby's chair creaked, he doubted the old man quite believed him.

'So,' said Dr Persikov, when Bobby had repeated his promises for the sixth time. 'If you're not here to kill me . . . why are you here?' The way Dr Persikov said this made clear that he regarded the idea of someone being there to kill him as perfectly normal and anything else as unlikely.

'Tell me about the night Natalie shot the burglar.' Bobby demanded.

So Dr Persikov did.

CHAPTER 40

Wednesday 10 March

'Grandpa . . .' It was what she always called him. So it was what Natalie called him that evening. 'Are you awake?'

She used *my grandfather* when talking about him at school to avoid being teased. There were teachers who thought he was her father but they were wrong, she'd asked the old man and he'd said this was untrue.

The old man sat in a leather chair even more ancient than he was. It had been made for the person who originally built this house and its battered red hide matched the scruffy inset to the desk at which he sat listening to Shostakovich. Symphony number seven from the sound of it.

'Of course I'm awake.'

Watching her grandfather drag himself back to the here and now, Natalie wondered where he went when he sat at that desk for hours, notebook and worn-out pencil on the red leather in front of him. She didn't ask permission, simply walked over to the old record player and lifted its arm from the plastic circle.

'Are you all right?'

Now was when she was meant to say yes, because that was what she always answered, anything else worried him. 'No,' said Natalie, 'I'm not.'

Maybe he really could hear tears fall because his face looked different when he turned towards her. 'What happened?' he said.

'I shot someone.'

It sounded so cold. So unbelievable.

'You . . . shot . . . someone?' His words were slow, with fear filling the gap between each one.

'Yes,' said Natalie.

It was the break in her voice which convinced the old man. Usually he would have said, *come here*, and she would have let him run his fingers across her face to read her emotions from whatever he found there. This time it was the old man who stood up and steered himself towards the child by the sound of her sniffing, and when he reached out he already knew what he was going to find . . .

'Why?' demanded Dr Persikov.

Even the slightest kindness would have tipped the child over the edge into full-blown hysterics, so he held back. Anything else would have been cruelty.

'He was trying to break in . . .' said Natalie, dragging a hand across her eyes. 'He'd smashed a window and was climbing . . .'

'Where did this happen?'

'In the dining room.'

Dr Persikov didn't ask where she found a gun because he already knew the answer to that. He kept an old Soviet revolver in a drawer in the kitchen. It was an old habit and old habits died hard.

'We'll tell the police I did it,' he announced.

'They wouldn't believe you.'

And beneath his fingertips Dr Persikov felt the slightest shake of her head. The tears were drying and iron entering her soul, he could feel it as surely as he could feel his heart flutter in his chest and his body draw breath.

Dr Persikov slapped the child.

It was enough. Ice turned to anger in her veins and when Natalie slapped back she hit so hard she almost managed to land her blow. Holding the child's wrists, Dr Persikov felt her anger rage and then die. She would never forgive him for that slap, but he had protected her from a horror she could barely imagine. The shrivelling of her conscience.

'We'll tell them it was me,' he repeated.

'No,' said Natalie, voice firm. 'We won't. They won't believe you. We'll tell them the truth . . .' For the first time she stumbled over her words. 'I'll call them now,' she said, and left the room before he could object.

'I thought your statement said you were asleep when she went upstairs?'

244

'It did.' Dr Persikov's tone made it obvious he regarded lying to the SFPD as a minor matter. 'It seemed cleaner that way.'

'So you believe Natalie shot the intruder?'

Blank eyes, white beard and a ruined face, Bobby had the man's full attention. It was like watching God plead.

'Are you saying she didn't?'

'We'll get back to that,' said Bobby, looking around the room. It was elegant and displayed such restrained good taste that those who didn't understand such things might have thought it shabby. What interested Bobby was the icon in the far corner. Actually, what really interested him was the frame. This was made from beaten silver, gone almost black with age and set with stones which looked like agate but might be much more valuable.

Last time Bobby had been here, that frame had housed a sullen-faced Madonna, the one later found at Midas Imperial, while Flic was still getting over being sick. Now it housed the sad-eyed Christ he'd caught in his torch beam on entering this room, with the blackened silver drapes making up the inner edge of the frame fitted the figure perfectly, in a way they never had for the Madonna and Child.

The icon was lighter than Bobby expected and he'd been right about the stones . . . They were something more than agate, rubies even. Anyone else would have had an elaborate alarm system linked to the picture. Dr Persikov had it hanging from a single nail.

'This is the icon that was stolen?'

Bobby put it carefully in the old man's hands and watched fingers brush its surface, tracing the lines of a cloak and the three-quarter silver circle of a halo.

'It wasn't stolen,' said Dr Persikov.

'Maybe not,' said Bobby, remembering the statement to which the old man's hand had apparently needed guiding, though his signature was firm enough.

Dr Misha Persikov.

'You also said it was police sirens which woke you. And, according to a statement from the first officer on the scene, you were in such shock he had to help you downstairs . . .'

'A good officer,' said Dr Persikov. 'Very thorough.'

Not Bobby's opinion of the man.

'When did you discover the icon was stolen?'

Dr Persikov sighed. 'It wasn't stolen,' he said. 'I got that wrong.

When I asked the officer if the icon was there he said, *What icon?* So I panicked. Natalie found it outside the window later, under a bush. That was when I called the SFPD and told them I was wrong, it wasn't missing . . .'

The old man paused to think about something. As he thought, his head turned a little to one side. 'Should I know who you are?' he asked finally.

'No,' said Bobby.

'Good . . . So much doesn't make sense any more. And you're really not here to kill me?'

'I'm not going to kill you,' said Bobby. 'That doesn't mean someone else won't. Tell me more about the icon.'

'Fifteenth century,' said Dr Persikov, 'possibly by Andrei Rublev. At least that's how it was catalogued in seventeen seventy-three, for Gregory Orloff . . . Catherine the Great's lover,' he added, hearing Bobby's unspoken question. 'It disappeared in nineteen-nineteen, during the Revolution and was found again in Vladivostok eighteen years later.'

Something in Dr Persikov's voice said the story was more complicated than this, but then, as Bobby was coming to realise, all stories were more complicated than this. His own apparently involved a nine-tailed fox, a daughter who didn't recognise him and a blind doctor who expected death on a daily basis and still believed Natalie was all that had stood between him and this happening.

'Describe the icon,' Bobby said.

Poached eyes turned in his direction and the ruined face became thoughtful. Dr Persikov was looking for danger, maybe searching for a trap inside that question. 'It's a Christ,' he said finally. 'Absolutely traditional . . .'

'So it's not a Madonna?'

The old man stroked the ornate frame on his lap, fingers retracing the silver folds of cloth which fell around the shoulders of the figure. 'Of course not,' he said. 'How could it be?'

Good question. Which didn't change the fact the last time Bobby saw it the figure behind those intricate silver folds had been female.

'So,' said Bobby, 'Natalie found it?'

Dr Persikov nodded.

'You're sure?' said Bobby. 'Natalie and not your gardener . . . ?'

'What gardener?' Dr Persikov said.

*

The fox came again that night. Walking through a wall into Bobby's bedroom like some bad CIA thought experiment. It shook itself dry and began to stalk around Bobby's room, examining the bed and looking at two paintings hung beside the door. It seemed particularly interested in a Dulac watercolour of a naked girl.

Nine tails flowed behind the animal like flame, and so fast did these flicker that Bobby found it impossible to know if there really were nine of them or if there was just one tail that was always in nine places at once.

In the fox's eyes were the stars and its breath was the rattle of rain upon the tiles of a roof. When it spoke it was with the dry growl of Bobby's grandfather, although its mouth never moved.

'So,' it said, 'what did that tell you?'

'That Professor Persikov doesn't remember hiring a gardener,' said Bobby, sitting up in bed.

The fox shrugged. 'Men get old,' it said. 'Get old, get vague, then die.' Its eyes were sly when it said this. Celestial foxes were not always to be trusted. His grandfather had told Bobby that.

'All right,' said Bobby. 'The icons have been switched around.'

Jinwei hu shrugged again. 'Slightly better . . . What else?'

'I think I'm falling in love with someone.'

'*Someone?*' Its laugh was abrupt, like the slam of a car door.

'Flic,' said Bobby. 'I think I'm falling in love with Flic.' He looked at the fox. 'That's not meant to happen, is it?'

The fox shrugged one final time. 'What would I know?' it said. 'You're writing the script. Have you told this girl about me?'

'A little,' said Bobby. 'Not much . . .' After that, the *jinwei hu* ignored Bobby for a while and spent the best part of a minute examining three Persian carpets, two on one side of the bed, one on the other, all of which carried variations on a tree of life.

'Costly,' it said, 'what else?'

It took Bobby a moment to work out what the fox was asking. 'Beautiful,' he said finally. 'Beautiful, costly and very intricate.'

'Also flawed,' said the fox.

'Isn't everything?' asked Bobby.

The fox grinned. 'Much better. Are you intending to keep this house?'

Looking around at the dark wood and Victorian furniture, Bobby

247

tried to imagine himself growing old among the trappings of wealth. Dinner parties at the long walnut table downstairs. Meetings with local dignitaries in the gilded drawing room with its ornate furniture, polished floor and French chandelier. No matter how hard he tried to summon up the images they refused to come.

'No,' Bobby said. 'I guess not.'

'Right answer,' said the fox.

It left with the clang of a window and claws like the scuttle of rats across an attic floor. 'Keep thinking of all the things you need to know,' it told Bobby, turning back, although by then it was little more than a flicker of flaming tails across the inside of Bobby's eyelids. 'And remember how little time you have left.'

When Bobby woke he was drenched in sweat and his teeth hurt from where he'd had them clenched. A window was open in the corridor outside his bedroom door; although there was no sign it had been forced, no clue that anyone had entered Begley House and nothing seemed to be missing.

Rain had soaked dark patches into a strip of carpet. If Bobby squinted hard and looked at them sideways, he could almost imagine the tracks of a large animal.

Walking naked back to his room, Bobby stopped by a mirror. The man who stared back was no longer a stranger. The face was familiar and even the eyes, sleep deprived and hollow, failed to raise their usual shiver.

He did, however, look terrible.

Sweat had darkened his hair still further, slicking it to his skull. He could smell the fear on himself, sour like stale sweat. His heart was hard in his chest, unforgiving in its rhythm. And then Bobby realised something else. He had seen the fox twice and, this time, when he saw the fox he had seen its reflection. Things had to exist before they could reflect, unless he'd merely dreamed the reflection too.

Each time you see a fox it takes a little of your soul. His grandfather had also told him that. A thousand years of knowledge is hard to look in the eyes. Especially when those eyes reflect all the stars in the night sky.

If the fox came a third time it would not leave Bobby behind when it went. *So little time, so much that he needed to know . . .* Was that all Bobby was meant to take from his dream?

CHAPTER 41
Wednesday 10 March

Purple skies hung over the Bay and the sycamores had begun to talk to each other in the way trees always did. A kind of dry whispering like an argument between librarians.

Hunkering down behind a bush, Louie dropped her trousers and did her best to ignore what the trees were saying. Other people saw ghosts but Louie heard them, it was one of the reasons she smoked crystal meth. Actually she smoked almost anything, even though she'd told Colonel Billy's friend she didn't. Louie guessed he knew she lied.

Whatever she'd had for breakfast, heating it on foil and sucking smoke direct into her hungry mouth, had been sold as meth. Quite possibly it was. Some days it got hard to tell.

Five in the morning, according to the watch Louie wore; but then it was always either five in the morning or late afternoon, because five was the only time her watch told and Louie was fine with that. She liked early morning, because no one else was around, and five in the afternoon was good because people were on their way home and sometimes that made them happy enough to give her money.

Pulling up her lycra trousers, Louie kicked dirt over a curl of shit and straightened her top. She wiped her fingers on grass and once her hands were clean, she splashed water on her face to clear sleep from her eyes and then set fire to another rock.

It was the cat's turn to have breakfast, although Louie took a little of the smoke for herself. In the rush of blood which followed the trees stopped talking, the sky ran through purple into black, the tree beneath which she sat shimmered a little and then the rush was done.

'Okay?' Louie asked.

Lucifer grinned.

People were friendlier to Louie now she had a cat tucked between her tits, with its head poking from the neck of her shirt. Even tourists, who'd yet to master that trick which allowed most of San Francisco to banish the homeless to the realm of ghosts and so had to work harder to render people like Louie invisible . . . even they laughed and nodded.

One, a middle-aged man in T-shirt, pearl earring and black jeans had pulled $100 from his pocket and then hesitated, trapped between impulse and embarrassment. Unless he'd just been trapped by the contrast between Louie's perfect body and the scars which uglied up her arms like notches on a stick.

'Thank you,' she said.

That had been his cue to hand over the $100 note.

Louie was impressed; mostly by the fact the man had pulled the note straight from his pocket instead of from a wallet or a money belt. In Louie's experience, you had to be her to have quite that contempt for the stuff.

So now she was dodging ghostly whispers and wondering when the sky began to turn turquoise and open out to reveal sunbeams. Louie wasn't stupid, she knew the sunbeams belonged on the ceiling of a church in Mission, and she didn't mind organ music in her head either, because both were better than the time she saw herself born, in a bloody and squalling bundle as the sky slit open, bled a bit and then died.

'*Stay off the brown acid* . . .' Louie was never quite sure what Colonel Billy meant by that, but he was probably right. Letting her sleep on his pitch, he'd protected her that night. Sat guard as she curled up next to a wall, so no one could get to her while the shakes were on and she was too upset to protect herself.

Colonel Billy said he didn't sleep that much anyway.

Of course, Lucifer was different then, older and less dark. All of Colonel Billy's cats carried the same name and he always insisted they were the same animal but she knew they weren't.

Louie had found the colonel his last kitten, this one. She'd found it in a squat and gone to get colonel Billy, and though they'd discussed telling the police about the three bodies, Colonel Billy decided not; someone would discover them eventually. Anyway, *discuss* was not really a word one used of Colonel Billy. He spoke and sometimes he made sense to others and sometimes he made sense to himself and sometimes he made no sense to either. Louie guessed that was true for everyone.

All the same, he'd been good to her and she didn't want to let him down. So she was doing what the colonel's friend had asked and talking to those on the streets. This was not as easy as it sounded. Particularly when dealing with someone like Volks.

Louie was in two minds about the Volks. Personally she thought he wouldn't last the winter, such as it was, but she'd been thinking that for five years now and this suggested she was wrong; although every time Louie met the boy she felt she was about to be proved right.

'You okay?'

Silly question really.

The kid with the dog on a string looked up from his pitch next to an ATM machine and prepared to be affronted. 'This is . . .'

'I don't want your pitch,' Louie said. 'And keep that ugly animal away from my cat.'

'Not ugly,' Volks said. 'Not your cat.' He took another look at the black kitten peering from the top of Louie's lycra T-shirt. 'Belongs to . . .'

'Did,' Louie said, dropping to a crouch. 'The colonel's dead.' If they were seen sitting like that by the SFPD they'd be in trouble. Two street people sat next to a cash machine counted as aggravated begging. It said so in *Street News*.

'How?' asked Volks. You could say that for him. He never wasted words on questions or anything much else.

'Don't know.'

Now she was doing the same. Louie shook her head in disgust. 'He's gone all right. A suit told me.' She'd been a suit once; or almost, back before. 'Said I should look after Lucifer. And he wants me to keep a look out for . . .'

'Dead babies,' said Volks.

Louie stared at him.

'The colonel told me. Look for dead babies. He'd give me food for every one I found and now he's dead.' Volks sat back, as if he'd just used up a week's worth of words, which he probably had. But Louie was interested in something else.

'You found one?'

Looking around him, Volks shrugged and dragged the dog closer. 'Might have done,' he said. A spider's web of new tattoo encased one elbow and Louie wondered if Volks knew what it meant. Double rape, male and female. She hoped not.

'I can still get you food,' said Louie. 'If you tell me where you found it . . .' When the suit had included dead babies in his list of things she should ask about, Louie had thought he was just being weird. Good clothes didn't mean you weren't weird. They just meant most people didn't notice.

'Well,' said Volks, 'it wasn't me exactly . . .'

Louie sighed.

'Not just one, either.'

'How many?' Louie asked.

'Zephyr found them,' said Volks, using up another week's worth of words. 'Out beyond the bridge. Hundreds. Got no heads . . .'

Plain-clothes police and private guards walk the Golden Gate Bridge, charged with stopping suicides from jumping into the Bay below. You can look hard without finding that piece of information in a guidebook. Some are men, some women, their age varies and the whole point, of the plain-clothes ones at least, is that they look just like everyone else.

So Volks and Louie took care to look happy and smile at everyone who glanced at them, and they got a lot of glances.

That was how the guards judged it, you see, by the expression on the face of the person they thought might jump; although if you put your bags on the ground and began climbing that would give it away too. Then the only problem was that running towards people to stop them jumping usually made them jump. It wasn't trained officers who ran at jumpers, it was everybody else.

All the tourists trying to do a good deed.

Weird really how it worked. The biggest attraction in San Francisco was as much an aid to suicide as a free plastic bag, free rubber band and a typed set of instructions.

That was what Louie told Volks anyway, as the two of them walked across the bridge, smiling brightly at everyone they met. Committees kept wanting to put up barriers, she added. Only the city kept turning the suggestion down.

'How far?'

'Long way,' said Volks. Further questioning resulted in the boy picking up his dog and striding ahead.

CHAPTER 42

Wednesday 10 March

'You've got a message,' said Flic.

She stood in the door of Begley House and behind her, parked kitty corner to the gates, stood an SFPD cruiser, siren silent but lights still flashing. Across the road half a dozen curtains twitched in the early morning sun.

'I've got a . . .'

'Message,' said Flic, holding out a twist of paper.

'Who from?'

'How would I know?' Stopping herself, Flic held up one hand in apology and took a deep breath. Whatever, she wasn't finding talking to Bobby easy. 'The lieutenant told me to bring it out here.' Flic's voice made clear what she thought about that.

'I'm sorry.'

'No problem,' said Flic. 'It's my job.'

'That's not what I mean,' Bobby said, 'and you know it.' Then he took a look at Flic and realised that she didn't know it at all. 'Come in,' he said. She was about to refuse, so Bobby pointed out that the message might need a reply.

The smashed Mexican glass stood in pieces on a tiled window sill in the kitchen. A couple of Chinese bowls rested on a marble work surface beneath. The room stank of last night's take-out and one pair of wooden chopsticks still floated in the washing up water. Although what Flic saw was the brushed steel cooker and huge walk-in fridge.

'Shit,' said Flic. 'You own this stuff?'

'Renting it,' Bobby said. 'They come with the house.'

'The White House pays for this?'

'I don't work for the White House,' said Bobby, then stopped. 'Fuck it,' he said. 'I'd really like to tell you the truth . . .'

'Yeah, so Felipe said.' Flic's voice was cutting. 'Only then you'd have to kill me . . .' She handed Bobby a twist of newspaper and, looking more closely, he saw an origami swan.

'Who delivered this?'

'A boy with a dog on a rope. He said he was working for you and wanted money.'

'What happened?'

'The lieutenant gave him twenty dollars . . .' If Flic found that surprising she did her best to hide the fact. 'I'm to tell you Lieutenant Que expects to be repaid.'

'Sure.' Bobby nodded, his attention already elsewhere. The swan had fragments about changes to the law regarding street people on one wing and bits from an advertisement for a co-op food warehouse on the other. Unwrapping the swan, Bobby found a crude sketch across part of the advertisement.

'What does that look like to you?'

'A map,' said Flic, having taken the scrap of paper. 'Does that say what I think it says?'

'Yeah,' said Bobby. '*Dead Babies.*'

'You know,' Flic said, 'I'm not sure any of us needs to know why you're here after all . . .'

It had taken Louie a good twenty minutes to draw the map and she almost came to blows with Volks over how far they were from the road.

In the end, to stop things getting ugly, they'd walked from the pines back to the twisting road while Louie counted the steps, and from the road back to the pines, with Volks counting, and finally, they made a third trip with them both counting aloud.

Five thousand paces made nearly three miles. And this was up and down, through bushes and over a fence with *Keep Out* written in red letters.

'Car,' said Louie, when a blue and white cruiser pulled into a parking area down below. Lucifer said nothing, just purred.

'Right,' said Flic, killing the engine. 'This should be it . . .'

Yanking on the handbrake, she pushed open her car door. A pale blue sea and dark rocks to one side. A slope of scrub and thorn to the other. They'd travelled without flashing lights or siren, Bobby having already put in a call to the local sheriff to say he'd be passing through. Probably due to a misunderstanding, the deputy came away from that conversation with the idea that Bobby was some sightseeing bigwig, the kind of man to use an SFPD officer as his personal chauffeur.

The view was spectacular. So Bobby made a point of staring out towards Alcatraz before turning to sweep the newly bought binoculars across the hills behind him.

'Up behind the rock,' he said. 'I can see Louie.'

Flic and Bobby climbed in the direction Bobby indicated and kept climbing, slopes leading to ridges and sudden dips which rose to slopes beyond. The headlands formed their own miniature mountain range but, by the time he was halfway there, Bobby felt as if he was facing something grander.

'You all right?'

He was gasping for breath, Bobby realised.

'Sure, I'm fine . . .'

Every time he looked Louie seemed to be the same distance away, so Bobby stopped looking and concentrated on climbing, until finally he reached the basalt outcrop. By which time his breath was ragged and Louie furious, her back to the rock as she stared crossly at Flic.

'She's a good friend,' said Bobby, dropping to his knees. It took Flic a moment to realise the man meant her.

Louie was right. The sign on the fence did say *Keep Out* . . . It also said *Private* . . . *Armed Patrols* . . . And, at the bottom, in much smaller letters, *Orloff Industries*. The best that could be said about the sign was that it was very old. So old in fact that it was made from enamel. Some of this had chipped at the corners, revealing cheap steel and smears of rust where wires tied the sign to the fence.

'First thing,' said Louie. 'You gave Volks his money, right?'

'I didn't see him myself,' Bobby replied. 'But he got his money.'

'Good. Sergeant Zha promised.'

That got Flic's attention, although whatever she was about to say got lost when Louie kicked the fence.

'Dead babies through here,' Louie said, lifting a section of mesh. 'You'd better come see.'

'How many dead babies?' asked Bobby.

'Um . . .' Louie thought about it. 'Hundred, two hundred. Dead everything,' she said. 'Really smells.' The way Volks spoke seemed to have rubbed off on her.

'We ought to make this official,' said Flic, sounding worried. She was already reaching for her radio when Bobby touched his hand to her wrist.

'It is official,' he said. 'You're here.'

'All the same, we should tell the Marin County sheriff . . .'

'No,' said Bobby. 'We shouldn't.'

'Are you willing to take responsibility for that decision?'

Bobby thought about his call to Washington, the fake cards in his wallet and the deal he'd reached with Lieutenant Que. About a nine-tailed fox stalking out of the darkness and the fact Bobby was pretty sure he was dying. 'Yeah,' he said. 'I guess I am.'

Ahead of them was low scrub and what began as path faded like mist in the sun and finally vanished altogether, leaving Bobby, Louie and Flic pushing their way through new bracken and treading down flowers. The air was warm, birds could be heard in the poison oak and eucalyptus around them. It seemed to be a morning in early March like any other until the wind changed.

Flic stumbled and stopped, one hand to her mouth.

'See,' said Louie. 'Really smells.'

'You weren't . . .' And then the process of vomiting stopped Bobby from saying much else for a while.

'Here,' said Louie, when he was done. 'Wash your mouth out.' The small black woman with the ruined face handed Bobby a bottle of water and watched him swig a mouthful and spit without even bothering to wipe the top.

'It's okay,' Louie said, seeing Bobby realise what he'd just done. 'I'm clean. Always been clean,' she added, sounding proud of herself. 'No needles and no disease. I look like this because this is the way I look.' She took back the bottle and offered it to Flic.

'Thanks,' said the officer, swilling out her own mouth and spitting into the dirt.

'You going to puke too?'

'No,' said Flic. 'I'm fine.'

'Don't look it . . .' With that, Louie tucked Lucifer slightly more tightly into her shirt, stroked the kitten to calm its fear and began to head for the stink. Leading Flic and Bobby around a strand of thorns, through something that looked like an attack of yellow bonsai and down a slope, the smell getting more cruel all the time.

'Found the first one here.' The woman pointed to a rotted patch of leaves near her feet.

'What happened to it?'

'Volks insisted on burying it. Said the thing looked too sad. Don't worry,' she added, seeing Bobby's face. 'There are plenty more . . .'

It was Flic who found the next one. 'Over here,' she said. Something about the tightness in her tone told Bobby she was on the edge of vomiting.

'Step back,' said Bobby.

'No.' Flic shook her head. 'You need to see this,' she said. 'It's got a tail.'

Pinpointing time of death can be done by insect damage or corruption, and though a number of factors can vary the rate of decay and even the behaviour of insects, nakedness is nakedness and corruption is corruption and the insect damage to the tiny figure curled at their feet was very severe indeed.

CHAPTER 43

Wednesday 10 March

Putting one hand over his nose and trying to breathe stale air from his cupped fingers, Bobby knelt next to the tiny corpse and rolled it over with a twig. This broke every rule he'd been taught, but Bobby was beyond caring and already suspected the corpse wasn't human. The eyes were too large and the face too flat, and the skin, what little remained, glistened purple and had a ripe quality that reminded him of wet leather.

'How many of the others had tails?' he asked Louie.

'All of the cats,' she said. 'All of the dogs and most of the babies, although some only had little tails. There are fresher babies over here.'

The slope down which they walked was greasy with fat leached from bodies tipped over the edge. Louie was right, the dead flesh at the top of the pile was slightly fresher than that underneath. So glutinous was the smell it stuck like jelly to the three people who halted near the bottom.

It was difficult to tell whether Flic was trying to hold back the stink or stop herself choking on blowflies clogging the air around her. 'This must be what hell is like,' she said, with a hand over her mouth.

Bobby had to agree. Holding his breath, he thrust his fingers into the slop and turned it over. At the bottom of the pile many of the animals were headless and a few had been gutted. All of the bottom layer had been skinned and some, the messier ones, looked as if it might have been done when they were still alive. Nearer the top, those with scraps of skin remaining had stubble where their fur should be and all had their necks broken.

'Monkeys?' said Louie, coming closer. 'You sure?'

'Absolutely certain,' said Bobby, as he stepped back and wiped his hand on grass and then wiped it again. Without anyone having to discuss their next move, Louie, Flic and Bobby began to retrace their steps to the top of the slope.

'Vivisection,' said Flic.

Bobby nodded. 'That's what I think. We need to find out who owns this land . . .'

'I can do that,' she said. 'I've got an old friend on the local force.' This was said in a voice so neutral that Bobby wondered why Flic blushed.

'What about me?' said Louie. 'What do you want me to do . . . ?'

'I need you to keep an eye on things.'

'What things?'

'Everything,' said Bobby.

Louie stared at him, her face serious. 'You know,' she said. 'That's going to take a lot of looking . . .'

One of the skinned monkeys lay in the boot, wrapped in a plastic shopping bag from Kwa Loon Supermarket, as Bobby and Flic crossed the bridge in silence. Louie had been offered a ride but refused.

'You sure?' Bobby said. 'I can drop you anywhere you want.'

'Quite sure.' The wiry black woman glanced from Flic to the SFPD cruiser. 'Here's as good as anywhere. There's stuff I've got to do.'

She caught Flic's look.

'Cold turkey,' said Louie. 'Comes to us all.'

'You're going to give up crack?'

The black woman stared at Flic as if she was mad. 'Me?' Louie said. 'I'm done with giving up.' Dragging the kitten from between her breasts, Louie held it up. 'Lucifer, now that's different. He's too young to be doing this shit.'

Complication is a matter of perception. Everyone alive has days when two simple but conflicting thoughts make matters so complicated it becomes near impossible to think logically and other days when a dozen shattered aspects of a worse problem flick by like invisible shrapnel, lost beneath the simple fact of living minute to minute.

Sometimes it's hard to recognise exactly when a problem begins or a situation changes and mostly it is already irrelevant, because by then the situation has altered beyond repair.

In retrospect, that 20:20 hindsight which passes for intuition after the event, there were three points when Bobby might have changed

259

what came next. He could have gone home alone, had a shower and sat in his new study while he thought things through. He could have gone straight to Chinatown Station with the suggestion that Lieutenant Que contact the sheriff's office in Marin County to tell him what Louie had found. And he could have decided then and there he was in too deep, called Washington and tried to get through to the general.

Or maybe there were six points . . . After all, he could have given Flic the coffee he offered instead of tightening his arms around her and returning a kiss. An hour later, when she was lying naked on his bed, he could have talked about her childhood, what books she liked and her favourite films, the things new lovers talk about in those moments after they've slept together. And after Flic was gone he could have taken a second shower and made lunch.

Simple things. Uncomplicated actions.

Instead, after lunch Bobby went to find his daughter. He went because he wanted to see Kris, although he told himself it was because Kris understood the anti-vivisection movement and he really needed to know what rumours were going round. But before all this, Bobby told Flic about the nine-tailed fox . . . Although he almost didn't.

'Say it,' Flic said.

'What?'

Climbing off him, Flic settled herself under the covers. That is, she tugged at a sheet until it came free and then wrapped herself in the thing until her body was hidden from Bobby's gaze and inaccessible to his hands.

'Say whatever it is you keep wanting to say . . .'

'That's the problem,' said Bobby, 'I don't know if I want to say it or not.' Sitting back, he settled himself against a carved headboard. It was very elegant and quite probably impossibly expensive and, like everything else in this room except for the sheet, it came with the house.

'Why don't you know?'

Bobby thought about that. 'Because,' he admitted, 'once said it can't be taken back . . . and I'm having trouble even admitting this to myself.' To Flic's credit, she gave Bobby the silence he needed to make his decision.

'It's about Sergeant Zha,' he said.

'I know.' Flic twisted round so she could see him better. 'I'd already guessed that.' Seeing Bobby's expression, she smiled, almost sadly.

'Going out to his grave to burn a paper gun wasn't exactly subtle. And then, going back to burn *bullets*, I mean, what was that all about?'

'You knew?'

'The whole bloody station knows. He worked for you, right? That's what Lieutenant Que reckons. Zha was working for some spook in Washington. All the apparent screw-ups and all those weird-shit friendships, his hanging round brothels and fixing favours for lowlifes. It all makes sense, at least, that's what people keep telling me . . .'

'Nice idea,' said Bobby. 'Only the screw-ups were for real and so was the rest of that shit. I'd love to say different.'

'But you knew him?'

Bobby shook his head. 'You know,' he said sadly. 'I'm not sure I can even say that.' Pulling his knees up under his chin, he wrapped arms around himself and thought about it. His muscles were still weak from lack of use and yet he liked this body, he liked its lack of scars and the way his mouth went up at both sides when he smiled. Mostly Bobby liked the fact there were things which could make him smile.

It was just a pity that . . . He thought last night through and decided he agreed with its conclusion. *It was just a pity that he was dying.*

'The fox came back,' said Bobby. 'It was here, last night. It walked through the wall and into this bedroom.'

Flic frowned. 'The Chinese fox?' she said finally.

'*Jinwei hu,*' said Bobby. 'The nine-tailed and celestial. It stood over there in the corner.' Bobby shook his head, almost helplessly. 'It wanted to talk about icons and carpets.'

'Why?'

'Oh shit,' said Bobby, 'because I'm Zha, okay?'

So shocked was Flic that she forgot all about her sheet and sat up, swivelling to face the man beside her, and it was Bobby who took the discarded sheet and used it to hide the darkness between Flic's thighs.

She barely noticed his movement.

'Zha's dead,' she said, then remembered something. 'You were at his funeral.'

'Mine,' said Bobby. 'You have no idea what that feels like . . .'

Whatever Flic saw in Bobby's eyes made her drop her gaze and sit back. When she looked at him again her face had settled to a mask so neutral Bobby wanted to shake her.

'Now do you realise why I haven't told anyone?' he asked bitterly.

There followed one of those awkward silences which end up almost

261

unbreakable and, just as Bobby became certain he'd lost her, Flic leant in close and ran her fingers down his face. It was a very simple gesture. Something that might be done by a mother to a beloved child or to mark a moment of understanding between first lovers.

'It's okay,' Flic said.

And then she was holding him against her and wrapping her arms around his head as he slid down and settled his mouth to one breast. 'Okay now,' said Flic, suckling him like an infant, her fingers twisting into his hair. 'You're allowed to cry.'

Darkness and the taste of salt.

Memories.

'Hey,' she said. 'That's okay.'

A stranger stalking out of the darkness. His face hard, gun in hand, flashing lights, shots. Alphonse daVilla. A sack of white crystals thrown down like a pillow. A medic, upset because things were going wrong.

'Bobby, talk to me . . .'

His hands were clutching at his chest while his breath dragged through a ragged hole where ribs should be. That had to be why he found it so hard to get his breath, the wound was still there, unseen unless one knew where to look. Dragging away his hands, Bobby examined his fingers.

No blood.

He looked again but muscle covered his ribs and pale skin covered the muscle. Bobby was up and on his feet before Flic moved, although when she did it was hard and fast. She'd learnt her lessons well.

Kicking out, Bobby fought like Colonel Billy at his worst but Flic kept her grip until his shouts turned back to sobs and he found himself naked on his knees, Flic having let go the moment he ceased to be a danger.

'Fuck,' she said. 'What was that . . . your wolverine impression?' Collecting up her uniform, Flic excused herself almost politely, leaving Bobby where he knelt on the carpet. It seemed kindest and Robert Van Berg, or whoever he was, looked to her like a man in extreme need of kindness, not to mention a psychiatrist.

Unless, of course . . .

Pulling on her bra and knickers, Flic shrugged herself back into a shirt that still stank of sweat and death, stepped into her uniform trousers and put on socks, tied her shoes and buckled her belt with unthinking fingers, checking her gun was present from habit . . .

262

Officer Valdez, the idea had taken longer to get used to than Flic first hoped.

Should she say goodbye or should she just leave? Alternatively, should she stay where she was and call the lieutenant? And say what?

Robert Van Berg and I were just fucking. Only he says he's not really Robert Van Berg because actually he's Sergeant Zha. Yeah. Come back from the dead. No, I don't know how it happened. Something to do with spirits and a Chinese fox. I thought you might know about that stuff.

Bobby was still on his knees when Flic went back into the room. On his knees and naked, holding his hands to his stomach as if hoping to keep his guts in place. He stank of sweat, the smell of her body and fear. Flic knew what fear smelt like and she knew what it looked like. There were a dozen reasons she'd given her mother and Felipe for joining the SFPD, all of them were good but none was entirely true.

'You want to talk to me?'

He looked at her uniform, at the woman who'd been naked in his arms only half an hour before and shook his head. 'What can I say?'

CHAPTER 44

Wednesday 10 March

As it turned out, he didn't need to say anything, not then and not for a while. Having removed her gun and jacket, Flic made him coffee, finding her way around the unfamiliar kitchen from instinct and common sense. And having made him coffee, she decided to pour one for herself. Somehow, between crashing cups and cupboards to tell him she was safely out of his way and Flic reappearing at the bedroom door, Bobby got himself to the bathroom and splashed enough cold water on his face to look vaguely like the person she knew.

His eyes were red and one hand still hovered near his gut, but Bobby was now dressed, inasmuch as he wore a silk gown with a purple dragon embroidered on the back.

'Where did you get that?'

'Lord and Taylor.'

Flic looked blank.

'On the corner of Thirty-third and Fifth,' said Bobby. 'In New York, the day after I woke.' He shrugged, and then because Flic just waited, he told her the whole story, from going to the warehouse with Officer Sanchez to waking in Manhattan, wired to more medical equipment than he knew existed.

'Pete Sanchez was with you?'

It was the first thing she'd said to suggest she might actually believe what Bobby said was true, he wondered if she realised that. 'Yes,' he said, 'Sanchez was . . .'

'What?' asked Flic.

'He was there when we arrived,' said Bobby, thinking about it. 'Only somewhere down the line he vanished. I'm pretty sure I went through that warehouse door alone.'

'You see him again?'

'Yes. After I was shot.'

Pete Sanchez on his knees, next to Bobby, cradling a dying man's head in his arms and telling him the ambulance was on its way, everything was going to be fine, as blood flowed from Bobby's mouth and a sucking chest wound let air into ripped lungs through a tear in reality.

'You saying he was involved?'

Is that what I'm saying? Bobby considered this point carefully, watching Flic perch on a stool next to a walnut dressing table. She sat uncomfortably, with the look of a woman uncertain about what she was doing there in the first place, and Bobby kept this in mind as he tried to frame an answer.

'He'd have his reasons,' Bobby said finally.

'And what were they?'

'Sanchez was fucking my wife.'

'*Your* . . . ?'

Belief, near as damn it, Bobby saw it then. A shift as doubt crumbled and Flic's face set.

'That how you think of her?'

'Ellen and I were married,' said Bobby. 'Possibly still are.'

'She's your widow,' said Flic, voice flat. 'Remember? You were there when she buried you . . . Oh, shit.' Flic shook her head crossly. 'I can't believe I'm having this conversation. That hospital in New York, give me its name.'

'*Flic* . . .'

'I mean it,' she said. 'You can give me the name, or I can walk straight out of here. Plus I want details for the bank, the lawyers, where you bought your flights . . .' Producing a tiny notebook, Flic opened it and extracted a matching pencil. 'Come on,' she demanded. 'I want everything.'

'Okay,' said Bobby. 'Okay. Let me get my diary and I'll give you the numbers.'

'No. I don't want the numbers. Just the names.'

So Bobby gave her five, spelling out each one and listening patiently when she insisted on spelling it back to him.

Though the walls were too thick for him to hear much and she'd slammed the door behind her, Bobby still got a low buzz of questions asked as she made the first call, then the second. It was when she made her sixth that he began to worry. Mostly because her tone sounded polite, still official but very polite.

A hospital, a banker, lawyers, a psychiatrist . . . No one on his list should be eliciting that level of deference from a serving SFPD officer. Not even one in her first few months in uniform.

'Okay,' said Flic, stepping back into the room. 'I'll give you Bobby Van Berg, waking up at LivingSoul after years in a coma and making di Simion, Barchetta & Rosenberg very unhappy. I'll accept you were under the care of a Dr Weyler, who ran his Lexus into a bridge outside San Francisco. And I'll give you a bank so upscale I had to take my chief's name in vain just to get the fact you've got an account there.'

Flic said this with an anger that spoke of oak-panelled offices and being patronised by Manhattan old money. 'I'll even accept you have friends in strange places. Dangerous friends and very strange places . . .'

Opening her notebook, Flic thrust the page towards him. The name meant little to Bobby but he recognised its rank and the number written alongside. Colonel Billy's old boss in Washington.

'He traced your cellphone, then used this to trace your bank. Henry Cabot felt you should know that. Oh, and the answer to your Liechtenstein question is, *a Russian*. Only now he's dead. If that makes any sense . . .'

Flic paused, seeming to sum up her thoughts. 'Right,' she said. 'So you're Robert Van Berg, who woke from a coma. I'm just not sure where you got all the Sergeant Zha shit.'

She gave him one of those stares, meant to feel like they see into your soul. 'You don't look mad,' she said finally, 'but then what the fuck do I know?'

'I died,' said Bobby, 'I came back.'

'Yeah.' Flic nodded. 'So you keep saying. The last person to claim that got his own religion, ask my mother.' Flic hesitated, on the edge of saying something else. 'Suppose you were brainwashed . . .' She thought that through some more, considering.

'Tell me about Ellen . . .'

'What?'

'Come on,' said Flic, 'tell me something about Ellen. Anything.'

'We met on a plane.'

'Which plane?'

266

'New York to San Francisco. We sat together near a window. Dr Goodman and Janice had the centre seats.'

'Who's Janice?'

'His second wife. She divorced him a few years later.'

'How old were you when you met?'

'Thirteen.'

'And how old was Ellen?'

'She told me fifteen. It was a lie.'

'When did you discover that?'

'Later,' said Bobby. 'After we finished making out.'

'Too much information . . .' Flic stood up and walked to the window, glanced outside and then looked more closely. 'There's a girl,' she said, 'staring over a gate . . .'

'Natalie. She does that a lot.'

Flic took a look at him. 'Natalie, as in . . . ?'

'Yeah,' said Bobby. 'As in Persikov.'

From the tone of her question, Bobby could tell Flic had missed the fact that Cicero Street backed onto Tamsin Steps. He was pretty sure the irritation was with herself.

'Let's get back to Ellen,' said Flic, sounding almost official. 'When did you get married?'

Bobby gave her the date. Then he gave Flic the name of the synagogue, the name of the rabbi, the address of the hall hired for the reception afterwards and a random selection of five wedding presents, with the names of who'd given what. He also gave her the room number at the hotel where they'd gone on honeymoon.

'*Too much information . . .*'

'Then stop asking,' suggested Bobby.

'No,' said Flic, 'you're missing the point . . .' Her voice suggested she'd got used to Bobby missing the point and also – entirely coincidentally and completely unspoken – that she was getting ready to forgive Bobby something he was too dumb to realise she still held against him. 'No one could have crammed you with that much information in the time available . . . When did you wake?'

Bobby gave her the date and tried not to mind when she checked it against a note in her diary.

'And Sergeant Zha died . . . ?'

He told her, but she knew anyway.

'One final question,' said Flic. 'When did you first realise Ellen was fucking Sanchez?'

Bobby blinked. 'I don't know when it started.'

'That wasn't what I asked,' said Flic. 'When did you *notice*?'

He thought about that. 'Maybe I always knew. I'm not sure.'

'I can see what Ellen got out of it . . .' Flic held up one hand, half apologising. 'Just being honest,' she said. 'But turn it round. Why would Sanchez fuck Ellen?' It said something for Bobby's memories that he didn't at first understand the question.

'She's in her late thirties,' said Flic. 'She's had a kid and it shows. Sure, Ellen works out and she looks good, but it's *for her age*. This is Pete Sanchez. You've seen Beatrice.'

'What?' she demanded, seeing Bobby shiver.

He shrugged, shook his head.

'Beatrice is young,' said Flic. 'She's rich. Her mother will probably make governor. Why would Sanchez risk that?'

'I don't know,' said Bobby, wondering if he'd imagined the look Ellen gave Sanchez at the funeral, the touch of their hands.

'Think about it,' Flic said, shutting her notebook with a snap. 'And I'll catch you later.' Flic didn't say where, so Bobby assumed she meant back here, which was fine because she did.

'Where are you going?' he asked.

'To find out who owns that piece of land in Marin County.'

'Then I'll go see Kris.'

'Okay,' said Flic, 'be gentle.'

CHAPTER 45

Wednesday 10 March

A pile of guidebooks rested on a table near the entrance. The usual collection of hip hotels, restaurant guides, back-packer bibles and small print, locally produced booklets that made up in enthusiasm what they lacked in production values or paper quality.

On shelves beside these, face out, stood the picture books. The Golden Gate Bridge in fog, Coit Tower, the murals that looked like they should be by Diego Rivera but were actually by someone else in his style. San Francisco leant itself to simplification. To the tourist family who queued by a till, it was somewhere to talk about afterwards, while the German girl behind them obviously regarded the city as a shrine to the Beats. Something Bobby could have guessed from her red jersey, high breasts and black jeans, even if she hadn't been buying a copy of Kerouac.

Borders was fine and probably close to her hotel but Bobby found himself wanting to give her directions to the City Lights Bookshop, home to Ferlinghetti and where followers of the Beats really belonged.

To Kris Zha, whom Bobby had yet to find, the Borders on Post Street represented something else again. The place she went when she could no longer stand being at home. And if Bobby was still waiting to find her, that was because he had yet to look in the place where he knew she'd be . . .

Black clothes, black hair, red lettering. At the third table along by the window, wearing shades and a T-shirt that read, *Death Cab for Cutie*, her hair tied back and so uncombed it came close to dreads.

'Can we have a word?'

All he got in answer was a scowl.

'*Please* . . . ?' Cutting Kris out from her friends was easy, Bobby simply introduced himself as a man who knew her father, and after a moment's hesitation, the other four kids got up as one and left. If adults had trouble dealing with grief, then teenagers were worse, because to them death wasn't simply a tragedy, it was an embarrassment, much like everything else in life.

'I'm not supposed to talk to you. We've been through this.'

'Yes,' said Bobby. 'I know, but I really need to ask you something.'

'About what?'

'Monkeys.' He nodded, stressing she'd heard him correctly. 'I just wondered,' said Bobby, 'if anybody in one of those chat rooms of yours has been talking about vivisection or monkeys?'

Kris considered Bobby's question for as long as it took to replace it with one of her own. 'How do you know I use chat rooms?'

'Your father,' said Bobby. 'He must have mentioned it.'

Looking up, Kris glanced across and something happened, because what Bobby saw reflected in her shades was not himself nor the café with its chrome counter, chilled staff and endless variations of death by carbohydrate. What he saw was what they hid, the sadness and loneliness . . .

His doing.

Getting killed was only the final insult.

'*What?*' demanded Kris. 'Why are you staring at me?'

'I . . .' Bobby stopped himself, rephrased what he wanted to say. 'Look,' he said, 'I knew your father.'

Kris pulled a scowl.

'Oh fuck it,' said Bobby. 'He loved you, okay? He might have been shit at saying it. Hell, he was shit at saying most things. But he loved you. You were the last thing he thought about before he died.'

'*You don't know that . . .*'

All it took to bring the café in Borders to a halt was a single shout. A woman at the next table was out of her chair and moving towards Bobby before her chair had even finished bouncing off the floor. Her clothes might be terrible and her expression self-righteous but it was the right reaction. Well, it was what Bobby would have done.

'It's okay,' Bobby said.

The woman glanced at Kris.

'Yeah,' said Kris, 'it's okay,' then added, 'My dad died.'

'Last month,' said Bobby. 'She's still upset . . .' He'd been right, there was nothing like death for making even grown adults retreat.

'How do you know what my dad was thinking?'

'Because I was there.'

'Did he tell you?' Kris's question was little more than a whisper. 'Did he really mention me?'

Only inside, Bobby wanted to tell her. Only where the darkness was and maybe a nine-tailed fox. Only in the snow wastes that remained between emptiness after everything else was gone.

But that was too complicated and she was a kid and he already owed her debts which could never be repaid. So Bobby lied and simplified the truth, even though he never meant it to end like this, with everything he believed in simplified so far it became a lie.

'Yes,' said Bobby. 'He talked about how much he loved you. How shit he'd been as a father.'

'He wasn't.'

'You know he was. The man never kept a promise to you in his life.'

'He was busy,' said Kris.

'That's what they all say,' Bobby told her. 'I'm too busy, work's too hard, the job's too grim, you've no idea what it's like . . . He fucked up. The thing you have to remember is your dad knew that and regretted it. Not just at the end, but for a long time before. All those months of not talking. All those times you couldn't stand to be in the same room.'

'You knew about that?'

'Of course I . . . Yes,' said Bobby. 'I knew.'

'It's weird,' said Kris. 'To think he talked to you. I didn't think he could talk to people. Mom says even Lieutenant Que couldn't get through to him and he was the closest thing Dad had to a real father. Maybe you need proper parents to be any good at it yourself.' She paused, considering what she'd just said.

'You'll be great with kids,' said Bobby. 'When the time comes.'

Which won't be for a long time, he wanted to add. *Because you have to go to college first and get over all that shit about what is life for and college means getting good grades, and babies means boys and you don't even want to go there yet.*

But all he said was, 'Your dad left you money.'

'What?' Kris looked suspicious. 'Mom would have told me . . .'

'She doesn't know yet,' said Bobby. 'It's in a trust for when you go to college.'

'You sure?'

'Very.' Bobby gave her the name of the lawyers in New York, the ones looking after his own money and made a mental note to fix the trust before he did anything else. 'You can go anywhere you want. Provided your grades are good enough.'

Kris pulled a face.

'And about that Goth make-up. You know why he hated it?'

'He just did,' said Kris.

'It's a kind of camouflage, a way of hiding. Your dad didn't like you doing that.'

'This?' said Kris, reaching up to smear black eyeliner down one cheek. '*This is about hiding?*'

Bobby nodded. 'Of course,' he said. 'You know it is. You're busy making people look at the surface, because you don't want them looking underneath.'

It was only at the end, after she'd finished a *grande latte* and he'd drunk his third espresso and they'd shared a fudge brownie between them that Kris brought up the original subject. 'What was that about monkeys?' she said.

'Doesn't matter . . .'

'Yes it does,' said Kris. 'Cruelty always matters. It's the standard by which we judge ourselves.' She said this with an absolutely straight face, and no suggestion she was simply repeating words read elsewhere.

'Come on,' she said. 'Tell me.'

Settling back, Bobby looked around the café. A dozen or so customers sat by themselves, a handful of couples faced each other and a large group of kids seemed to be having trouble getting their wireless internet connection to work. As good a snapshot of early twenty-first-century San Francisco as anyone was likely to get, and about as removed from the lives of Kris's own children as '30s Shanghai was to him.

'You visit chat rooms about animal rights.'

It was not a question but Kris still nodded, her head turned to one side.

'I wondered if you'd heard stuff about experiments on monkeys . . .'

'In the US?'

'Locally.'

Kris frowned. 'Locally?' She said this as if she might have misheard him, and it was Bobby's turn to nod. 'No,' Kris said finally. 'But I can ask around . . .' She paused, hesitated. 'I thought primate experiments were illegal in California.'

'Maybe they are,' said Bobby. 'You'd know better than me. However, these are not nice people.'

'You're saying the tests are illegal?'

Remembering the dead animals rotting in the hills, Bobby decided someone had to be breaking the law, even if only about dumping. Although maybe he'd got it wrong, maybe this wasn't about vivisection at all.

'*This has got something to do with Dad.*'

Bobby looked up.

'Doesn't it?'

'No,' said Bobby, pushing away his cup.

Kris smiled and shook her head, face softening. 'You're almost as crap at lying as he was . . . I'll check out some chat rooms and call you if I hear anything. Let me have your number.'

'You've already got it.'

'I threw that away,' said Kris.

Bobby gave the number to her again.

CHAPTER 46
Monday 15 March

Wednesday bled into Thursday and Friday became the weekend and nothing much happened except that Bobby paid off Latif and got his head around Flic suddenly refusing to sleep over Sunday night. It was to do with keeping her independence, apparently. The only other thing to happen, late Monday morning, was that Natalie Persikov kicked a ball over the hedge of the Begley House, and then came knocking to collect it.

Actually she rang the bell.

When Bobby answered the door he found the girl red-faced and out of breath; but then getting the ball into Bobby's garden had required her to climb a tree, because that was the only way she could kick it high enough to manage. Bobby knew, he'd been watching from a first-floor window.

'It's on the grass at the back.'

'What is?' asked the startled girl.

'Your ball. I'd get it but I figure you want to collect it yourself.' Bobby smiled at the child's bemusement. 'It's fine,' he said, 'you can go through.'

Bobby's study had French windows at the rear leading onto the small area of grass, which was all that remained of the original garden. Never big to start with, the space had been arranged into borders and rockeries and a tiny patch of lawn.

Going back to his desk, Bobby shuffled his way through copies of SFPD files, letting Natalie take her time. The files came from Lieutenant Que, via Flic, who was now liaison to whichever department the lieutenant thought Bobby was meant to represent. It might be unofficial, but it was still official enough for Flic to have been moved off other duties and told to make herself available, should Bobby require her presence.

That was how the lieutenant put it. *Should Bobby Van Berg require her presence.* Sometimes the old man had a sick sense of humour.

'I've got the ball,' said Natalie.

Bobby glanced towards the French windows. 'Any time,' he said, then waited. Now was when she was meant to say something, anything would do. A comment about his garden, an apology, a few words to open the way to whatever it was she actually wanted to say. Instead Natalie walked around Bobby, glanced back at the study door and shrugged.

'What exactly were you expecting to find?' asked Bobby.

The girl hesitated.

'It's okay,' said Bobby, 'you can tell me.'

'No, I can't . . .' And with that she was gone. A flash of blonde ponytail and speedwell blue eyes, a twist of thin shoulders and both ball and girl disappeared down the hall and out of the front door, which shut with a slam.

'You want to tell me what that was all about?' asked Flic, from where she stood at the top of the stairs. She wore a T-shirt, not much else and was carrying a laptop. Bobby could see enough of her thighs to make the sight distracting.

'She's scared of something.'

'Yeah, right.' Clattering down the stairs, Flic hit the space bar on her laptop and thrust the machine towards Bobby. 'Take a look at this,' she said.

The site in Marin County had been derelict for a dozen years. It was, according to all records, still derelict. An argument between Marin County, the US Military and a pressure group set up to protect the Mojave toad looked likely to keep it that way.

'And then there's this.' Flic pulled up another page. This one had a long list of calls taken from a logbook at the sheriff's office.

'How did you get that?'

'I asked.' Flic smiled. 'Sometimes doing the obvious works wonders. Here . . .' Pointing at the screen, she indicated half a dozen calls from a small-time vineyard and tourist hotel. The owner wanted to complain about a truck cutting through her land. All she could say about the driver was that he wore a cap pulled low. Oh, and his truck had *CFO Medical Disposal* down one side.

'Don't tell me . . .'

Flic nodded. 'The vineyard's right between a side road and the dumping area. I've arranged for us to see CFO.'

'When?' Bobby asked.

'Now,' said Flic, and by the time a Marin County sheriff's car had pulled up outside the Begley House, she was back in uniform and Bobby had dressed in his best black suit and was wearing shades.

'Okay?'

'You'll do.'

The sheriff's car was green and white, a Cadillac, and the deputy who climbed out to meet Bobby looked absurdly young. An impression made stronger when he saluted.

'Tom Vassa. We're going to CFO, right?'

Flic nodded. 'You know them?'

'Know of them,' said Deputy Vassa. 'Never given us any trouble. Renew their licence on time. That's why we didn't pay much attention. Woken Field on the other hand . . .' He was talking to Flic but his glance was aimed at Bobby.

'Trouble?' said Bobby.

'East Coast people,' said the deputy, then paused, aware that might not have been the most tactful thing he could have said. 'They been in touch with you . . . ?'

'No.' Bobby shook his head. 'I'm here about something else.'

The offices of CFO Disposal were low and modern in an adobe walls and sheet glass sort of way. It was one of the ironies of style that what most people thought of as modern actually developed out of 1930s fascist architecture. At least, it did according to Janice Goodman, Ellen's ex-stepmother. A woman who left no more mark upon her stepdaughter than a hatred of earthenware and a liking for hard-edged design.

'What are you thinking?' Flic whispered.

'About . . . Kris,' said Bobby, which was as close to that particular truth as he was willing to go.

Although Bobby had a distrust of most men in suits, himself included, he found the way Will Milling came down the steps reassuring. Whether or not someone met you at the door said nothing about their guilt or innocence, but it could say a lot about their attitude. In Bobby's experience, the only ones to cause trouble were those who came to the door because they hoped to stop you getting inside, and those who remained inside because they were fucked if they were going to come to the door.

The owner of CFO Medical Disposal met neither of these categories.

'Is everything okay?'

Given that a Marin County police cruiser had just drawn up outside his offices with its lights flashing – and Flic had insisted on the lights – the answer to that should have been obvious.

'Will Milling?' asked Flic.

The man nodded.

'Mr Van Berg would like a word.' That was Bobby's cue to step forward. All of this was running to Flic's script and all of it twisted the rules, even without Deputy Vassa knowing Bobby Van Berg was actually someone else.

'It's about dumping in the Marin Hills.'

'About . . . ?' Will Milling's chin went up. 'We don't dump,' he said firmly. 'CFO Medical Disposal are not that stupid.' He was a man sure of his ground and quite happy to defend it.

'Good,' said Bobby. 'That means you won't mind helping me find out whose been using your trucks.' Looking around, Bobby asked, 'Where do you keep them anyway?'

'In the garages.' A raised flowerbed supported by field stone walls turned out to roof a sunken lot where gleaming trucks were refuelled, steam cleaned and sent out again.

'This is big business,' said Bobby.

The man nodded. 'That's why we wouldn't dump,' he said. 'We've got too much to lose. We do half a dozen of the new bio start-ups, three hospitals, two universities and a vet . . . That's from the old days,' he added. 'When my father ran the business. What kind of waste are we talking about anyway?'

'Monkeys,' said Bobby.

Will Milling blinked. 'Not CFO,' he said firmly. 'We don't do anything involving live experiments.'

'Moral objections?' Flic asked.

'Commercial common sense. I'm not interested in having my office picketed by a bunch of activists or whatever they're called these days. We don't do animal experimentation. We don't do anything involving human foetuses. It's just not worth the grief.'

'So it isn't one of your trucks dumping dead animals in the hills behind the Marin headlands?' Flic Valdez kept her voice strictly neutral. As if this was just something she needed to get cleared up.

'Not us,' said Will Milling.

'Despite the fact the truck had CFO Medical Disposal written down one side . . .'

Pulling out his phone, Will Milling said, 'Did anybody get the number?'

Flic had been the one to talk to the owner at Woken Field Vineyard and the woman had been positive the truck had no plates. Since this would be enough to get a truck pulled over by the first police car to pass that seemed unlikely, which suggested the number was deliberately obscured.

'What happens to your trucks when you're through with them?' asked Deputy Vassa.

'We trade them in.' Will Milling barely bothered to keep *you idiot* out of his voice.

The deputy flushed. 'So you've traded in *all* of your trucks? No exceptions . . .'

'That's what I . . .' A sudden thought stopped the man mid-sentence.

'What?' demanded Bobby.

'The thing is,' said Will Milling. 'We gave a truck away a few years back. Well, not exactly gave it. More threw it into a leaving package. We'd been having trouble with one of the foremen and he'd been here a while.'

Bobby could write the rest himself. It had been easier to pay the man off than fire him and if an old truck helped sweeten the package . . . Probably tax deductible into the bargain.

'What's he doing now?'

'He set up on his own. We helped him get the licence, sold him an old butane rig and promised him work. But Eddie was still pretty erratic, so after a couple of years we let the deal lapse.'

Sweet and easy.

'You know if Eddie's still in business?' asked Bobby.

'I haven't heard otherwise.'

'And he still has your old truck?'

Will Milling shrugged. 'Again, so far as I know. We welded sign-boards over the old lettering. Someone I knew came up with the signs and I had the local garage . . .' He stopped, aware he'd just admitted doing everything he could to get his ex-employee to leave, short of asking the man to name his price.

'What was he doing?'

'I'm not sure I understand the question.'

'Yes, you do,' said Bobby.

'We were losing stock,' Will Milling said. 'Nothing big. Just gas from the pumps, the occasional tyre from the stores. We lost three laptops over one weekend. A window was broken but it wasn't really big enough for anyone to get in . . . That's on file,' he told Deputy Vassa. 'I can give you the crime number.'

'Not necessary,' said Bobby. 'Just give me the name and address of this man and we'll leave you in peace.'

'You won't tell Eddie it was me?'

Flic smiled.

CHAPTER 47
Monday 15 March

Built from breeze blocks, Eddie Skoda's incinerator featured a tall chimney with some kind of weird metal box at the top. A peeling sign on a razor-wire fence read *Skoda Waste Management*. A dog on a chain behind double gates let them know they weren't welcome.

'You think Eddie's here?' Deputy Vassa asked.

Flic checked her watch. 'It's two-thirty p.m., Monday afternoon. Seems like he should be here to me.' Something about the way Flic said this made Bobby decide she and Deputy Vassa had been more than just friends. He was unsure if the fact he felt jealous was good or not.

Jealousy wasn't something he'd suffered from in quite a while.

'We could always try the rear,' said Deputy Vassa.

A burnt-out oil can and a collection of truck tyres piled like some piece of modern sculpture. The mongrel tried to follow them round, but its chain was too short and once they'd passed out of its sight and behind a tar-paper shack it seemed to forget them.

Skoda Waste Management was so low rent Bobby could only assume Eddie Skoda did all his business by phone. And what with the razor wire, guard dog and keep-out signs, he definitely seemed like a man who valued his privacy; unless he was just a man with something to hide.

'I'm going in,' Bobby said.

'You can't do that.' The words were out of Deputy Vassa's mouth before he had time to think about them. 'It's illegal,' he added, slightly embarrassed. 'We don't have due cause and we don't even have enough to get a warrant.'

'Why don't you two take a ride?' said Bobby.

Flic looked at him.

'I mean it,' said Bobby, voice neutral. 'Have a coffee and catch up on old times. You could meet me down there in about ninety minutes.' He nodded to where the track vanished through scrub towards a minor road.

Only when Bobby was certain Flic and Deputy Vassa had taken him at his word did he turn his attention to the locked gates. Although first he had to take a call on his phone.

'What?' he demanded.

A disembodied operator told Bobby he had a voice message. Please key his voice mail retrieval code. After a few seconds, the computer told him helpfully that if he hadn't set up a code for message retrieval then his default code was 444.

This was the number he punched into the phone.

'It's Kris . . .' Her voice was hesitant, slightly embarrassed, the way most people are when talking to machines. 'I've met a boy who knows someone who wants to talk to you. Call me, okay?' Maybe she intended to add something else, because there was a long gap in which Bobby could hear only background noise and then the static ended.

'Push one to delete. Push two to store. Press three to replay . . .'

Keeping the message, Bobby toggled his phone onto vibrate and slipped it back in his pocket, then rattled the gate. He needed to talk to a dog about a man.

Animals, children and street people . . . It seemed Bobby hadn't lost his touch. The dog was some bastard cross between a Rottweiler and something already mixed and the old whip marks around its ribs told Bobby all he needed to know about its life. A torn ear, crusted nostrils, one eye blind. The animal was ferocious because it was too scared to be anything else.

They had a difficult moment when Bobby first came within reach and the animal lunged because that was what the dog believed it was meant to do. So Bobby stepped back and sat, talking softly and endlessly about nothing that really mattered. Mostly about how complicated life was when you weren't sure who you really were, but how being chained and beaten for years was undoubtedly worse and how Bobby didn't envy the dog his life.

The mongrel listened and then listened some more, and although it had trouble understanding a single word, something about the tone muddled it. So the animal kept listening and puzzling and puzzling and listening right up to the point Bobby bent close, stroked its skull until it lifted its head to meet his caress and then, as the animal closed its eyes in unexpected ecstasy, broke its neck and laid it on the crushed cinders that had made up its entire world.

'Sorry,' Bobby said.

At first sight the tar-paper hut contained little of interest. A calendar for the previous century in which a naked blonde expressed unlikely interest in the handle of a torque wrench, a cup enamelled with mould, the remains of a pizza so hard it could have been cast from concrete. The place was sour with dust and tainted from a soiled lab coat hung on a hook near the door. A pair of industrial gloves lay discarded on the floor underneath.

Bobby was about to check the contents of a cardboard box when his jacket vibrated.

'Call me,' said the message. It was unsigned . . .

'This is Kris Zha . . . *Hi, I'm not here right now, but please leave a message at the sound of the tone* . . . She'd downloaded a snatch of Laurie Anderson and hacked out the lines she wanted, that was Kris all over.

'Later,' Bobby told himself. He'd fix coffee, thank his daughter for her help and ease himself out of her life without Kris even realising he'd tried to make himself part of it; he should have never asked for her help in the first place and besides he now had what he needed, it was parked outside, next to a dead dog and a wheelbarrow with rancid grease in the bottom.

A Toyota Hilux, originally blue but resprayed white to match the livery of CFO Medical Disposal. Bobby only knew about the respray because whoever levered off *Skoda Waste Management* had done more than break the weld holding the panel in place. Some of the surface paint had flaked away to reveal the original blue beneath.

The truck would give him Eddie Skoda, ex-employee of CFO Disposal and owner of this establishment. Eddie Skoda would give him whoever was trying to dispose of the waste. There was a good chance that person could give Bobby whoever was behind the murder of Colonel Billy, from there it would be a short step to finding out why.

Colonel Billy, dead monkeys, Natalie . . . Those were the ends that Bobby wanted to tie together, because all of them seemed to lead back to the late Sergeant Zha.

A metal plaque on the incinerator door announced that Skoda Waste

Management was licensed to incinerate '3.7 cubic tons of waste per 24-hour period', with exclusions for weekends and official public holidays.

If the hut looked squalid, it was nothing to the filth awaiting Bobby behind that door. The burner was out and had been out for weeks from the look of things. A panel had been taken off a wall and brass piping was piled into an untidy heap. Eddie had even tried to use paper, brushwood and logs to finish a burn that had obviously been interrupted by mechanical failure.

A dead pig had bloated and split, something that might once have been simian was reduced by corruption to oddly familiar bones and a smear of alien goo. Those were the animals which could be identified. The only other objects to which names could be put had been inanimate in the first place. Sanitary napkins from a rest home, medical waste and operating gowns, a bundle of files marked *shred and destroy*.

More from duty than because he expected to find anything, Bobby shuffled through the files. A dot com take down, a couple of bio start-ups, banking records from the late 1980s . . . None looked critical or even interesting.

In fact, the only paper to matter Bobby found by accident, long after he'd decided there was nothing to find, and he found it not in one of the files marked for destruction but pushed under the kindling that someone, Eddie Skoda most probably, had tried to use to restart the flames.

It was the bottom copy of an old invoice, *paid* scrawled across it in red biro. *Job as discussed*, told him little, but what interested Bobby was the date, address and the name. *Dr M Persikov, 3 Tamsin Steps*, four months earlier . . . Around the time Colonel Billy first came to Bobby with stories of cats disappearing and then their owners. About the time the rumours began.

Folding the invoice and wishing he had an evidence bag, Bobby began to sift through the rest of the charred papers and then gave up. Some were rank with unspecified slime and the rest so friable they crumbled beneath his fingers. A CSI team would have a field day in here, but they weren't going to get the chance, at least not yet.

'God,' said Deputy Vassa, when he stopped to collect Bobby from the road side. 'What's that smell?'

'You don't want to know,' said Bobby.

They drove back in near silence, Deputy Vassa talking only to his radio, and Bobby and Flic staring out of their respective windows, lost in thoughts unknown to each other. Flic's were personal and mostly revolved around the fact that she no sooner got close to Bobby than he seemed to disappear inside his head.

And inside his head, Bobby thought only of his last meeting with Dr Persikov. Anger made up most of those thoughts, anger and puzzlement. He might be shit at many things but Bobby regarded himself as someone able to read others. If the invoice in his pocket was to be believed, even this was now beyond him.

'Where do you want me to drop you?'

'At the station house,' said Flic, before Bobby could answer.

'Sure,' said Deputy Vassa. 'That good for you?' He glanced in the mirror at his other passenger.

'Tamsin Steps would be better.'

Bobby watched Flic realise he'd just given Dr Persikov's address and wonder how to undo her earlier request. So maybe he could still read people after all. At least, he could read Flic and she was one of the most difficult people to read he'd ever met.

'Want to come with me?'

Flic nodded.

'More dead animals?' Flic asked, standing on a sidewalk just before the start of Tamsin Steps. Inside his car, Deputy Vassa was waving a studiedly casual goodbye, though Bobby doubted if Flic even noticed.

'The incinerator is broken,' said Bobby. 'I'm guessing that's why Eddie took to dumping his rubbish in the hills. I'm also guessing he didn't tell anybody about the change of plan.'

'So why aren't we chasing down Eddie Skoda?'

'Here . . .' Bobby pulled the invoice from his pocket. He would have said more, only his cellphone started vibrating again and it was all he could do not to flip it open and bark, *Sergeant Zha.*

He needn't have bothered.

'It's Kris . . .' The message was tense, almost terse. 'What's the point of giving me this number if you never answer? I don't know what's going on, but I think someone followed me home from school . . .'

Bobby's whole body froze.

'What?' asked Flic.

'Kris,' said Bobby, still listening to his voice mail. 'She's being stalked.'

'. . . *jogging pants. It's really weird, she's carrying a cat.*' By the time

284

Bobby got to this part of his daughter's message, Flic was already unclipping the radio from her belt.

'Leave it,' said Bobby, catching Flic's hand. 'It's Louie.'

'The woman with the cat?'

'Yes,' said Bobby. 'I'd better call Kris, tell her not to worry.' Dialling from memory, Bobby reached a computer. It was his turn to leave a message.

CHAPTER 48

Monday 15 March

Detection was meant to be the cool use of facts and intelligence, both kinds. Reality had always proved rather messier, and from the moment Natalie Persikov opened the door Bobby realised this time would be no different.

'You stink.' The girl made no effort to be polite. Although it was hard to fault her accuracy or dedication to the truth.

'I know,' said Bobby. He turned to Flic. 'This is Natalie, Dr Persikov's granddaughter.'

'She knows that,' said the girl.

'She does?'

'Of course she does . . .' Natalie Persikov looked between them as if suspecting some trap. 'Officer Valdez drove me out here when that weird sergeant wanted me to show him how I fired the gun . . .'

'Except you didn't,' said Bobby. 'It was someone else.'

As Natalie opened her mouth to protest a voice came from an open door behind her. Old the voice might have been but it carried natural authority and there was no mistaking Dr Persikov's accent.

'Who is it?'

'A policewoman,' said Natalie. 'And the man from next door.'

'What an interesting combination,' said the doctor. 'Maybe these days burglars bring their own officers with them.'

Flic glanced at Bobby.

'I told you,' Bobby said, 'I dropped by the other night.'

'Via a window in the attic,' added Dr Persikov. 'And he left with a priceless icon. I'd been planning to call the police but there doesn't seem much point, does there?'

'Believe me,' said Flic. 'If I thought for a moment this man had stolen from you I'd be the first to arrest him . . .' And listening to her voice, Bobby understood that she meant it.

'When did you notice the icon was gone again?' asked Bobby.

'*Again?*' That was Flic.

'It's in the original report,' Bobby said. 'Ask Natalie. She shoots a burglar, supposedly. Her grandfather reports an icon missing. The crime team turn up footprints, broken glass, crushed flowers, even ash from a Russian cigarette but no icon. The next day Natalie finds the icon under a bush in the garden. Amazing . . .'

'You leave my granddaughter out of this.'

'I'd like to,' said Bobby. 'Only you should have thought of that before you let her take the rap for that shooting.'

'And I've told you . . .' Dr Persikov's face was bleak. 'She pulled the trigger. Much as I'd like to say otherwise.'

The child said nothing while this was going on. Merely shuffled her feet and glanced sideways at her grandfather. It was Flic who noticed the whiteness to Natalie's knuckles and realised this was because the child was digging nails into her own hands. Although the SFPD officer only mentioned it to Bobby afterwards.

'Okay,' said Bobby. 'Here's what we can do. We can arrest the doctor now and take him down to the station . . .' Bobby shook his head, to keep Natalie from protesting. 'Let me finish,' he told the child. 'It will be better for your grandfather if you do.'

'I'll hear what the man's got to say.'

'We can do that,' said Bobby. 'Or we talk about what's really been going on. About who killed Ibrahim Nasra. And just maybe . . .' Bobby hesitated, interrogation was more difficult when the suspect was blind. There was no holding Persikov's gaze. No value in significant nods to Officer Valdez or resigned shakes of the head.

'Maybe what . . . ?' Dr Persikov asked, which was when Bobby realised that sometimes silence and darkness could work just as well.

'We cut a deal. You're old, a distinguished art collector, a well-known philanthropist. I'm sure the Governor would look leniently at any appeal you decide to make.'

'Why would I confess to something I didn't do?' There was real anger in the old man's voice. 'All this is because Natalie shot the burglar,' said the old man. 'It's over. Why can't you just leave us alone?' Tears slid from under Dr Persikov's glasses and his fingers shook. He had the hands of an old man, skin so thin his fingers were bruised with age.

'You know,' said Flic. 'I think we should sit down.'

Bobby Van Berg and Flic Valdez watched the child take the hand of her grandfather and lead him towards the dining room, hesitating only slightly at the door.

'We can use another room,' said Flic.

'No.' Up went Natalie's chin and they both watched her shake her head.

Dr Persikov was right, the icon was missing and all that remained of where it had been was a pale patch of wallpaper, which the picture had protected from the light.

'You never thought of keeping it in a bank?'

'The Rublev? Icons are meant to be seen and no one but an idiot would steal the thing.'

'Why?' asked Flic.

'Because no one could ever sell it.'

'Not on the open market,' agreed Bobby. 'But there are collectors who'd buy it tomorrow . . . Twenty years from now you might get the icon back if it came on the market, maybe even fifty years, but a hundred or more?'

'You're missing the point,' said Dr Persikov. And Bobby figured they were. He was there to confront an old man with his part in whatever it was the old man had a part in. Something nasty enough to involve dead animals and quite possibly dead people as well. Yet here they sat discussing icons.

'Which point?' said Bobby.

'The icon was already stolen.'

Bobby thought back, remembering. 'You told me it was a present.'

'I did not . . .'

'Yes, you did. One with sentimental value.'

That was when the old man's face began to change, not in the way people's faces change when they remember something, but in shock. And as Bobby suddenly remembered for himself that he'd been Bobby Zha back then, the shock on the old man's face turned to fear and he jerked forward, one hand reaching blindly for the arm of his chair.

'No,' he said. 'Impossible. I told them it couldn't be done.'

'Grandpa?'

'Impossible,' he repeated.

'What is?' demanded Flic.

'This . . .' said Dr Persikov. 'Him . . . Not possible. I told your government. So they took it away from me and began to run a programme of their own. I told them, even the Boss couldn't get anybody to make it work.'

'The Boss?'

'Joseph Vissarionovich,' said Bobby.

'Vissari . . . ?'

'Stalin, the Boss of bosses. The man for whom millions once died. Come on,' Bobby said to Dr Persikov, 'what couldn't Stalin get to work?'

The old man was staring blank-faced at a wall, mouth open and spittle dribbling from his lips. Hands which only seconds before gripped the chair and Bobby's sleeve now gripped each other, their fingers twisting together so hard that veins stood out like highways on his wrist.

Natalie's demand that they get help was unnecessary. Flic was already onto the station house, putting in a request for an ambulance.

CHAPTER 49

Tuesday 16 March

Louie was having a *what* day, which was better than a *how* day and infinitely preferable to any day that demanded she concentrate on *why*? All the same, she could have done without it . . .

So much of life was an imitation of itself that deciding whether a thing was real gave her problems. Sometimes really obvious things weren't real at all, they were merely pretending. Union Square was a case in point. Was it real or simply a good imitation?

Certainly it wasn't the original square where crowds used to gather to support the Union side during the American Civil War, that conflict where everyone remembered the North and South and then blanked when it came to the world out West. These days Union Square was the roof to a car park, little more than a slice of real estate kept green by sprinklers and existing in the minds of most merely to keep apart the stores which made up its sides.

In the middle of the square – and Louie loved this bit – was a ninety-foot-high twist of candy with a dancing boy on top. 'Wow,' said the tourists, as they stood admiring what the rest of the city chose to ignore. 'Look at that pillar . . .'

A monument to Admiral Dewey's victory at Manila Bay during the Spanish-American war of 1898, an utterly artificial conflict, dreamed up by Randolph Hearst to help sell more newspapers. Real, fake and hyper-real. It was upsetting how few people worried about the things that really mattered.

In an odd way, Louie could see something of herself in the black-clad teenager she followed through the door of Borders Books. The girl's obvious irritation with idiots who had no idea where they were going, plus her reluctance to pay much attention to traffic lights on the way were qualities with which Louie could identify.

Her friends were also cool, although the man who went upstairs behind them was weird, and the way he kept scowling at Louie was just plain stupid. The fat girl with red hair and a nose ring was better. Although, after Kris, Louie liked best the Chinese boy who plonked himself in a café chair, and promptly stuck his foot through the strap of his laptop case to stop anyone from stealing it.

They were the kind of kids who knew the world offered more than café lattes, blueberry muffins, blonde girls reading teen mags and grown men looking at glossies designed to show them this month's toys. One could appreciate that.

Louie expected and got the occasional sideways glance, but the staff never refused to let her in and they even smiled at her kitten on both occasions she followed Kris up the stairs and into the café. Kris was the sulky one, her red-haired friend was Zabel, although Louie thought that might be made up, the thin man with the cap was Eddie and the boy with the computer was Mouse.

Eddie was the one Mouse wanted Bobby Van Berg to meet and the one getting fed up at being kept waiting. In fact Eddie had just announced he was leaving San Francisco, it was safer apparently. He didn't want to talk to somebody anymore . . .

This gave Louie a problem. Van Berg had told her to watch *everything*, which was far more than one person could manage. So Louie had delegated a number of the jobs, a concept familiar to most of the people that Louie knew. A surprising number of whom had been in the Marines or the army, with a few from the navy and fewer still in the air force. Maybe because it cost so much to train navigators and pilots that the air force were less willing to let them go.

Louie had been in the first Gulf War. Back then, of course, she'd been someone else. In fact, she might have been a man. Louie had trouble remembering. In the end, Louie decided to follow Eddie because he seemed most frightened and that suggested he knew something.

Also, there seemed to be a large fox following Kris around like some dog. It grinned at Louie when she noticed it, and grinned harder still at all the people who decided it was invisible and then shivered when it walked straight through them.

Following Eddie turned out to be a bad mistake. Not because it wasn't interesting, it was; particularly the bit where Eddie's fears turned out to be real and a tourist wearing a scarf caught up with him in the Stockton tunnel.

Eddie had come down from North Beach, Louie knew this because she'd overhead him say so. And knowing this, Louie had gone ahead. It was an old trick and mostly it worked. People never expected to be followed from in front. When the woman in the Hermès scarf caught up with her target, Louie was the swaying heap in a bricked-up doorway, squatting over a puddle of her own urine.

Instant invisibility, just add piss.

'I won't tell,' said Eddie. You had to admire the man. It took courage to be that scared and still defiant. The woman grinned, and her grin said, *that's not what this is about.* Which was when Louie realised the man wasn't being defiant at all; it was a promise he'd just made, a plea for his life.

That grin remained in place as the woman with the scarf reached into her bag for a small automatic, yanked back its slide and put a bullet right through the middle of Eddie's forehead.

Dropping her weapon, the woman peeled off surgical gloves and put them in her bag. At the other end of the tunnel, she stopped to buy lychees, bamboo shoots and a packet of plastic chopsticks. Louie she simply didn't see.

For a second Louie considered doing something totally out of character, like calling the SFPD, but the only officer she trusted was dead and Eddie's death made her frightened for Kris. So Louie doubled back instead, taking a left and walking as quickly as possible to China-town gates, where she found Volks sat under his ATM machine, the dog curled up around his feet.

'My pitch,' he said, before Louie had a chance to open her mouth.

'Your pitch,' agreed Louie.

'Your cat,' said Volks, nodding towards Lucifer.

'Yes,' Louie said. 'Still my cat.'

'My pitch,' Volks said.

Louie sighed. 'I need help,' she said, cutting the conversation short. Volks was about to say he didn't help people, and then he remembered, he'd helped her before.

'Still my pitch,' he said.

'Yes,' Louie agreed. 'Still yours.'

Volk had never been in trouble with the SFPD. This was a fairly incredible statement for a homeless person to make, but it happened to be the truth. Alcohol gave Volks a headache and crack made him sick. If not for the voices in his head he'd still be pruning vines and bringing in the grapes in Napa Valley like his father and grandfather had done.

'NeedToSeeVanBer . . .'

The officer who looked up from the desk in Chinatown Station saw a dog, a string and a bundle of rags, with a copy of that day's *Chronicle* pushed into what could have been a pocket. A closer look revealed that the twist of cloth was an old fatigue hat, the kind with a neck flap to protect against sun. The rest of the clothes also looked as if they might once have been a uniform.

Since the person speaking was not intoxicated or under the influence of narcotics and since there were no members of the public to be offended by his dress and since Ramon Habiro regarded himself as that rare beast, a liberal, he actually tried to work out what Volks had said.

The fact that it made little sense was to be expected.

'You need a place for the night?' Habiro knew of a Catholic mission with a bed still available, and if that was no good, the mayor's latest initiative still had spare tents according to a recent memo.

'VanBer,' Volks said. 'It's important.'

Ramon Habiro sighed.

'Look,' said Volks. 'Somebody got killed. I have to tell VanBer.' And that was the point Officer Habiro stopped practising tolerance and started paying attention.

'Go on,' he said.

'On where?' asked Volks, normal people could be odd.

'Who got killed?'

'Who knows?' asked Volks. 'Why would it matter . . . ? Call VanBer, tell him about the girl.'

'Which girl?'

Officer Habiro was gathering an audience. A couple of his colleagues, one of the civilian computer geeks, a cleaner who also brought in lunch for three of the Hispanic officers. Some were smiling, a few trying not to smirk. Only Officer Habiro was taking the situation seriously and then only because he was trying to make a point. All this changed the moment Volks looked round his audience and announced, 'One of yours.'

'One of our what?'

'Cop girl,' said Volks. 'Her dad got shot.'

A single voice cut through all the others. Lieutenant Que coming out of his office to see what the commotion was about and walking slap into Volks' last comment. 'Kris Zha?'

Volks nodded, wondering if he recognised the man from somewhere. 'In danger, Louie says. I need to tell VanBer.'

'Get Robert Van Berg,' said the lieutenant. He turned to the nearest officer. 'Start by putting in a call to Officer Valdez.' Catching the man's glance, Lieutenant Que scowled.

'Valdez is handling our liaison,' he said. 'Where's Kris now?' Lieutenant Que demanded of Volks. '*Come on,*' said the lieutenant, '*tell me.*'

'Louie's going to find her.'

'And where's Louie going?'

'I don't know,' said Volks apologetically. 'She didn't tell me.'

'Start looking,' Lieutenant Que told the nearest uniform. 'Start looking and don't stop . . .'

CHAPTER 50
Tuesday 16 March

After she left Volks with his message, Louie doubled back to throw anybody else off her scent. It seemed unlikely she'd be followed but the homeless woman with the kitten took her job very seriously.

Along the way Louie collected a couple of men she knew and using threats, blackmail and promises on which she would never deliver got them to start looking. How hard could it be to find a girl dressed in a *Death Cab* T-shirt, carrying a spiky rubber rucksack and followed by a huge fox? Not least, when most other white kids were wearing Gap or T-shirts advertising synthetic bands. (Louie had strong opinions on the state of punk. Mind you, Louie had strong opinions on most things.)

Virgin Records was full of tourists and empty of anyone Louie wanted to see. The other music shop on Union Square was equally see through. Maybe the girl had gone home? Louie considered this for all of three seconds, which was how long it took Louie to remember that in nearly a week of being followed, Kris had barely used her home as more than somewhere to sleep. Whatever the fight with her mother was about, it must have been bad to leave Kris that rootless.

'Hey.' A girl Louie barely recognised was waving her arms from across the street. 'You Louie?'

'Who wants to know?'

'Dix . . .' The girl dodged a cable car and bared her teeth when a taxi almost clipped the shopping trolley she dragged in her wake. Louie could remember when people still had proper names but it seemed so long ago now.

'Someone said the kid's heading up Columbus.'

'Who said?'

Dix shrugged. 'Don't know,' she said. '*Tell Louie the kid's heading up Columbus*. You're Louie, so I told you . . .' The girl turned away, job done.

Shit, thought Louie, I was right first time. Kris was heading home. Alternatively, Colonel Billy's friend had a house on Cicero Street and that old doctor had a place on the Steps behind, Kris could be going to either of those. Although why she'd be doing that . . .

Clambering aboard a cable car, Louie slumped into a seat near the back. A girl in a green T-shirt pointedly changed places and a couple opposite suddenly started to take great interest in the shops behind them. Since these included a Wendies, a wholesale jeweller and some outfit offering cheap deals on computer cases, Louie wasn't convinced.

'Two dollars.'

Louie looked at the brakeman as if he was mad. She'd seen him a week earlier, laughing with the tourists and pulling faces at kids. So she knew he was one of the good guys. All the same . . .

'It's two dollars, lady.'

Louie almost paid up just for that final word. Only people like her never took cable cars and never paid when they did.

She shrugged.

'Lady . . .' As the brakeman with the ponytail became aware that a dozen people were watching to see what he would do next, he decided to do nothing. Crazies were a part of this city. Without crazies and the threat of earthquakes San Francisco was just somewhere else.

'I have to get off at Russian Hill,' Louie announced. 'Find a girl and a fox.'

'Sure,' said the man. 'I'll let you know.'

Why would he lie? All the same, when the car ground to a halt at a crossing and the brakeman smiled at Louie, saying here would be a good place to get off, she almost refused, convinced he wanted to trick her.

It didn't look like Russian Hill to Louie, but then nothing looked right from the seat of a cable car. The angles were odd and mostly all Louie could see was the top of people's heads.

'*Hey . . . Louie, wait up.*'

Another voice she didn't recognise. Between them, Herbie, Volks and Zephyr must have spread the word across half the city. Within an hour, they'd probably know about it down in Mission but by then it would be too late.

'You Louie?'

'Yeah,' said Louie. 'That's me.'

'Thought so,' said the old man. 'Black, little cat, small tits. Walks bent at the hip like she's in a hurry.'

'I am in a hurry,' said Louie.

'Okay,' said the man. 'She's over there.'

'Who?' demanded Louie, wanting it spelt out.

'Rubber rucksack. White skin, black T-shirt, frizzy hair, stud under her bottom lip, talks to herself a lot . . .' He recited the list from memory. 'That's the one, right?'

'Sounds like her.'

'Good. Can't see the fox, though. Tell Volks he owes me.'

Another one gone while Louie was still trying to form a reply. Not that it mattered. He'd got it right and Kris was coming up the road. In fact, she was walking right towards Louie.

'*So*,' said Kris, '*what do I do . . . ?*' The question was addressed to no one in particular. Although the girl answered it herself. '*How should I know . . . ?*'

She wasn't mad, Louie could recognise what passed for mad. Kris was just working stuff out for herself and doing it aloud; age and embarrassment would cure the girl of that. Behind her trotted the fox, eyes sweeping the street and mouth open in a toothy grin.

Stepping back, Louie watched them pass. It all depended where the girl was heading. If she was going to the suit's house and Colonel Billy's friend was at home then Louie could leave it at that.

The kid would be safe. 'Come on,' said Louie, holding her breath as Kris Zha paused, glanced once at the small black woman and began to climb Cicero Street. 'That's right,' said Louie. 'Almost there.'

Sure enough, the girl stopped outside the Begley House, looked round her briefly and walked up to the bell.

'. . . Eleven, twelve, thirteen, fourteen.'

Surely someone should have come by now? This was too long to wait for Colonel Billy's friend to answer the door. The kid had to know that, which didn't stop Kris from ringing the bell again.

'. . . Eight, nine, ten, eleven.'

Louie counted off the seconds, remembering to add *elephants* after each. She couldn't remember when she'd been taught to do that. Probably around the time she was learning to jump out of aeroplanes.

297

Counting elephants stopped your parachute getting wrapped round the tail.

As Kris was about to turn away, and Louie was getting ready to intercept the girl and tell her she was in danger, the door opened . . . So Louie stepped behind a hedge and watched a woman in jeans greet Kris by name. Behind the woman stood a man. Louie didn't recognise him either, although it was obvious he knew Kris.

'Where have you been?'

Kris seemed puzzled.

'Everyone's been looking for you,' said Sergeant Sanchez. 'You're in danger.'

'*I'm what?*'

'You're in danger,' said the woman. 'There's no time to explain, but you have to come with me.'

Despite herself, Kris glanced from the woman to Sergeant Sanchez, who nodded. 'You'll be safe with Ozzie,' he said, and when Kris still looked uncertain, Sanchez added, 'You'll just have to trust us.'

The woman looked as if she planned to say something, until Sergeant Sanchez shook his head . . . Another woman might have scowled, this one just grinned. She was harder to recognise without her headscarf, but she still carried her bag, the one containing a gun.

Out of there, Louie wanted to shout. *Get out of there now.* Only the words strangled in her throat and shouting might make things worse; if things could be made worse, so Louie chose silence and continued to watch.

'Look,' said Sanchez. 'I know about your argument with Ellen and I understand you hate the fact your mom turned to me for comfort . . . But we both care for you and know how hard you've found the death of your dad. I also know that nothing I'm feeling about your dad's death can come close to what you feel.'

He's lying, Louie wanted to say. *Can't you see that he's lying?* Only Kris just nodded, half in agreement and half to acknowledge she might actually have misjudged the man.

Seconds later, a cab drew up and the woman opened the door for Kris, waited until the girl was inside and climbed in after her. Whatever she said to the driver, it made the man lock all his doors.

'Sanchez,' said Sanchez, pulling a small box from his belt. He listened intently. 'Shit,' he said. 'In danger . . . You're sure about

this? The lieutenant himself . . . Okay, I'll get right on it. Where am I?'
Sergeant Sanchez stared up and down the slope of Cicero Street, with
its picture-book houses and elegant trees.

'Just off Union Square,' he said. 'I'll get moving right away.'

CHAPTER 51
Tuesday 16 March

The woman with the weird-shit baby contraption looked puzzled. Maybe she had trouble understanding Louie's question or maybe she wondered why it was being asked of her; either way, having considered the problem for a second, she did what most people in most cities do when confronted with one of the homeless, tried to circumvent her problem.

This was a mistake, largely because Liz Orton had no idea how fast the small homeless woman could move and because Liz forgot to allow for the fact she was wheeling a pushchair.

It was the fox's fault. Louie had waited for it to do something useful, like follow the car, but it had just turned, grinned at her. And its grin said, *So what are you going to do now?*

'I need your phone,' said Louie, materialising right where the woman intended to go. She spoke slowly, just in case her original words had been jumbled or the woman was hard of hearing. 'Do you have one?'

Liz Orton nodded. She regretted this the moment she did so. Only, by then, it was too late because the tiny woman with the kitten tucked into her shirt was holding out a hand.

'It's an emergency,' said Louie.

The jogger looked doubtful.

'If I don't make this call,' said Louie, 'someone could die.'

Liz, whose afternoon until this point had been very ordinary, wondered if that was a threat, and decided she probably didn't want to find out. All the same, some weird kind of pride refused to let her give in immediately. 'Who do you want to call?' she asked.

'The police . . .'

The jogger thought about that and decided there was absolutely no way she could refuse this request.

'You want to call the police . . . ? And if you don't, someone might die?'

Louie's nod was emphatic.

'I'll call them for you,' said Liz Orton, pleased with herself for having come up with such a sensible solution.

'Okay . . . Tell them I need to talk to the suit. Say it's about Kris . . .'

'Kris?'

'Her dad died. He was SFPD. She's in danger . . .'

The jogger juggled the facts, thought about them and came up with an obvious question. 'Who from?'

'I don't know, but there's a sergeant involved. And a woman called Ozzie, who was in the Stockton Tunnel . . .'

Liz Orton handed Louie her cellphone. 'I think you'd better call them yourself.'

'The suit,' Louie demanded, the moment the 911 call was picked up at the other end. 'No,' said Louie, 'I don't have an address. I need to talk to the Colonel Billy's friend . . . No, I don't know the number of this phone.'

She listened some more.

'No,' Louie said, 'just put me onto the suit.'

When she gave the cellphone back to the woman with the blades it was with a puzzled shrug. 'They don't want to help,' Louie said, and walked away, unaware that Liz Orton would spend the rest of her day explaining to assorted SFPD personnel she'd simply lent her phone to a homeless woman and no this wasn't a habit of hers.

By then Louie had long since tracked down Colonel Billy's friend. Well, Volks tracked him down to the public library on Larkin Street, where he was frantically databasing articles on Stalin, Gregory Osip and a Soviet surgeon from the 1950s called Vladimir Demikhov.

Louie tracked down Volks by telling everyone she met to get him to find her the moment they saw him. Eventually, the messages all caught up with each other and Volks went back to Chinatown Station to tell the lieutenant what Louie had seen.

The man told Volks he didn't believe it, but something in his eyes said he did and Volks left with another $20 and a warning from Lieutenant Que to keep his mouth shut. As she was seeing Volks out, the SFPD officer who'd been in with the lieutenant dug into her bag to produce another $20 and wonder, casually, if Volks knew where Mr VanBer had been heading. The man she went on to describe sounded more like Colonel Billy's friend.

Volks thought it best to lie.

CHAPTER 52

Tuesday 16 March

When Louie found the suit he was looking older than she remembered, his face sunken and haunted. A fine sweat covered most of his forehead and she could smell something close to fear.

'It's going to be okay,' she said.

'Maybe,' said Bobby, closing down his library computer. 'You've got news for me?'

'Kris is in danger . . .' The waif-thin black woman with the lycra top kept her statement simple. It seemed best to explain quickly what happened. 'I saw it,' she added.

'You saw what . . . ?'

So Louie told him, she left out some bits and got muddled in a couple of places but she got in the facts that mattered. The man being shot in Stockton tunnel. A single shot to the head, small gun. This was the detail which convinced Bobby she was telling the truth, because he'd already heard about that. So Louie told Bobby some more, like the stuff about the woman in the door of Bobby's own house and the SFPD officer behind her.

Louie had been expecting Bobby to be interested in the officer but he was much more concerned about the woman. And when Louie told him she was called Ozzie, Bobby buried his head in his hands and began to swear, a low and vicious litany that mostly involved the words *idiot* and *fuck*.

'Sanchez definitely called her Ozzie?'

'Yes,' said Louie, 'I've got good ears. It was the woman from the tunnel. I recognised her.'

'No,' said Bobby. 'You didn't, no one did. You know how to hide in this world?'

303

'How?' asked Louie, looking interested.

'Become someone else . . .'

Louie laughed so hard that a librarian came and asked Bobby and Louie to leave the building. On their way out people stepped aside to let them through. So much fear in this world, beneath the cappuccino froth and milky certainties. At Louie's suggestion, they ended up on a bench in front of City Hall. It might have been mid-March, but the early evening sun still glazed the black dome in front of them and was hot enough to prickle the back of Bobby's neck.

'What do you need?' Louie asked.

He thought about that. 'I need to know I'm not going to die,' he said. 'At least, not before this is through.'

'You're worried by death?'

'I can taste it like blood,' said Bobby. 'Smell it on my fingers.' This showed an unusually developed sense of intelligence for someone not living on the streets, at least that was Louie's opinion.

'You expecting it soon?'

'That's my problem.' Bobby shrugged. 'I don't know.'

'No one knows,' said Louie firmly. 'And worrying about it only brings it closer. Isn't there anything sensible you need?'

'A rifle,' said Bobby, 'laser sights, as much back-up as possible.' He listed these with little expectation that Louie could help.

'We could simply call the police,' Louie said, surprising herself.

'They'd only arrest Sanchez.'

'You don't want him arrested?'

Bobby shook his head. 'I want him dead, and Kris is my responsibility. I got her into this.'

'Fine,' said Louie, 'we'll do it your way. Everyone will get knives because blades are easiest to find and they're silent. This rifle, you have a model in mind?'

'Let me make a call . . .' Walking over to a tree, Bobby parked himself beneath it and punched in Latif's number from memory. For all Bobby knew someone was tracking his calls. If so, let them.

'Me,' he said.

The man at the other end grunted something which might have been a greeting. Alternatively Latif could just have been feeling non-committal.

'I need a rifle.'

'Thought you said we were done,' said Latif. 'All square.'

'We are. I'll pay the going price.'

'What are you hunting?'

'Something big . . .'

Another grunt, then a question. 'Big as a pig, maybe a little bigger?'

'Yeah,' said Bobby, 'that's about right.'

'Okay, you're going to want a clean kill. That means stopping power. How close are you going to get to this animal?'

'As close as I can,' said Bobby. 'But not so close I spook it.'

'Laser sight,' Latif said. 'Long barrel, thirty-ought-eight slugs . . . Yeah, we should be able to do that. When do you want to collect the gun?'

'I don't,' said Bobby. 'I'm going to send someone.'

Understandably enough, Latif didn't like the sound of that. 'How am I going to recognise them? More to the point, why should I trust them?'

'Because I'm sending them,' said Bobby, dealing with the second problem first; then he said, 'You remember my Evidenza?' Of course Latif did. It was the rose gold, three-dial model and this was a man who wore two watches at the same time. 'I'm going to send it with the person, okay? That's the sign they're for real. And you get to keep the watch . . .'

Yeah, he thought that might make a difference.

'It's all fixed,' Bobby told Louie. 'You take this to Latif and bring back the gun.'

'Me?' Louie looked at Bobby as if he was mad. 'I'm not taking anything anywhere,' she said. 'I'm coming with you. Zephyr can fetch it.'

'Who . . . ?'

'Used to be in the Marines,' Louie explained, seeing Bobby's expression. 'He likes that stuff. Me, I regard weapons strictly as hardware. We'll need to talk to Zephyr about back-up.' She looked at Bobby. 'Do you have any money?'

He gave her what he had.

'Fuck,' said Louie, and this was a woman who made a point never to swear. 'You any idea where that woman's taken Kris?'

Of course he had. 'White Drop,' said Bobby, at least, he hoped so because Bobby was about to bet his life on it, Kris's too . . . and the whole of San Francisco knew where White Drop was. Well, the bits which read the *Chronicle* and paid attention to *Atlantic Monthly* and the

New Yorker. White Drop was where it had always been, slung into the side of a cliff overlooking the Pacific and staring down with Olympian detachment on jagged rocks and slate-grey waves alike.

'You know who she is? That woman.'

'Yes,' said Bobby. 'I know.'

'And Kris . . . Why her?'

Bobby had trouble understanding Louie's question.

'I mean,' said Louie, 'why did they kidnap *Kris*?' She looked at Bobby. 'That's what just happened, right?'

'I think so.'

'So why?'

The man standing in front of Louie thought of all possible answers to that question and didn't like any of them; but one of them, the one which made the most sense, he absolutely hated.

'She's my daughter,' said Bobby. 'I think the woman who took Kris knows that.' He was ready for more questions and mentally preparing his answers, wondering how to keep them short when Louie just nodded, like it all suddenly made perfect sense.

'Wait here,' she said. 'I'll have Zephyr fetch your gun.'

In the end Bobby went on by himself to White Drop. Louie was less than keen, because, Bobby finally realised, she felt it was her job to keep an eye on him and waiting for Zephyr prevented her from doing this.

Bobby didn't know whether to be amused, irritated or reduced to tears.

'You take care.'

'Of course.'

'There's no of course about it,' said Louie. 'I mean look at you. When did you last eat?' She said this with all the authority of a woman so thin she could still fit into the clothes of a child.

'I'm fine,' said Bobby.

Louie snorted.

That was how they parted, Bobby half wondering if he'd see Louie again and half hoping he might. Quite apart from liking her he needed that gun, and would do his best to make himself wait until it arrived.

CHAPTER 53
Tuesday 16 March

One gull circling on the evening air is a noble sight; the lost soul of a mariner and a reminder that the air we breathe is not simply a mix of molecules but a living and moving medium. Even a handful of gulls have something about them. It is only when gulls gather in their dozens, raucous and cruel, that they become something else, something uglier. Something close to human.

Hunger, superstition and a wish to stay alive . . .

The instincts which drove him were simple, Bobby knew this. Even after he realised his single gull was actually two, maybe three riding the dregs of a thermal and disappearing and reappearing from behind a promontory, he was still impressed enough to let his eyes follow the flight.

A steeply sloping jumble of scree leading from the roadside to the water's edge had been cut back by some contractor and shaped with such casual disregard for what was originally there that it came close to genius.

Next to the road stood a gate, something that sounded simple, until one realised the gate stood twenty feet above a garage cut into the cliff; and the gate only existed because in-filled stone walls created the ground on which it now stood. The drop from this gate to a hairpin in the drive was so steep it probably needed to be negotiated with one foot on the brake. Having rounded this bend, an equally steep stretch led down to the garage. Steps from the garage led down to the house.

So closely did White Drop fit into the cliff that it was almost entirely hidden from the road above. Because of this, Bobby had positioned himself on a slope to one side of the house, half sheltered behind a rock. The more he looked at the house, the less likely it seemed that he could enter by any way other than walking up to the front door and knocking.

Its walls were cast concrete, the angles brutal. Only a semi-circular room facing the sea softened the lines, and even then, the jutting curve of its floor provided the ceiling for a cubist cave that overlooked a triangular pool.

Anyone who didn't already know the architectural details could have discovered them simply by checking back issues of any newspaper for the end of July 2004, the week Gregory Osip bought White Drop and announced he was about to move in.

He never did.

Excitement turned to disappointment and then boredom as the long-awaited arrival of one of Russia's richest oligarchs failed to happen. Letters of complaint to the *Chronicle* about White Drop being left empty grew so frequent a local pressure group was invited to tour the property.

Far from being allowed to go to ruin, repairs had been made, some of the field stone walls had been rebuilt – to the highest standards, reported one of those inspecting the house – and even the famed Mediterranean garden was being tended, bushes pruned and cacti replanted. According to the *Chronicle*, a skeleton staff were on hand to keep the house in top condition for when Mr Osip felt safe enough to move in.

Safe from *what* went unreported. Although few who bothered to follow such things had much doubt that Osip meant safe from Moscow, safe from the reach of Colonel Putin, ex-KGB officer and breaker of oligarchs.

Everyone knew what happened next. *Princess Alisa*, Gregory Osip's yacht anchored off White Drop (and yacht was a very loose description for a vessel that featured three staterooms, five bedrooms, satellite navigation, two 480bhp Volvo Penta engines and its own casino).

After a month the yacht left, only to reappear about three months later. This happened twice. It was on the second return that, according to everyone's best guess, a Russian agent blew up the yacht, sinking the *Princess Alisa* and killing everyone aboard, including Gregory Osip.

Except that wasn't the way it went at all, was it?

Bobby knew that now. In fact, he was probably one of only three people who knew what *did* happen. If Bobby was right, then his daughter was in more trouble than Bobby could even contemplate. And if he was wrong? Bobby reached into his pocket for his phone. If he was wrong, things weren't that much better.

'This is Felicidad Valdez. I'm not answering calls right now but leave a message and I'll call you back, promise.'

Bobby sat with his back to a rock, watching the gulls still circle overhead and listening to Flic not answer his calls. It was nothing personal, at least Bobby didn't think so. Flic had her phone turned off and her service provider kept switching Bobby through to voicemail. Since that was the way the system was meant to work he could hardly blame them.

Sometime soon he was going to have to add some words to his silences. It would help, of course, if he knew what he wanted to say. Just in case Flic had got back yet, he called her home. He'd tried that once already and got Mrs Valdez, demanding, *Quién?* To which he'd been unable to give an answer.

All he got this time was an answering machine. 'Niva Valdez, Felicidad and Felipe aren't here right now. Please leave a message and we'll get back to you.' Again it was Flic's voice, you could tell a lot about a woman from her voice, or maybe he was just making that up.

'Flic, it's Bobby . . .' He needed something else to fill the silence, like words and meaning. 'You know I told you I might not always be around? Well, I wanted to say I love you.' Bobby sighed, he probably shouldn't have said that. For a moment, he considered breaking the connection, calling her own phone and leaving his message on that, but he was too far in and there was little he could say more revealing than what he'd just said.

One should say that kind of thing face to face. He should probably have said it already. God knows, it would have been true. Maybe he'd still get the chance.

'I'm not sure what's going to happen next and I'd like to be able to tell you where I am, but then you'd want to come out here and I've probably got you into enough trouble already. That's it really. I'm sorry for hurting you. I'm glad we were able to make our peace. I'll catch you later.'

A click, a change in the quality of silence and then a voice, breathless and anxious. 'Bobby . . . Are you still there?'

Yes and no. Bobby cut the connection, switched off his phone and settled back against his rock to watch a fat sun sink into the ocean.

Everybody cried, it didn't necessarily mean anything. After a while, he began to wonder where Louie was.

A bundle of rags thrust out its hand, so Bobby shook, then stepped back as the bundle yanked a smaller bundle off its back and crouched beside the rock.

'This is Zephyr,' said Louie.

Kneeling, the ragged man unrolled that day's *Chronicle* to reveal a Remington 7400, with telescopic sights and laser pointer slung under the barrel.

'Got a message,' said the bundle. 'The black man says this was what he can do in the time, the number's been acid etched and over-stamped and the barrel is virgin. Oh, and thanks for the watch . . .' Message delivered, Zephyr stopped talking. The stubborn determination on his face vanishing as he glanced around him, apparently puzzled to find himself on a side road overlooking the Pacific.

'Louie?'

'Good job,' she said. 'Well done.'

Zephyr smiled.

'Here,' said Louie, 'I want you to take this.' She handed Zephyr the kitten from the front of her T-shirt and watched his smile disappear.

'That's your cat.'

'Colonel Billy's cat,' said Louie. 'I was just babysitting.'

'Is the colonel coming back?'

Louie thought about it. 'Doubt it,' she said finally. 'Don't think he'd want to anyway. Once was more than enough.'

'So what do I do with this?'

'Look after it,' said Louie. 'Or let it look after you. Lucifer's a lucky cat,' she added, inspiration suddenly striking. 'Okay? He's very lucky. Things are going to be much better from now on.'

Zephyr started to smile again.

'Right,' said Louie, reaching for the rifle. 'I'll take that.'

Keeping his grip, Bobby blinked as Louie simply twisted it from his fingers. It wasn't strength that gave her the rifle but a trick of the wrists. He'd seen Louie tense and only realised his fingers had released their grip when the gun was already in her hands.

'You ever used one of these?'

'No,' said Bobby. 'Have you?'

'Oh yes.' Louie nodded. 'Latest model, at least it was when I knew about stuff like that.' As she talked, her fingers adjusted knobs and checked the sight was solid and the settings correct.

'You can't go in there carrying a rifle,' said Louie. 'They'd kill you before you reached the door. You got to go in naked.' She caught his look. 'Not actually,' she said, 'but no visible weapons. Think about it . . . Why did they kidnap Kris in the first place?'

Bobby had been thinking about it. He'd been thinking about little else. The only answer he could come up with was that Kris knew something she shouldn't or they wanted something.

'So what do they want?'

'Me?'

'How would I know?' demanded Louie, sounding exasperated. 'It's your daughter they've kidnapped.' Behind her, Zephyr looked suddenly serious, upset and almost comically sympathetic, while an elderly man behind him, whom Bobby hadn't even seen arrive, sucked his teeth in disgust at the state of the world.

'This is Leroy. He was a friend of Billy's.'

'We were in the same unit.'

Bobby looked at him. 'Which unit was that?'

'Hundred and first Airborne. Tat Defensive. Spring of 1968 . . . We didn't really know each other back then. Hell, guys like me didn't talk to spooks like him. And they didn't talk to us.'

'Colonel Billy was black,' said Bobby.

The old man shook his head. 'Not back then he wasn't. He was pink as a baby and almost as useless. A couple of the brothers would have fragged him, but he kept trying to get it right, and he kept trying not to get us killed. You can't ask more from an officer than that.'

Bobby sighed.

'Take a knife,' said Louie, pulling one from the bottom of a bag. 'And you've got a gun, right?'

'How do you know that?'

Smiling, Louie said, 'Shoulder holster. You think I don't notice stuff like that? Take this as well.' She handed him a revolver so tiny it looked like it belonged on a key ring. 'Three shots,' she said, 'use it real close, back of the skull or behind a knee . . .'

He put the gun in his sock.

'Now take this,' said Louie, handing Bobby an old Colt, the 1911 government model.

'What do I want with that?'

311

'You need stuff you can give up,' Louie told him. 'You worked out what they want yet?'

'Me,' said Bobby. 'I think.'

There was one way to find out . . . Actually, there were two, although Bobby only realised this when he'd already broken cover, so he ducked down again, avoided questioning looks from Louie, Zephyr and Leroy and reached for his phone. 'Ellen, hi . . .' Listening to the woman on the other end struggle to put a name to his voice, Bobby was tempted to say, *Hey it's me* . . . Only that would be cruel and counter-productive and Bobby was shocked to discover he didn't want to be either.

'I'm calling about Kris,' he said. At which point Bobby had to hold the phone away from his ear, so loud was Ellen's anguish. Everyone waited while Bobby let Ellen have her say, and none of it differed very much from what he felt himself.

'Has there been a note?'

A wail of words from the other end suggested there had.

'You know what it said?'

She didn't and that was interesting. If the note had gone to Ellen then obviously she'd have known, and if it had gone to the *Chronicle*, the whole city would have known. Bobby could think of no reason to keep the contents from Ellen, unless what the note threatened was unusually horrific or security demanded it.

Bobby was ahead of the SFPD and he was behind them, a tricky space to occupy, so he decided to take a risk. Something he began to regret as soon as he opened his mouth; as things turned out, it was okay.

'Look,' Bobby said, 'you're not going to like this.'

Ellen waited.

'The thing is . . .'

'Just say it.' Ellen's voice was brutal.

'Sanchez, you shouldn't trust him. The kidnapping was witnessed. Sergeant Sanchez was there.'

'I know,' Ellen said. 'Pete Sanchez told me. He saw Robert Van Berg bundling my child into a car. And you're him, aren't you?' said Ellen. 'We've been waiting for this call.'

'I didn't take Kris,' said Bobby. 'Sanchez did.' He was about to say more, when he realised the obvious. 'This line is tapped, isn't it? They've got a wire on this . . .' Nobody used wires anymore but the old words stuck.

Ellen said nothing.

'Good,' said Bobby, 'then this is for the record. Pio Xavier Sanchez is involved in the kidnapping of Kris Zha and he was behind the murder of Sergeant Bobby Zha, the girl's father. There are witnesses to both of these events.'

Street people and a ghost, or whatever the fuck he was.

'Pete . . . ?'

'He might not have pulled the trigger, but he still knelt beside your husband and watched him die.'

'How do you know?'

'I was there,' said Bobby. 'That's a fact. Deal with it.'

If the FBI were involved then that would go into the record. If not, and the kidnapping was still being handled by Chinatown Station, then the moment the lieutenant saw a transcript of this conversation he'd brand it a lie, and probably demand both transcript and tape be destroyed immediately.

He'd done it once before, for entirely noble reasons. There would be no loose ends, no dirty washing still on display when Lieutenant Que retired. A lot of things were finally beginning to make sense.

CHAPTER 54

Wednesday 17 March

The front door to White Drop was some weird German design that pivoted slightly off centre and opened within its own space. Although Bobby only discovered this several minutes later, after he'd wasted time pressing his thumb into the centre of a bell push and heard ringing in the distance.

Nothing the first time and nothing the second, just the sound of a bell chosen for its perfect pitch. When he got fed up with waiting, Bobby rang a third time and kept his thumb on the button.

'Okay, okay . . .' The accent was thick. 'We're coming.'

Steps thundered down wooden stairs and Ozzie threw open the door. She was looking very pleased with herself. 'At last,' she said. 'I was beginning to think Peter had got it wrong.' Beckoning to Bobby, she stepped back to give her guest more room. 'Come in . . . I'd love to say my house is your house but . . .' She shrugged. 'I make it a policy not to lie.'

Gregory Osip had been handsome, wide cheeked and slightly plump. The woman in front of Bobby was almost rat-faced, her breasts pressing hard against her vest. A faded razor-wire tattoo circled the wrist where Osip had worn his famous and fabulously expensive watches. The gold rings were gone. Five simple gold studs ran up the outside of her ear.

It took courage or desperation to do what Gregory Osip had done to his body and yet they both knew it wasn't enough. A yacht destroyed, its crew dead, extreme surgery, sleight of hand and still Russian intelligence had tracked Ozzie down to Dr Persikov's house.

'Through there,' said Ozzie.

Bobby walked into a semi-circular room made famous by interior design magazines the world over, and found himself facing a 180 degree vista of the Pacific. A view so staggering that, for a second, Bobby could almost forget the gun held to his back. The magazines had got it right. The view was perfect.

'You see why I bought White Drop?'

Yes, Bobby could see. Money might not buy happiness but it could buy space, it could buy time and from the look of things, it could also buy a sliver of dawn creeping across the dark surface of the planet's biggest ocean.

'Sanchez,' called Ozzie.

A metal gate clanged below a window, feet slapped on concrete steps and Sergeant Pete Sanchez came through the door. He was still in uniform.

'He's investigating a crime,' said Ozzie, catching Bobby's surprise.

Sanchez laughed.

'Fetch the girl,' Ozzie ordered.

Somehow, from everything he'd seen, Bobby expected Kris to be dragged in blindfold or with her hands cuffed behind her back. Instead Sanchez disappeared down the steps and came back seconds later with Kris, who was clutching a towel.

Ozzie shrugged. 'I've got a pool,' she said. 'It seemed a pity not to let Kris use it.' She smiled at the girl, who did her best to smile back. Apart from a bruise on one cheek, she looked fine.

'You okay?'

'So far,' said Kris, though her fingers found her face, feeling for the ache.

Ozzie sighed. 'Sanchez can be a bit crude at times.'

'Yes,' Bobby said. 'So I've heard.' He was about to leave that comment hanging, until a tightening around the sergeant's eyes made him decide to push it further. 'You should hear his girlfriend on the subject . . . I fucked her,' Bobby added, when Ozzie looked puzzled.

'Can't get it up without using a dildo, right? Or is it handcuffs?'

Two steps brought Sanchez close enough to drive a fist deep into Bobby's side. 'Liar,' he said, dragging Bobby to his feet again.

'Yelped like a dog,' said Bobby. 'Crawled on all fours.'

'Later,' Ozzie said, when Sanchez raised his fist a second time. 'First, search him.'

'Believe me,' said Sanchez. 'There will be a later . . .' Glaring from his target to the rat-faced woman, his eyes revealed a darkness he'd kept

315

hidden behind wry smiles the whole time Bobby knew him; except Bobby hadn't known him. No one did, except maybe Bea. In those eyes was a cruelty to burn villages and impale children on sharpened stakes.

'I'll ask her,' Sanchez added. 'Find out from Bea if you're telling the truth.' That was when Bobby knew he had to kill this man, he'd left himself no choice.

'Begged for more,' said Bobby, and Sanchez hit him anyway.

'Enough,' hissed Ozzie. 'Search him, *now*.'

That was the difference, Bobby realised. People like Sanchez burnt villages to order and those like Ozzie had it done.

'Stand,' Sanchez said.

The woman held her gun to Bobby's head while the sergeant opened Bobby's jacket and removed a regulation-issue Sig Sauer P229. Next Sanchez patted down Bobby's back until he found the 1911 Colt tucked into his belt, Zephyr's offering. The gravity knife he found in the right-hand pocket of Bobby's jacket.

'Boy's toys,' said Ozzie.

Sanchez grinned.

'At least,' said Bobby, 'I can get it up without . . .'

When the pain receded, Bobby got to examine White Drop's floor at first hand. It was, obviously enough, of the highest quality; hand polished *cinza rajado* from Brazil. Had Sanchez's kick landed where it was meant to land, Bobby would have been beyond caring, unconscious or curled around himself and fighting waves of darkness.

As it was, he curled around himself anyway and stayed down, his cheek cool against the tiles. He could hear gulls beyond an open window and the sound of waves breaking against black rocks on the shoreline, the thud of his own heart . . . And he could hear Ozzie being angry and Sanchez busy justifying himself, and somewhere behind all that was Kris in tears.

'Get the scissors.' Ozzie's voice was sharp. 'Go on . . .' Footsteps vanished up wooden stairs and clatter came from above. 'In the bathroom,' she said.

Clatter from a different room and then more feet on the stairs.

Bobby felt himself being lifted roughly and slammed into a chair. 'Yelped,' he said, through broken lips.

'*Sanchez* . . .'

Gripping Bobby's head, the woman pulled it back. 'Look at me,' she demanded. When Bobby finally did, he found himself staring into the dead eyes of one of the world's richest people. A woman, who looked no happier than anyone else. 'Stop it,' suggested Ozzie, touching her thumb to Bobby's eye and wiping away blood. 'Or I will hurt you myself, and believe me, that will be a very different thing.'

Bobby shrugged.

'Alternatively,' she said. 'I could hurt the girl.' Ozzie smiled, satisfied with whatever she saw in Bobby's eyes. 'Everyone has a weakness and it's mostly their family. Why do you think I never had children?'

Outside a gull continued to cry, circling above waves that spent themselves on distant rocks. The city would be waking, couples fucking, quarrelling or preparing for work. Flic would be out there somewhere, wondering how much of what she'd been told by Bobby was true. An old Chinese detective would be deciding whether he dared wipe a telephone record. Ellen would be waiting for news of her missing daughter. And the girl, whom Bobby could just see out of the corner of his eye . . .

Bobby wasn't sure what would happen about the girl.

'You,' Ozzie said. 'Come here.'

Kris flinched.

'Come on,' said the Russian, so the girl did as she was told.

'Do you know this man?'

Kris Zha shook her head.

'You've met him?'

'Yes.' Kris nodded, reluctantly. It was heartbreaking, the kid was trying to work out what was best for him and not for herself. *You don't know me*, Bobby wanted to say. *We've never met.*

'He was friends with my dad.'

'Is that what he told you?'

'That's true,' said Kris. 'I promise.'

When the rat-faced woman smiled it was to reveal teeth stained with age and broken. The only example of reverse cosmetic dentistry that Bobby could remember. Her vest was cheap, her nipples prominent beneath thin cloth. She stank of untipped cigarettes and sweat. Moscow had promised it would break the oligarchs. *Make them wear a hair shirt*, was the phrase used. What Ozzie had done to herself seemed far worse.

'You see these scissors?'

Kris nodded, her eyes wide.

'Right . . . You ever cut anyone's hair?'

She shook her head.

'Now's your chance to learn,' said Ozzie. Turning to Bobby, she asked, 'Do we need to tie you?'

'I'll behave,' Bobby promised.

'Good, then we're agreed. No sudden movements or rude comments to our friend.' Ozzie was smiling, which was more than could be said for Sanchez. For a second, Bobby wondered if the woman understood how dangerous Pete Sanchez could be and then realised Ozzie must have spent a life surrounded by such people, only experience could explain the casual indifference with which she treated Sanchez, like a handler with a half-wild dog.

'A bit rusty,' Ozzie told Kris, handing her the scissors. 'But they should be up to the . . .' Glancing from Sanchez to her prisoner, Ozzie shook her head. 'Don't say it,' she told Bobby.

Sanchez flushed.

Taking the scissors, Kris hesitated. 'What am I meant to do?'

'Cut off all my hair,' said Bobby. 'Come on. Do what Ozzie says.'

She was methodical and careful, thinking first about what she had to do and the best way to do it before she began. The very qualities her school reports always accused Kris of lacking.

'Come on,' said Sanchez. 'Hurry it up.'

So Kris cut faster, tears rolling down her face. She thought this was some kind of ritual, Bobby could see that in her eyes. A way of preparing him for execution. Her view of crime was very simple.

'Okay,' said Ozzie impatiently. 'Enough . . .' Yanking Kris aside, she grabbed Bobby's skull with calloused fingers, turning it this way and that; and she kept turning his head, her eyes examining its cropped surface for proof that Robert Van Berg was what Sergeant Sanchez had promised, Dr Charles Weyler's only successful experiment. The brain of Bobby Zha transferred to another body.

'These aren't them,' Ozzie said, nodding to the faint creases left over from Van Berg's childhood accident. '*Where are the new scars?*'

'They have to be there, unless . . .'

'Unless what?' demanded Ozzie.

'Maybe Dr Weyler had a way to make scars invisible. That's what happened, isn't it?' he demanded of Bobby. 'The scars from your operation are invisible . . .' So animal were the eyes staring into Bobby's face that it was all Bobby could do not to shiver.

'What scars?' he said.

Sanchez hit him. 'Tell me,' demanded Sanchez, picking Bobby off the floor. 'How could Ozzie's doctor transfer your mind without opening up your skull? It's impossible.'

Bobby spat blood onto the floor. Red on white. So many memories, although now was probably not the time. So instead he looked Ozzie straight in the eyes. 'My name is Robert Van Berg,' he said. 'And I have no idea what Sergeant Sanchez is talking about. I work direct to the White House and I can give you telephone numbers if those help. Numbers to call and names to check.' Reeling off a couple, beginning with Morgan Cabot and the general in Washington, Bobby saw the woman blink.

The Osip intelligence machine was as good as rumour said.

'Check my inside pocket,' suggested Bobby.

Stepping forward, the Russian pulled open Bobby's jacket and did as suggested, albeit reluctantly. Maybe she thought his pocket was poisoned or sewn along the edge with hooks tipped in fugu. Something equally stupid.

'What is this?' she demanded.

'Read it.'

Ozzie handed the envelope to Sergeant Sanchez. 'What does this say?'

Sanchez read. 'Bullshit,' he protested, voice furious. 'It's a lie.'

'*What does it say . . . ?*'

'It says I work direct to the President of the United States of America,' said Bobby. 'That all agencies are required to provide any help I might need. And that I outrank all other agents in the field . . .'

Bobby's smile was slight. 'I don't know what lies Sergeant Sanchez has been feeding you, but that's the truth. And if you think I'd come after you without the CIA, FBI and NSA knowing then you're a fool.'

He stared hard at Ozzie. 'You may be many things,' said Bobby. 'I don't, however, think you're that. We want what you have. The working notes Dr Persikov carried out of Stalingrad. The notes you gave to Dr Weyler.'

So much made sense. The original laboratory must have been on the yacht that Ozzie had bombed. So, God alone knew where Charles Weyler had been working from in his last few days. Out of a cellar somewhere, maybe . . .

'It's a lie,' Sanchez said. 'He's Bobby Zha.'

'*Dad?*' said Kris. It was close to a cry of pain.

'He *is* Zha,' insisted Sanchez. 'You should have heard him call CSI. Watch this.' Grabbing his own revolver, he put it to Kris's head. 'Tell the truth,' he told Bobby. 'You're Zha, aren't you?' Pete Sanchez flicked back the hammer on his gun.

'Dad?'

'Jesus fuck,' said Bobby. 'No wonder Bea thinks you're a sad little cunt. Tell me.' He grinned at Sanchez. 'Is there anything you *can* manage without mechanical help . . . ? Howled like a dog,' Bobby added. 'Said it was the first decent—'

This time when Sanchez moved Bobby was waiting. He tried to roll with the punch, going over backwards and half splitting his skull when his chair hit the floor. The first kick splintered a couple of Bobby's ribs, but he avoided the second, rolling out of its way. By the time Sanchez had positioned himself for a third kick, Bobby was ready.

Louie's derringer was badly made and rusty, the bullets small calibre and Bobby only had three of the things, none of which mattered. He rode out the kick, locked one arm tight around Sanchez' ankle and pushed the muzzle of the tiny revolver against his attacker's knee.

Sanchez screamed.

As an already flattened slug lost its battle to shred cartilage, Bobby fired again. The second bullet made it almost right the way through Sanchez's knee, before it too came to a halt, twisted and flattened beyond recognition.

By then, Bobby had pulled his attacker to the ground and crawled on top of him, twisting the screaming man's head so he could reach the back of his neck.

A final shot, silence and then the sound of Kris vomiting.

'Get up,' said Ozzie.

Bobby did as he was told.

Looking from the dead man to where Bobby now stood, tiny gun still in his hand, Ozzie shrugged. It looked like a toy. No, it was a toy compared to the Colt that Ozzie held.

'Give me a single reason why I shouldn't kill you.'

'Because,' said Bobby. 'Then there would be two presidents who want you dead or behind bars and you're having enough trouble coping with one.'

The Russian smiled. 'Good answer. I intend to leave now,' she said. 'Are there really soldiers and police waiting outside?'

'No,' Bobby said.

'I'm glad,' said Ozzie, 'taking hostages can get messy. I try to avoid messy whenever possible.'

'Then why murder all those animals?'

It was a reasonable enough question. You could see that from the way Ozzie and Bobby both turned to the girl, giving her their full attention.

'Well?' Kris demanded.

'That wasn't me,' said Ozzie. 'That was our good Dr Weyler failing to get his details right.'

'What details?'

Ozzie sighed. 'Fat Ivan,' she said. 'Heard of him?'

Kris hadn't, although Bobby had. That is, he'd seen the news.

'Cosmetic surgery,' said Ozzie. 'New name, fake passport, the best English bodyguards money could buy, even a wig. Moved to Istanbul, converted to Islam. You know how they found him . . . ? He didn't wear a condom and the prostitute was KGB. Fat Ivan was dead the day he booked a second massage.'

Ozzie turned a circle, raised her hands in the air and turned another one . . . 'Look at me,' she said, 'Tits, hips, buttocks, no balls . . . You can fuck with everything except DNA.'

'Yes,' said Bobby. 'I can see the problem.'

'Imagine being able to hot-swap bodies . . .' Ozzie's voice was almost wistful. 'No more obsessively having to clean where you've been. No more wondering if even haircuts can be used to find you.'

Bobby could guess the rest. 'You tracked down Dr Persikov. Got him to give you the notes he told Washington he didn't have.'

Ozzie patted his pocket. 'Persikov's real name is Misha Petrov. Fat Ivan found him, copied his original notes and gave them to Dr Weyler, a brilliant but particularly amoral example of the species. Only the Fat One died before Weyler could deliver. I was Dr Weyler's second choice.'

'And you wanted proof?'

'Who wouldn't?' said Ozzie.

A hundred animals and half a dozen homeless people died while Dr Weyler tried to prove transplanting brains, skulls or entire heads was possible, maybe a thousand animals. Yachts burnt, cars crashed, and all the while, White Drop stood empty as its owner cut the grass and trimmed hedges at the house where Dr Persikov lived. Bobby was willing to bet the laboratory had been aboard that yacht.

'He failed,' said Bobby.

Ozzie nodded, almost sadly. 'Three near misses. All human and all insane. He begged for one last chance and I agreed.' She nodded towards Kris. 'I offered him her father. Dr Weyler swore it would work this time. Instead he ballsed it up almost before he'd begun.'

'No.' Bobby shook his head. 'Your pet gunman ballsed it up by cutting out the bullet before Dr Weyler was ready.' He caught the surprise in Ozzie's eyes. 'I guess you didn't know that. And there's something else,' said Bobby, feeling the final pieces come together. 'It was you who shot the burglar and took the icon, then you had to give it back, until you decided to take it again.'

The Russian said nothing.

'Natalie was convinced you'd saved her grandfather's life. That's why she covered up for you.'

'I did save his life,' said Ozzie. 'He was the target. The KGB have been tidying up a lot of loose ends lately.'

'The KGB doesn't exist anymore,' said Kris, voice cross.

Ozzie smiled at her. 'You're such a child,' she said, turning for the door.

CHAPTER 55
Wednesday 17 March

Louie would always maintain the Russian fired first. The man Louie was talking about was actually an ex-East German spetnez who saw the sun reflect off Louie's telescopic sight and snatched for his own weapon, intending to provide cover for his boss who, by then, had almost reached the jetty.

Catching the sudden movement, Zephyr stood up and raised a revolver.

At this, Ozzie's bodyguard raised his own gun and while Zephyr was changing his mind about standing up, Louie put the Remington to her shoulder, drew a bead on the skull of the woman now sprinting towards a waiting boat and succeeded where a dozen of Gregory Osip's agents had failed.

It was over, Louie could go home.

None of this made the papers, television or even the wilder reaches of the internet. By the time the news was released of Gregory Osip's sudden reappearance and equally sudden death, the US government had already made a formal complaint to Moscow, claiming to have irrefutable proof that Osip had been shot by a member of the Russian secret service.

This was denied totally by the Russians, who blamed his death on rivalry between oligarchs; a group of men, the spokeswoman added, little better than gangsters.

The death of Sergeant Pete Sanchez was noted. His commander, a Lieutenant Que, spoke movingly of the officer's devotion to duty and his own shock at the way Sanchez had so obviously been tortured by Gregory Osip.

It was the death of Robert Van Berg which attracted most attention.

He was variously described as a friend of a recently murdered SFPD officer, an agent for a special ops unit based in Washington, and directly under the control of the President. After initially denying it had even heard of the man, the White House admitted it might have used him on certain missions.

This admission came shortly after a Select Committee announced that Mr Van Berg had undoubtedly been instrumental in preventing critical information falling into the wrong hands. The information in question was written in Russian on the back of an icon, handed to the authorities two days after the events at White Drop. The homeless woman who gave it in had been at White Drop on the day in question, according to some reports. Other reports suggested she'd found it in a bin.

No one ever really discovered what happened inside White Drop, after Gregory Osip left and before the SFPD, the FBI and CIA arrived to find Osip shot on the steps outside, Sanchez dead inside and a girl in her early teens sat in tears, cradling the head of a man most reports claimed she barely knew.

What actually happened remained a subject about which Kris Zha found herself unable to talk. Trauma, agreed the doctors who examined her. Kris was willing to let them think this, just as she was willing to let them think it was her idea to call a number in Mr Van Berg's wallet and talk to a general, whose name she never knew.

The general had wanted to know what happened right at the end. In fact, he wanted to know so much he took a military flight to San Francisco, and then had himself driven out to Kris Zha's house. He got no more out of the teenager than anyone else.

'I can't,' said Kris.

'Why not?'

She looked at him. 'Because I promised.'

After that, the general left. He understood about such things.

It had been growing light in White Drop and the waves were rising. Kris was unsure whether the two things went together. Geography bored her. When the shots first happened, she'd wanted to move towards the windows, find out what was happening.

'Stay here,' ordered Robert Van Berg.

'Why?' asked Kris. She expected him to say it would be safer. Instead, he told her he was dying and needed the company. There wasn't really much of an answer to that.

'I need you to deliver a message to Officer Flic Valdez.'

Kris knew the name. 'What should it say?'

'It should say I'm sorry and I told her I might not be around. Tell her, I meant every word I said.' Bobby paused. 'There's something else,' he added. 'That trust we talked about? It's all fixed up. So I guess the lawyers will be in touch.' He wanted to say, *work hard at college, get good grades, behave yourself.* But it didn't seem appropriate.

'Let me get a doctor,' Kris begged, when Bobby's eyes shut for the second time and his breathing became shallow. 'I can use the phone over there.'

'Too late,' said Bobby. 'And besides it's time.' One eye was swollen shut and Kris knew that some of his ribs had been broken, plus he'd split his head, but that didn't seem enough to kill someone like him.

Kris stood up. 'Look,' she said. 'I'm going to make that call.'

'No. Kit, listen.'

She turned back, looked at him. 'Kit was . . .'

'What your father used to call you, right?'

Kris nodded.

'Let it be,' said Bobby. 'Everyone has to go sometime.'

'You really knew my dad?' Kris asked, with all the anxiety of a child who believes the person questioned might die before she can get an answer. 'I mean, for real.' Kris hesitated. 'You see, no one else did, not really.'

'Yes,' said Bobby. 'I guess I did. He told me one of your mother's sayings once. About repentance.'

He waited, but Kris just looked blank.

'It's being in the same situation,' said Bobby. 'It's being in the same situation and not doing the same thing . . . Your dad could be hard to like, but I knew him better and liked him more by the end. And he loved you.' Looking into eyes made vast by sadness, Bobby shrugged. 'We've been through this already. So you'll just have to take my word for it.'

'You really don't want a doctor?'

'No.' Bobby shook his head. 'I'm expecting someone else.' Those were the last words he spoke.

His grandmother came first, the English one. She wore her old tweed coat and walked with a stick that scraped noisily against the floor. Behind her was his aunt, and someone who looked like his aunt's reflection. The mother he'd never met, most probably. All of them smiled at him, rather seriously.

The young man who came next just grinned, shrugged and brushed dust from the lapel of his white suit. Even dead Johnny Zha had trouble behaving. Bobby's grandfather came last, his coat flowing behind him like a cloak. He wore a uniform Bobby had never seen before and was smoking a thin cigar.

And then, as Bobby watched, they stepped aside to let the fox enter. It was huge, with red eyes and backlit by sun streaming through the window. Nine tails flowed above it like war banners.

The *jinwei hu* spoke with the voice of his grandfather and wore his aunt's sour smile. Its claws scratched like rats on the expensive floor. Bobby could feel the noise inside his head. Turning, the fox glanced at those standing on both sides of it, then stepped forward.

'Now,' it said.

Grandfather Lau nodded.

What happened next didn't happen (because such things cannot happen). As Kris heard sirens wail on the road above and reached over to shake the man whose head was already settling into her lap, Bobby opened his eyes one final time. Reflected in them Kris saw a celestial fox. She recognised it instantly, from the tales her father had told her as a child.

Instantly she understood that White Drop was now empty of all living things except her. Just as she knew that what she saw was impossible. But as the dead man's eyes began to glaze, Kris watched the *jinwei hu* turn, smile at her and slink from the world's most perfect room. It didn't look back.